Jessamy
Court

RANDOM HOUSE  NEW YORK

Anne
Maybury

Jessamy
Court

FOR
JEAN MANN

Jessamy
Court

I

IT WAS LIKE the refrain of a song sung by all the people I met as I drove through the dazzling autumn afternoon.

"Lovely day." . . . "Lovely day, Miss Fleming." . . . "Lovely day."

And each time I nodded and laughed and agreed. I had no warning, as my white car joined the crawling lines of traffic, that I was at the beginning of an experience that would nearly cost me my life.

My journey began at a hospital in North London, on the third floor, in a room that had slatted blinds and walls the color of young spring leaves. The only flowers were those I had brought with me, not the chrysanthemums that made golden mosaics of the flower stalls at street corners, but phlox—pink and mauve and white.

Stephanie loved them, and I could imagine how her face would light up at the sight of them.

The middle-aged nurse who took me to Stephanie's room said as we walked along the quiet corridor, "We found a letter from you in Miss Clair's purse. That's why we contacted you. There was nothing else by which to identify her."

I remembered vaguely that I had written about ten days earlier, saying, more or less: "Hey, I haven't seen you for a long time. Call me and tell me what's happening."

"I'm afraid she won't recognize you," the nurse said. "She's suffering from some emotional collapse. But the doctor will explain. He is somewhere in the hospital and I'll ask him to come and have a word with you. He will want that. You see, Miss Fleming, you're the only contact we have, but now you are here, you'll be able to tell us who her relatives are and who will take responsibility for her." She opened a door at the end of the corridor.

The girl on the bed glanced at me without recognition, her eyes vacant and wandering and obviously not seeing the slanting sunlight or the scented flowers I carried.

In the moments it took me to reach the bed I thought how curious it was that until that moment I had never thought Stephanie beautiful. But the bitterness of her usual expression had been wiped out by her illness, and even with her hair dragged back from her face and the unnatural gleam on her opaline skin, she was lovely.

She remained unaware of me, her eyes staring at the ceiling. Her eyelashes stood out like little stiff threads, as if they were wet with the tears she had no idea she was shedding, and her small white hands lay quite still on the sheet.

I leaned over the bed, noticing how thin she was: her shoulder blades too prominent; her pointed breasts under her thin night-dress like those of a skinny child.

"Stephanie, if you can hear me, don't try to talk, just nod your head."

The only movement she made was to close her eyes.

"Darling, it's Rachel. Rachel Fleming." I waited and then looked at the nurse.

She shook her head. "She's not even hearing you," she said. "I'll go and find the doctor."

Left alone with Stephanie, I touched her hand, murmuring her name, my name, trying to get through to her. But all she showed was a blank indifference.

"Good afternoon," a voice said from the doorway. "I'm Dr. Wilde."

He was a very self-composed man, middle-aged and blunt-featured, and he was looking at Stephanie with neither pity nor indifference. His expression was that of a man prepared to use all his skill to help those needing it, but careful not to become so identified with his patients that he wore himself out.

Aware that I was watching him, he shook his head, answering my obvious but unasked question. "She can't hear what we're saying."

I felt free, then, to talk. "How did this happen?"

"She collapsed in the street. There was no one with her, and we have no idea who she is."

"She is the daughter of Tatiana Livanova."

He showed immediate surprise. "The dancer who was found dead a few days ago?"

"Yes."

"Then why in the name of goodness did no one report that she was missing?" He sounded angry.

"She lived alone, and I suppose if friends telephoned her and received no reply, they would think she was away."

"You can tell me," he said, "who her relatives are."

"There are none—at least, none that she knows. Her mother's family are scattered in Russia and Austria and France, but she broke with them many years ago. Stephanie's father's people never approved of the marriage, so there was no contact there, either."

"Someone has got to be found to take responsibility. A reliable friend of her mother's, perhaps; someone who knew them both very well."

I shook my head. "Stephanie and her mother led completely separate lives."

"Then some mature and reliable friend?"

"Unless Stephanie has made new friends this past few months, I don't think that those she knows are anything but acquaintances. I doubt if any of them could, or would, help. She was inclined . . . well . . ."

"Go on, go on."

"She was inclined to have sudden relationships that soon burned out."

"No emotional staying power," the doctor said. "I understand. And you?"

"Oh, I'm her oldest friend."

"Then you must help."

"Of course, in any way I can. But please tell me what is wrong with her."

"You could call it shock. People react to stress in different ways and some develop physical symptoms. I've known cases of temporary blindness and even paralysis, though there's no real physical disease. Put simply, Miss Fleming, it's an escape from some intolerable situation."

"Her mother was dancing in *The Snow Maiden* only a few nights ago—I read the rave notices—so her death must have been a terrible shock."

"A sudden and accidental death is always a shock," the doctor said. "But Miss Clair's reaction is unusually violent. Now, first of all, if she had some of her personal possessions around her, they might touch a chord—" He turned to the door as a man with an enormous nose and the eyes of a predatory eagle looked in. "Mrs. Ransome in number seventeen . . ." the man began.

The doctor by Stephanie's bed nodded and said, "Coming now," and then turned to me. "I'll be back in a few minutes. Please wait."

I was alone with Stephanie. I touched her hand, but there was no response from her fingers. The ribbon that tied her hair back looked too tight, and I eased it a little and then spread her hair fanwise over the pillow. It curled at the ends like the petals of very pale daffodils. I smoothed it at her temples, but it was like playing with a doll. She lay absolutely still, too far away to be roused by anything I could do, plunged deep in the cocoon of her shut-away mind.

Stephanie had never loved her mother, and since Livanova had always looked on her as an aggravation and a nuisance, her daughter could have none of the sense of guilt which people sometimes feel at omitted kindnesses, withheld affections which, upon death, can haunt and shame. Livanova had never wanted anything from Stephanie except that she keep out of her way.

The morning papers had streamed the facts of the great dancer's death across their pages, and shocked at reading the news, I had telephoned Stephanie, but there had been no reply from her apartment. I had made three unsuccessful attempts to speak to her, the last one immediately after hearing a report on television of the inquest on the dead dancer.

The result was an open verdict and none of the evidence given had indicated that there had been what was called in criminal jargon "foul play." Yet neither was there anything to show any reason why Livanova should have slipped and fallen so heavily against the wrought-iron balustrade of her apartment balcony that the impact had been fatal. According to newspaper reports, there had been no sign of a struggle, or of a robbery.

Livanova had recently celebrated her forty-second birthday. She had lived a life dedicated to dancing, guarding her perfect health and escaping to her Dorset home to relax after the tremendous expenditure of energy during her stage appearances.

In more than one newspaper her previous "close friendship" with Fabian Seal was mentioned. Most reporters also reminded their readers of the sudden and publicly unexplained estrangement between the great dancer and the man who had been architect, artist and mountaineer—"the three-gifted man," as he had been called.

At the inquest Fabian Seal had been closely questioned, and behind each newspaper report was a subtle, implied doubt that Tatiana Livanova's death had been an accident. The ominous words "open verdict" meant that the police files had not been closed on the case. Something could yet be discovered about the dancer's last hour of life.

In one Sunday newspaper there had been an overcolored description of how Livanova had been found "lying limp and graceful, curiously reminiscent of the final pose of the Dying Swan—the dance the great Pavlova had immortalized and which Diaghilev had hated." Poetic words; journalese. But at the root of that news a radiant and magnificent dancer was suddenly dead.

One of the great difficulties the police met with was that on that particular night the porter at the block of flats had been taken ill and there had been no one on duty in the front hall.

I wondered, as I sat beside the unheeding girl, how the police were continuing their lines of investigation, but I knew nothing of their ways and they were most certainly not making anything public.

When the doctor returned I asked, looking at Stephanie, "She can't even indicate if she's in pain, can she?"

"She isn't. In fact, physically she's reasonably fit. I've told you, it's a matter of escape, Miss Fleming, and I have to find out what it is she is escaping from. That's where someone must help me. There's a block somewhere in her mind, and until I know exactly what it is, I can't help her."

The girl lying in the white bed moved her hand, plucking at the sheet. She was murmuring to herself, and bending over her, I heard one word: "Jessamy."

I looked quickly at the doctor.

"Jessamy," he repeated. "What I want to know is whether that is someone's name. It's the only word she has spoken."

"It's the house Livanova owned in Dorset." I spelled it for him, explaining, "It's odd, but Stephanie always pronounces it as her mother did, with a soft 'J,' as if it were a French name. But then, Livanova was partly Russian and brought up in Paris, so she spoke with an accent. Stephanie didn't, but I suppose she thought that was the right way to pronounce it; perhaps it is. It sounds French somehow . . ." My voice trailed off as I saw the doctor's surreptitious glance at his watch. I was being garrulous and it was all irrelevant, anyway.

"You say you are Miss Clair's closest friend?"

"We were at school together, and afterward she came to rely on me. She had no one else." I paused, wanting to explain without resentment how a mother had separated her life from her daughter.

The doctor helped me. "So Livanova put her career first. Well, yes. Go on."

"She wasn't allowed to meet her mother's friends or those who worked for her. There was no family life for Stephanie."

The doctor had moved to the door. "I suggested, before I was called away, that Miss Clair should have some of her personal things about her. Perhaps, Miss Fleming, you would go to her apartment, or wherever it is she lives, and fetch some for her—pretty nightdresses, make-up, a hand mirror. You know the kind of thing."

"Yes, of course I'll do that."

"The duty sister will see that you are given whatever keys were in her purse and you can sign a receipt for them."

"Yes," I said again, adding, "Anything I can do to help . . ."

"Anything?" His eyes challenged, but he didn't wait for me to speak. "Then find out why the name of that house is troubling her so much. That's the most important thing. Ask among her friends. Pronounce it any way you like—soft 'J,' hard 'J'—but see if anyone can give you a clue. I must get through to her, and the longer we leave her in this state, the more difficult it will make my task."

"I doubt if anyone knows as much as I do about her."

"Then you're the one to help me, aren't you?"

For a moment we seemed to be adversaries, meeting each other's eyes without warmth across the room.

The doctor could keep the silence longer than I. He had authority, and I saw, in the cool glance he gave me, the determination of a man who would not listen to refusal. He was prepared to toss me, whom he had never met before, into a sea of difficulty that I was certain was beyond my depth. "I wouldn't know how to begin to help," I protested in despair.

"The house—Jessamy," said the doctor.

"But how can I interfere there? I'm not even a relative."

"You've already told me that she has no family—or none whom she sees—so it leaves me no alternative but to ask a friend, her closest friend." He gave me no chance to protest. "Miss Fleming, if you had worked with sick people as long as I, you would know the truth of the French proverb 'A good friend is worth a hundred relations.' But perhaps I'm cynical. Never mind." He moved his shoulders with a gesture of impatience. "To get back to our discussion. Miss Clair needs help. This place, Jessamy . . ."

"I don't think you quite understand. Stephanie never knew Jessamy Court. Her mother refused to allow her to go there and she had no interest in the place, anyway."

"Then perhaps someone who lives in the house could help."

"I believe there is a man down there who was Livanova's accompanist when she practiced her dancing. His first name is Dominick, but that's all I know. I'm not even certain if he's still there. And I don't think Stephanie ever met him. She never told me that she did, and I was the one she talked to about everything. I don't think she minded much about being kept away from the house—she didn't like the country. She only resented not being asked to her mother's house, because it would have made her feel more wanted."

"This man could still be there."

"But I don't *know* him. I don't know anything about the house, except that Livanova owned it."

"Miss Fleming, I have a dozen patients in this hospital desperately needing me. So I'm afraid someone will have to do the basic work of finding out what is troubling Miss Clair. And since she has no known relatives here, then I'm afraid a friend—"

A friend. *You, Rachel Fleming.*

There came a movement and a sound from the bed. "Jessamy . . ."

"You see?" The doctor paused halfway to the door. "There is so obviously a link. And in cases like this, where a patient has repressed into unconsciousness the emotional problem that she can't cope with, we must, as I've already told you, find out what the problem is."

"Perhaps it's just that her mother is dead and she will inherit the house."

"I've never heard of anyone collapsing through knowing of an inheritance. Something happened to her at the inquest on her mother, or just after, because that must be when she became ill."

"Her mother's solicitor—" I began.

"Of course. Of course. But one thing at a time. It's not much use finding him while Miss Clair is in this condition. She wouldn't know or understand anything that he might say to her."

"But she has that name on her mind," I said. "Jessamy."

"She doesn't even know she's saying it. She is a long way away from awareness of anything, even her identity. In any case, the solicitor has probably been in touch with her already. You could have a look round when you go to her home and see if she has a diary with a date in it which might refer to his name or to some future meeting with him. But it's useless to think of practical matters until Miss Clair comes out of this trauma. So we must find out what it is about that house. Or rather . . ." He left the sentence in the air.

The cool, commanding implication was there. "Or rather, you must. *You,* Miss Fleming . . ."

I wanted to shout at him, "I'm only two years older than Stephanie. Why expect me to take on this responsibility?" But he did, and I knew that wherever it led and whatever the outcome, I couldn't refuse.

"Very well. I'll help if I can."

A faint smile touched his face. "That's what I hoped you'd say." The door opened and someone called his name again, softly.

He nodded and turned back to me. "Thank you for understanding that something must be done apart from hospital treatment. Just help us. If you can find the link between that house and my patient, we may be able to pull her through. It's urgent, Miss Fleming."

The door closed and, again, I was alone with Stephanie. I bent over the bed and laid my fingers softly against her cheek. "Darling, please try to understand. You said 'Jessamy' just now. Why?"

She lay, eyes on the ceiling, unmoving, unheeding. "Jessamy," I repeated softly.

But there was no reaction. The doctor was right. She had not been trying to communicate with either of us. The name of Livanova's house belonged somewhere in the nightmare behind which she had escaped. I was quite certain that if the name had been even a semiconscious effort to give us a message, my questioning would have produced some small reaction. And there was none.

I kissed Stephanie's damp, glazed cheek, said quietly, "I'll be back very soon," and went in search of the keys to her apartment.

On my way back to the West End of London the elements had changed as if to fit their mood to mine. Light cloud now covered the sky. A wan sun appeared, haloed in the way that always threatened rain.

During the half-hour journey to Stephanie's Thames-side apartment, she was scarcely out of my thoughts. I understood very little about illnesses caused by hysteria or shock, but I had known for a long time that Stephanie had a streak of instability. Livanova's wild, mixed blood, English and French and Russian, was Stephanie's too. Unlike her mother, though, she had never found any outlet for her temperament, so that it had been driven inward, resulting in sudden outbursts of anger against life and resentment of Livanova.

In anyone else, this persistent rancor would have irritated me, but something very strong had been forged between us back in our schooldays when, young as I was, I had recognized Stephanie's loneliness and deep sense of being unwanted. Her need for me as confidante, sympathizer and prop against the situations she could not handle herself was, in a way, a satisfying one, giving me a sense of responsibility which I enjoyed. When we both left school, Stephanie's habit of coming to me to talk everything over remained. She lacked ambition and had drifted into a series of small, unimportant jobs. She had no real interests and little talent. All she had ever wanted to do was to model clothes, but although taller than I, she was not quite the height to compete with the goddesses of the photographic studios.

She was twenty-three, but she retained a curious innocence in spite of her sophisticated talk, and while my friends found her faintly irritating, to me she had the appeal of a lost kitten. Of course, now that she was so ill, I would help her in any way I could.

II

STEPHANIE'S APARTMENT was on the third floor of an old house very near where the artist Turner used to sit and watch the sunsets across Chelsea Reach.

When I opened the door I found three envelopes on the mat, but since they were obviously all bills, I left them on the hall table.

I didn't expect the apartment to be tidy and it wasn't, but the rooms were charmingly furnished and from the wide windows the pale sun glinted on the swift-flowing river.

I found a suitcase and packed it with nightdresses, slippers, make-up. Then I went to the desk. There were bills but no letters and nothing in her small green diary that seemed of any importance.

Stephanie could, of course, have met her mother's solicitor at some time during the inquest on Livanova's death, in which case they might have arranged a date for a visit which Stephanie had characteristically forgotten to write in her diary.

I remembered the name of Livanova's manager; Stephanie had spoken of him many times. She hated him because he had often acted as a buffer between her mother and herself. He had for years guarded Livanova as closely as if she had possessed the crown jewels.

Even if I could contact him, I wasn't at all certain that he would help me, but I had to try. I reached to the ledge under the table and pulled out the telephone directory.

"Farson, James L." was listed with a Mayfair number. His secretary answered the phone, said Mr. Farson was busy, but could she help me. I explained that Stephanie Clair was ill and I wanted to contact her solicitor. Immediately I sensed a caution, as though, because she had no proof that I was a bonafide person, she must be careful what she told me. I managed to persuade her finally that I really was a close friend of Livanova's daughter, and after much searching, she gave me the solicitor's address.

When, still refusing to be intimidated by my role as outsider, I telephoned his office, I was told by a woman's clipped voice that Mr. Vincent Crewe was out of London on an important case in a Midland court.

"Then perhaps I could speak to his assistant."

I was asked my business; I gave my name and explained that Livanova's daughter was ill and I felt that the solicitor would want to know that she was in the Royal Channon Hospital.

The voice relaxed some of its stiffness and thanked me. Mr. Crewe would be informed as soon as he returned the following week.

"But there must be someone I could speak to *now*," I said desperately. "Someone handling Mr. Crewe's work while he's away."

The voice became brisk again. "I will pass on your message, Miss Fleming," she said and hung up the phone.

I felt some sense of relief. At least, when he returned he would know that he must contact the hospital. It was even possible that by then Stephanie would have recovered sufficiently to be able to talk to him.

I crossed the room to the closet and reached for Stephanie's dressing gown. A letter hung half out of one of the pockets. My

first thought was that it could be from the solicitor, but as I unfolded it, I saw, at the top of the fine-quality paper, a printed
address:

Jessamy Court
Pilgrim Abbas
Dorset

I sat down on the dressing-table stool, and without shame, read
what was written in black, flowing handwriting:

> It is some years since we met, and then it was only briefly.
> I tried to get in touch with you after the inquest, but you had
> disappeared and the pressure of work made it impossible
> for me to remain in London.
>
> We have something important to discuss, haven't we,
> Stephanie? So I suggest you come down here. Come on Mon-
> day. If you travel by train, the best is the 10:30 to Dorchester.
> Change there for Pilgrim Abbas. I will meet you.

The letter was brief and peremptory. Stephanie was given no
choice. "Come on Monday."

I might not have been able to decipher the very black signature
had I not known the name so well. Fabian Seal. "The three-gifted
man."

The swiftly formed letters gave the impression of something
dashed off in a hurry, and I wondered if that accounted for the
fact that there was no form of address, no "Dear Stephanie." Instead, the letter seemed charged with an air of command. I reread
the meaningful line "We have something important to discuss,
haven't we . . . ?" With my senses sharpened by Livanova's death
and Stephanie's illness, the words seemed to hold sinister over-
tones.

The strong, racing signature evoked a memory of the first night
of a new production of *Scheherazade* I had seen some months
before. I remembered, too, the gist of what the critics had written
about it the following day in the newspapers.

> Fabian Seal may not be a prolific theatrical designer—he
> has, as yet, only worked on three plays, a highly successful
> musical, the controversial *Tempest* and two ballets—but his
> sets have a tremendous impact. . . . There is nothing small
> in Seal's work; he does not design pretty little pieces in which

the actors move as if afraid the stage scenery will fall on them. He gives space and grandeur to every scene. Nor does he indulge in gimmickry.

I had once read a "Profile" of him which had appeared in a Sunday newspaper. Architecture had been his first choice for a career, but he had rejected it and gone to the Sorbonne, where he had shown considerable promise as an artist. Then, entirely unexpectedly, he had tossed all his promise away in order to climb mountains. The article had been sentimentally headed "The Man Who Loves Solitary Places."

Two years ago Seal had been involved in an accident, and his left leg had been so badly injured that he now walked with a limp. His mountain days were finished, but with the passing of one great professional passion, another took over. His architect's knowledge and his talent as an artist had been combined in his first effort as a designer. He had created the sets and the costumes for a new ballet—*Mazeppa,* the story of a page in the court of the King of Poland—and had found instant success.

Fabian Seal . . . Livanova's one-time lover.

Yet by the time he had to turn his back on his loved mountains, the rift with Livanova had already occurred. He had never collaborated in creating a ballet for her.

It was possible that the dancer's intimate friends had heard why they had quarreled and parted, but Stephanie never knew, and since I was as intrigued as she, we had speculated together.

I had said, "I remember your telling me that she didn't really like close attachments. Perhaps Fabian wanted marriage."

Stephanie had tossed my suggestion aside. "I think she threw him over when he became lame. Being Mother, she couldn't continue an affair with someone who wasn't perfect. That would have injured her vanity. I wish, oh, how I wish, that my father hadn't died."

I had wished that for her, too, but he had been a victim of an influenza epidemic only three years after his marriage to Tatiana Livanova.

The letter could be important, and I put it in my purse. Then I finished packing the suitcase and left the sunny apartment.

I was sitting in my car, held up by traffic lights, when a thought leaped out of the air and struck me. Stephanie's collapse could be connected with the receipt of Fabian Seal's letter.

The lights changed to green and I moved slowly forward in the tightly packed column of cars. As the traffic fanned out and I had a fairly clear run along the wide road that led to the hospital, I began to think again about Fabian Seal and recalled newspaper accounts of how closely he had been questioned at the inquest, how he had admitted seeing Livanova at her Dorset house on the morning of her death. His last sight of her, he had said, had been as she drove through the gates of Jessamy. Yes, he assured the court, it was positively the last time they had met. The next question put to him was one which the newspapers had highlighted. Was he aware that it was an established fact that he had been seen in London only hours after Madame Livanova had arrived? Fabian Seal agreed that he had driven there on business. The court seized on his cool reply. Two people leaving the same house for the same destination and yet traveling separately? Why had they not traveled together?

"Because we both needed our cars."

It was a straightforward answer, and I remembered speculating, as I read the report, why the same question had been put to Fabian Seal three times.

I wondered if Stephanie knew something, which through caution or fear she had withheld at the inquest. I wondered also if she had read in the wording of Fabian Seal's letter a threat in connection with that knowledge, and if this had frightened her so badly that she had escaped into her deep trauma.

It seemed that I had found something which I could tell the doctor and on which he might be able to work. But as I turned into the hospital gates and drove along the flower-bordered paths, I faced the fact that he wanted something more from me than what was, after all, a wild supposition.

I unpacked the things I had brought for Stephanie and put her make-up in the drawer by her bed. Then I laid the letter, face upward, on her limp hands.

"Do you remember reading this?" I watched her expression closely, but she had escaped too deeply into her jungle of oblivion, and there was no reaction. I wandered to the window, not wanting to leave her, yet not knowing why I should stay. I looked through the slats of the blind and saw, below, a small paved garden. Some hospital patients were walking along the paths; the sun had broken through the light cloud and their mauve shadows were following them slowly along the walls.

14

A nurse entered, and her smile said clearly, "You have been here long enough. Please leave my patient."

"Dr. Wilde—?" I began.

"Oh, he has already left the hospital."

It didn't matter. If he had been there and I had shown him the letter, I was fairly certain that he would hand it back to me and tell me again to contact the man living at Jessamy Court.

The nurse stood waiting. I touched Stephanie's limp hand, said, "Goodbye, darling. I'll be back," repeated my assurance to the nurse, and left the hospital.

I walked toward my small car, opened the door and breathed in the lingering scent of the flowers I had left in Stephanie's room. Then I sat for some moments behind the wheel, wondering what to do next.

But I knew. I had to telephone Dorset and speak to Fabian Seal. I switched on the engine of the car and joined the great stream of traffic bound for the West End of London.

The Lincoln Royal Hotel where I worked stood in Piccadilly facing St. James's Park, defying the twentieth century by being proudly and audaciously Gothic. Towers and turrets of dark-red brick rose elegantly to the sky. It was old, it was loaded with history, and its hundred years had not dimmed its importance. The famous and the rich still walked through the wide marble halls; the public rooms glowed with ruby velvet and crystal chandeliers.

I worked among this splendor of liveried porters and small pages in tight uniforms, but my office was a small room at the back of the hotel, looking out onto a narrow street. If I wanted to see the sun, I would have to open the window and almost overbalance to get the glimpse between the rooftops.

The term "assistant" meant in my case that I was a kind of glorified Girl Friday to Jock Graham, head of Public Relations at the hotel. I coped with the less-important visitors, arranged press meetings and photographic sessions, and very often I was called for to soothe a star who had been elbowed out of front-line treatment. It was I who had to supply the gin and the extra bouquet of flowers and try to compensate by any means I could think of for the loss of the brightest limelight.

Life in our office was at times very demanding, but I loved the work and I dreamed of one day being a press-relations officer in my own right. In the meantime Jock was a good and generous employer and I was happy.

When I arrived back at the office, Fleur, his secretary, told me Jock had been looking for me. I slid out of my coat, put my purse in the drawer of my desk and went into his office.

He was a small, square man with bright dark eyes and receding hair. "Well, and how did the hospital visit go?"

"Abortive," I said. "Stephanie didn't even recognize me. The doctor told me that she is suffering from very deep shock."

He lifted his heavy eyebrows. "Because of her mother's death? Oh, come off it! I can't believe she has collapsed through a broken heart. Livanova didn't give a damn for her daughter, so why should her daughter care whether she's alive or dead?"

It was pointless to protest that perhaps we didn't know the truth and that the dancer had an affection for her daughter, because Jock knew everything about everyone who was famous— it was his job.

"But something shocked her," I said and told him of my conversation with her doctor.

"So what's going to happen now?"

"I don't know. The solicitor is away on some big case in the Midlands, and when I called his office I was more or less politely told that as an outsider, no information about Livanova's affairs could be given me."

"Did you explain the circumstances?"

"Whoever I spoke to was guarding her employer's clients," I said, and added hopefully, "Perhaps by the time the solicitor returns to London, Stephanie will have recovered. I hope so, because I gather that delay will make her cure all the more difficult."

"And what are you supposed to do about it?"

"I don't know. That's the awful thing. I can understand how the doctor sees her case. He can't work in the complete dark and it seems there's no one who knows as much as I do about her— or cares," I added.

Jock picked up a pencil and drew a triangle and a circle. His hands were always busy when he was thinking. I stared at the elaborately patterned blue-and-green tie some film star had given him from his own collection.

"I think you'd be a charming bedside contact for an ailing man," Jock said, "but I can't see what help you can give an unconscious girl."

16

"It seems that since she collapsed she has spoken only one word."

Jock tossed the page on which he had been scribbling into the wastebasket. "Your weakness, my dear Rachel, is an exaggerated sense of responsibility. I've told you that before."

"Perhaps it's that I can't resist interfering."

"Oh no. Only tactless people really interfere, and you wouldn't be working for me if you were that. What was this one word Stephanie Clair spoke?"

"Jessamy."

"What's that?"

"It's the name of her mother's house in Dorset."

He flicked over some papers on his desk. "All right. The doctor tells you the obvious, that someone has got to help him get through to her, but I think *you* need some advice too. Don't let this business obsess you. We're none of us so enormous that we can take on the troubles of a continent."

"This isn't a continent. It's one rather lonely girl."

"You know me, I exaggerate. But you also know perfectly damn well what I mean."

I did. My own job at the hotel was to cosset people, but good advice was so often difficult to take. I left Jock and tried to drown my anxiety in work.

The following day I telephoned the hospital, and the nurse on duty told me that there was no change in Stephanie's condition.

I coped with a foreign stage star's demand for a generous meeting with the press when he came to London the following month; I arranged for a photographic session for a French novelist whom the critics decided would be a second Colette; I staved off would-be starlets who were prepared to pose in the elegant lobby of the Lincoln Royal clad in a bikini or less. Yes, they were beautiful and I was sure they would pose in the nude if anyone wanted them to. But *not,* dear Miss What's-your-name, in the foyer of the Lincoln Royal.

At the office and at home in my Bayswater apartment, Stephanie remained vividly in my mind. Past memories of her plagued me. Stephanie curled up in a chair in my apartment, saying bitterly, "She doesn't want me. She never did. She gives me an allowance on condition that I keep away from her." She—Tatiana Livanova. Stephanie crying over a broken romance. "I can't keep lovers; I can't even keep friends. Rachel, what's *wrong* with me?"

And I, in my limited wisdom, reassuring her. "Nothing is wrong with you. It's just that so far, you've been unfortunate in your choice. One day you won't be."

"It's horrible to find that in the end no one wants you."

"They do."

"Who does?" she had challenged.

I had said, "I do, for one. We're friends."

And now that she needed friendship, I didn't know how to help her.

Stephanie's problems had always been tricky to solve because she was still emotionally a child. But this time it wasn't Livanova's daughter who demanded my help, but an experienced and responsible doctor.

It took me three days to decide what to do, and Jock Graham was, quite innocently, the one who led me to it. It happened at the end of a long day. It was eight o'clock and I was hungry and tired after a day of almost ceaseless crises.

"You look drained."

"I feel drained."

"Of course, you haven't had your holiday this year, have you?"

"Except for a few days in the spring, you haven't yet offered it to me."

"Then I'd better do so. For the next few weeks we shall be as slack as we will ever be, so why not take a break now? Get a booking . . . go somewhere abroad. Relax for a while before the winter influx arrives to wring the souls out of us and wear us into the grave."

I laughed at his heartrending outburst. Jock loved every moment of his life. He adored the stars, even the difficult ones. I once heard him say, "No one gets to the top the easy way, so I give them all grudging admiration."

I watched the low sunlight slant across his rocky face and thin ginger hair, and said that September was a lovely month for a holiday but I couldn't leave Stephanie. So I would take a week off and stay in London to be near her.

"Doing what? Feeding her grapes and holding her hand?"

"Perhaps," I said, refusing to rise to his bait. "But first of all I shall telephone the house in Dorset—Livanova's house. Fabian Seal is staying there."

"Ah-h-h-" It was like a soft, long-drawn-out whistle. "So he turned up again in Livanova's life. Well! Well!" It was the first glimmer of real interest he had shown.

"Do you know Seal?" I asked.

"No. But I've heard rumors."

"Why did they part?"

"I suppose they had a final almighty row. It's the old story of the coin, one side love, the other hate, particularly between two temperamental people. You flip the coin and"—he shrugged—"bang goes sweetness and light."

"Is Fabian Seal temperamental?"

"I should imagine so." He grinned at me. "But then, our world is full of gossip, isn't it, Rachel?"

"Yes. What have you heard about Fabian Seal?"

"It's ancient history, my dear. He's out of the real blaze of lime-light since the famous break with Tatiana Livanova, but they said then that he was unpredictable, ruthless and devious. Oh well, every successful man has his enemies."

The telephone rang and I went back to the small office I shared with Jock's cool, dark and efficient secretary. I stood with my back to her and ran my fingers lightly through the leaves of the plants we grew on the window sill—azaleas and a spindly avocado we had encouraged from a stone.

"We're slack at the moment, so I'm going on vacation."

"Try Turkey," Fleur said.

"Try South Africa," an insouciant voice called from halfway inside the drawer of a filing cabinet.

Richard—Rikky to us all—was Jock's godson and he was in the office to learn the business.

"I'm taking a week now and the rest later," I said, "and I doubt if I shall be leaving London."

III

THAT EVENING I put *The Song of Summer* on the record player and began composing a letter to Fabian Seal. I ruined four sheets of notepaper before rejecting the idea of writing to him. The telephone was a far more revealing communication than a letter and it would be easier to judge him from speech rather than something where every word could be thought out carefully before being committed to paper.

I would call Fabian Seal and tell him that Stephanie had collapsed with some kind of shock and that the doctor needed help in finding the cause. I would ask him if he had met and talked to her at the inquest; if he knew whether she and her mother had quarreled sometime before Livanova's death and if, possibly, remorse had struck her so vehemently, and because she was highly sensitive, she could not face it.

The church clock at the end of the road struck eight. I unfolded Fabian Seal's letter, reached for the telephone and dialed the number.

A woman's slow, soft voice answered me.

"I'm speaking from London," I said. "Miss Clair . . . Stephanie Clair . . ."

"Oh." The voice at the other end interrupted me. "Oh, Miss Clair, Mr. Seal has been waiting for you to call him. But he's out at the moment. He left word that you would be met—"

"I'm afraid you don't understand. You see—"

Again she interrupted me, her voice quickening, her tone agitated. "I'm the housekeeper here and Mr. Seal is expecting you."

"Please ask him to telephone—"

"But, Miss Clair—"

"I'm not—"

"Oh dear! Oh dear, the music . . . I can't hear." Her agitation increased. "I'll tell Mr. Seal you'll be down, as he says he told you, on Monday."

Piano music made a background for the housekeeper's voice.

"Please listen a moment—" I began loudly.

There was a crash of angry piano chords and the line went dead.

Defeated, I replaced the receiver and walked about the room. I would give Fabian Seal time to return to the house before I called again. I didn't want a further abortive conversation with the nervous housekeeper.

But as an hour went by, I found my heart beginning to thud with excitement as if my mind were anticipating something that was still only stirring in my unconscious. I had had the same sensation before in my life and it had always preceded some important decision I had not even been aware I was going to make. I tried to think calmly. I went into the kitchen and made myself some coffee, and drinking it in the quiet of my sitting room, I kept remembering the agitated protests of the housekeeper at Jessamy Court.

"Mr. Seal is expecting you." . . . "But, Miss Clair . . ." Breathless words spoken as if she were looking over her shoulder all the time.

I wondered whether Fabian Seal had in fact been in the house and if it was he who had played the piano I heard in the background and had crashed those last chords.

I wondered, too, what the house was like and why Livanova's

one-time lover was living there, inviting Stephanie down to a place that should, by right of inheritance, be hers. He, acting host; she, the guest.

The open verdict at the inquest meant that somewhere there were loose ends which Stephanie might know and had dared not tell at the time. Whenever Fabian Seal's name came into my mind, I felt a faint quiver of fear, although, since I had never met him, my reaction had no reasonable basis.

If I went down to Dorset and introduced myself as a friend of Stephanie Clair's and explained about her illness, it was possible that he would come to London to see her. And since I could not rid myself of the suspicion that her collapse could be connected with the letter she had received from him, I might be doing her great harm.

Pilgrim Abbas was probably one of those small, enclosed communities where visitors from London would be looked on as "foreigners" and treated cautiously, so I could not hope for much help from the villagers if I went down there and mixed with them and tried to get them to talk. Only one place and one man could perhaps supply the links I needed to help Stephanie: Jessamy Court and Fabian Seal. I wanted to see both, and the more I tried to stop thinking about them, the more urgent and inevitable the desire became, the more alarming and the more exciting.

The doctor had made it clear that time was not on his side. It was also obvious to me that as I was no relative, I would learn little that would be of any help to the sick girl.

Involvement was the only way—some kind of false impression to those concerned that I knew more than I did and had a right to know the rest.

Involvement. The word clung to my mind with the tenacity of steel fingers. As Rachel Fleming, I was not fundamentally involved. Friendship and simple humanity were all I could claim, those and a doctor's words: "Find the link between my patient and Jessamy Court."

Had I been Stephanie's sister, I would have had more right to question; or had I been her identical twin, I would have played a part and gone to Jessamy Court as Stephanie, although as a twin I would obviously have known a great deal more than I did.

If I could *be* Stephanie . . . My imagination played with the idea as people play with dreams of great riches. If such an impossibility could become a reality, I would learn what the link was between Stephanie and Jessamy Court; I would come face to face with Fabian Seal.

The fantasy took clearer shape and became like some nagging, persistent picture that I could not erase from my mind. Finally, in despair, I slid into my coat, seized my purse and fled from the apartment.

But the streets and the lighted shop windows and the crowds hurrying to restaurants and theaters were like part of the backcloth on which my fantasy of complete involvement became terrifyingly possible. Myself as Stephanie Clair. The idea so shattered me that I bumped into a woman who was passing, apologized, swung round and collided with a man coming the other way. The two impacts brought me to my senses. The idea was as impossible as if I had said I was going to the moon. And anyway, to masquerade as someone else was probably a criminal act.

I returned home, still no more relaxed in my mind. I walked my apartment as if I were in a cage.

Ethically, even the thought was wrong. I could not play the role of Livanova's daughter. I could not . . . How could I? *Because it is Stephanie whom Fabian Seal expects.* And also because of a salient point in Fabian Seal's letter: "We have something important to discuss, haven't we, Stephanie?" There was only one way to know whether the menace I read in the words was real or just a figment of my stimulated imagination. But something even stronger than instinct told me that whatever it was, it would not be told to an outsider.

I stood looking at myself in the three gilded panels of the dressing-table mirror. Both Stephanie and I were small and slim and fair, but my hair was many shades darker than hers and my eyes were gray; hers were blue. Relief flooded through me. For impersonation, two people needed to be absolutely alike, and Stephanie and I were not.

I went to the record player and restarted *The Song of Summer*. I began to sing to it as if I were freed from some terrible burden. But soon the music seemed to fade and I was back in the same room four years ago and Stephanie was saying in her light, protesting voice, "I saw Mother today in Bond Street. She was with that man, Fabian Seal. She was in a hurry because they were going down to Jessamy Court that afternoon. And she never even said 'You must come down sometime.' She just introduced this man and then whisked him off. She couldn't bear to remind him that she had a daughter as grown up as I am."

I had said, "But she was only nineteen when you were born, so—"

"She needs to be considered ageless."

"Suppose you just take it for granted she'd like you to see the Dorset house and go down there? Walk in on her, look round and say 'How lovely!' even if you hate the place, and act as if you felt you were welcome."

"If I did that, she'd cut my allowance, and then I'd really be in a spot. It's a case of blackmailing me into staying away from her. Rachel, I hate her so much, it's terrible! And there's everyone saying how marvelous she is and this man, a whole seven years younger than she is, in love with her."

"What is he like?"

"Not good-looking. Dark. Not very tall. But you can't, somehow, seem to take your eyes away from his. They're greenish gold and bright and amused, as if he's laughing at some secret."

"Did you like him?"

"I wasn't given a chance to find out. Mother snatched him away. I don't think I registered at all with him, either. I was wearing dark glasses and a head scarf and I might have been anyone walking down Bond Street."

Anyone . . . Rachel Fleming, for instance . . .

Outside the window, the sky was like shadowed sapphire and the harvest moon had not yet risen. There was a continuous faint rustle as the wind danced through the dry leaves of the plane trees.

Twice I reached for the telephone and each time I held back. Fear and suspicion of this man I had never met warred with an increasing certainty that only by coming face to face with him as Stephanie Clair, would I know what it was that made him so anxious to see her. The letter had held no gentleness, no hint of kindly interest. Something important lay between Stephanie and Fabian Seal. The more I sat hunched by the telephone thinking about it, the more possible it seemed that it could be a fact that was dangerous for Stephanie to be confronted with and for me to find out.

The third time my fingers closed around the telephone receiver I knew there was no more argument. Rightly or wrongly, on a foolish impulse or because circumstances had offered no other course if I wanted to help an unconscious girl, I called Jessamy Court.

While I listened to the prolonged ringing tone, I told myself that two days would be the most that I could manage in my masquerade as Stephanie Clair. If I were there any longer, someone, or something, would catch me out.

The same slow, slurring voice answered me.

I took a deep breath. "Is Mr. Seal there, please?"

"Oh, that's Miss Clair, isn't it? I'm sorry, but Mr. Seal is still out."

"Then will you please tell him that I will be arriving sometime Monday afternoon. I shall drive down."

"I'll tell him, Miss Clair."

Rachel Fleming into Stephanie Clair—the preliminary transition had been made.

All that day and the next I told myself that there was still time to draw back. I telephoned those of Stephanie's friends whom I knew; I even went to see three of them in the vague hope that someone might have a bright idea that could help. None did. Even their sympathy was not quite genuine.

"She was always excitable, wasn't she? She once had hysterics at someone's party, and for nothing at all, really. I don't wonder she had a breakdown; she's that kind of person." . . . "Stephanie in the hospital? Oh, do give her my love. I must fly now, I've got a host of people coming in for drinks."

I asked them all the same question. "Did you see Stephanie between the time her mother died and her collapse?" I believed them when they said they hadn't.

So, I was on my own, committed and involved.

I spent the next three days before leaving London recalling everything I could about Stephanie and her life, practicing answering imaginary questions as Stephanie might answer them, subduing my own personality as a rehearsal for subduing it in front of Fabian Seal.

Since Livanova had made her daughter a small allowance on condition she stay out of her life, I doubted if Fabian Seal had learned anything about Stephanie that I did not know. But up to the last moment of leaving for Dorset, I clung to the hope that she would recover consciousness and that I could telephone Jessamy Court as myself and offer some excuse that Stephanie would not be able to make the journey just yet. I would give her Seal's letter and then let her choose whether or not she would go down to Dorset.

But my last telephone call to the hospital only five minutes before I left London was anything but reassuring. "Miss Clair is still unconscious and very weak."

I was committed. And down at Jessamy, Fabian Seal waited for Stephanie Clair.

IV

MONDAY MORNING was cool and gilded, and if I hadn't been so intensely nervous of what I was about to do, I would have enjoyed the drive down to Dorset.

The car, however, had no anxieties. It purred through the suburbs of London, through Hampshire and Wiltshire like a contented white cat. In between watching the signposts, I went over once again all that I knew about Stephanie.

I had been careful to make myself as physically like her as I could just in case Fabian had registered something about her when he had met her so briefly in Bond Street. But I doubted if, absorbed in his own love affair, he still remembered anything about a girl he had met four years ago. I was fairly certain, too, that Livanova had not shown him any photographs she might have of her daughter, fearful that her aura of perpetual youth would be destroyed.

Even so, I took great care with my appearance. I had had my hair tinted from its own darkish blond to Stephanie's pale honey. I had also taken the precaution of having it set the way she wore hers, straight, with the ends slightly curled under.

Although Stephanie had been just too short to be a model, she was two inches taller than I. But neither that nor the fact that I could not change the color of my eyes worried me much. Stephanie's volunteered information at the time—and my good memory —about the head scarf and the dark glasses must have made her very anonymous to Fabian Seal.

Since I knew that Livanova lived an isolated life in her Dorset house, I doubted if she had mixed with people in the county and I doubted even more if she had ever spoken to them about her daughter. I was reasonably safe, and if by any chance there was anyone around the Dorset villages who might know Stephanie, I had a car and I could slip away before it was discovered that my name was Rachel Fleming.

I sped over Salisbury Plain, driving south and west. The spire of the great cathedral rose like a tall gray arrow into a sky over-laden with a faraway golden mist. I drove past lambent green fields and little copses where the bracken was like a tufted russet carpet. The journey was easy until I passed Dorchester. After that, I had to ask the way at least six times before I found the village of Pilgrim Abbas.

By that time I was in one of the most enchanting corners of Dorset. The cottages were of stone, their roofs thatched. Tall elms broke the skyline and a stream of very clear water ran through the main street. A weathercock was perched on top of a lovely old stone gatehouse and I slowed down, wondering if this was Jessamy Court. It wasn't, but a farmer, leading a great chestnut shire horse, told me the way.

"Oh, Jessamy be along the road that runs across a corner of Ellen's Heath and then past Maiden Forest. You go straight on toward the sea."

It didn't sound quite like that as he said it, for his Dorset 'a's' were long and his speech like a rough caress.

I thanked him, and driving on, came to the Heath. Heather made amethyst patches and the scattered trees bent eastward, flung that way by the prevailing southwest winds. In the distance I could see the dusky line of Maiden Forest, and the loneliness and isolation had a strange beauty. There was no wind; everything stood still. As with people, if you looked hard enough, you saw a pulse beat, a breath draw in and out again, so with landscape. It seemed to me, looking ahead into the golden afternoon, that the stillness moved, quivered, trembling almost imperceptibly in the sensuous joy of the sun.

I came at last to a long lane, and at the far end I saw some tall gates. I had come to Jessamy Court.

I stopped the car, got out and stood looking up at the two battered and time-worn stone griffins which topped the pillars. The fabulous beasts gazed over my head, smiling at nothing. Beyond the gates was a lime avenue and in the distance three gables of tawny stone rose up.

I was facing the moment of no return and I felt intolerably alone. If you lose your identity, however voluntarily, everything that goes with it is also lost—personality and preferences, relatives and friends. There is nothing to cling to except the hope that forms the reason for the masquerade.

The car slid almost too easily between the gates and up the long drive between low rhododendron bushes and tall lime trees. The house came into full view around a bend.

I had no clear idea of the period of its architecture, but I guessed that it could be at least three hundred years old. The golden tint of its stone, which seemed so much part of western Dorset, glowed in the late sunlight; the windows were mullioned, heavily leaded and jutting out into angled bays. Over them were heavy stone carvings, weathered by wind and rain, and the lower walls were half covered with the pointed leaves of creeper, already turning the color of flame. Up the short flight of steps the huge mahogany double doors, with the black lion's head as a knocker, gleamed in the late-afternoon light.

It was not a palatial house, but it had an ancient beauty and it stood solidly in its valley, the boundaries being the Heath, the forest and a great cliff on the sea's edge.

There were paths and tangled lawns and splendid old trees. I could see no flowers. Jessamy was surrounded by a green world, except for one maple blazing its scarlet leaves across the main lawn.

In that breathtaking lull, as I sat in the car, I heard only the serpent hiss of the invisible sea. When I was very young we had a cleaning woman who came from the North of England. If my brother or I couldn't make up our minds about something, she would say, "Now stop your havering and get on with what you have to do." *Get on with it, Stephanie Clair* . . .

I got out of the car and climbed the five steps to the double front door. The bell at the side was huge and belonged to a far-gone age. Although I pulled it tentatively, I heard it clang through the house with great power.

Almost immediately the door opened and a tall woman with dark hair dressed with a Madonna simplicity, small, restless eyes and a weather-burned face said, "Miss Clair?"

I offered my first lie to her. "Yes," I said.

"I'm the housekeeper, Mrs. Manfred. I hope you didn't have much trouble in finding the place. We are very isolated here." The voice sounded like the one I had heard on the telephone, although it was no longer agitated.

"I've had a lovely journey down." I gave a glance over my shoulder.

Trees and hills and the puffs of gilded cloud were all motion-less, as if they watched the house and waited for Rachel Fleming to make her first mistake as Stephanie Clair.

Then the door closed behind me. The portrait of a woman in white hung over the huge fireplace and dominated the hall. A refectory table glowed in the broken light from the windows and a copper-colored cat sat on a window sill flicking its tail and watching me.

A staircase curved up to the next floor, the banisters of wrought-iron curlicues so delicate that I felt they would tremble at a breath.

"Come in. Come in, Stephanie."

At the sound of the man's voice, Mrs. Manfred moved quickly away. And then I saw him.

Framed in a doorway on the left, outlined in low sunlight from some window in the room beyond, he seemed completely the host, holding out both hands to me. He was of medium height and his hair was dark, with a lick of curl in it.

"It's good to see you here," he said.

I had apparently passed the first test. Fabian seemed satisfied that I was the girl he and Livanova had met on the street in London. I remembered what Stephanie had told me about the amuse-ment in his eyes. There was none for me. The formal smile on his lips and the welcome of his words were all he gave me. His eyes remained narrow and tawny and watchful. It was very possible that in spite of the invitation, this meeting with Livanova's presumed daughter was embarrassing to him. But I decided that Fabian Seal seemed to be the very last person who would ever be embarrassed.

He went to fetch my suitcase from the car, and I stood by the window of a huge white paneled drawing room looking out onto the grounds that enclosed Jessamy.

Outside the two French windows was a covered terrace supported by slender columns spiraling and supporting autumn-tinted creeper.

I turned back into the room. Although it was expensively furnished, it bore no strong flavor of a man's or a woman's influence. As I looked about me, a curious sense of urgency seized me. It was as if some drama had been enacted here at Jessamy Court and its highly charged atmosphere still clung to the house. I told myself impatiently that my reaction was merely the result of my own nerves.

In spite of his lameness, Fabian Seal moved with speed, for I seemed to have had time only to notice the yellow brocade of the deep chairs and the satin-gloss of old mahogany before he said from the doorway, "I've taken your suitcase to your room. And now I'm sure you'll want to freshen up after your journey. Mrs. Manfred will show you the geography of the house."

I had always supposed that people of the ballet world were gentle in face and manner, allied to the romantic poets. There was nothing of this about Fabian Seal. He was essentially male, the mountaineer of his more vigorous days rather than the theatrical designer he had become.

"You had tea on the way down?"

I assured him that I had stopped for some in Blandford.

"And saw its six-arched bridge?"

"I crossed it," I said and laughed, "lost my way and found it again. Then when I got here your gates were open to receive me."

"Oh, they're never closed. No one trespasses here—we are too isolated."

Mrs. Manfred was hovering in the doorway. "Shall I show you to your room, Miss Clair?"

"Thank you."

I decided, as I went up the wide staircase with her, that she was the perfect discreet housekeeper. If I had had any hopes that I might lure her into gossip, I could forget it. I wasn't even certain, as I made one or two complimentary remarks about the house, that she welcomed me. But then, she had probably been at Jessamy for a long time, and because of her devotion to Livanova, had no time for her daughter.

At the top of the staircase was a gallery that ran around three sides of the house. Mrs. Manfred crossed it and flung open a door. "The room faces south and, as you can see, has a view over the bay and that cliff which is called Gideon's Rock. 'Tis a fine sight to see the fishing boats go out from Pilgrim Abbas. But if you would like, I'm sure Mr. Seal would let you have your mother's suite. It's at the far end of the passage."

"This is lovely, thank you, Mrs. Manfred."

She nodded. "I told Mr. Seal when he said to put you in your mother's suite that you'd prefer to be in this room. It be too early yet to . . . well, to . . ."

"I understand," I said. "And you're quite right, I would prefer to be here."

"This leads to the bathroom." She crossed and opened another door. "I think I have remembered everything. Please tell me if there is anything else you need."

There were books on the bedside table, a cookie tin and a carafe of water. There were some Michaelmas daisies and crimson maple leaves in a green jar on the large serpentine-fronted chest.

"Mrs. Manfred, you've thought of everything. Those leaves are beautiful."

"You passed the maple tree when you came up the drive. Madame Livanova's suite looks out on it. She loved that tree, but only when it were green." Her voice changed, throbbing with emotion. "It was terrible, Miss Clair, the way . . . the way she died. But I mustn't talk to you about it. The shock . . ."

"Yes, it was a shock." In that, I spoke the truth.

"Miss Clair, it's been bothering me." She gave me a clear, straight glance. "I must have seemed rude the way I rang off when I spoke to you on the telephone. Madame always said I must wait for the caller to ring off first. But you see, I'm nervous because I don't hear too well and Mr. Dominick was playing the piano. I didn't mean to be rude."

"You weren't, Mrs. Manfred. I know what it's like to try to listen to a conversation when noises are going on round you, because—" I stopped. I had so nearly said "I work in a busy office." But it was important not to tell too much and get myself deeply into explanations. The less information I offered, the safer I would be.

I stood looking out onto the rich stretch of emerald lawn. Beyond a line of low bushes, the land sloped to the sea, which moved gently, rippling like steel ribbons. I opened the window and leaned out. There was a ship on the horizon, and on my left I saw Gideon's Rock rising up. Its land side seemed gradual and richly green, but I could also catch an angle of its sea face. From the shore it rose, sheer and bare and threatening. I turned away and looked about me, only half listening to Mrs. Manfred in the bathroom, enumerating the things she had put there for me.

"Madame always used this particular French lotion—perhaps you know it? It smells of her favorite sandalwood. And the bath soap matches it, and this talcum powder is very special—so light, so soft."

"Thank you for thinking of everything," I said again because there was nothing else to say.

When she left me I made a slow tour of the room. It was large and the furniture was of antique walnut polished to a sheen like glass, and the evocative scent of herbs and wood hung in the air. I wondered vaguely how many trees had been felled hundreds of years ago to make that great carved bed, the highboy, the serpentine chest. I brushed my fingers lightly over the surface of the dressing table and it was like touching silk.

I had brought very little with me because I planned to stay only two days. If I asked my questions carefully and kept my eyes open, it would be long enough to discover the link between Fabian Seal, Stephanie and Jessamy Court.

I began to unpack, opening drawers and putting things away. And while I did so, the atmosphere of the house enveloped me. Tatiana Livanova must have walked with her light dancer's step through this room, showing around the few guests who were ever invited to her Dorset hideout.

As I moved about the room, I went over once again even the most minor details of Stephanie's life as far as I knew them, going right back to the time when I had first met her at school.

It had taken me a long time in those days to overcome my envy of this daughter of a great ballerina. But I came gradually to realize that she was imprisoned in her own self-doubt and that anyone could bully her—and did. It was I who acted as a buffer between Stephanie and the astringent world of school. And when she grew up I was the stake to which she anchored herself; I who listened to her plaintive stories of repeated failures.

In order to augment the small allowance her mother gave her, Stephanie had to find work for herself. I remembered her saying once, "She has two mink coats and masses of clothes. She doesn't like jewelry, but she lives in that fabulous apartment that must cost the earth in rent. If she would only *buy* a London house, it could be mine one day and I'd have some sort of future security. But that's Mother. She spends today and thinks nothing of tomorrow. I don't even get enough to live on."

And to Livanova's discredit, she had never bothered to insist that Stephanie be trained for anything, nor did Stephanie herself possess the moral stamina to train herself. I tried to remember all the jobs she had taken and lost, so that Fabian Seal should not trap me.

The first one was at an art gallery, marking pictures with the little red "Sale" tab, selling catalogs, listening to art talk, none of which she understood, so that boredom overcame her and she was dismissed for carelessness. After that, there was the bookstore, where she was in trouble because she could not understand the adding machine. Then she found work with a well-known florist, and had enjoyed learning how to make bride's bouquets until one day she had pricked her finger on a rose. This had become infected, and she was so frightened that she refused to handle roses and left. Job after job . . . I wondered whether Stephanie herself remembered them all. But *I* had to. All those experiences had to be mine.

I walked into the drawing room. The late sun had shifted, throwing its rays onto a tapestry, lending a suffused glow to the somber fawn and café-au-lait colors.

"It's not a Bayeux tapestry," Fabian Seal said from the far end of the room, "and I'm afraid I can't tell you its history. It was bought, like almost everything here, with the house. The only room your mother had altered was the one she used as a practice room—I'll show it to you later—and, of course, her own suite. But now . . ." He went to a side table. "You do drink, don't you?"

I said I did.

"Good. Your mother only touched half a glass of champagne."

I chose a dry martini, and he gave it to me well iced. He drank whiskey, sitting in a chair by a lamp which threw his shadow spread-eagled onto the wall.

"So you drive a car." Head slightly bent, he looked at me from under drawn brows. "That means you won in the end."

Won what? I did the obvious thing. I said nothing and waited for him to explain.

"Trying to blackmail your mother into giving you a car." The lightness of his tone robbed it of insult. "You threatened to tell everyone how she paid you to keep away from her unless you got your car, didn't you? As if threats ever scared Livanova. You never understood your mother, did you? Or perhaps I'm wrong. Perhaps you did, since you got what you wanted in the end. That's a nice little Allegro you've got. Did you choose it or did she?"

"I . . . I did." I lifted my glass and drank. I had made my first mistake. I should, of course, have come to Pilgrim Abbas by train. Stephanie had no car. I gave silent thanks to the law which did not demand the owner's name on the license stuck to the wind-shield.

"You still have your apartment in Chelsea, then?"

I hoped a nod was sufficient. I would have to get used to glib lies for the next two days.

"I once had a house in Royal Square," he said. "It was the place I went to between climbs."

"You miss the mountains?"

"Of course."

It was a stupid question, but it was a panic effort to keep the conversation away from myself.

"Everest?" I said.

"Good God, no. The nearest I got to that was Annapurna. But never mind about mountains. I invited you here to get to know you."

"That sounds rather one-sided, Mr. Seal . . ."

"Fabian."

"Fabian, then," I conceded. "But I want to know more about you, too. Your life is interesting, mine isn't. So you won't mind if I also ask you questions, will you?"

I felt that I had startled him by my challenge, but he answered easily and with authority. "Not if you answer mine first." He paused, then gave me a direct look. "You know, of course, about the relationship between your mother and me."

"Yes."

"And that for the past two years we hadn't met at all."

"Of . . . of course."

"We met again a few weeks ago. Did she tell you? Or hadn't you seen her lately?"

I bent my head, watching my fingers play with the little crystal glass, and did not answer.

"I'm sorry." He misunderstood my seeming evasion. "It's too early yet to talk about your mother."

"Oh. Oh no, I don't mind. In fact, I want to. It . . . helps."

I had come to Dorset to hear him talk, to sift the conversation, to find out exactly how Stephanie was involved. But I had to remember that there had been an open verdict on Livanova's death and that Fabian Seal might have been involved; I had to remember, too, that I was Livanova's presumed daughter.

"Are you working at the moment?" I asked.

"That's why I'm at Jessamy. I'm designing the scenery and costumes for a new ballet. But you don't want to hear about it."

"Why ever not?"

He said, disinterestedly, "For the simple reason that you don't like ballet."

"Why should you think that?"

"Because it's natural for people to dislike that which they think has come between them and the person from whom they want love."

We were getting too deeply involved in words that might trap me. I tossed off a flippant answer. "Oh, all that is too intense for me."

To my surprise, he laughed. "But you *are* intense, my dear. You're intense—*and* tense—sitting there now, half wanting to fight with me." His strong fingers curled around his whiskey glass. "All right, then. What shall we talk about?"

The things I want to know—and most of all, what is the important matter you had to discuss with Stephanie?

I did not dare rush the essential questions. They must be introduced casually into the conversation. I was on safer ground asking him about his work.

"This ballet," I said. "I'd like to hear about it. Will it be one of those short ones they do nowadays?"

36

"We're breaking with modern ideas and mounting a three-act ballet on classical lines. But we can only do it because we have the essentials for such length—a strong cast, music by Hannaford, choreography by Freyberg, artistic director Gilderoy, the theater Covent Garden. Anything else?"

"And *you* are working down here? I'd have thought you all planned a ballet together."

"When I first start a design, I like to go away from the rest of those involved. I'll submit my designs for the scenery and the costumes when I'm ready, and after that we'll all get together in London and the discussions will begin. In the meantime this is an ideal place for me to hide out and work."

It seemed to me that he needed to be either strong or ruthless or without sensitivity to stay on in this house where he and Livanova had been lovers.

"There are other reasons why this is a fine place for me," he said. "Livanova's practice room is ideal for planning sets and lighting and effects, and there is also a witch living almost on the doorstep."

"Oh!"

"Don't look so startled. Her name is Hobbin. And the ballet is about witchcraft."

"Bell, book and candle," I murmured. "What is it to be called?"

He said, as if he had been asked many times and was a little bored, "*The Witch and the Maiden*."

"Based on an old fairy tale, like *The Sleeping Beauty?*"

"No. A perfectly new dance drama."

"Was . . . my mother going to dance the leading role?" It was the first time I had called her that and it gave me an odd sense of personal involvement.

"No," Fabian was saying. "Miranda McCall will be dancing the bewitched girl. She has all the attributes of innocence and evanescence; her head and arm movements are quite wonderful and her name will pull in the crowds."

"I . . . see."

"Do you?" It was obvious that he thought my ambiguous statement quite pointless, which it was. I was too on edge and wary to make sensible comments and I felt that he didn't care whether I was interested in the new ballet or not. It was as if we were both trying to gain an entry into the other's mind, each of us alert and watchful.

37

Whatever his personal feelings, whatever emotions might touch him, lightly or deeply, he could control them as he wished. He wore not one inch of his heart on his sleeve; I felt his strength and it frightened me.

I watched him fondle the cat, which had settled on the arm of his chair. Fabian was capable of long silences, which were fine if two people enjoyed harmony, but not when one, at least, was nervous and on edge.

"It's strange to create a ballet on witchcraft these days."

"Why?"

"It seems so medieval."

"On the contrary, there is as much witchcraft now as there ever was. A great many people possess occult powers, and much that we do today in innocence, or in a rush of romanticism, has its origin in old witchcraft."

"Touching wood for luck," I murmured.

"Too obvious, too simple, too silly." Again he looked a little bored with me, as if my comments were on such a pedestrian level that it was a waste of time to continue the conversation. He turned to the purring cat. Then, remembering his function as a host, asked politely but with no real interest, "Have you never lit candles on your table?"

"Yes."

"When a man was coming to dinner?"

(To show him what a charming apartment I had, what a good cook I was . . . and all for nothing. We had quarreled that night over a silly thing like a party he hadn't been asked to, and I had.)

Fabian was saying, "Lighted candles originated in order to evoke magic forces."

"My lighted candles didn't evoke anything marvelous for me," I retorted.

"Perhaps you didn't believe enough, or want badly enough."

"Yes, perhaps so," I said. It was true. I had wasted no sleep on that probable lover.

"As I told you just now, we have a witch almost on our doorstep."

"What does she do, look in a crystal ball and tell the village girls that their husbands are going to be good-looking and rich? And do they cross her hand with silver?"

He didn't echo my laughter. "If you believe that all there is in the world is what you see with your eyes, then I'm afraid you're arrogant, my dear. But let's not get into some deep discussion; it's far too big a subject." Suddenly he laughed. "And by the way, don't let anything I have said disturb your sleep. There are no ghosts at Jessamy."

"That's fine, because I enjoy my sleep. I usually have such nice dreams."

I saw his eyebrows lift, and I supposed even that light remark could be dangerous. For negative people—and Stephanie was negative—perhaps didn't have bright dreams. I would have to be cautious even in trivial conversation.

"I'm glad you could get away and come down here. You'll stay a week, at least?"

"I . . . I thought . . . two days."

"Are you between jobs?"

"Well—"

He took that as an embarrassed admittance of still another failure to earn a living. "Then that's settled. There's no hurry for you to return. Or have you anything lined up for yourself?"

"Yes."

"Doing . . . ?"

"Oh, nothing remarkable. Assistant to a man in public relations."

"Assistant? Without having to train first?"

He was too quick. I said, "Oh, I mean . . . I'm joining his staff. I expect I shall be a sort of Girl Friday for quite a long time." To steer a course between a truth and a lie was going to be difficult to sustain. I thought with mounting horror of a week spent here in masquerade, and I knew that I would have to find some excuse to escape before those seven days were up.

"It's such a pity your mother dropped her relatives and so unlike the Russian side of her. Young people should have a sense of belonging. It's only when you reach my age that you can choose to be like Kipling's cat and walk alone."

"Oh, Livanova *did* belong—to her dancing. That was her world."

"Every time you speak of her, you use her name, Livanova. She was your mother." His voice had the sudden timbre of ice.

"But everyone talks of her that way."

"Even her daughter?"

I could find no immediate answer and so I resorted to a shrug. The man who sat opposite me was too alert. Talking to him, even being with him, was like fording a stream, moving from stepping

39

stone to stepping stone, avoiding the swift currents between them.

Fabian rose and crossed the room, standing with his back to me. In the brief silence I made my first plan for next morning. I would have to find a place from which I could telephone the hospital in private. The house would be too dangerous, but it was desperately necessary to know if Stephanie had recovered consciousness. I would first ask to speak to the doctor, tell him what I was doing and explain that he had been the cause of my wild decision. I would bring him into the plot because I would feel stronger with an ally, however unwilling he might prove to be.

I knew I couldn't possibly telephone from the house and ask after the health of a girl I was supposed to be. Ears would flap and voices would whisper. "Shock has made her a little mad, calling up London to ask how she herself is." *Mad . . .*

V

"STEPHANIE . . ."

I started. *I was Stephanie.* But there had seemed to be a long silence after our curious preliminary conversation, and with so much to think about, I had relaxed my vigilance about my new identity. It shattered me that in the first quarter of an hour in Fabian Seal's company, I had forgotten.

He was glancing over his shoulder at me, features questioning.

"I'm sorry," I said quickly. "I was looking at *that*." I nodded toward the first thing that caught my eye. It was a tasseled banner with tongues of fire embroidered on it.

"That's Oriflamme," Fabian said, "the banner the kings of France carried into battle. But it's not, of course, an original. I expect the real Oriflamme was copied by some bored little princess, stitching away in a cold stone room in a French château. Even as a copy, though threadbare in places, it's rather fine, isn't it? But this is what I wanted to show you. Come here."

I went to his side. He reached up and switched on a light inside a display cabinet, and I saw rows of fans, some made of lace, some with painted crinolined figures, one of Chinese men, their clothes decorated with what looked like tiny precious stones of ruby and sapphire and turquoise.

"Your mother's collection," Fabian said.

"They're beautiful."

"You remember them, surely. But perhaps you don't. You were a very little girl when you lived in the London house with her. When she took her Park Lane apartment, you were sent to boarding school."

I remained tactfully silent.

"When Livanova bought Jessamy, the fans came down here."

I had never heard of the collection of fans.

"She inherited some and collected others. There is one that is said to have belonged to the great Anna Pavlova. That one—" He pointed to it.

It was of ivory, gently yellowed with age, and it had delicate bird paintings on each narrow panel.

"Though that was probably someone's story told in order to sell it. Your mother adored them. She gave you one, didn't she?"

Then I remembered that little fan of fussy frilled silk which Stephanie had once ripped out of a drawer and begun to tear apart in impotent fury because her mother had refused to increase her allowance.

Fabian held out his hand for my glass. A second martini was usually quite safe with me. But his were stronger than any I had tasted before and I drew my glass away.

He reached over and took it firmly from me. "This is a celebration. And quite frankly, I think you'd better unwind, don't you?"

"Oh, I'm fine." I looked up at him and met only mockery.

"My dear Stephanie, you're as nervous as a little cat in a storm. And there's no need."

I sat down and hoped I looked physically relaxed, although every muscle behind my outwardly slack attitude was tight with alarm.

I wondered what he knew about Livanova's will, but I had no idea what circumstances had brought him to Jessamy. The rift between the dancer and himself could have been healed. Or Fabian could have come to Jessamy in order to discuss some professional point with her, and for some reason, stayed on.

The "important matter" he had written about in his letter was something I knew I had to wait for him to mention. As I had no idea what it was, I could all too easily ask in a way that would reveal to him my ignorance, and that I didn't dare do. On the other hand, I had sensed in his letter a hint of menace which made me far more confused and alarmed than I had imagined I would be. Fabian Seal was a sophisticated and supremely self-possessed man.

I had been certain that I had planned answers to most questions that I would be asked, and in a way, I had. But I realized now that there were snags I had not considered. One was the fact that questions could be phrased in more than one way. Certain ways were easy to answer and others more difficult. Fabian seemed to choose a direct and difficult way. I was troubled, too, by the curious glint in his eyes. I was reasonably certain that it had nothing to do with a doubt as to my identity; it was rather a kind of natural mockery. The face belonged to a man of strength, of independence, of powerful emotions, but the eyes were those of a man who laughed at life. He was an enigma, and that was why I was uneasy. I had no idea how to behave toward him. I only knew in that first hour with him that I was going to need far more caution than I had anticipated.

Darkness had fallen and Fabian closed one of the tall French windows and returned to his chair, pausing to fondle the cat.

"He's beautiful," I said.

"We call him Jupiter, but no one now remembers why."

"Did he . . . was he . . . ?"

"Your mother's cat? No, he came with the house. Take Jessamy and you take Jupiter."

"Things usually go in three's," I said. "There should be something else here with the name beginning with 'J.' " I was making polite conversation.

"So you decry magic but admit to superstition?" He didn't wait for me to answer. "You know what your mother's particular favorite was, don't you?"

Oh yes, I knew that. Stephanie had told me more than once. "She always had something green about her room or on stage when she danced—a certain green," I said triumphantly, able to answer at last.

"A rich grass-green," he said. "Always that. The color of the famous peridot necklace she once had, which was stolen."

I nodded, remembering very well. It had been just one more bitterness for Stephanie: "She's so careless with her possessions and yet she's too mean to give me nice things. That necklace belonged to my great-grandmother; it could have been mine one day. But no, she goes and loses it and shrugs her shoulders. Nothing is of any value to her but her dancing."

Her dancing. I wondered if, when Livanova had patched up her quarrel with Fabian and lent him her house, she had expected to dance the Maiden in the new ballet. It was something important to find out.

A sound outside the house broke the stillness.

"That will be Dominick," Fabian said. "You've heard of him, of course."

"Mother's accompanist down here. Yes."

"He's staying on until he can find work—never an easy thing for a young pianist whose experience has been no more than accompanying a dancer when she is practicing alone."

The door opened and a brush of cold air swept in with the man who seemed, on entry, to light up the room.

"You see?" Fabian said. "She has arrived. Stephanie, this is Dominick Hunt."

I guessed, as he paused in the doorway, that he was in his late twenties. His manner was hesitant, as if he felt he might be intruding. But the hesitation was too long for that and it was rather as if a new tension had entered the room, one that was not mine and yet for which I could be responsible.

My heart began to thud like a drum. I waited for Dominick Hunt to denounce me. My hands were clasped together in my lap and my nails dug into my palms. It was such a moment of sheer agony of apprehension that I had to do something to stop myself breaking out into a cold sweat of guilt. I held out my hand to him, and with a fierce muscular effort, managed what I hoped was a smile. But as he crossed the room to my side, his evident surprise at something about me held me in my state of alarm.

"It's uncanny," he said, "the way you hold out your hand to me exactly as your mother used to. I'm afraid it gave me a moment's shock."

I glanced down and saw that I greeted people as Stephanie did, and as Livanova must have done, as if I expected my hand to be kissed. I was not only acutely embarrassed because of its affectation, but shaken that I could so unthinkingly have absorbed one of Stephanie's gestures. People had laughed at her for this pretension, but I knew that it was something she had watched her mother do many times before Livanova had decided that her daughter was reaching an age when she could no longer be dragged around as a small, pretty appendage. Reared in Continental towns, where in the old days exaggerated gallantry was the ritual, such a gesture was natural to Livanova. It had also become a habit Stephanie had never bothered to unlearn.

I covered the silence with a quick flow of explanation. "Oh, people always think I'm trying to be grand or foreign or something. But I'm not. It's quite mechanical, I don't even know I'm doing it." The explanation came with such ease that for a moment or two I was pleased with myself. Then I became faintly frightened. It mustn't be so easy that my own personality became submerged.

"I always found it charming," he said.

I didn't answer, but as I glanced at Fabian Seal, I thought I saw a shadow of amusement cross his face. Livanova never offered herself except for adoration. *This is my hand, which can express every emotion, can tell any story by a movement of my fingers. I do not offer my hand to you as others do; I am not like others . . .*

While I interpreted Livanova's mannered gesture, I answered Dominick Hunt's kindly questions. Yes, I had a very pleasant journey down . . . No, I didn't know Dorset, adding, "very well," just in case Stephanie had ever been there and I had forgotten.

Fabian asked Dominick how the audition went that afternoon in Dorchester, explaining to me, "There's a new ensemble being formed to play at concerts. They plan to concentrate for the time being on the west of England and they're looking for a pianist."

"But something has come up in London that could be far better," Dominick was saying. "You were working this morning when the call came through. It's to join the Forrester Piano Trio. They're known over the whole of Britain and it would be a tremendous thing for me. Palmer says there's just a chance I'll be called for an audition for that."

"Palmer," Fabian said, "being Dominick's London agent."

I listened and made appropriate comments. But other thoughts ran parallel. My grandmother had treasured a photograph of Ru-

45

pert Brooke, the poet who had died in the First World War. She had known him at Cambridge when he was at the university there.

This man, Dominick Hunt, had the same golden glamour, the same marvelous profile, with forehead, nose and chin in clear sculptured lines. The lamplight caught his hair, which was a gold that neither Stephanie, with her pale-corn tint, nor I, with my darker blond, could match in richness of tone. His eyes were deep, dark gray; his mouth, sensitive and sensuous.

I thought: This man has everything. Talent . . . looks . . .

"We met once. Do you remember?"

I dared to look straight into his eyes, playing for time. A lie could catch me out.

"It was in Berkeley Square," he said. "I was in town because your mother wanted to work through an arrangement of a dance. We had practiced it at Jessamy and she wanted me to hear the full orchestration. You were coming toward us and your mother introduced you. But we were late, so it was a very brief meeting. I remember I wished you'd take off your dark glasses so that I could see you properly. Your hair was loose, like it is now. I remember, too, that you wore the most enchanting aquamarine earrings. Your mother remarked on them, and you said that they were always falling off and you were on your way to have them adapted for pierced ears."

"Oh no." I put up my hands quickly. I had never even thought to have my ears pierced. But Stephanie had. And as Dominick said, those little blue jewels she had adored had kept falling off because the lobes of her ears were so small. I said, "I . . . I didn't have them pierced, after all."

Two men watched me, on the surface kindly, indulgently. But underneath, I had no idea what thoughts were in the minds of either of them.

"Have you still got the earrings?"

"No. I . . . I lost them." I lifted my voice a little, making it lighter, more like Stephanie's, caught up with a new fear that Dominick might recall her voice. But then, traffic had probably been roaring through Berkeley Square at the time and it would have distorted sound.

"I tried to get in touch with you once," Dominick said. "I had seats for a first night. But there was no reply from your number."

"I'm sorry."

"So was I. But that's put right now, isn't it?" He smiled at me.

For the next ten minutes, while Dominick accepted a drink, the conversation touched on nothing very important. Fabian Seal was setting the tone and the pace. It was he who asked the questions, who steered the talk between the three of us into the channels he chose.

Then, as Dominick had his second drink, Fabian turned to me. "I think we've got time for me to show you your mother's practice room before dinner. That is, if you would like to see it. If not, if you'd prefer to wait a few days . . ."

"I'd like to see it, please."

The lamps had been turned on in the hall and the painting over the stone fireplace glowed in the lights. It was unmistakably Tatiana Livanova, in a flimsy white ballet skirt molded to her figure and a tiny silver crown on her head. Her dark hair was drawn back in the classical style and the artist had painted her face in a strange magnolia color that gave it a luminous quality. Even so, nothing could soften the power of her features—the broad forehead, the slanting, slightly Magyar eyes, the strong, narrow lips.

"You aren't in the least like her," Fabian said.

"No. I'm not."

"Of course, your father was fair."

I didn't answer. My father's hair was dark red, his eyes as blue as gentians.

The cat was following us, tail erect, purring softly. I bent and stroked him as Fabian opened a door. "Come along in."

I doubted if there was another room in an English country house like the one I entered. The lights Fabian switched on found strong reflections in the great mirrors stretching to three-quarters of the way up the high walls.

I followed Fabian's casual upward glance. The ceiling was heavily molded—a vast spread of white arum lilies had been sculpted there, flower and leaf, leaf and flower, and each one was reflected in the enormous walls of glass, so that the massed lilies seemed to become incandescent.

There was a white piano on a dais and a *barre* fitted up for Livanova's practice. Even at Jessamy Court, where she came when not dancing, she could not relax from the disciplining of her body—rehearsing an arm, the curve of a hand until she had achieved perfection in the slightest movement.

In a far corner was an alcove framed by off-white curtains. In it was a divan piled with green cushions, by its side a small mother-of-pearl table. On it stood an empty cut-glass decanter and a crystal goblet.

"Your mother used to lie and rest there after practice. She loved this room. I was here when she planned it, and it took ten men to carry each panel of glass. Mirrors for dancers are not an expression of vanity, they need them for seeing themselves with truth. For dancers, mirrors have to be pitiless." He crossed the room. "Here, each one hides a closet." He drew on a slot cut in the glass. The mirror slid back and I saw a line of ballet clothes, frothy and feathered and sequined. "All used long ago and cast off. But she could never bear to throw them away. So she housed them here. And this"—he had closed the closet and opened another —"contains old props."

It was much deeper than the first one, and I saw little artificial trees, a small round ebony table, a gilded chair, a broken column that could have been part of a stage ruin.

"Your mother liked to use props even when she was practicing. It gave her a sense of theater." He kicked gently at a carved footstool. "She was essentially traditional; she hated gimmicks as much as I do."

I turned and looked about me. The only out-of-character thing in that room was the trestle table by the door. On it was piled an untidy conglomeration of sketches, colored crayons and charcoal sticks. I would have liked to know whether it had needed a great effort in forgetfulness to work in this room that had been Livanova's, or whether, in here, Fabian felt close to her. But before I could summon the courage to ask so personal a question, a sound stirred the quiet. It could have been a bell or a gong. It rose as gradually as a rustle of wind in the distance and grew in volume so pure, so haunting that it seemed to express all the joy and the sadness of the world. A sound hinting at things beyond realities.

I looked quickly at Fabian.

"Mrs. Manfred never knows where we are, so she summons us to meals with the bell."

"I've never heard one like that before."

"I doubt if you will. It's rare in the West. It's Tibetan and was given me in Nepal after a climb. The Sherpas say that it summons the good spirits, so you see even religion has its magical side. Shall we go and eat?"

The reverberation took a long time to die away, and I could imagine such bells echoing through the lower slopes of the Himalayas.

Our conversation over dinner was very general. We talked of the theater, music, travel, and my contribution consisted of cautious comments and vague answers. It was lucky that Stephanie had had no professional training or I might have been asked questions on subjects I could not possibly answer. No one mentioned Livanova's name.

During the delicious meal I found opportunities to ask questions, trying to probe behind the façade of this man who could possibly hold the key to Stephanie's illness. Did he enjoy living so deep in the country, I asked, and in a place that was so far from London? Did he intend to stay long at Jessamy?

"Oh, I can work better if I am left alone, and in my London house there is always the telephone to disturb me. Here, Mrs. Manfred guards me from callers."

"The house is very beautiful, isn't it?" I said, peeling a ripe peach.

"Yes."

Every attempt I made to break through the superficialities was met with a nonchalant answer and very little that enlightened me. He replied politely enough, but he gave nothing away.

I discovered one fact, important only because I was intensely interested in people. If appearances illuminated character, I would have said that Fabian would have been the one who took life seriously. I was wrong. While he talked and listened, his light tawny-green eyes were brilliant with something between interest and mockery. He was like a master who knows his pupils too well to be fooled by pretense, a man understanding the world and its people, a sophisticate without illusions. But if I were already suspect, he had every intention of playing my game—and that thought alarmed me. Now that it was too late, I wished I had resisted all arguments, but I knew that if I had had that meeting with the doctor over again, I would act in exactly the same way.

Dominick interested me, too. I would have expected him to be the more light-hearted. But I was wrong. He entered into the conversation at table easily enough, gave opinions, ideas, but all the time there was a seriousness about him, so that only very occasionally a fleeting smile would light up his marvelous face. I wondered what childhood unhappiness had drained the laughter out of him, or whether Livanova's death was a shock he had not yet been able to shake off.

Mrs. Manfred finally brought in oranges soaked in kirsch.

"I see you appreciate food." Fabian had not missed the way my eyes had lit up. I loved oranges.

"I'm no connoisseur," I said, "and my cooking isn't very imaginative."

"Your mother had a sparrow's appetite."

And now that she was dead, it seemed that Fabian could talk about her as if he felt no more deeply for Livanova than an acquaintance. Or it could be that he was the complete master of his emotions and nothing that was said or done could shake his iron control.

Fabian was saying that he had to go out. He paused in the drawing-room doorway. "I doubt if I'll be long, but it's a matter concerning fishing rights on the stretch of river our self-styled Lord of the Manor owns. I'm fighting for his tenants, who want to fish there, and I wish we were still in the age of pistols at dawn. It would give me pleasure to shoot the mean old bastard. And don't worry, I'll see you'll never meet him and suffer his pomposity."

Fabian was one of those people who, upon deciding to leave, left. He didn't hover in the doorway, asking me if I'd be all right, wondering what Dominick was going to do. He left us as quickly and silently as Jupiter, who followed him, probably because "fish" was a word he understood.

I said to Dominick, "He takes an interest, then, in country affairs."

He was looking out the window, and instead of answering me, he said, "It's a lovely night. Would you like a walk?"

"Yes."

"Then go and fetch your coat. It may be cold."

VI

HE WAS IN THE HALL as I came down the stairs, my coat worn like a cloak over my shoulders.

"Stephanie Clair," he said slowly, watching me.

I hesitated for a moment on the last stair, holding my breath. For one awful moment I thought I heard doubt in his voice. Then he held out a hand to me and I knew that my imagination was playing tricks.

"Would you like to go through the woods or down to the sea?"

I chose the sea. The high cliff that shielded Jessamy was black against a sky turned indigo by the slit of a moon. Seen from the beach, it resembled a great bird with serrated, outspread wings. These were lower than the central body of the rock and less steep. I could even see in the dim light small, sparse bushes that had dared to find a footing on the ledges of the two wings. There was a slight wind and the tide was far enough out for the tumbled rocks to be visible like black teeth against the wide smooth sea.

We walked near the waves and my feet sank into the water-saturated sand.

"Liv . . . my mother loved this place, didn't she?"

"Yes. And so do I. Jessamy was all I wanted for the moment. I worked for a great artist, and when Livanova wasn't here I could concentrate on my own career." He paused. "I've got a long way to go, and opportunities in music don't come easily." He walked a little away and then reached a hand back for me. "Shall we sit here for a while? It's sheltered."

There was a low ledge on the cliff face and we sat together, both of us hugging our knees and looking out over the faintly moon-flecked sea. Dominick was restless. He lit a cigarette, stubbed it out and kept glancing about him as if he were expecting someone.

I broke the silence. "It's very deserted."

"It's almost Jessamy's private beach. Livanova used to bathe if the weather was very warm, though she wasn't much of a swimmer. We had good times down here, and now . . ." He broke off, turning his head away.

So at least *he* mourned her. I asked gently, "Have you known Fabian long?"

"Only since he came back to Jessamy. And that was about three weeks ago."

"I don't understand," I said, frowning at the sea. "Livanova died in London. And she was guest artist with the Ashenden Ballet Company, so she couldn't have had any plans to stay down here with Fabian. She couldn't possibly commute between Dorset and London. I'm sorry," I added quickly, "but you see, I know so little about my mother's movements. That doesn't make sense to you, does it?"

"It does if you knew Livanova," he said sadly.

"How long is Fabian staying here?"

Dominick got up and walked away from me and stood at the sea's edge. His voice came back, sharp and vibrating, "God knows . . . God knows what is in his mind."

I wondered why it hadn't struck him to say "It's your house now. It's up to you to tell him how long he can stay." I could think of no way to approach the question without giving myself away.

Yet I knew if I kept the conversation flowing, I might learn more about Fabian.

"He tells me he's working on a ballet."

"Yes. *The Witch and the Maiden.*" Dominick turned and faced me. The sliver of moon was behind him, so that his face was shadowed. But his voice was angry. "That's the reason given for his being here."

"You make it sound as if you think there's another."

"I'm sorry. I didn't mean that. It's just that I can't answer for Fabian. I don't know him any more than you do. Perhaps no one has ever really known him, except Livanova." He paused. "It's curious that we can't establish some kind of friendship. After all, he had loved her and I was devoted to her—or perhaps grateful is a truer word. You see"—he kicked the sand with the tip of his shoe—"Livanova more or less picked me up out of the gutter. I was bankrupt when she met me in Dorchester, where I had gone to plead with them not to take away my few bits of furniture. The authorities had said, with the cold indifference of the law, that I would be left my clothes and the 'tool of my trade.' That meant they could not by law take my piano from me, though they looked as if they wanted to. Livanova happened to be in Dorchester. Her accompanist in Dorset had just become ill and was old and about to retire. She was looking for another. The point was that she needed one who would live at Jessamy Court," he said wryly. "I had hoped for London, but she had all the necessary people there—her housekeeper, her secretary. So I came here. And I'm the outsider. Fabian Seal is a stranger to me, and so are you. Though I think I know why you're here."

I felt a rising panic and refused to meet his eyes. Whatever he thought he knew, it couldn't be quite the truth or his voice wouldn't be so gentle. I pretended that the clasp of my thin gold bracelet was loose, checked it and waited. Silence was so often the best ally.

"You came here," Dominick said, "to find out why your mother did what she did."

"What . . . did . . . she . . . do?"

"Oh, Stephanie, you don't have to pretend with me. It's no secret, after all. Your mother even told me once what she intended to do with Jessamy Court, and she said you knew, too."

Without realizing that I had moved, I found myself standing

facing him. The wet sand felt cold through my shoes and the waves were sleepy and hushed.

"What am I supposed to know?"

"How guarded you are! That Fabian would—and has—inherited the house, of course."

The moon was only in its first quarter but it seemed suddenly to pour too mercilessly onto my upturned face. I moved away, watching the polished black and silver water, trying to reassure myself.

I was safe. I was also, by a single sentence, very much wiser. I knew now that Stephanie had been aware of Fabian Seal's inheritance. It was something she must have learned very recently, during the weeks I hadn't seen her. But since she disliked the country, I couldn't imagine it would upset her to the point of collapse. She might resent it, considering the place as hers, but most certainly even Stephanie's characteristic overcharged emotions wouldn't plunge her into such a state at hearing the news. Something far deeper was involved, and if I was to help her, I had to know what it was.

I began to walk on slowly, stepping between the black rocks. "Fabian must have loved the house, too," I said.

"Loved it? Or wanted it?"

"I don't know. I know so little," I added with absolute truth.

Dominick laid a hand lightly on my arm. "You aren't upset, Stephanie?"

"Why should I be? My mother had a right to . . . leave her possessions as she wished."

"If you say that, you're being very generous."

I accepted the undeserved praise. "And you," I said. "What will you do?"

Dominick said, "For the moment I have nowhere to go. This was my home, and no one could possibly have foreseen the dreadful thing. As soon as I can, I'll get away. Fabian is being good to me, and yet, dear heaven, I can't feel grateful. That's bad, isn't it? Perhaps it's because shock has numbed me."

I didn't comment. There was a more important question I wanted to ask. "Were you here with Fabian the night Livanova died?"

"Neither of us was at Jessamy. I had given myself a few days off and was staying in Lulworth. Fabian had gone to London."

"And gave evidence at the inquest."

"Yes. He had gone to a meeting of the administrators of the

Ashenden Company, something to do with the amount of money he was to be allocated for scenery and costumes."

"And to decide that Miranda McCall would be prima ballerina," I said softly. "I wonder if Livanova minded?"

"It's strange the way you speak of her."

"Because I call her Livanova? Fabian said the same thing to me. But she's more the dancer than my mother. *You* should know that, since she probably seldom talked to you about . . . about me." It was disturbing that my own identity was becoming easy to crush under Stephanie's pale personality. "I suppose it's natural that Fabian should want Jessamy," I said. "After all, it was *their* place, wasn't it?"

For a moment Dominick was silent. Then he said with a low intensity, "Do you realize that Fabian must be very afraid of you?"

"Why?" It was a purely automatic question, because I knew. I stepped carefully over a rock, bent and picked up a ribbon of brown seaweed, ran it through my fingers and waited.

"You could be here to make trouble," he said. "You might go to court and some judge could revoke your mother's will in your favor, so that the house reverts to you."

"I have no intention of fighting the will." It was a wild presumption. I had no idea how Stephanie would feel when she was well again.

Dominick said quietly, "Just one thing, and please listen to me. If you should change your mind and decide to fight the will, just be very careful."

"Careful? How?"

"Don't mention it down here. Keep your decision to yourself until you're back in London."

I looked toward the distance, where the lights from a cluster of houses shattered the darkness. A fear stirred inside me like a coil of ice unwinding and spreading through my whole body.

"And now," Dominick said, "let's stop this difficult conversation. You're here and it's a lovely place to be. But you're cold." His hand was on my arm, so that he must have felt my shaking limbs. "Let's get back into the warmth of the house."

He led me up the beach and onto a rough path that ran around the base of the cliff, between thick bushes and trees. An owl streaked across our faces on silent wings, dive-bombing a tiny animal, probably a field mouse. I raced after it to scare it away.

"You may have saved that small rodent," Dominick said, "but he'll try again when you're out of sight and he'll catch the next one. You're not a country girl, are you, Stephanie?"

"Oh yes, I—" I stopped suddenly. I had nearly told him the truth. *I was brought up in a village in Berkshire.* But Stephanie had lived almost all her life in London.

"There are predators everywhere," Dominick said. "You have to let them have their way. Humans, animals, birds—they live off each other, and we call it the balance of nature. Don't be too soft-hearted."

We were very silent as we walked through the woods of silver birches to Jessamy's smooth lawns.

When we arrived back at the house Fabian was in the drawing room listening to music. He sat relaxed, his head resting against the tall chair back, a brandy and coffee by his side.

I checked my footsteps at the door.

"Go on in," Dominick said.

"I'll take my coat upstairs first."

As I went up the steeply curving staircase, it struck me what a strange choice this house was for someone as light, as ethereal as Tatiana Livanova. Yet, by thinking that, I was being concerned with her as the dancer, not the woman. She wasn't ethereal. She might tear the heart out of an audience who saw her in classic or modern dramatic roles, but she herself had been powerfully ambitious. She was a woman whose loveliness of movement, whose perfect grace and faery quality had been created by harsh discipline and iron determination. Perhaps this great house, darkened by its medieval windows and the paneling in the hall, was not such an odd choice, after all.

I pushed open the door of my room and paused before I went in, looking behind me. The carved posts of the gallery, which surrounded three sides of the hall, flung deep shadows across the floor and at the far end I saw the line of moonshine piercing the walls of the west wing. That, Fabian had told me, was where Livanova had had her suite. Lying there in her bed, surely she must have felt the great loneliness of that long, dark passage that led from the gallery to her suite of rooms. But of course, when she first came to Jessamy, there was Fabian; and when they parted, there could have been, for all I knew, someone else who countered the silence and the hollowness and the isolation of that suite in the west wing.

I walked into my room. There was a soft fluttering sound and a cold draft of air blew about me. I switched on the light and a bird flew past me. I backed, startled, and saw it perch on the heavy gilt frame of an old, heavily varnished landscape painting.

One of my windows was open. I tried to urge the bird toward it, but every movement I made only sent it fluttering and stupefied from one picture frame to another. It was a fully grown sparrow, yet its short, panic flights about the room were like those of a clumsy fledgling.

I went to a second window and opened that. As I did so, I glanced down into the garden. A shadow moved on the lawn. The creaking of the window as I flung it up caused him to raise his head—Fabian stood for a moment, face lifted, so that his features were faintly outlined in moonlight.

The bird made a fluttering circle around the room and flew near enough for me to lift my arm in a curve to drive it again toward one of the open windows. Blinded by its own futile fear, the sparrow flew into my face, and I ducked.

If it hadn't been for the obvious panic in that diminutive body, the whole game would have been one of exasperated amusement, like playing "touch" with a child. As it was, we circled the room, the sparrow and I, he—or she—perching always just out of my reach, as if I were a predatory animal.

I did not know whether the hammering on my door startled the bird as it startled me. But I swung around, called "Come in," and Fabian entered.

"I saw from the garden," he said. "I'm so sorry." He crossed the room to where the sparrow was perched on the landscape painting. "Bridget, a village woman who comes morning and evening to help Mrs. Manfred, always opens the windows when she turns down the beds, and the bird must have flown in. They're not usually so stupid, but I suppose even the bird world has its idiots." His movements toward the sparrow were exactly as mine had been, and yet, where I had succeeded only in making it flutter hysterically, Fabian drove the bird quietly toward the window.

"These rooms always have to be well aired. Otherwise, with so much old wood about, the house gives off a fusty smell, which I dislike. But the windows are supposed to be closed after about a quarter of an hour. I'm so sorry, but Bridget must have forgotten."

The bird, having almost exhausted itself, just managed to hurl itself through the window, crouching for a moment on the outside sill while it collected its strength again. Then it flew off.

"I'm sorry this should have happened in your room." Fabian closed the window.

"Oh, that's all right. I'm sorry for the bird. It's probably the only sparrow in Dorset still awake."

"I know how terrified you are of anything feathered." He was looking at me over his shoulder as he pulled the heavy silk curtains across the second window.

Of course. *Stephanie was afraid of birds*. And I had forgotten. Had she been there, she would have fled and huddled behind a closed door until someone drove the bird out.

"You knew, then, that . . . I was afraid of birds?"

"Your mother told me once. I believe you were scared of some feathered costume she was wearing for *Fire Bird*. Wasn't that one of the few times you saw her in her dressing room after a performance?"

I supposed that was correct. I nodded and didn't feel so badly about an implied lie. "Thank you for coping."

"Think nothing of it. I'll see that it doesn't happen again."

The door closed and I was alone. "Thank you" I had said, as if I were really grateful to him for saving me from my fears of a harmless sparrow. I was standing in the middle of the room, and as I listened to Fabian's footsteps fading down the long passage, I faced the shocked fact that when he had reminded me of Stephanie's fear of feathered things, I had actually felt that fear stir in me. Perhaps I was an actress *manqué*. Perhaps, if I tried hard enough, I could think myself anyone I chose. It was, of course, too stupid. I knew who I was, and any mannerisms I copied from my long friendship with Stephanie were unimportant. I was merely playing a part too well. But it was just a part and the important thing was to see myself in my new role: Rachel playing Stephanie and being the observer in complete control of the situation.

VII

I AWOKE UNREFRESHED, slowly got out of bed and drew back the curtains. It was a day of bleached light, the sky hanging above the land and the sea, silver-gray like the inside of an oyster shell. There was a stillness everywhere as a clock in the hall below struck seven.

I had been told that breakfast would be brought up to me. I went back to bed, lay on my stomach and faced the fact that last night had been merely a rehearsal for the day—or the two days—that lay ahead. Not more, please heaven, not Fabian's suggested week.

Mrs. Manfred brought me breakfast. Eggs delicately scrambled, crisp dark toast and honey, and coffee. There was also a note from Fabian.

I have to go out on unexpected business. Will see you at lunch. Enjoy your morning. Ask Mrs. Manfred to show you the staircase down to the vaults. They are all that is left of the monastery which stood on this site four hundred years ago.

When I had dressed, I took my tray and went to find the kitchen. Mrs. Manfred was busy giving cleaning instructions to a village woman whom she introduced to me as Bridget.

"Mr. Seal told me there was a bird in your room last night, Miss Clair. I'm so sorry."

Bridget's Dorset dialect was far more difficult to translate than Mrs. Manfred's. But her smile covered her entire rosy face, kindly, anxious, apologetic. Her eyes were quick and darting.

"That's all right," I said. "Mr. Seal coped."

I left the kitchen and went on a tour of most of the house. For a while I stood looking out the window at the gray and silver mist lying so lightly over the green landscape that it seemed a dream setting. Later, the day would have that faraway golden shimmer that made September my favorite month.

I wandered around the gallery that encircled the second floor, looking at the few portraits of some previous owner's ancestors. They were slightly dull, but painted with such care, it was sad that they had been sold so casually with the house. Only when I leaned over the balustrade and looked down into the hall did Jessamy Court take on its other personality. Livanova, looking from her great portrait, gave the house its new life.

I wondered what Livanova's suite was like, but I knew that even as her presumed daughter, I could not explore the rooms without Fabian's invitation. I was quite certain that Mrs. Manfred would not suggest that I visit them without his direct instructions.

I went into the main rooms, interested to see them in daylight. The dining room was dim and the crimson décor did not lighten it. I went from there to a small book-lined room with a typewriter on a low table and files in rows on shelves.

As I went through room after room I remembered reading stories of the old days in Russia, of the heaviness of the draperies that hung over their windows, the dark solidity of their furniture. The Russian side of Tatiana Livanova would have felt at home among the furniture and the chandeliers of Jessamy and would not have wanted to change them.

Although I had never known her, I felt her personality even more strongly that morning, as though she were somewhere near me, challenging my right to play her daughter.

I pushed open the door of the practice room. The great mirrors blocked any windows there originally must have been, and I switched on the light. In the alcove on the far side of the room, it was as if Livanova had just left her couch. There was even a faint dent in the green velvet where her head could have lain, as if no one had shaken the cushion since she had last rested there.

I turned full circle. Three reflections met me. *Three Stephanie Clairs* . . .

I walked slowly toward one reflection. Except for my coloring and height, I was so unlike Stephanie that I was appalled at what I had done. In London, I had imagined that I had thought all around the wild project so that it was fairly foolproof. I faced the fact, now, that I had been so determined to become Stephanie Clair for a few days that I had swept any snags which I could not face into a corner and hidden them. Such was impulse and head-strongness, and such—as I had been told so many times by my family—were my characteristics.

But I was committed, and short of packing up and escaping secretly at night, there was no way out. *Stephanie Clair*. I said the name aloud to my reflection and saw movement in the doorway.

Mrs. Manfred was watching me. I had no idea how long she had been there, but as I swung around to face her, she slipped away out of sight.

I went out and closed the door of the practice room behind me. I found Mrs. Manfred busily dusting the long refectory table in the hall.

"Mr. Seal suggested I go down and look at the vaults," I said.

"Of course, if you wish," she said reluctantly. "I'll show you the way, though I think it's a horrible place."

"Why?"

" 'Tis said that bad things went on down there once, a long time ago."

"Oh, Mrs. Manfred, surely . . ."

"Hobbin says she knows and she be a witch. She says that people round these parts tell stories that their folks told them, that once, long after the monks left Jessamy, someone started a witches' coven there. A hundred, two hundred years ago, they said, in the days when they burned them that they found. But if a place be once used that way, something stays. That's why I never go down there. It'ud give me the creeps. Madame Livanova went down sometimes, but then Hobbin told her about the old tales and she never went down again—she being half-Russian, she believed things."

"Then no one goes there now?"

"Only Mr. Seal to fetch the wine. That's all it be used for these days."

"Since I don't believe in witchcraft, I won't be afraid of old vibrations."

"That be the word Madame Livanova used. Vibrations." Mrs. Manfred slurred over it. "But you be careful if you go down there, Miss Clair. There's bound to be rats."

"I don't think Mr. Seal would suggest I go if there was a risk of meeting them in daytime."

She gave me a strange, long look. "Well, if you really want to see that old part of the house, you go down the passage to where the kitchen is. Before you get there, you'll see a door on your left. You go through it. 'Tisn't locked, though it should be. But the key got lost. Don't shut the door after you, Miss Clair, just in case."

I laughed. "I won't. And if I see a rat or a ghost, I'll run."

The long flight of stone steps curved around a thick column and I found myself in a huge, cold medieval hall.

This, then, was all that was left of the monastery on whose foundations Jessamy had been built. There was one corner where the vaulted ceiling and two stone columns were in a magnificent state of preservation. For the rest, the arches and columns were eroded by time and probably by the vandals of the Middle Ages.

It was intensely cold and the damp rose from the uneven stone floor. But Mrs. Manfred's alarms were unfounded. I felt no "presence," no ghosts walked, and I had no sense of evil.

I wandered around the huge place, which obviously ran underneath a greater part of the house. The old stone pillars were rough to my touch and the only light was from two high and age-encrusted windows which seemed to give on to the green of ivy, so that from outside they must be almost completely hidden.

There was an open door at the far end of the vast chamber and through it I saw a well-stocked wine cellar. The bottles lay on their sides in neat rows, some of them cobwebbed, as if the wine had been laid down to mature for a great many years.

There was a silver goblet in a niche, as bright as if it had been polished that very day. I picked it up, knowing nothing about silver, but I guessed from the lovely chasing and the elegant line that the cup was very old. Somewhere I had heard that red wine was best sampled in a silver goblet.

As I put the cup back, a movement in the shadows startled me. Silently, with a leap and a skid, Jupiter came from behind a pillar. He was playing with something soft and yellow, pouncing and withdrawing, paws soft and curving delicately around the plaything.

"What do you think that is, a yellow mouse?" I bent down and saw that it was a mangled chrysanthemum and that it had a tiny tag attached to it.

I picked it up, and the cat turned his back on me and began washing himself. The tag was a cut-down luggage label and on it had been printed *Stephanie Clair* in a thick black felt pen.

My first thought was that the flower was part of a bouquet someone had intended for me. But if that were so, I could not see where the rest of the flowers had got to.

The cat's slitted golden eyes watched me without blinking. He must have found the single flower somewhere and then carried it, as he would have carried a mouse, following me into the vaults.

"If I hadn't seen you, you'd have been shut in down here, you ass." I picked him up. He was soft and beautiful to my touch, a paw on my hand that held the flower, claws sheathed.

I set him down in the hall and found Mrs. Manfred in the dining room. "Jupiter was in the vaults. I was afraid he might get trapped down there."

"I suppose he followed Mr. Seal down. He went this morning to check the wine."

"I found him playing with this." I held the mangled flower out for her to see the tag. "It has my name on it."

A curious expression, part suspicion, part knowing, crossed her face. She looked from the torn flower to my face and back again. Then she snatched the chrysanthemum from me. "You forget it, Miss Clair. That be someone's silly joke."

"To send me one flower? But I don't know anyone down here well enough for them to joke with me."

"No. Of course you don't. It be some child's foolishness." She spoke soothingly. "You take no notice. I'll throw it away."

"I hate throwing away something that's still living," I said. "It could revive." I looked at the low bowl of Michaelmas daisies on the refectory table. "It can go in with those."

"Do as you like with this one, miss, but if there be any more, don't you touch them."

"Chrysanthemums aren't poison."

"No, but— Oh well, never mind. It must have been those children hearing you were coming and playing some nonsense game."

"What children?"

"Hobbin's grandchildren. They be staying with her because they both had measles and their doctor sent them out of Dorchester to get well. They be strange, and don't you let them play tricks with you."

"I won't," I promised, "and thank you for warning me." I laughed, but Mrs. Manfred didn't laugh with me.

"Mr. Dominick be gone to the village, but he won't be long. He usually plays the piano in the practice room in the morning. At least, he used to. It's different now. I suppose there's no heart left in him to play in Madame's house." She picked up some knives from the table and fingered them absently. "He says, if you'd like to go later with him to see the Swannery at Abbotsbury—it's lovely, Miss Clair, all them swans—then he'd be happy to take you. Only he hasn't got a car, but you have."

"If you see him, thank him for me, but I'd just like to wander around this morning."

I unlatched one of the tall French windows and went on to the terrace. From there I could see the Heath, like a soft amethyst carpet, and to the left, the beech forest, the branches of the trees absolutely still in the quiet morning.

I remained for a while, looking through the slender rope-patterned stone columns of the terrace. To my right I could just see the silver-gray of the English Channel, and on the horizon, the long, low line of a tanker probably making for Southampton.

Mrs. Manfred's voice came clearly from a room behind me. ". . . didn't tell her. It weren't for me. But who would have done it? To Madame's daughter, too. Who?"

"It be rubbish, anyway."

"Of course. I wonder if Hobbin—"

"Don't you go asking her anything. I be feared of her."

One of them must have seen me standing on the terrace, for I heard a sharp "Sh-h-h," and then the loud burring of a vacuum cleaner.

I guessed they were talking about the flower but it didn't alarm me. Small village communities were often riddled with superstitions and odd local beliefs, and it was possible that someone—a dismissed servant perhaps—had a grudge against Livanova and was working off his resentment on her daughter. Mrs. Manfred had called it someone's joke. It could be that or it could be part of an old wives' tale. Whichever way, a chrysanthemum couldn't possibly harm me.

I went down the steps and across the lawn. There were no walls enclosing the Jessamy estate, just a thick line of laurel and rhododendron bushes encircling the mature lawns and broken only by a gap through which a path meandered to the sea. The tall wrought-iron gates at the entrance to the drive were mere formalities of exclusion and privacy, since anyone who wished to trespass had only to push his way through the bushes.

I crossed to the Heath, where the wild heather seemed to stretch to the horizon. The air was soft and the ground under my feet rich with the purple and amethyst of ling flowers, and touched with white where the gleaming quartz sand revealed the entrance to a rabbit's burrow. I walked in a semicircle toward the forest, and the sun, breaking through the morning mist, played on the great trunks of the beeches, the boles black in the earth shadows. It was so quiet that when I stood still, I heard a whisper of sound as a leaf dropped from a branch, and in the distance, like background music, I listened to the rhythmic beat of the waves against the rocks strewn under the great cliff that guarded Jessamy.

In the distance I could see a man scything the dry bracken to make winter bedding for some animal. His back was to me and he worked with a slow, steady movement in tune with the gentle life in this remote corner of Dorset.

The forest was pathless, so that I had to try to keep a sense of direction. The trees were rich and full and their branches intertwined, making arches above me.

Great forests always gave me a sense of the wonder of being young in places of such immense age, a feeling that although I was a microcosm, I was part of all that was past.

Quite suddenly I saw movement and two deer, a stag and a hind, appeared between the trees. There was more movement behind them, where the rest of the herd was following. Someone had once called them "the sons and daughters of the forest." The stag's proud antlers were sharp against the filtered light, and the muted russet coloring of the hind turned it into an animal from a medieval tapestry. I forgot Jessamy, I forgot my own mixed identity, as I walked toward them on what had become enchanted ground. The stag appeared to be lying down, and as I crept as silently as I could toward the animals, it rose, lifting its head and moved toward the hind. Then, as suddenly as I saw them, they vanished and I knew that my human scent had drifted their way.

I had come to a shallow pool of muddy water thick with the scum of rotting weeds. It wasn't beautiful and yet the magic remained, for I stood in a circle of light in the leaf-shadowed forest and it was like a stage set for some miniature spectacle, spotlit and green and waiting for the actors.

Soft little giggles brought me out of my fantasy. Two children watched me, a boy and a girl of about ten. Gypsy-haired and dark-skinned, they could have been twins.

I greeted them. "Hello."

At the same moment there was a rustle of leaves and two birds flew up with swift, flapping feathers from a tree behind them.

The children swung around and looked up. Then, with their backs to me, their hands at their sides, they bowed to the birds and said in unison, "Good morning, my lords."

The next moment they turned to me, their expressions almost solemn.

"Why did you do that?" I asked them.

"Do what?"

"Bow and say good morning."

"We allas do when we see magpies. It be lucky to bow to them and call them my lords! Didn't you know?"

"I'm afraid I didn't. And I hope they bring you luck."

The girl nodded. "Oh, we know we're going to get luck."

"Yes," said the boy.

"What are your names?"

"I be Robin. She be Lucy." Their accents were broad Dorset.

"And you live around here?"

"With Granny."

The boy bent and picked up a dry rust-colored leaf and blew through it, making a queer husky sound. He wore a single earring in his left ear and he was grinning between his efforts to use the leaf as a kind of trumpet. They weren't to be rushed either into letting me get to know them or finding out who I was. They behaved as if curiosity was nonexistent between us, strangers though we were.

There was an aura of poetry about these children. Their faces were long, with little pointed chins; their eyes dark and tilted at the corners, like deers' eyes. The girl's hair was tangled and chestnut-colored; the boy's was chopped off unevenly on a level with his ears. They both wore thick woollen sweaters and shorts, and nothing about them was clean. Yet they had a curious attraction, and I had a feeling that however long they lived, they would always be closely identified—two against the world. Something dark and strange, drawn from the depths of wild and too-wise forefathers, clung to them—a kind of innocence and non-innocence.

"You aren't at school, then?" It was a fatuous comment, since they were in the forest, but they showed no signs of wanting to leave me and something had to be said.

"We got measles and now we be sent to Granny till we can go back to school."

"She lives over there." The girl pointed, and I could just see another clearing to our right and what looked like a small graystone cottage. "She'll tell your fortune if she likes you. You see, miss, she's a witch."

It was their exit line. They ran off, laughing at me over their shoulders.

I wandered in the direction of the cottage and found myself back on the edge of the forest, not far away from Jessamy. I had walked in an arc, and the trees thinned out behind the cottage until the land was again heath and furze and briar.

The cottage itself was very small, with two tiny windows and a tall chimney. Creeper and ivy clung to a kind of little stone out-house. My footsteps must have cracked on the untidy gravel path littered with broken twigs, for a woman came to the door. Her face held strong traces of earlier good looks, dark and powerful. Her lips were very full and red and her thick hair was twisted into a coil on top of her head with hairpins half falling out. Her dark dress wasn't particularly clean, and as she wiped her hands on a cloth, I saw that her nails were black. But pride glowed on her face and her narrow eyes held wisdom.

"I be Hobbin"—her accent was as broad as that of the children—"and you be the little lady from Jessamy." It was the kind of expression not used these days, but then, this was a corner of England where time had halted. She gave a thick, low chuckle. "Don't 'ee be surprised. There be few secrets at Pilgrim Abbas.

Some of 'em that lives here don't know all. I know all and a lot besides."

Village grapevines were strong and swift. I was not impressed.

"They say you be the daughter of Madame Livanova."

I implied that this was so.

"Strange you be not like her."

"No. I . . . I'm like my father."

"You be stayin' some time?"

"Oh no. Only a few days." Her steady stare made me nervous. I said the first thing that came into my head. "It's very beautiful here."

"Ah, 'tis so. Once, though, in my Granny's time, that were all garden." She swept a hand toward the green lawns of Jessamy. "Flowers, lots of them, and rich people walking and laughing, and a summerhouse that burned down."

"The green is very restful."

"Restful? Jessamy? Ha . . . it never been restful since *she* took it over. And now that *she* be dead"—she shrugged—"what now?"

"Mr. Seal is the new owner."

"Aye." She gave me a strange, penetrating look. "Don' 'ee be sad. It be justice, bitter justice."

"What is?"

"Never 'ee mind. Hobbin don't talk. She knows all the secrets hereabouts and she don't ever talk."

"But Livanova . . . my . . . my mother . . . I think if there is anything to know, I must know."

She shook her head. "What you don't know won't trouble 'ee." Then she leaned across and touched my forehead with a light finger. "Star-crossed," she said.

I started back, and she shook her head at me. "Don't 'ee be feared. Hobbin won't hurt 'ee. There be signs written on foreheads, but only some as can read them. You take care. The stars don't move easily across your life."

And that, I thought, was telling me about the present, not the future.

It was a brief enough meeting and yet it disturbed me: I wondered if she had really known anything that would help me but wouldn't tell, or whether to pretend secret knowledge was part of the distinction of being a witch.

Meeting Hobbin had had a curious effect on me. I no longer wanted to find my way to the village, which I could just see across the distant ridge of the heath. There had been no change in Stephanie's condition when I had left London yesterday and I doubted if anything dramatic had occurred in twenty-four hours. I had been given no hope that she might come out of her mindlessness until the doctor could find a way of getting through the shock blockage in her brain. So I could safely leave telephoning the hospital until the next day and return to Jessamy. Fabian or Dominick might be back by the time I reached the house.

The gleam of the sun breaking through the high mist shone on the beeches and the purple heathland. Here and there on the low bushes, spiderwebs shimmered in the light, each woven trap fragile and deadly in its perfect symmetry.

Where the heathland narrowed at the grounds of Jessamy, there was a field, and I saw two huge dappled shire horses, with white feathered hoofs and gentle Roman noses, plodding along the furrows. In these days of fields worked by machinery, I watched the beautiful, serene link with the past, and heard the farmer's call "Whoa! Whoa!" as he gentled the horses around a curve in the field.

VIII

FABIAN WAS IN the practice room. There was a ladder in one corner and a net had been stretched on hooks near ceiling level from one side of the room to the other. Between the net and the mirrored wall was a small table with three green candles on it, their flames flickering slightly in a breeze I couldn't feel.

The white object in the corner behind the net no longer looked like a grand piano but seemed transformed into a crouching beast. The mirror behind the net gave me back my reflection. I looked unreal, as if I were a colored shadow without essence. But then, I *was* unreal, existing in a no-man's-land between two people, myself and Stephanie Clair.

Fabian was standing by the littered trestle table.

"It was lovely in the forest," I said.

"Was it? Yes, I suppose it was." He answered abstractedly.

"I saw some deer near a pool that was more mud than water."

"Oh, stags roll in it. It helps to blacken their coats and make them appear ferocious to other predatory stags." He kicked gently at a stool and sent it spinning lightly across the parquet floor. "This is their mating season." He hadn't once looked at me, and now, stepping back, he stared at the group of props behind the net curtain. "It's phony. Damn it. Candles and mirror and bell . . . all the obvious trappings of witchcraft. I loathe being obvious."

"If you really want to give the impression of a dream sequence, surely the net is just right."

"That's not the object. In fact, this isn't my idea at all and I'm damned if I'm going to be persuaded by Gideon Gilderoy, our artistic director, to resort to old tricks."

"But surely, if the story line is about witchcraft, it's full of what you call 'old tricks.' "

"There are more sophisticated ways of portraying magic," he said, "than dealing a pack of cards and lighting colored candles, but I can foresee sparks flying when Gilderoy and I meet."

"What other magic is there?"

"Plenty, but your mind has its limitations in this area, hasn't it?"

"How can a man who has seen the world as you have, believe in something so . . . so intangible."

"But that's just it. Intangible things exist."

"Oh, Fabian, really . . ."

"Do you imagine your mockery shows intelligence?" He sounded angry.

"Enlightenment," I corrected him. "Twentieth-century realism."

"Then the latent powers that exist in many people mean nothing to you?"

"Convince me." I spoke lightly, to hide confusion.

"No, that would be a waste of my time. Or perhaps I might hand you one thought. It's that science has begun to accept that something may exist beyond their own hard facts. I am not alone in believing that there are facets of human personality that we don't yet fully understand. In other words, I believe that some people have highly developed senses. Properly used, they can work marvels. They are the magicians of the world."

"You talk of magicians?"

He went to the table and began flipping through the pile of sketches. "You can call them what you like." He sounded bored with me, as an adult would be with an obstinate child.

Fabian intrigued me. I would never have thought of him as the lover of an older woman. He was too poised, too free a spirit, too uncompromising. But then, perhaps Livanova had developed these characteristics in him.

"You love ballet, don't you?"

"Not particularly. I like design, and even then I only work at what I think will be a success. I choose my commitments. You see, I hate failure."

"I don't know . . . my mother never told me . . . where your home is."

"London, St. John's Wood. A house in a tree-lined street, with a surgeon living next door to me on one side and a psychiatrist on the other. So you see, I'm well guarded if I fall ill or go mad."

I moved to the trestle table and glanced at the piles of painted sketches of scenery and drawings of dancers executing a step, arm and leg movements so real, I felt that any moment the drawn figures would come alive.

"Where did you study art?" As soon as I had asked, I knew that I sounded impertinent. But I was ill-at-ease, which in a way helped my masquerade, for nervousness when meeting strangers was a characteristic of Stephanie's.

Fabian reacted with a touch of amusement. "Are you wanting the history of my life?" he asked. "Because if you are, my dear Stephanie, I'm afraid I'm not good at being cross-examined."

"I'm sorry."

"You don't have to apologize. Most men would be flattered by your interest, as I'm sure your own experience has already taught you. But I'm not 'most men.'"

"If you think I'm trying to flatter you, then I'm afraid you'll have to be disillusioned. I . . ."

"All right, all right." He burst out laughing. "Point taken. You're not wanting to flatter me, just showing a polite, cursory interest in me. And before you protest again, just give me time to answer your question. Yes, I studied art after I had passed my preliminary examinations in architecture. Then, after that, the mountains. You see, I have a restless mind."

"But you would never have left the mountains if it hadn't been for your accident, would you?"

"How can anyone say? *I* can't."

"I think it's easy to imagine you in solitary places."

"That's not particularly perceptive. You probably read an article about me. They were all fairly inaccurate."

"Yes, I did read one some year or so ago. But can't you give me credit for forming my own opinion?"

"Not entirely." He still sounded faintly amused. "Well, go on. What more do you want to know?"

There was no encouragement in the question, and I said, sounding a little indignant, "Isn't it a two-way thing—getting to know someone?"

"Then go ahead."

I looked across the room at our reflections in the mirror. That, I thought, was exactly the way our relationship was at the moment —a reflection of what we were, nothing deep or real yet known.

Fabian picked up a stub of crayon and tossed it into the bin by the side of the table. "All right, I'll give you a brief picture of my background and then you won't have to spend your time trying to pluck up courage to ask me. I'm British, I come from Wiltshire. My father is a scholar, an expert in Oriental languages and at the moment in China. My mother is dead. She was a small, restless woman who never quite knew what she wanted out of life. I've probably inherited her restlessness, although I know what I want."

"What *do* you want?"

He looked at me, and his eyes, reflecting the lights of the room, had a brilliant clarity. "To be master of anything I undertake and to find the truth behind the image."

The image: Stephanie Clair. The truth: Rachel Fleming. I felt a sick fear tighten every muscle. I couldn't meet his eyes, I couldn't speak.

"Oh, I doubt if I shall ever find the truth," he broke through my fear. "Nobody has; perhaps nobody can. We're shadows *and* substance, aren't we, Stephanie?"

We were on dangerous ground. Although I realized that my fear had been quite wrong and he was speaking generally about the duality of everyone, and although I longed to hear more, I didn't dare continue on such a level. If I, as Rachel, were interested, then he could trap me because I would be so absorbed in what we were saying that I would forget I was Stephanie. She wouldn't be the least bit interested, anyway, so I must not be.

The realization of why I was at Jessamy didn't leave me for a moment, but I seemed unable to ask the right questions or find a way to ferret out any information. It was as if Fabian Seal had cast a spell upon me. Or it could be that, caught between being Stephanie and being Rachel, I was somehow lost and uncertain.

"Well?" Fabian urged, breaking the long silence. "Don't you think we're paradoxes—shadow and substance?"

I said, trying to speak casually, "I hope I'm mostly substance. I wouldn't want to melt away like a shadow." I walked toward one of the great mirrors and smoothed my hair with a calm I didn't feel. "Fabian . . ."

"What is it?"

"When you first knew my . . . my mother, you were still climbing, weren't you?"

"Yes, yes I was. But you should surely know that."

"Of course. Only, she told me so little about herself. You and she . . ."

"We what?"

A memory had risen triumphantly to the surface, and I said, "You met at a party after she had danced in a new ballet. I even remember the name—*The Fox and the Fire,* wasn't it?"

"That's right."

"But you never designed sets for her, did you?"

"No." The word had a finality about it that discouraged more questions. I didn't dare push my luck too far. I remembered that it had been around the time of Fabian Seal's accident when Stephanie had told me they had ceased to be together. It was after that, when he could no longer climb mountains, that Fabian Seal designed his first sets and costumes for a ballet.

"This new ballet has the same team that worked on *The Fox and the Fire.* The choreography is by Freyberg. We think alike along the same ideas of either classic or modern ballet, but we both prefer a strong story line and character depth."

"You say the ballet you're now working on is traditional?"

"So far as poses and steps are concerned. I think I prefer the modern dance technique, rejecting the old formal posturing and accenting strong drama and strong music, though I draw the line at electronic music. Working with Freyberg is rewarding because although he tends toward the classic, he doesn't muddle his decisions. He makes careful plans whether he is going to make his ballet a story or a mood, and then doesn't deviate."

"It must all be very expensive."

"Oh, it is if you want the best musicians, the best choreographer, the best designers. I, for one, am expensive. So with all that money being paid out, no one in the profession becomes a millionaire."

"Mother loved spending money."

"Remember, she earned it all. She worked, and dear heaven, how she worked! But since we're talking of money, at least she put a little aside for you." He paused.

I felt that he was expecting me to say something—perhaps how much Livanova had left to her daughter—and I made a small, vague gesture as if I didn't want to discuss it.

Fabian said, "I suppose every daughter of a famous mother dreams of egg-sized diamonds in the jewel box and furs of exotic animals. But as you know by now, Livanova left nothing like that for you. There's her famous white mink, of course, and a sable—neither very suitable for a working girl. But you already know the contents of the will, so we won't discuss it."

I thought carefully before I spoke. "Mother was always erratic and unpredictable."

"What do you mean?" His voice sharpened.

I said, avoiding his eyes, "It . . . it was just a comment. But she was, wasn't she?"

He was silent and I felt his eyes on me. I seized hold of my flagging courage, faced him and said, "You wrote in your letter that there was something important we had to discuss."

"And you thought I had asked you down here to find out if you minded that the house had become mine?"

It was all too easy to say the wrong thing, to give myself away at this crucial moment. I let the question hang in the air.

"Well, *do* you mind?"

"No. But somehow I . . . I have the feeling that there is something else you want to discuss with me."

"All in good time," he said.

It was as if he found it amusing to keep me guessing, playing some stalking jungle game with me.

"She—my mother—must have known how you love Jessamy."

"It has history and nobility." His voice was detached.

And, my dear Fabian, it has a price. Aloud, I asked, "You will live here?"

"Oh no." He picked up a sketch of a dancer in a swirling mist of a green skirt. "Are you in love? No, don't answer. That's entirely your affair. Instead, tell me, what do you intend to do with your life?"

The quick changes in the direction of his conversation nonplused me, but I answered cautiously in case this was a trap. "I told you, don't you remember? I've had the chance of a job."

"In public relations. Oh yes. I wonder how long you'll keep it?"

"Why should you ask that?"

"Because one of the few things I've heard about you is that you have no staying power." He reached out, and with an unexpected gesture, laid the back of his hand against my cheek.

I drew away quickly. The mixture of relentless questioning and sudden change of mood into a gesture of friendliness floored me. I wondered if in the end Livanova trusted him, or whether, had she lived, the will would have been altered and Stephanie might have inherited Jessamy Court.

I had been so confident that two days would have been sufficient for my masquerade, but now I was less certain. For some reason best known to himself, Fabian Seal was tossing information at me so lightly, so nonchalantly that I felt certain he was not in the least concerned with my reactions, and his inquiry about whether I minded his inheritance was a mere formality.

He was watching me in a silence in which he seemed to be perfectly at ease, but which I had to break because I was still too on guard, too tense for silences.

"Am I allowed to ask about the new ballet, or is it a secret until the opening night?"

"Not at all. It's the story of a young girl spellbound by a magician who meets her and falls in love with her. He masquerades as a mortal, and when she rejects him he lays a spell on her. So far, it's the old fairy-tale routine. But he makes a mistake in his spell and she finds herself caught up in strange and fabulous dreams, some so joyful, some so chaotic that they send her temporarily a little mad. All the dreams promise opportunities open to her when she wakes, like roads leading out in different directions. And she can choose. There they are, the ways she can take to happiness, to destruction. And to the discerning, who see more than a dancer's clever steps, the ballet has another level of meaning." The seriousness suddenly left him and he laughed. "Did you know that verbena should be gathered when neither the sun nor the moon is shining? Then it becomes a love potion."

I said, matching his laughter, "Have *you* ever gathered verbena?"

"My dear girl, I don't even know what it looks like. And no . . ." The laughter left him. "Magic is not the collecting of toads' feet and serpents' eyes and mandrake. It's real. But even superstition can, in itself, create a magnetism that people call magic. I believe in men's latent powers, and this ballet, for all its seeming mumbo-jumbo, has a clear indication of those powers. But it's impossible to explain. Nothing can put into words what is pure meaning. You don't understand, do you?"

"No."

He was looking at me, eyebrows drawn down over his strange, light eyes. "Don't try. But don't try, either, to make me explain the deeper levels of the ballet, because if you ever see it, you understand or you don't."

"I want to see it," I said. "I'd like to feel that I understand."

"You're very young," he said.

Watching him turn away from me, I felt young and inexperienced and frightened at what I was doing. He was a clever man and a deep one. If he was not teasing me with his talk of magic powers, if he really believed in them and perhaps could put them into practice, I had not the slightest hope of carrying my plans through to a conclusion that would help Stephanie.

I felt I had to know more, or rather, to have him explain in clearer language what he meant by his belief in magic.

"It all sounds rather obscure. I'd like to know—"

"Leave it," he said. "Leave it, at least for the moment. I can promise you'll understand soon enough." The way he spoke made that particular line of conversation final.

He could have meant me to leave him then, but I didn't. I said, "I went down to the vaults this morning."

"They're rather fine, aren't they?"

"Was it a burial place?"

"Oh no. They're called vaults because they're such fine examples of medieval architecture, but they were the monks' cellars."

"Mrs. Manfred says she thinks they were once used for witchcraft."

"Mrs. Manfred has a lively imagination fed on old wives' tales." He saw me glance at a beautifully bound book on a high reading stand by the trestle table. He picked it up. "I've borrowed this from Gilderoy. He found it somewhere and needs it himself. But

77

I know from experience how long he keeps research books and so I'm using it first for the costumes and sets. You see?" He held it out to me. "There are illustrations. In fact, it's a translation of a book published on the Continent in the last century. I should think the writer dug up every spell he could find, even in the remote villages of Eastern Europe."

I had taken the heavy book from him and was leafing through the pages. The book was divided into headed chapters, and I scarcely gave any time to the colored illustrations of peasants in various costumes and werewolves and startling drawings of witches' "familiars." I had no idea whether there was a chapter on flower spells, but I turned the pages on "Cards," "Numbers," "Potions." I glanced at masses of small sketches depicting candles and circles; I saw a drawing of an old alchemist busy with his dream of turning metal into gold; I read that in small isolated villages superstition can create a magical ether that makes spells possible . . . Pilgrim Abbas.

I looked up at Fabian, who was watching me with amusement. But it was only a flashing glance, for at the same time I had turned a page and in the right-hand corner I saw the drawing of a flower laid on a cottage doorstep. There was a tag attached to it but it was too small to read the name. Not that that was important.

I slapped my hand down on the page and held the book out to Fabian. I said, "I found a flower this morning in the vaults."

"Blown by the wind."

"Brought there by Jupiter," I said. "And look, this book describes it."

"Well! Well! So now Jupiter is a witch's 'familiar.' "

"The tag had my name on it; the flower was a yellow chrysanthemum."

"You must tell me if chrysanthemums are particular favorites with the witch sorority." In spite of the faint amusement in his tone, the expression in Fabian's eyes was wary.

I turned to the book again, searched for an allusion to the drawing and found it on the next page. "It says here that a revenge spell is to send a flower—the same flower—anonymously to someone each day for nine days. It means the wrong they have done you returns to them."

He reached out and closed the book. "If you read any more of that, you'll start seeing ghosts. Come on, let's walk down to the sea."

I held back. "Who could have sent it?"

"How should I know? Hobbin's grandchildren, perhaps, reared on her spells. But how do you know it wasn't one of a bunch someone kindly intended for you and the flower you found was the one that got away?"

"Then where are the others? And since I know no one here, who would have sent them?"

"You are Livanova's daughter. It's possible you'll get acknowledgments of that for quite a time. It's called reflected glory."

"I don't believe it. And," I added, more scared by the strange thought, "would they just put 'Stephanie Clair' on the tag? Wouldn't there be a short message and the name of the sender?"

"Why ask me? Come and let's see if there's any coffee around. And then we'll go for that walk."

"So I can expect a flower every day for nine days?"

He didn't answer me.

"It's too stupid." I was suddenly defiant and angry. "I suppose it could only be the children. I saw them this morning. They're strange and there must be very little to amuse them down here. I suppose they thought this . . . this idiocy up for me. After all, they must see spells being worked by their grandmother and thought they'd try to scare me just for devilment. Well, they can stop, because no rather tired yellow chrysanthemums are going to scare me."

Fabian was at the door of the practice room. I took one last look at the book. "I've got an idea. I threw the tag in the wastepaper basket in my room. If I get it, perhaps you could tell, from the way the letters are printed, who sent it."

"Go and fetch it, then." He looked toward the bowl of Michaelmas daisies on the refectory table. "I suppose that droopy yellow flower there is the one?"

"Yes. I didn't see why it should be left to die. It wasn't its fault it was chosen to play some idiot game with me."

"I've never thought mauve and yellow, even in flowers, is a particularly attractive combination. Now, go up and get that tag."

I sped up the stairs, and the warm sunshine spread around me as I entered the room.

The wastepaper basket was empty. Of course, Mrs. Manfred must have cleared it. I went downstairs again and found her in the kitchen, peering hard at the engraved silver forks as if checking Bridget's morning work. In answer to my question, she said she had found nothing in my basket.

I thanked her and returned to Fabian, who was leaning against the ivied wall of the terrace, sketching a slender stone column on a small pad. "Anything and everything can come in useful," he said.

"The tag is gone."

"Mrs. Manfred does her work," he said disinterestedly.

"I asked her and she said my wastepaper basket was empty."

"Then perhaps that's magic too. A flight into invisibility. Don't worry. I doubt if I could have traced the printing. And since I possess no gifts as an amateur detective, I doubt if I could find the sender of your flower."

"If I'm to get nine of them," I said, "surely someone will see who comes to the house with their revenge gift."

"Children can crawl through hedges undetected."

"*If* a child delivered it."

"An adult would look pretty silly walking up the drive carrying a single flower."

"I think somebody was being very silly in sending it, anyway," I retorted.

He glanced over my head. Mrs. Manfred stood in the doorway. "Your call from London, Mr. Seal."

"Settle for the children," Fabian said over his shoulder as he walked unhurriedly away from me. "Your mother used to have Hobbin here sometimes because she hated going to the hut—she said it smelled of candle grease and frying bacon. And sometimes the children came to play in the garden while your mother listened to Hobbin's forecasts for her. During that time they probably found the vaults—children have a way of discovering exits and entrances we haven't the imagination to look for."

"I wonder," I said, "if Hobbin warned my mother that she would die." But I spoke to the air. Fabian and Mrs. Manfred had vanished into the house.

It must be obvious, of course, to whoever dropped the chrysanthemum near the house that I would learn of the spell. It was obvious that I would consider it childish and Robin and Lucy would be blamed. Perhaps someone planned it just that way, because they believed—or wanted me to believe—that spells worked. It was unimportant. After nine days their inane magic would have been seen to fail, and in any case, I would be gone long before nine days had passed. But he—or she—or they—would know that I would eventually realize that someone was acting through the children, if the children were indeed involved.

Behind it all, whether the flower was sent to me as Stephanie Clair, or as her impersonator, it contained a warning message for me.

Although Dominick had talked to me about the beauty of Abbotsbury, it was Fabian who took me there the following afternoon. We walked together in the marvelous gardens between the ilex and the eucalyptus trees, watched the white cloud of swans preening themselves among the eel grass, as they had done on those same acres for five hundred years. The wind whispered in the reed beds and the lagoon was full of silver light.

The sun disappeared as we went down to the sea and watched the mackerel fishers bring in their catch. The nets were dragged slowly through the waves, and men and water and struggling fish were like pieces of mobile steel under the lowering skies.

I had a feeling that Fabian had watched the scene many times and might be growing impatient, but I knew that I could talk to him more personally here, away from Jessamy. It was as if the house were a thick curtain between us.

"I suppose flat land has no attraction for you," I said.

"Why not? Scenery is like people—you learn to admire differing types."

"When did you start to climb?"

He turned and perched on the sea wall and held out a hand to help me up. "When I grew tired of architecture and tired of art. As I told you last night," he said, "I am a very restless man, and I suppose climbing was a search for something."

"Something you found?"

"Yes and no. It's a tough life up on the high peaks. You're thrown together with a strongly individual group of men. It's competitive as well as a personal challenge."

"That didn't spoil it for you—the competitiveness, I mean?"

"Why should it?" His tone had hardened. "Men climb for different reasons. Some for money, some for fame, some because they love the publicity of conquering an impossible mountain."

"And you . . . ?"

He watched the gulls wheeling and screaming over the mackerel catch. "Oh, perhaps something of all three reasons. One mountain in particular for the challenge. Cuernos in the Andes."

I tried to remember if that had been Fabian's last climb before his accident, and couldn't.

As if he were reading my thoughts, Fabian said, "Cuernos was four years ago. I climbed twice in the Himalayas after that. And then it was over."

"I know I'm repeating myself and you hate repetition, but it *is* such a strange mixture. I mean climbing and designing stage sets."

"Odd things go together," he said. "Unexpected choices complement each other. Like music and cricket, tales for children and philosophy. Remember *Alice Through the Looking Glass* and *The Lord of the Rings* and their authors. Just think of any two opposing interests, and somewhere there will be someone to fit the oddity."

"And you loved Cuernos more than anywhere else?"

"Yes," he said. "Climbing in the High Andes, we would look down and think we could see the golden cities of the Incas half hidden in the great forests below us. Of course, there was nothing to be seen except trees and vegetation. But imagination teases us all, doesn't it, Stephanie?"

"I . . . I wouldn't know."

He said, as if my limitations bored him, "That's right. I doubt if you would."

The Bentley stood royally in the shade of a group of trees. Fabian opened the door on the passenger side and gave me a long, strange look. "The mother . . . and now the daughter . . ." he said slowly.

"What about us?"

"So different."

"But you said *and now* the daughter."

"Now I know you both," he said. "Get in the car."

"You know *me,* after less than a day?"

"Superficially, yes. And one thing is very obvious, you and your mother are utterly different."

"You don't have to remind me."

"It's just as well. It should reassure you. Livanova lived life to the full and died before the decline of her great talent could break her heart. You would never break that way."

"Oh, I'll just crumble because I'm ordinary."

"I can't make categorical decisions about you yet. After all, as you say, I've known you for only twenty-four hours and I learned very little about you from your mother."

"She didn't want to know me," I burst out, and was appalled at the emotion in my voice. I had spoken with the feeling that Stephanie would have shown, as if some magic power of acting had caused me to be so identified with her that it had taken momentary control.

Fabian was saying, "Why do you have to be so bitter about it?" Once more flashes of something close to animosity sparked between us. "Livanova was perfect when she danced. Did you expect her to be perfect in other ways, too? Do you expect no flaw in an emerald?"

"She . . . she could have wanted me a little."

"And *you,* my dear, could have stood occasionally on your own two feet, couldn't you? Instead of which—Oh, forget it." He had got into the car, and leaning forward, switched on the engine. "After all, I didn't ask you here to quarrel with you."

"Why did you invite me?"

"I've told you. I knew your mother; I wanted to know her daughter."

The car moved forward, accelerating swiftly. The car's size filled the twisting Dorset lanes. We purred through the villages of Swyre and Pucknowle, between the amethyst hills and the chalk streams. My hands were folded in my lap and I stared ahead of me. I knew that I appeared relaxed, but actually, I was tense with alarm. I felt as if some force outside myself was at work taking over my mind, so that I was reacting to Fabian's remarks as Stephanie would have. It was, of course, the reaction I had hoped for when I made the journey to Jessamy, but the ease with which I was identifying with another human being frightened me.

I sat stiffly in my seat in the car and tried to reassure myself. I knew who I was. Rachel Fleming was still there, the personality behind the impersonator. It was merely that I was a better actress than I had supposed.

Some horses were galloping in a field, their russet tails swinging behind them; a golden plover rose, startled, from in front of the car into the gray sky. The beauty of the movement made me think of ballet.

"I once saw Miranda McCall," I said. "She was dancing in *Agon.*"

"She was totally out of harmony with that ballet," he said shortly. "Stravinsky's music is not for her. She is essentially a lyric dancer. That's why she will be the supreme choice for *The Witch and the Maiden.* We will work on the music, the choreography, the sets. McCall will achieve the miracle."

And Fabian Seal could have been in love with her before Livanova had died . . .

Such small, seemingly irrelevant things could be important, things perhaps like Miranda McCall's place in a ballet and in Fabian Seal's life. It was all conjecture, but I filed the thought in my mind along with all the others. One thing was becoming evident, I would need to stay longer than the two days I had planned, and that dismayed me.

We were driving through a great avenue of trees darkened by the fading light. It was like entering a green cave, at the end of which I could see the glow of the sunset.

"How did it happen?"

"How did what happen?" His voice was sharp and he turned his head slightly my way without taking his eyes off the road. "What?" he asked again more sharply.

"Your accident."

"What a girl you are for leaping from one thought to another."

"I know. Someone once said that my mind was like a kangaroo hopping over ideas."

"And questions," he said.

In the silence that followed, I felt an easing of tension and I wondered whether he had been afraid my question had referred to Livanova's death. As yet we had both avoided mentioning it.

It had begun to rain, falling lightly in tiny spears, spattering the immaculate bonnet of the Bentley and glistening on the leaves of the trees as if they were being dipped in silver.

"I like rain," I said. "It washes the world."

He laughed. "You never cease to astonish me. Your mother once told me that you hated water and refused to learn to swim."

Mistake number three? Four? Five?

I said vaguely, "I claim the right to change my likes and dislikes."

"Of course," he said, and drew the car out and around a cart pulled by a fat, sleepy horse, its flanks covered with an old shawl.

84

IX

"IT REALLY ISN'T NECESSARY," Dominick said after breakfast when we were alone. "I can walk back from the station—I've done it often enough—and if I cut through the forest, it really isn't that far."

He was going to London to see his agent, and after insisting on driving him to Dulverley to catch the connection from Dorchester, I had suggested meeting him that evening.

"A day in London will be tiring after the long journey and I'd like to see Dulverley. If I take you to the station there, I shall know the way to come and fetch you."

It was Fabian who as he strolled out onto the terrace heard what I was saying, and made the final decision. "Never refuse a charitable act, Dominick. The chance may not come again."

"Oh, but I hope it will," I said. "I want to see the countryside."

Dominick took two violent puffs on his cigarette, then stubbed it out against the stone balustrade. "It's absurd, isn't it, but I don't want to go to London. I've got a feeling that I'm going through a phase of bad luck and the whole journey will be a waste of time."

"Nothing is a waste of time if the effort is genuine," Fabian said and walked away from us down the five stone steps to the lawn.

I asked Dominick, "If I hadn't been here, would he have driven you to Dulverley?"

"I doubt it."

We stood together watching Fabian limp across the smooth, wet grass that glimmered in the capricious sunlight.

"On the surface," Dominick said, "he has no weaknesses, and however much he tells me never to refuse an opportunity offered to me, if our positions were reversed, he would himself choose to walk to Dulverley. He accepts no favors." Then he repeated softly, "On the surface."

"You say that as if you knew him deeply."

"I don't, but I suppose we all have two sides to us and I have often wondered about the side Fabian never shows."

"An Achilles heel. We all have them. I have."

"Have you?" A trace of a smile touched his face.

"Of course. Didn't my mother tell you?" Suddenly, unbidden, I was Stephanie again. I felt her helpless honesty about herself take over. "My Achilles heel," I quoted Stephanie, "is being scared of life, hating to take chances."

"Yes, that's what I've heard. And yet you don't seem to me to be timid. I'd have said you were a very self-assured person."

Once more I saw the peril of a too close analysis. I glanced at my watch. "Don't you think we should start for Dulverley?"

"Perhaps," he said absently, staring toward where Fabian had disappeared into the forest. During the instant before he was aware that I had turned toward him, I surprised a mixture of animosity and suspicion in his expression, and it shocked me because it seemed alien to his usual masculine gentleness.

It was obvious in that unguarded look that Dominick didn't trust Fabian. But then, neither did I. The difference between us was that while I was free to leave Jessamy at any moment, Dominick was not. He needed money and help in order to escape. I realized how very much this journey to London was going to mean to him.

The single yellow chrysanthemum was on the third step down from the double front doors. Like the other, my name was printed on the tag.

I picked it up and held it out to Dominick. "This is the second one I've found waiting for me somewhere."

He looked startled, and then said, "The second what? Flower? Is someone strewing them around?"

"You could say that's the idea."

"I don't understand."

"Nor did I until I read about it in Fabian's book on witchcraft. Now there are seven to go. I'm sorry . . . you don't know what I'm talking about, do you?"

"Not really."

I told him about finding the first flower in the vaults. "I don't know where it was originally left, but Jupiter found it, thought it was a mouse and brought it for me to see." Then I explained about the spell.

"And that," Dominick said gravely when I had finished speaking, "is the kind of stupid practice they'd get up to in this village. Throw it away and forget it."

"I can't do either." I went past him back into the house and put it with the other in the bowl of flowers on the refectory table. The hall was deserted and only Tatiana Livanova watched me through her painted eyes.

I hadn't meant to close the front doors with such heavy hands, but I heard them thud and echo like a doom crack. And that was idiotic. I checked my nervous imagination. I had just been clumsy shutting a door. The finding of the flower hadn't affected me in the least. Or so I told myself, until I joined Dominick and heard myself say, "You told me to forget it, but I won't be allowed to, because there will be another tomorrow. Who around here grows yellow chrysanthemums?"

"There's no one living near except Mrs. Hobbin, and she grows nothing. She rakes the forest for what she wants, and I believe she eats the most amazing things that she finds there, things you and I wouldn't dare touch for fear we'd die of poisoning."

"Someone must grow chrysanthemums," I said.

"Perhaps Fenney, Fabian's gardener. He lives somewhere in the forest, though I've never seen his cottage."

"So Fenney—"

"I wouldn't suspect him. He's very earthy, and a man of seventy wouldn't play at spells."

"Wouldn't he? I wonder. Especially if he's earthy. Simple people are closer to magic than the sophisticates of the town."

"And you believe all that?"

"I don't know. I'd never really thought about it until I came here. Then, that book Fabian has . . ."

"Oh, Fabian . . ."

"There's an enormous intelligence there," I said, "and I'm not being clever recognizing it. And he believes in magic, so how can I not think that perhaps there is something?"

Dominick stopped me with a hand on my arm as I stumbled over Jupiter, who had leaped out from behind a lilac tree. "You should have thrown that flower away somewhere where anyone passing could have seen it; it would have shown whoever is hanging round Jessamy dropping chrysanthemums, that to you, it's nonsense."

"But the intention is there, isn't it?"

"To play silly games with you?"

"No, to make it clear to me that someone thinks I have harmed them and is warning me of revenge. Or dislikes me and wants me to know it."

"Who could dislike you?"

I heard my sudden laughter. "Do you know, Dominick, I really do hope someone does. It's only the people without personality and without the courage of honest convictions who want to be liked by everyone."

"But who down here even knows you well enough?"

"That's it. Who? I'd like to find out."

We had reached the garage. Dominick stopped. "Stephanie, please don't let this upset you. It's probably only children playing some silly game."

"How many children live in this area or know that I'm a visitor at Jessamy?"

"There are a few in the village."

"And what wrong could I possibly have done them or their parents?"

"It's worrying you, isn't it?"

I walked into the shade of the garage. "Oh no. I'm about as impressed by bell, book and candle as I am by fairy tales. But I'm not at all certain that if children are doing this, some adult isn't behind it."

"Fabian must have told you about Hobbin and her grandchildren, Robin and Lucy," Dominick said. "That's your explanation."

But I was scarcely listening. A sequel to the chrysanthemum's message had struck me, and I spoke my thoughts aloud: "Suppose . . . my mother did someone a serious injury, and because she died before whoever had suffered could retaliate, I'm the target?"

"That's a thought you'd best forget. Here, let me look at that tag." He took it from me. "It's just a cut-down label and the printing is very ordinary, absolutely without a single trace of a personality—no fancy twists to a letter, no dashes. Anyone could have done it. Perhaps you won't get any more. These things tend to die out if nothing is made of them. But if you do find another, leave it where it is. Don't even pick it up."

I had been walking a little ahead of Dominick and suddenly I stopped and looked back. "Are you saying the best thing to do would be to ignore it?"

"Not that exactly, but—well, I think it would be better to do just that. Ignore it."

I saw the way his eyes veered from mine: troubled, puzzled. And I felt that behind his apparent disbelief in village spells and charms, he was taking it all a little more seriously than he would have me believe.

He said, "You could, of course, send the tag to an expert. The police . . ."

"Oh, Dominick." I burst out laughing. "What would they say if I walked into the police station carrying a solitary chrysanthemum? They'd probably tell me to go and see a psychiatrist."

There was a waste bin in the corner of the garage and I threw the tag in. "That," I said, "is the end of today's little spell."

Dominick guided me through Pilgrim Abbas to Dulverley, through the lovely, lonely country of wild blue hills and forests and the water meadows.

Driving through Dulverley, with its ancient winding streets and buildings that leaned like bent old men, was full of hazards, but we reached the station with time to spare.

I left Dominick there, found a parking lot for the car and went in search of a telephone. I found one at the corner of a narrow street and from there I called the hospital in London. I was put through to the sister-in-charge, who told me that Stephanie's condition was unchanged. She then asked me if I was a relative.

"No. A friend. Rachel Fleming. I came to see her—"

Someone tapped on the glass door of the telephone kiosk. I looked over my shoulder and a man glared at me.

"I'm so sorry—" I said into the telephone. And then I stopped. The line was dead. Either the nurse had been called away or we had been cut off. It didn't matter. Stephanie was still in her traumatic world. I replaced the receiver and slid the kiosk door back. The man and I looked at one another.

"I hope I didn't keep you waiting too long," I said. "It was a London call, and urgent."

"For a smile like yours," the man replied, "I would forgive you anything."

I went on a leisurely tour of the city. The great Minster stood surrounded by a moat, swan-haunted and serene, so old that Saxon kings and Norman knights had worshiped there.

Outside the precincts of the great church, the warm, pungent smell of roasting chestnuts came from a little cart on which a brazier glowed.

After lunch, Fabian drove me to Upwey and we tossed a coin into the wishing well and I made my secret wish. "You should make a wish too," I said to Fabian.

"Perhaps for me there are other, more certain ways of getting what I want."

"I can well believe it."

He laughed and said, "Let's find a place for tea."

During the next hour, while we had tea and walked along by the millstream, I recognized how strong were Fabian's changes of mood. He seemed to forget I was Livanova's daughter and was an excellent and easy companion, talking of Dorset, which he loved, pointing out an avenue of ash trees leading to some hidden mansion. "They call the ash the Venus of the Woods. There are none, unfortunately, at Jessamy." He bent and picked up a stone and held it in the palm of his hand. "Do you see? It's just a stone and yet, looking at it in the light, it has some of the colors of a pheasant—titian and sapphire." He tossed it away. "However hard he tries, no artist can ever catch the real depth of that which he copies. Nature evades us just as we evade one another. Not that people, as a rule, want to. Most of them have a need to be known, to be understood to the depths, but scarcely any of us are."

"Do *you* want to be known deeply?"

"Oh, there are exceptions. Personally, I would find it very uncomfortable to be utterly understood."

I wanted to say "So Livanova never really knew you?" But in her dominance, she would have needed to know in order to control. Perhaps Fabian's self-containment was what had parted them. Strange that a pebble picked up from a path should have brought us back to Tatiana Livanova.

When we arrived at Jessamy, I kept glancing at my watch, anxious not to be late in meeting Dominick's train.

"It will take you exactly a quarter of an hour to get to Dulverley," Fabian said, "so stop fussing. And listen to music or put on the television or something to amuse you. I have to go out for a while on some frivolous village matter about an old barn that should have been pulled down years ago. It's of no use to anyone except the rather bloody-minded old colonel who owns it, and he never uses it. They shouldn't be bothering me with their village arguments, since I'm not a landowner here."

"But you are. Jessamy—"

"My dear Stephanie, nothing of this"—he waved an arm—"is mine yet. Surely the solicitor told you that it takes a very long time to probate a will?"

"I know. But everyone here must have heard that Jessamy will eventually be yours."

"Why?" His voice was cold. "The facts of the will haven't been broadcast. However curious the public are with regard to Livanova's will—*if* they are, that is—nothing can be publicized until probate."

I wondered if Mrs. Manfred had been mentioned in the will, and supposed that since she had been Livanova's housekeeper for as long as I could remember, she must have benefited. And it was likely that although Dominick had not been with Livanova for very many months, he, too, would have been left some small legacy.

While we were talking I had sat down on the window seat, and I could feel Jupiter's soft copper tail flicking the back of my neck as he perched above me on the sill watching the birds on the lawn.

Fabian, who had been sorting through a pile of newspapers left on the table, said, "Mrs. Manfred will never throw anything away. I think she must have been a squirrel in a previous incarnation."

I sat quietly as the black and gold lacquer clock struck the hour.

"Just remember," Fabian added, "that there are three forked lanes from here to Dulverley. Take the left one each time; the right lanes all lead on to the Heath, and if you drive for long enough, you'll end up in the Thomas Hardy country, and who knows, you might see the ghost of Tess of the d'Urbervilles." He lifted a hand in slight salute and was gone. The great front door closed quietly behind him.

X

I LEFT FIFTEEN MINUTES later, driving down the long lane from Jessamy, the sunset behind me. I could see in the driving mirror streaks of crimson flaring fanlike over Gideon's Rock, and in those burning reflections I played with fantasies. They said this was part of King Alfred's place—he of the ragged disguise and the burned cakes. But could it be, perhaps, King Arthur's country? Was this the Camelot? And were the knights sleeping somewhere hidden in that great limestone cliff and not, where other stories had it, in Cornwall or that lonely place in Wales they called Gwynedd?

The countryside was empty of people. No man strode across the Heath with a dog bounding in front of him; the great shire horses were stabled for the night; the birds were silent. Only I, driving through the winding lanes, disturbed the peace of Pilgrim Abbas. The open Heath on my right gave way to high hedges;

dust-dry oak leaves choked the ditches. I slowed down at a forked lane, then recognized an isolated cottage Dominick had pointed out to me. The car's headlights lit up the rust-colored spires of sorrel in the untidy garden, the walls matted with ivy and the unlit windows. That was the spot where I had to take the second of the left-hand lanes.

Darkness was almost total, and because of the lingering warmth of the day, I had the windows open. The pungent scent from an autumn bonfire drifted in, bringing with it a nostalgic memory of days when I was very young and helped my father burn the fallen leaves in our Berkshire garden.

The Dorset lanes wound like serpents, lonely and secretive, the lovely vistas hidden by shadows. I rounded one of the bends and saw a light ahead of me. For a moment I thought it was a lamp thoughtfully placed at some cross lane, but at the moment when I realized it was too small and far too low down to be a street lamp, it began to swing from side to side and then disappeared around another bend.

I slowed down and thought I knew what had happened. Dominick had caught an earlier connection, and since I had not been at the station, had decided to walk. He had seen the car coming toward him, guessed, in this isolated place, that it could only be mine and was signaling me to stop.

But then I remembered being told that the connections from the main station at Dorchester were very few and far between, and if he had caught an earlier train, he would surely have arrived at Jessamy before I had even left to meet him.

Somewhere on the way, I had obviously missed the right turning, and a farm worker, walking home, was probably warning me of a danger ahead—a possible blocked road or a dead end. I drove slowly to the next bend and saw the light again. It was to my right and stationary. I was being guided by some benevolent stranger. But I knew the hazards of English country lanes only too well, and before I could turn the car around, I would have to find out whether there were ditches on either side, hidden by darkness, into which the wheels could tip and leave me helpless.

I opened the door and got out, and above the purr of the engine I heard the sound of church bells over the fields. The Pilgrim Abbas bell-ringers were practicing for Sunday and the cadences were poignant and evocative as they flowed toward me in that black, narrow lane.

To my relief there were no ditches, but as I got back into the car I could still see the light glowing steadily to my right.

I drove on slowly for some few yards until I came to a place where the bushes seemed thinner and the light just ahead and to my right. But there was no turning in the lane.

Puzzled, I got out again and went to the bushes. The light remained steady. I called out, and my voice rang clearly in the night: "Who is it?"

There was no answer.

Small sharp twigs caught my hair and scratched my legs as I pushed through the bushes. Then, as I stepped free of the hedge, feeling my way over the black earth, my left foot touched something that swayed under it. I drew quickly back, but my foot was held in what felt like soft mud. There was a queer sucking sound and I remembered that once, long ago, I had heard that same sound on Dartmoor—the wet, sinister thirsty hiss of a bog.

With that step, the realization of danger flashed through my brain and I flung my hands out, catching hold of the spiky bushes on either side of me. I gave an enormous heave, and leaning my whole weight backward, I dragged my foot free of the insidious suction. I felt the weight of mud clinging to my ankle and the icy cold of the stagnant water. But I was safe on the dry bank, shaking with relief, heedless of the small, vicious branches of the hawthorn bushes that dug sharp points into my face and hands.

I stared down at the black mass, not knowing how deep it was and whether, had I gone less cautiously toward it, I could have fought my way safely out—or if the swirling mass would have engulfed me.

In the distance the church bells rang with a purity that mocked the evil place across which a single light made a thin golden path too faint to reveal the danger beneath it. I wondered how the light could lie so gently on that sinister, semi-liquid mass. It was possible that the bog was little more than a wide ditch and the flashlight that beckoned me was in a lane on the far side. If so, someone must be there, someone who could have seen what was happening to me but hadn't called out to try and stop me. Had watched—and waited.

"That be a bog," said a voice behind me.

I knew, before I turned, who spoke.

The children, Robin and Lucy, stood side by side, their faces shadowed and eerie in the darkness.

"You'd be taken right under if you'd gone in there," the boy said matter-of-factly.

"Do you know where that light came from?"

"What light?"

"Look through the bushes and tell me if there's a lane on the other side. But take care. Just look, don't step forward."

"Oh, we knows the bog," the girl said impatiently. "All of them as lives round these parts knows the bog." She went to the hedge and peered through. "There do be a light, Robin," she said.

"It can't actually be on the bog," I said, "or it would have sunk by now. So where . . . ?"

"Oh, there be only bits of bog and there be places you can stand on, if you knows them. We call them—the bits where you can stand —the Little Purple Men, because they be bright in summer daytime. Granny says 'tis some flower that grows there. Don't know what it be called."

"Did you see anyone with a flashlight?"

"No," they said in unison.

They had moved, and now their small, pointed faces, with high foreheads and eyes like black diamonds, were half lit by the car's headlights.

"Did you *hear* anyone?"

"Oh yes. Someone were coming along the lane."

"Who was it?"

"Dunno. It were dark."

"A man?"

They nodded.

"Surely there can't be many people living round here."

"There be the village up the road," they said reasonably enough.

So anyone could have stood in the lane and signaled me to a halt, then led me to that dank, foul place.

"Why don't the authorities fence it off?"

"Oh, we all knows it, and no one goes through them hedges. Hedges is meant to keep people out."

"*I* went through."

"Yes, you did," they said in maddening unison.

"Why aren't you at home?"

"We be going now to our supper. But Granny sent us out; there were someone from the village wanting her to tell the cards. She'll tell them true for you if you ask her."

"Thank you, but I know what my fortune very nearly was, and

for the moment, all I'm interested in is who shone that light and then threw it onto the bog, and why did it just happen to land on one of your Little Purple Men."

"That's because that bit where the light is be near the bushes. He'd just have to bend down and put the light there."

I said, "Haven't you any idea who was here and shone the flashlight?"

"No. We just knows where he put it. You come with us," Lucy said, "and we'll show you where the light be. It be all right," she added comfortingly, "there won't be no one there. He be gone."

"Expecting me to investigate?"

The word floored them. They tried twice to repeat it, as if it were part of a game, and gave up. "You be very grand," Robin said.

"Oh no, just puzzled."

"You don't get folks down this lane," Robin said. "Only them as is going to Jessamy or to Granny's for their fortunes."

"You could've been dead by now," Lucy said ghoulishly.

"Oh, I shouldn't think so," I replied lightly. "It's probably quite shallow. But anyone else who tries to attract me with a flashlight, even if it's in the middle of the main street in Dulverley, will be unlucky. In the future, I stay in the car."

"Yes, miss."

I turned. "Can I give you two a lift?"

"Oh, our place be just through the forest on the other side of the lane. Don't you *know* that?"

I accepted their reproof in silence, got into the car and, holding the door open, called, "By the way, does your grandmother grow yellow chrysanthemums in her garden?"

"Oh, we don't have no garden; there be just the forest."

And as far as I was aware, chrysanthemums didn't grow wild. "I see," I said, but knew that I saw and understood very little.

The children disappeared before I had settled in the car. On an impulse I got out again, parted the hedge and looked through. The light had disappeared; either the particular Little Purple Man on which it had rested could not take its weight and it sank, or it had rolled off and been sucked down into the bog.

There was no proof now that there had ever been a flashlight, and I wasn't at all certain that the children were sufficiently reliable to back me up if I brought them in as witnesses.

I shut myself in the car and reached for a box of Kleenex, took off my shoe and wiped it as clean as I could. But the bog slime clung to my ankle, and after using the whole box of tissues, I gave up and I drove uncomfortably away. I reached the station just as the branch train from Dorchester was slowing down. I parked where I could see across the pretty station garden to the whole length of the platform. Only a few doors opened and Dominick stepped down from one of them.

"I call this a noble gesture," he said when he joined me, "and I'm grateful."

"Was the trip successful?"

He shook his head. "Musicians aren't at a premium and the piano trio are postponing their audition for the moment. My agent suggests I move up to London, but there's still a chance that I might be accepted for the quintet which is being started here in the southwest. So I'm on a kind of seesaw—London or the West Country. But let's forget it. Have you had a good day?"

I made noncommittal noises. I would let him relax from his journey before I told him what had happened to me. I drove steadily, watching for the place where I had been dropped by the signaling light. It was never easy finding a particular spot in a strange area in the dark, especially when driving in the opposite direction. But counting the bends in the lane, I eventually knew I was near the place.

"Did you know that there's a bog behind those bushes?"

"Yes. How did you hear about it?"

"I nearly sank into it."

I heard him catch his breath sharply. "But you can't have. If you'd gone for a walk, you'd have seen—"

"It was dark."

"There's a thick hedge all round. What reason could you possibly have for going through it?"

"But I did. It happened just now when I was on the way to meet you."

"You mean you skidded going round that bend? I've always said it was too sharp, and sometimes a hare or a rabbit will streak across the road in front of a car and you swerve to avoid it. Is that what the trouble was?"

"No." I stopped the car and switched on the interior light. "Look. Proof." I showed him my wet, stained shoe and muddied ankle.

"Then—what happened?" He put out a hand and touched my

wrist. "You've got scratches. Stephanie, what happened?" His voice and his expression were harsh, almost as if he were angry with me for alarming him.

"Someone was around," I said and told him of my adventure. When I had finished, he burst out, "Then it was those damned children."

"I don't think so. If they had been guilty of mischief, they wouldn't have dared to stay and speak to me."

"It doesn't follow." He got out of the car and went over to the hedge and parted it. "Look—come and look. I think I can guess what happened."

I joined him, and he said, "You see how very near the surface the bog water is in places? So what you saw must have been your own reflected headlights."

"Waving me down just ahead?"

"Tricks of light on pools of water, perhaps ruffled by a wind."

"Well, there's no reflection of my headlights now, is there?" I sounded bad-tempered and I felt it. I wanted to be believed; I resented cool reasoning because I knew perfectly well it did not apply in this case. And I needed an ally.

"Oh, let's go," I said impatiently. "I want to get back and clean up. There's nothing pleasant about having bog mud clinging to your ankle."

Dominick broke the silence as we drove on. "There's just one thing that strikes me. A farmer could have lost an animal—a pony or a sheep could have wandered and he went looking for it. He could have stumbled into the bog."

I let out a startled cry and the wheel jerked in my hands. Dominick reached over and steadied it.

"I'm sorry," I said. "But I never thought of that. Of course. Someone could actually have stumbled *into* the bog. Suppose . . . it's horrible, but suppose someone . . ."

"Just a minute before you get upset. That bog isn't one of those deep, dangerous places you get on, say, Dartmoor. No one quite understands how it functions, but it's shallow and a man wouldn't drown in it. It would be hideously unpleasant, but he'd be able to fight his way free and—" He stopped and turned to me. "But you, heaven help us, you're so little, *you* could have been dragged down quite a way."

"Then I'm grateful for my quick reflexes," I said weakly.

"This part of the country is so isolated that I suppose whoever came here searching for a lost animal—and that's the only sensible thing I can think of—didn't dream that the car coming his way was being driven by someone who didn't know the bog was there and might investigate the flashlight."

I remained silent, my hands guiding the car along the black lanes. Some sixth sense warned me not to believe in easy explanations. Someone had deliberately tried to attract my attention; to beckon me, by means of a light, to a frightening and sinister place.

". . . no one would do such a thing, even for some nefarious thrill," Dominick was saying. "Why should they? People don't go around harming someone without any reason, unless they're mad. And so far as I know, there isn't even a village idiot in Pilgrim Abbas. No one here dances naked in the full moon. So I'm sure there's a simple explanation—a farmer losing an animal."

Or someone wanting to frighten me badly because they thought I was Livanova's daughter. Or because they knew that I was not . . .

XI

THE LANES ON THAT DRIVE BACK seemed interminable, the long shadows of the trees, flung crisscross by the car's lights, making our journey seem like plunges in and out of ebony caves.

"I must tell Fabian," I said.

"Fabian?" Dominick sounded startled, as if I had brought him back from some far-removed thought. "Yes, of course. I think you should."

"He'll probably telephone around to the farmers to see if anyone lost an animal and went looking for it tonight."

"He might."

"He *must*," I said and turned the car into the last lane.

The hedges had disappeared; the ridge of Maiden Forest was behind us. We were in the wide stretch where heath and sea and rock met. The moon swam clear of the great cloud and I saw the three gables of Jessamy and the lovely mullioned windows lit by moonshine.

It was theatrical, but there was nothing sinister about it. It was a house that had been loved and lived-in for centuries. Even as I told myself that, I remembered the rumor that between the time the monks had had their monastery on that site and Jessamy as it was now, certain strange rites had been held in the cellars there. Medieval witchcraft was so far in the past that nothing could remain. Yet as I drove between the gates and up to the house, the curious dread of arrival grew stronger. I didn't want to walk through the door, to cross the hall dominated by Livanova's portrait. I didn't want to meet Fabian Seal.

I thought angrily that had it not been for the doctor's intervention, I might at this moment be lying on a Mediterranean beach or wandering through the fountained gardens of Granada.

"The lamps are on in the drawing room."

"So Fabian is home," I said.

"Oh, not necessarily. He always wants plenty of light."

I turned off the car engine and sat looking up at the house, where moonlight and house lamps met and blazed in a soft diffusion of silver and gold. "I still wonder why I was invited here," I said. "I think Fabian made up his mind long before he ever met me—while he was still my mother's lover—that he didn't like me. So *why* ask me down?"

"Perhaps," Dominick said, "to try to change his mind and like you. Perhaps he felt it wasn't enough to know you by hearsay; he needed to meet the real Stephanie."

The words jerked me out of my preoccupation. I shot a swift look at Dominick. But his face, illumined by the lights from the house, was calm and I felt that the suspicion of something sinister in his words came purely from my own unease. Yet remembering the letter to Stephanie, I was quite certain that Fabian's reason was not that simple.

"I wish I knew him," I said and opened the car door. "Fabian, I mean."

As I got out I thought I heard Dominick say, "Perhaps it would be best for you if you never did." But my movements drowned his voice. He came with me to put the car away, and gathering up the box of muddy tissues I had used to clean my shoe, said, "I'll take these round the back and throw them away."

He disappeared through the gap into the small kitchen garden and I made my way to the terrace. One of the tall French doors of the drawing room was half open, and I paused before entering the room and got my compact out of my purse. Turning sideways so that the moon was behind me, I held the mirror up and did quick repairs to my face, acknowledging a futile vanity where Fabian was concerned.

"This isn't Halloween, my dear."

I jumped like a startled rabbit and lowered the little compact mirror which, held close to my face, had screened the doorway.

Fabian stood watching me with amusement.

"Am I only to look in my mirror on Halloween?" It was a weak quip but I was embarrassed at being caught.

"Don't you know the old superstition?"

"I know some. Which one?" My question was polite and quite disinterested.

"When you lift a mirror and look into it and see the moon, you must light a candle and then—Oh, let's forget it. It's all nonsense, charming or idiotic, depending on how you feel about such things. Come along in. I hope you're hungry, because there's a mighty great casserole for dinner. Are you?"

"Oh yes. Yes." My words came hesitantly, as Stephanie often spoke, answering even a simple question doubtfully. And once again I was alarmed. I must not find it too easy to be someone else; I must not lose myself in another woman's identity.

"What in God's name have you been doing? Playing mudlarks?" Fabian was looking at my foot.

"I nearly fell into the bog. You do know there's a small one on the way to the station, don't you?"

"Well guarded by bushes. Yes, I know. Come inside. Moonlight blazing on us might become you, but I don't think it enhances my looks." He stood aside for me to enter the room, then closing the French window, he said, "Now tell me what happened."

I used almost the same words as I had when I told Dominick. Fabian paced the room slowly, listening and not speaking until I had finished. Then he said, "Someone looking for a stray dog, and finding himself on the edge of the bog, stumbled. Then in trying to save himself, the light got flung out of his hand."

"Dominick said something like that, too. Couldn't you telephone to see if any farmer has lost an animal?"

"If he has, I can't do anything about it."

"But it would—" I stopped. I had nearly said "It would relieve my mind." But that would sound as if I feared that the whole thing had a personal and sinister meaning.

"It would what?" Fabian was watching me.

"If . . . if it was an animal, I'd like to know that it had been rescued."

"What a lot I'm having to relearn about you, Stephanie," he said softly. "I thought you disliked animals. You hated your mother's little dog."

"I . . . oh no . . . no. She was wrong," I protested lamely.

I thought I heard him laugh as he went to the door. "Very well, I'll call up a couple of farmers I know."

The main telephone was in a small room, furnished as an office, at the far end of the hall, and I could not hear him speaking.

Dominick entered through the French doors.

"I'm going to have a bath," I said.

"Of course. Anyway, dinner won't be for some time. Mrs. Manfred is busy on the telephone giving the butcher a piece of her mind about the lamb for the casserole. And Livanova used to say that Mrs. Manfred's mind was often a mile long when she got near a phone. She's so nervous of it, she either talks too much and never listens, or mumbles and puts the receiver down."

"But it's seven o'clock. Whoever the village butcher is, he'll have gone home long ago."

"Dear Stephanie, you aren't in a city. The people owning the few shops here live over them. And it's just possible the butcher went to Black Agnes for a beer after he'd finished with his customers, so Mrs. Manfred couldn't contact him earlier."

"Black Agnes?"

"The local inn. It's an odd name, and no one knows its origin except that Black Agnes was the name of Mary Queen of Scot's horse."

As Fabian and I met at the drawing-room door, he said, "I've called our two nearest farmers and neither has lost a dog, a cat or a sheep, so the mystery of the flashlight remains."

I darted a look at Dominick and I was certain in that moment that the same thought crossed both our minds. Even if Mrs. Manfred had used up her anger with the butcher in a single minute, there would still not have been time for Fabian to telephone two people.

"I thought I'd have a quick bath, if you don't mind. But if it's not convenient—"

"Why should I mind?" He sounded impatient, as if I were interrupting with superficialities other more important things. "You can lie and luxuriate in your bath for the next two hours if you want to. We aren't primitive here. We don't bring Victorian hip baths up to your room and we do have constant hot water. So don't be apologetic about it."

Stephanie again, twining hesitant fingers through my usually positive mind, irritating Fabian. "Oh, I'm not apologetic," I said too loudly, as if trying to reach her in London. "I'm just mad that I've probably ruined a perfectly good shoe."

"Give it to me later. Fenney, the gardener here, can get a polish where no polish ever before existed or was ever likely to. Now go along."

I lay in the pale-green bath, kicking up the water. The first movement of the Pastoral Symphony rose from the room below and was a beautiful background to my unbeautiful thoughts. No one but I had seen the light in the lane flashing me to a stop, and only the children and I had seen it remain steady and beckoning from the bog. I had, from the start, dismissed Robin and Lucy because I wasn't certain how much I could trust them. And I felt that even if they corroborated my statement, I could be suspected of bribing them. Who, after all, in this village would trust the grandchildren of a witch? So I had no real proof of what had happened or any way of knowing whether Fabian and Dominick believed that someone had deliberately led me to that odious place.

Lying in the scented water, I was fairly certain that my ugly adventure had been intentional, and there was only one possible reason. Someone wanted to frighten me away from Jessamy. But whatever happened, I knew I must not lose my nerve. Nor must I leave until I had made more effort to find out what was the secret I was not supposed to know.

Back in the bedroom, I found myself wandering aimlessly around, changing my mind about the choice of a dress, putting on shoes with heels and changing my mind and wearing pumps. Lethargic and uncertain, unlike myself: like Stephanie . . .

I crossed to the mirror, sat down, and resting my chin on my hands, looked at my reflection. In that curious moment I could almost have been prepared to see her looking out at me as if some metamorphosis had taken place and I had become Livanova's daughter.

But all that was happening was that I was playing a part too well. I needed to hold on to myself, to be the observer, and so, in complete command of a situation I had chosen.

Fabian and I went into the drawing room for coffee after dinner but Dominick didn't follow us. Mrs. Manfred carried in the tray with the Crown Derby coffee service and set it down.

"Pour, please, Stephanie," Fabian said.

I looked at the three small crimson and gold cups. "For Dominick, too?"

"I think we'll leave his. Listen."

The music of Chopin's Revolutionary Study flamed in tumbled chords from the practice room.

Fabian went out into the hall and said, "He's shut the door on himself, but I don't see why he shouldn't have an audience, do you?" A few seconds later the music stormed round us.

"It's marvelous," I said. "So defiant, so strong."

"You like music?"

I answered, after a moment's cautious thought, "I should imagine my mother told you that I did."

"Yes. But she also said that you liked sentimental tunes. She didn't, as I suppose you know. She loved the wild, melancholy music of the Slav people, the Tartars most of all. I never quite knew what race her grandfather came from; I doubt if she knew, either. Did she?"

I said, knowing too little, "She . . . my mother . . . was just . . . Russian," and then changed the subject. "Dominick plays well."

"Chopin and Scarlatti and perhaps a Bach toccata. But you'll never hear the glory of a Beethoven or a Bartók sonata. Livanova forbade him to play deeply intense or passionate music. She said he wasn't capable. And she couldn't bear to listen to savage music —as she put it—played with as much fire as dead ashes."

"How unkind."

He answered, with characteristic impatience, "Do you measure truth by its yardage of kindness?"

"It wouldn't have hurt her to let him play Bartók if it gave him pleasure. And anyway, how can Dominick ever improve if he's not allowed to play difficult music."

"You don't understand, do you?"

"No." I sat cradling my cup, feeling the heat of the coffee warm my fingers.

"Livanova praised or criticized with absolute honesty; she was fearless of resentment. She was also violently jealous." Fabian's voice had a faraway note. "I understood all those fires of feeling in her. You never did. Had you done so, she might have loved you more."

"She couldn't have loved me less."

"Dear God, she said you were bitter."

The pity I had felt for Stephanie throughout the years broke into a wave of resentment against Fabian Seal. "I wonder how different you would have been, how *you* would have looked at life, if my mother hadn't caught you young and trained you her way." I hurled the words at him, drowning Dominick's flowing music.

Fabian rose. "Yes," he said softly, "I wonder," and turned his back on me.

For a few moments only the music broke the stillness. Then Fabian turned to me, leaned against the heavy carved table and said, "You see? You hurl a truth at me and I can take it. I can say, 'Yes, Stephanie, I was a young man fascinated by an older woman, ready to learn from her, to be molded by her.' I admit it—so I stand by my own adage, the adage that she taught me: truth."

Utter truth, even if it hurt, because anything else, for a man like Fabian Seal, was an assault on integrity.

For a man like Fabian Seal. But all I was certain about him was that he was difficult to know, so there was no yardstick by which I could measure his character. And anyway, however high his principles, I had no proof that he lived by them. My feelings when I was with him were of unease, of a need for watchfulness without in the least being able to prove my suspicions.

The strain of the impersonation into which I had voluntarily plunged, and the shock of that evening's ugly experience at the bog, made me so tense that as I sat listening to Dominick's playing, I had a wild urge to jump up out of my chair and face Fabian with the unpalatable facts. I wanted to shout, "This house should belong to Livanova's daughter. And since I'm in a truth-telling mood, I'll tell you something else. I am not Stephanie Clair."

If I did that, I had a feeling that his light eyes would just laugh at me, because somewhere in the two days I had been at Jessamy, I had given myself away.

I had no way of knowing what would have happened had we sat together much longer listening to Dominick's playing—if my will power would have snapped and I would have done what my impulse tempted—for suddenly the music stopped and footsteps strode loudly across the parquet floor of the hall.

"Can't I even bloody well play to myself in peace?" His voice was low and violently angry and his usually gentle eyes were like gray fire.

Fabian lifted his head. "Surely you don't object to Stephanie and me?"

"You know that I only like to play to an audience when I know they're listening. Otherwise, to me, it's eavesdropping. My music is a personal thing unless I am voluntarily playing for the public."

"I'm sorry," I said. "But I enjoyed it so much."

"We both enjoyed it," Fabian told him.

"Like hell you did!" Dominick gave him a cold stare and turned on his heel and left us.

Without knowing why, I started up out of my chair to follow him.

"My dear Stephanie, sit down and don't fuss. Temperament should always be left to cool itself. Would you like more coffee?"

"No, thank you. Fabian, there's something I must tell you." I waited, but he made no movement. He sat with his face half turned away from me, focusing on the glow of the fire of ash logs in the grate. "I think I ought to go back to London tomorrow," I said.

"Good heavens, you've only just come."

"I didn't plan to stay long. You remember . . ."

He turned and looked at me. "What do I remember?"

I thought, with secret anger: It's as if he enjoys seeing me flounder over an explanation it's not easy to make.

"That I explained when I first arrived, and you didn't tell me in your letter how long I was expected to stay."

"Ah, the letter." He gave me a long, thoughtful look. "Are you always so long answering?"

"I'm sorry."

"Oh, don't be. You probably found the decision difficult. 'Do I want to meet this man'?"

"Yes," I said. "I did find it difficult."

He crossed the room, saying, "If you go tomorrow, you will

108

make a tricky situation for me. You see, I have accepted an invitation for us for tomorrow night." He put a record on the record player. *"The Karelia Suite,* do you know it?"

"No."

He sat down again. The music was in direct contrast to what Dominick had played. It was as if it came from somewhere outside the house, as if a goat-footed god were playing and the things of the forest were dancing to it.

"The people who live at Lys Manor are giving a party for Marian Homer's birthday. It will be quite a big affair and Dominick has been asked to play. It could lead to some engagements for him, since the Homers move in artistic circles."

"But they won't have asked me. I don't know them."

"I do and so did your mother, slightly, and they have invited you."

"It's kind of them, but I can't go. I must get back to London."

He asked, sounding amused, "Some man?"

"No."

"You answer that so emphatically. Don't tell me you haven't had affairs."

I said, with truth, "Of course, and I've made mistakes. It's part of growing up, isn't it?"

"Yes." He leaned his head back, eyes narrowed, listening to the music.

I said, "Fabian, I *must* get back to London."

"We'll talk about it after the party. I hope you've brought something attractive to wear. If not, go into Dulverley. I believe there's one good dress shop there."

"Thank you, I'll manage."

"Good." He settled back again, relaxed, and reached for Jupiter, who leaped purring onto the arm of his chair.

It was a strange evening, at once intimate and remote. To anyone looking through the window at us, we would have appeared as two people sitting quietly, drawn close by understanding, by friendship or by love. In the firelight and the lamplight and the soft shadows, no one would have dreamed that we were poles away from understanding one another and that the emotion that enveloped us was neither friendship nor trust. No one, looking in, would have dreamed that the girl in the green dress and the small pearl earrings was there in the uneasy position of impersonator.

Lying that night in the fourposter bed, I heard the clock strike one. Sleep seemed a long way off and the bog incident was still too real in my mind. Neither Fabian nor Dominick had mentioned it again, and the obvious reason was that they didn't believe I had been in as much danger as I had made out. Stephanie, coming to see me after a meeting with her mother, had once explained that Livanova had said to her, "Where I am temperamental, *you* are neurotic. And that I can't stand. You bore me with your wild stories and your stupid fears."

Perhaps, in a fit of irritation, Livanova had repeated those words to Fabian and to Dominick; perhaps both of them had decided that the flashlight on the bog had been in my imagination and they had just played along with my story in order to keep me quiet.

But someone knew it to be the truth: the one who had flashed the light at me, and then, according to the children who had heard him walking away, left the place knowing that sooner or later I would be reported missing.

As sleep evaded me, a depression, physical as well as mental, overcame me. I tried to take myself in hand, fiercely denying the sense of loneliness and desolation that was increasing with every hour I spent at Jessamy Court. It was entirely unreasonable. I had parents and relatives who cared for me; I had friends I loved; I had work that I enjoyed. Yet none of those comforts were quite relevant to me while I was in Fabian Seal's house. I was like a web hanging too fragilely between two people, clinging to both— Stephanie Clair and Rachel Fleming—yet belonging to neither.

XII

THE FIRST THING I had to do in the morning was to telephone again to the hospital in London. When I told Fabian that I wanted to drive around and see the countryside that morning, he said, "I'm glad you are one of those people who can amuse themselves."

"But you were afraid I wasn't?"

"That's right," he agreed cheerfully. "I have to see Hannaford this morning."

"That means going to London?"

He shook his head. "He has a country house near here. It was he who found Jessamy for Livanova. It's useful that he's down at the moment, because we have things to discuss. Yet he's far enough away not to be on my doorstep."

Mrs. Manfred was outside my bedroom, dusting the carved pillars of the balustrade that ran around the hall.

"I'm going out," I said. "I thought I'd drive round the countryside. I'd like to see Dulverley again."

"It be a pretty town." She stopped and followed my eyes to a small brooch she wore on the collar of her dark blouse. Her face went scarlet. "Oh, miss. I'm so sorry."

"What for?"

"This." She fingered the brooch. "You was looking at it. I shouldn't have worn it while you be here. I didn't think. But it cheers me sometimes. It were she who gave it to me. Your mother."

"Did she? It's pretty."

"Do you really think so?" Her dark eyes were puzzled. "But I thought you didn't like it because of the color of the stones. Madame said you thought green was unlucky. She said she gave it to you, but you would never wear it and so she took it away from you and gave it to me. By rights, 'twere yours, miss."

I acted quickly. I smiled and laid a hand on her arm. "Keep it, of course. I love green on other people. It's just that I feel it's unlucky for me." *But on the previous night I had worn a green dress* . . . "It's one of those stupid things I try to fight," I added lamely.

I wasn't certain if I had convinced her, for her eyes still rested speculatively on me. Then, as if to accept that I didn't resent her having the brooch, she asked, "Have you seen Madame's suite of rooms yet?"

"No."

"Perhaps it be too soon—"

"Oh no."

"They be along the passage." She pointed. "Right there, at the far end."

"Thank you. I'd like to see them now, in the morning light."

"*She* loved the morning too. But the nights were her real time, with the music playing and everyone cheering her and throwing flowers . . ." She broke off and turned back to her dusting.

Double doors led to Livanova's suite. I had formed no idea of what I might see. I stepped into a room dominated by a chandelier that glittered like a cascade of jewels.

The walls of the large room were covered in embossed white velvet, and a magnificent painted screen stood against a far wall. The colors of the room were yellow and lettuce-green, and the whole effect was made exotic by three panels of silk embroidered with birds of paradise. Two torchères on either side of the carved fireplace had crimson shades.

But the room was entirely without background. There were no photographs of family or friends. It was as if Livanova had just "happened," and claimed nobody as belonging and wished nobody to claim her.

I crossed to the second pair of double doors, opened them and walked into her bedroom. Here, too, was the same "unbelonging": no photographs, no small, valueless and sentimental mementos. Only elegance again—cherry-red and white. There was a screen in this room also, but again obviously not for the purpose of hiding anything, merely for its decorativeness. I recognized the type, for I had seen a similar one in a great house in Scotland and had it described to me as a Chinese Coromandel. The large bed was lovely, too, with a headboard and coverlet of white silk with a thin peony pattern in dark red.

Livanova's own rooms, personal and yet supremely impersonal. I stood looking about me, taking in every detail as if it were important to me—as in a way, it was. The more I could understand this woman who had the world at her feet, the easier I would feel in Fabian and Dominick's company, the more I could help Stephanie.

Stephanie's hesitant, negative voice came back to me, complaining: "She hasn't even got a photograph of me. I know that because she has never ever asked for one. But then, I don't exist. I shouldn't *be* existing."

I went over to the carved white desk on which stood a mirror and which obviously served as a dressing table. All her creams and powders had been emptied from their original containers into covered crystal bowls. Her favorite scents seemed to be L'heure bleue; her lipsticks were gathered together into a cut-glass dish and ranged from pale-pink to damson-red.

I opened a drawer; it was full of varicolored scarfs. Another had handkerchiefs and gloves. Either Livanova was extremely tidy or, which was far more likely, Mrs. Manfred watched over her possessions as carefully as if she were guarding museum pieces.

Outside the window the maple blazed theatrically crimson against the many shades of evergreen—yew and cedar, laurel and thick peridot-green grass.

She had lived here with Fabian; perhaps they had slept the night together in that silken bed. Or perhaps, after making love, Livanova had banished him to his own rooms and slept alone.

I wondered if all of Livanova's lovely things now belonged to Fabian. Stephanie might know, but I did not, and I had already discovered that Fabian Seal was not the man to be asked anything outright. Even had I not been at Jessamy under false pretenses, I would still have been cautious of this man. It was absurd to be careful of what I said because I minded his reaction to me. But the truth was there. *I wanted him to like me.* And since he was a man I didn't trust, I knew I was being illogical.

I was still certain that he hadn't invited Stephanie to Jessamy merely to get to know her. But he was going to discuss whatever was important in his own good time.

I had heard so much about Livanova's powerful personality, her supreme self-will, that I wondered if Fabian had had much influence over her. He had been considerably younger—youth fascinated by a marvelous talent and a beautiful maturity. I had no idea whether he had loved her genuinely, as a man loved a woman for being a woman, or had loved her as an artist. I was quite certain that if I remained here for a century or beyond, I would never know. Fabian walked alone and his motives, bright or dark, were his affair. I was up against a will stronger than mine, and although I hated defeat, I could not see that I would gain much by remaining at Jessamy.

I walked around Livanova's lovely room, touching things, smoothing a silken cushion, aware of a lingering scent of sandlewood and jasmine.

There was a sadness about a beautiful room belonging to a woman so suddenly dead, and with it I felt my own sadness. I had learned nothing that could help Stephanie. Yet behind my sense of failure was the knowledge that I would remain a little longer. I had survived the initial difficulties of my fraud and I could continue for a few more days. Miracles happened and I might yet discover something of use to Stephanie and her doctor.

I was standing by the bedside table and picked up a slim green book lying there. It had been published in the days of gilt edgings and splendid bindings. I turned the pages and came across a verse that was lightly underlined in pencil:

> Sleep; and if life was bitter to thee, pardon,
> If sweet, give thanks; thou hast no more to give;
> And to give thanks is good, and to forgive.

I wondered, as I laid the book back on the table, who asked for forgiveness, whose message was there in Swinburne's poem.

I had hoped Mrs. Manfred would follow me into the room and, perhaps, gossip a little, but she let me be. So I closed the door on those two beautiful, silent rooms, gave a glance out of a window in the passage and went to fetch my coat.

The garage doors were open, and the first thing I saw as I got in behind the wheel of the car was the yellow chrysanthemum on the passenger seat.

It must have been put there very much earlier, for the tips of the petals were already turning brown and the flower looked too tired even to be refreshed by water. There was no tag on it, and as I drove out of the garage I tossed the flower into a lilac bush and tried to stop thinking about it.

Halfway down the drive an old man was bending over the grass border. I slowed down and he turned and looked around at me, and the two words he called to me must have been "Good morning," but spoken in his deep, throaty voice and in Dorset dialect, it sounded rather like a great cat's purr.

"I be Fenney," he said.

"Ah yes, you keep the grounds here looking beautiful."

He had narrow blue eyes and stiff hair the color of mixed pepper and salt. His trousers were tucked into a pair of old boots and his skin looked like brown leather.

"To be zure, it be fair green 'ere."

"Please," I pleaded, "would you speak more slowly. I'm afraid I'm rather dense and I can't quite understand . . ."

He took no offense. Instead he chuckled, and when he spoke again, even more slowly, I translated madly and understood.

"You be my lady's daughter from town and we speak strange, don't we, miss?"

"I like it. Yours is a gentle dialect. But do tell me, do you really look after all this by yourself?"

"Aye, I do. It be easy these days. Not like when I were young and flower beds were everywhere and my grandfather and my father had three working lads under them. Now there be only the lawns and the bushes to trim. My lady would have no flowers. And you be her daughter?"

"That's right. I'm just going to drive round the countryside," I said to stop any possible questions about Livanova. I restarted the car, waved to him and drove on up the avenue.

I was quite certain that the only public telephone in Pilgrim Abbas would be in a corner of the local general store. And since I needed to call London from some place where no one knew who I was and where I could not be overheard, I would have to go to Dulverley. But this time I would look for a row of telephone booths so that I would not have to risk an impatient man.

When I came to the lane where the bog lay hidden behind the hawthorn bushes, I kept my eyes firmly fixed on the way ahead. Two minutes, three minutes of remembering, and then I saw the gray tip of the village church and I threw off the final husk of memory. In the serenity and the brightness of the morning, it was easy to argue that there could be an innocent reason for what had happened. At least, that was how I chose to argue as I reached the village.

The cottages were rich with late roses and the rooks were noisy in the tall trees. The little stream that ran so cleanly and brightly toward its mother river reflected the sunlight in dots and dashes.

I slowed down as I neared the diminutive general store with its sign *Post Office,* and knew at once that I had been right in thinking that the telephone in Pilgrim Abbas would be a very public thing. It was. I could just see, as I passed, someone standing near the counter with the receiver to her ear. Nothing could be spoken there that would not be overheard, and certainly Livanova's supposed daughter could not call London inquiring about Livanova's real daughter.

I drove on through the village and took my time getting to Dulverley, on a road so free of traffic that I could drive in a leisurely way without being hooted at by irritated motorists. I enjoyed speed, too, but this part of Dorset seemed to go so far back in time that I would not have been surprised to have passed a coach and horses and heard a horn pierce the quiet and seen a feather curl around a woman's cheek as she leaned from the coach to look at me.

I passed a beautiful stone gatehouse guarding an avenue which seemed to stretch into an infinity. The sky was softly blue between thistledown clusters of white cloud. It had rained during the night and in places the small pools of water glimmered like crushed crystal.

Dulverley lay neatly among its low guardian hills, slumbering in the soft morning, crowned by its Minster and exuding an aura of complacency, as if its few remaining medieval streets were a display for visitors.

I found the post office, shut myself in a booth and put in a call to the London hospital. I was told again that there was no change in Stephanie's condition, but this time I asked for Dr. Wilde. I was informed that it was not his day at the hospital.

"Will you give him a message, please?"

"Of course, Miss Fleming."

"Will you tell him that I am in the country and I will call him in a few days."

"Very well." The voice on the telephone sounded cold, as if the nurse thought I was abandoning Stephanie.

But I had to let it be that way. I wasn't at all certain how the doctor would react if I told him of my method of getting into Jessamy Court. It would be easier to explain when I saw him.

I said, just before replacing the receiver, "Please believe, I am trying to help."

I left the booth and spent the morning exploring the town.

XIII

THE GATEHOUSE I had so admired on the way to Dulverley was
the entrance to Lys Manor. Ahead of us as we entered the house
was a double staircase, the two shallow flights sweeping out and
meeting where an archway led into a great formal room. Stephanie
would have loved it all—the rich gathering of people, the chandeliers, the elegance. It was the life she had always said her mother
should have given her.

But Livanova, in her ivory tower of ballet, had probably seldom
entered such a world herself. Ballet and high living were not good
allies, and Livanova's devotion to the perfection of her art was
absolute.

The Homers of Lys Manor were the leaders of the social set
for that corner of Dorset. Lord Homer was sixtyish, handsome,

with a high domed head, a halo of gray hair and a charm of manner that drew every guest, as he greeted them, into a warm welcome. His wife, whose birthday was being celebrated, was also tall and very dark. There was an un-English air about her, as if somewhere far back, she had oriental or gypsy blood.

I saw her glance with kindly amusement at the rose-colored dress I wore. She, too, was in rose-red, but where I wore a necklace of garnets, inherited from a Victorian great-great-grandmother, pearls were in her ears and at her throat. She was charming, and I caught the bright, meaningful glance she shot at Dominick and then at me. I interpreted it and was amused. It was almost as if she were thinking aloud: "These two young people look so well together. Livanova's daughter and Livanova's accompanist. I wonder . . . ?"

I drank champagne and watched how the women gathered around Dominick. Yet at no time when I caught sight of him across the room did I see him laugh. It was as if the gods at his birth decided that it was enough to give him that marvelous face, and as payment, denied him the gift of laughter.

The dazzling facets of the chandeliers shone on his bright head; Dominick was surrounded and feted, and yet I felt I wanted to go to him and protect him—although heaven knew from what. He had been Livanova's accompanist; he had had experience in playing before audiences; and he must have met many women. He was therefore perfectly capable of looking after himself.

While I watched Dominick, I was aware that Fabian was watching me, and even at a distance I saw the glitter of those alert eyes.

Dorset society was friendly. People talked to me. A woman in a red dress sang in a beautiful voice some Brahms songs. We wandered obediently from reception room to music room and back, listening, applauding, accepting champagne, talking.

Someone touched my elbow. I turned. She was middle-aged; her hair blond *cendré,* her skin suntanned, her dress dead-white.

"I knew your mother slightly, Miss Clair. I do charity work in Dulverley and we once asked her if she would appear at a fete we were having and bring you with her. The children had seen her give a wonderful performance in *Symphonic Variations,* and they wanted to meet the little girl who was, to them, so marvelously fortunate in having a prima ballerina for a mother. But then, two days before the fete you became ill."

Other people had joined us; I saw their faces, like smiling inquisitors.

"Oh yes . . . yes," I said vaguely, and gave a wild glance in the direction of the music room, where the guests were already gathering to hear Dominick play.

"Measles," someone said.

"Yes," I said again, out of my depth and grateful for the help.

"Oh no, it wasn't." A woman in a black gown and aquamarines spoke firmly. "It was pneumonia. You were very ill. Surely you remember?"

I had forgotten that illness of Stephanie's. "Oh," I said brightly, "*that* time!" as though I had had a succession of illnesses.

Something impelled me to look over my shoulder. Fabian stood near me.

"We're asked to return to the music room," he said.

He didn't touch me as he walked behind me, but I felt his strength, as physically uncomfortable as it was mentally disturbing. I didn't want him to sit close to me and found an isolated chair in the middle of a row. Almost immediately, as if he had willed her to do so, the woman on my left got up to join someone across the room and Fabian slid into the vacant seat. I felt the accidental brush of his arm against mine.

The room became quiet. Dominick sat down, flexed his hands, bent over the keyboard and began to play. I glanced about me at the guests and wondered how many of them were as interested in the music as in the player. I was quite certain many of those women, young and not so young, would have enjoyed being singled out by Dominick—to have his interest, his companionship, and to make him laugh. So many women. Me, for instance . . .

Applause broke out as the music ceased and then Dominick began to play again.

"Brahms," Fabian said, and I was childishly annoyed that he should be so sure I wouldn't know.

When Dominick had played two encores, there was an announcement of a buffet supper and we filed into a paneled dining room where a long table was laden with so much food that the choice was bewildering.

Fabian said, "You'd better have some caviar. It's the Beluga kind that Livanova used to have sent over from Russia."

I had tasted caviar before as an experiment in sophistication and liked it. But the roe from this royal sturgeon of Beluga was so much less harsh, so much richer.

"If I were you," Fabian said, "I'd try to eat it in more comfort. Go and find a seat somewhere and I'll join you when I've bullied someone to fetch me a whiskey. I don't drink champagne and I hate parties."

"Then why did you come?"

"For your entertainment," he said curtly and left me.

Dominick was with some people in the drawing room near a fine Adam fireplace, and I crept gratefully to his side. He had his back to me, but before I could slide into one of the few vacant chairs I heard him saying, "Of course she left it to him out of guilt."

A middle-aged woman with dark-red hair protested, "Oh, surely not. She was so wonderful, she couldn't have had anything to be guilty about."

"I thought it was common knowledge, since it all happened down here."

"What was common knowledge?"

"Never mind," he said quickly. "It's over. It was over a long time ago."

Someone in the small group said, "You can't just half tell a story. What was supposed to be common knowledge down here?"

"That Livanova caused the accident that lamed Fabian. And now can we drop the subject, please?"

I backed away from the little green-velvet chair, bumped into someone and apologized.

Dominick heard my voice and turned and gestured with his hand. "Oh, Stephanie, there you are. Here's a chair, you'd better seize it before someone else does."

He gave me a questioning, sideways look and I had a strong suspicion that he had known I was behind him and had intended me to hear what he said. It was very likely that his sensitivity had prevented him from telling me to my face something that was detrimental to Livanova. And yet he must have felt it was important that I should know. A vital link flung at strangers—Livanova had left Jessamy Court to Fabian Seal in expiation, and Fabian had forgiven her, or he could not have chosen to live there. I remembered the verse I had seen underlined in the book of Swinburne's poetry in Livanova's bedroom: "And to give thanks is good, and to forgive."

I ate caviar and wafer-thin toast without really tasting it. Then Dominick took my plate away and brought me chicken and salad.

"I heard what you said just now about Fabian's accident being my mother's fault. I didn't know."

"Nobody did at the time."

"Why did you tell those people?"

"In a way, to save you."

"Save me from what?"

"There's always gossip in small places. I've heard plenty here. They have talked among themselves and decided that, since Fabian is still at Jessamy and seems to be host there, the house is now his. From that piece of deduction they have concluded that you must have been rather a bad daughter otherwise Livanova would have made it clear that, on her death, the house would be yours. So I thought I would give them a clue as to why the house was left to Fabian."

"It doesn't really matter. I shall be away from here in a few days."

"But perhaps it matters to *me* what they say."

I put down my half-tasted plate of chicken on a small, marble-topped table. "How did you know how Fabian's accident happened?"

"Your mother told me. There were times when, if she had been overworking, she would be plunged into deep melancholy. I was the only one here she could talk to. There was Mrs. Manfred, of course, but she was not someone Livanova could confide in. I didn't know that *I* was until one night when I found your mother huddled on the floor in the practice room. She was unhappy and overwrought. It was then that she told me about Fabian's accident."

"How did it happen? How was she involved?"

I sensed his immediate withdrawal. "Don't ask me, ask Fabian," he said in sharp protest.

"I can't."

"And I can't tell you." He looked unhappy and embarrassed. "I'm sorry. I thought I was doing the right thing, letting you know that your mother was involved, so that you shouldn't think she left him Jessamy because she didn't want you to have the house. Now I'm not so sure that I should have said anything."

"It *was* the right thing," I said. "As far as I remember at the time, the whole affair was hushed up. But why? If it was an accident, then no one was really to blame. Unless one of them had been careless."

"Yes, one of them was. But now, let's forget it."

He had taken the plate with my half-eaten chicken and vanished before I could tell him that all I wanted was coffee. I stood by the carved fireplace and remembered how Stephanie had said with glee, "The great love affair has ended. Fabian Seal is in hospital nursing a crushed leg. I wonder if Mother, being Mother, told him it was all over between them and he tried to commit suicide? That would flatter her vanity."

Now that I had met Fabian, I was quite certain that if he tried to kill himself, he would make a success of it. And more important, he would die for no woman. I doubted he was even capable of living for one, solely for one.

Dominick returned with pink and green ices in smoky glass cups. I took one and murmured my thanks. "Did Mother tell you what their quarrel was about? Did she say whether it happened before or after Fabian's accident?"

Dominick put down his glass of ice as if he had decided it was the last thing he wanted to eat, and took a cigarette from an open box on the table. "Let it rest, Stephanie. It's better that you shouldn't know any more."

"Why?"

"Because you mustn't be drawn into this." His voice was distressed. "I don't understand a lot that's happened and *is* happening any more than you do. I've puzzled about it—oh, not from the point of mere curiosity. But Livanova was my employer and she was good to me. *I've* tried to think out what happened before and after that day when Fabian got hurt. And when you were invited down here, I asked myself—Lord in heaven, what am I saying?" He stubbed out his unsmoked cigarette with a violent movement. "As I've said, forget it all. I'm sure the crazy things I'm thinking are just a matter of letting my imagination get the better of me because I'm worried about my future. I don't *know* what happened between them, either before the accident or after it. Your mother didn't tell me that. All I can do is guess, and I've got to stop thinking about it. Everything starts spreading and getting out of hand, and that's dangerous."

While Dominick was speaking, my own thoughts raced. It was possible that the house was not enough compensation. The sins of the mothers, like the sins of the fathers, could be visited upon the children. On the daughter . . . On me, as Stephanie . . .

Dominick was saying, "Do you want to dance?"

The music had begun in the large round hall and a few couples had taken the floor in a dignified foxtrot. It wasn't my kind of dance, but I knew that Dominick had no intention of telling me anything more that night.

"Yes, let's dance," I said. "I think that third glass of champagne was a bit unwise, but you can prop me up if I seem about to fall flat on my face." It was a silly, aimless comment, since I didn't feel in the least unsteady. But I liked the comfort of his arms around me.

We danced twice around the room, and then his voice came softly against my hair. "Livanova should have let me meet you long ago. But then, you were in London and I was living down here. Anyway, I'm no use to any woman at the moment. I promise you one thing, though. When I get a job, the first thing I'm going to do is take you out to dinner. Will you come?"

"Yes," I said, and looking away in a vague and happy dream over his shoulder, saw Fabian watching me.

I felt a sudden resentment against him. It was as if he were deliberately denying me my happy moments dancing in this lovely room. But that was unfair. I was blaming him for my own flight of imagination. Fabian was merely watching me. I glanced at him again; he had turned away. I gave a small, audible sigh of relief.

When I came downstairs the following morning the house seemed very quiet and I walked down to the sea. As I watched some fishing boats far out near the horizon, a plane flew overhead, the first I had heard since I came to Jessamy. The noise of the engine only accentuated the silence of that Dorset coast, and watching it disappear into the distance was like leaping into another world. For only the men at Jessamy Court belonged to the twentieth century. Even Mrs. Manfred and Bridget, for all that they used modern domestic gadgets, could be wisked back easily a hundred years.

I left the sea and returned to the house. Fabian was sorting sketches in the practice room.

"Yesterday I found another chrysanthemum. It was in my car and I threw it out. Today I haven't seen one."

"Well, children get bored with games," he said abstractedly, "and anyway, I'm glad not to see any more drooping yellow flowers in that bowl in the hall. When I next go into Dorchester, I'll get you some really beautiful flowers—Crown Imperials. Do you know them?"

"They have a row of golden bells," I said. "I've seen them in the windows of expensive flower shops. They're rare in England."

"Some are grown at Lys Manor, and Dorset people call them Roundabout Gentlemen. I've seen carpets of them in the hills above Esfahan." His voice trailed off into some remote memory.

I brought him back sharply to the present. "I asked the children, and they said they knew nothing about the chrysanthemums."

"What did you expect them to do? Own up sweetly?"

"Why should they play a stupid game with me, unless someone else is using them? They wouldn't think it up on their own."

"Which means," he said, "that you know very little about children."

"Then I'll ask them again when I see them."

Fabian changed the subject. "I'm afraid I have to work this morning," he said. "Time isn't on our side and the sets and costumes have to be made. I had hoped that Dominick would be here to amuse you, but he disappears after breakfast until lunchtime." He drew a few swift lines with a thick black pencil, and from them came a ballerina, arms stretched and fluid as if she had been caught by the artist at the pinnacle of a leap. "Perhaps, later, you'd like to go down with me to Black Agnes and watch our local life go by." He turned quickly toward the table. As he did so he stumbled slightly and I saw a flash of pain cross his face.

"Is your leg hurting you?"

"Only when I forget that I'm not an athlete," he answered lightly.

"Men who climb mountains must be very sure-footed, so how did the accident happen?"

He picked up a crayon and turned from me, sharpening the point by rubbing it on a piece of paper. "Is it important? It's done, that's all. And the past is gone forever. The present is all that matters."

"I'm sorry. I shouldn't have asked you."

"Oh, don't be sensitive about it. I'm not. I just find looking back rather a bore."

"I don't think like that. I want to remember the times when I was happy."

"We're not talking about ecstasies, we're talking about an accident. It happened."

"I don't think we can forget even the bad things completely—something of the past surely rubs off on us."

"But if the will takes over and tells you that today is more important than yesterday, then you can lock the cupboard door on old history. But now I'm about to go back on my words, because it interests me to hear you talk of the past. So far, you've done little of that, have you, Stephanie?"

Caution made me choose my words. "It isn't particularly interesting."

"You could let me be the judge of that. And you know, I find your relationship with your mother very curious."

"So do I. But that wasn't my fault," I retorted. "Do you want me to tell you of our brief meetings when no one else was near, no one who might look at my mother and then at me and think: Well! well! So the legend is destroyed. Livanova has a grown-up daughter." I clapped my hand over my mouth as a child might do and felt my lips sting with the sharp impact. Again Stephanie speaking, Stephanie feeling. It frightened me that the moments were growing more frequent when I was no longer aware that I was acting a part. Once more I was seized with the outrageous fear that I might look in one of the mirrors and not see myself.

The telephone began to ring somewhere in the house and Fabian left to answer it. I sat down limply in the chair by the table. My arm brushed some drawings and I turned to look at them.

Strong crayon strokes, full of movement. A lighted candle; a dancer, transparent skirt swirling, with a mirror behind her, and no reflection.

No reflection in a mirror—the sign of a witch.

The room swam about me, twisting as if distorted, then settled and seemed to be transformed into my apartment. I saw my large cream sofa, my tangerine cushions. I saw the porcelain eagle—wings extended—that crowned my mantel. And Stephanie sat on the goatskin rug, saying, "I asked Mother for a bigger allowance. Everything is so expensive. I said, 'You spend so much on other people—your secretary, your dresser and all the rest of them. Why can't you give me more? *Why,* Mother?' And she had been angry. 'For God's sake, don't keep calling me Mother. I'm Livanova to you, as to the world. Remember that.' If she could have shut me up in a convent, she would have—my mother with her damned eternal youth."

"My dear Stephanie, you haven't changed in the least during this past few minutes that I've been out of the room."

I came back with a jerk from that sad memory-sequence. "Of course I haven't." Cross with Fabian for having found me so absorbed in a reflection, as if I were anxious about my looks and the effect I was making on him.

"Then why that expression of surprise, as though you don't recognize yourself?"

"I was . . . thinking."

"Or remembering?"

He was too perceptive. "Yes, if you like, remembering." I admitted it because there was quite enough on which we might fight without making difficulties over unimportant observations.

He touched my cheek lightly as he moved past me to the table. "I asked you once before if you had ever been in love. I don't think I let you reply."

"Why do you expect me to now?"

"I expect you to answer, or not, as you wish. For my part, you're Livanova's daughter, so naturally you interest me."

As Livanova's daughter, not as myself. Or even, perhaps, as an impostor . . .

Instead of answering, I replied to his blatant curiosity with a question of my own. "I might ask you why you never married my mother. If you loved her . . ."

He had been half turned from me, looking up at the great lily ceiling as if some idea, perhaps concerning me, but more likely not, were forming in his mind.

Then, at the moment when I had given up hoping for a reply, he swung round. "My dear, I have woven a circle around myself to guard my freedom."

"And did my mother find the fortress so impregnable. Was that why . . . ?"

"Say it. Was that why we broke up—because I didn't want marriage? It's quite a question, but it remains unanswered." He laughed. "You see, I'm not chivalrous. I don't set out to please women by pandering to their curiosity; but on the other hand, I do not blame them for not satisfying mine."

"That's fair enough."

"Oh, I'd never have been a successful jousting knight in the

Middle Ages, with a woman's kerchief tied to my lance. And that reminds me, one of these days I'd like to do a genuine spectacular. Richard First, I think, and the Third Crusade. But that's for the future. It's odd, isn't it, how we talk glibly about the future when no one can ever plan with sureness for it. I can't; *you* can't."

Things that could happen in a flash of time . . .

"Sometimes we act because it is a challenge. But it doesn't always work, does it, Stephanie?"

I sensed a trap somewhere in his words and made no comment. But it was I who broke the silence that followed. "It must be so satisfying doing work you enjoy that it can't really be a challenge."

"It will be satisfactory," he said, staring at the mirror, "if I can get the hackneyed idea of bell-book-and-candle magic out of Gilderoy's head."

"But you believe in magic. You told me so."

"Oh, I do. And I think I also told you that I don't believe in the abracadabra of village superstitions. Real magic is a faculty for good or for ill-wishing. There are marvelous potentials inside some people. A few recognize them and develop the gift, others never know they have it."

"You said something like that when we first talked about magic. You haven't told me, though, whether you have the gift."

"Guess," he said and laughed and walked away from me. "Now I have to work." His manner and his voice changed, became brisk and efficient. "I must rethink the whole of the set for the second act." He looked at his watch. "But if you'd like to come back later, we'll go into the village together."

XIV

MRS. MANFRED WAS POLISHING a heavy carved table near one of the French doors that led to the terrace.

"I know so little about antiques," I said. "I wonder if that is early Georgian?"

She stopped rubbing the glossy surface. "All I know is that it polishes like glass, it does. Not that your mother was ever interested. She used to say, 'I bought all this furniture with the house, but none of it would be my choice. It doesn't matter; only my own rooms are important.' And they are lovely, Miss Clair, aren't they?"

"Yes," I said, "they are," and went to the terrace and stood in the open doorway.

"It's terrible, her rooms up there, all empty. Doors closed, nothing but— Oh, I don't understand."

I swung around. "You don't understand what, Mrs. Manfred?"

"Never mind, never mind." Head purposefully bent, she rubbed harder at the glowing surface of the table, then, thinking better of her refusal to explain, said, "I just don't understand how nobody saw that Madame Livanova must have been exhausted—so she was dizzy and she fell."

I offered a silent congratulation on that piece of fairly quick thinking. I knew by the tone of her voice that she didn't believe a word of what she said any more than I did. They were devious —Mrs. Manfred and Fabian. Perhaps even Dominick, too. But I had a feeling that in his case he was trying to save me from some truth he only suspected. I was as far as ever from any idea of what that truth could be. It was as if the three people who lived here had woven a cocoon around Tatiana Livanova, and inside it was some salient fact that I was not allowed to know. It could be that I had unwittingly revealed myself to one of them without knowing how I had done so.

I crossed the terrace and went down the moss-encrusted steps to the lawn. Overhead cumulous clouds of fair weather swam across the sky. A west wind blew and the air was strong with the scent of dying leaves and grass. No birds sang and there was a curious, echoing silence, as deep as that in a cathedral after the crowds had gone. It was as if I, human and noisy, walked in the forest on enchanted ground, my feet making the only sounds there by stirring the leaves and cracking the fallen twigs.

I wanted to forget Jessamy and Fabian, but I could not. As I walked from the shade of trees into patches of sunlight, I wondered if Livanova had planned to stay at Jessamy with Fabian, if the love that had been so talked about had remained strong, bridging the gap of their long estrangement.

The house was obviously Livanova's grand gesture, her way of saying "Forgive me" in the unlikely event that she did not outlive Fabian.

Stephanie had said, "She believes herself to be immortal." The critics had called her supreme. And they who gathered around her in a kind of "queen's court" had bowed to her and lapped up her lavish gifts—payment for their adulation—as cats lick up cream.

In the end the queen could have decided to return to her former lover. What happened after that was all conjecture. Only Fabian knew.

There was movement far ahead of me through the trees, a

glimpse of a fawn body, the swing of antlers as a stag bent to eat. But wild and shy, I knew it would come no nearer.

I sat for some time on a small hillock of moss, making my plans. I would tell Fabian that I must leave the next day and give work as my excuse. Fabian had still not discussed the details of Livanova's will with me. I could toss a coin to guess the reason. The kindest could be that he did not want to distress me over his inheritance of the house. On the other side of the coin was the uneasy feeling that he was playing a waiting game with me. The more I thought about it, the more possible it was that he had invited Stephanie to Jessamy Court because of something they both knew and which was harmful to one of them. But Fabian was not to be hurried. I had to wait and look and listen, because somewhere in the labyrinth of tragedy and doubt must lie the reason for Stephanie's collapse.

After a while my thoughts destroyed the enchantment of the forest and I got up and stood for a few moments, looking about me, trying to orient myself. My own good sense of direction and the position of the sun guided me on the right way back to Jessamy.

Returning, zigzagging over the boles of the great trees, I came to Hobbin's cottage from behind. She was standing at the door as if waiting for someone, her arms folded, her black hair disarrayed, and yet she was splendid in some strange way, straight-backed, heavy-breasted, like a tattered Brünnhilde.

She must have heard my footsteps crackle on the withering leaves, for she turned and saw me, and then greeted me as if I were the one whom she had been expecting.

"Missy, you come to see me?" She didn't wait for an answer. "I be thinking of you. You come in."

She stood aside and I went into the dark, stuffy little room as if I had planned to call on her.

"Sit down. Sit down." She pulled out a battered old Windsor chair which must have first found its place in the kitchen of some early Victorian house. There was a red cloth on the table and a pack of cards. She touched them. "I tell you things?"

I had no desire to listen, nor would I believe that there was wisdom in a pack of worn playing cards. Yet I held my breath.

She laid her palms flat on the table and leaned toward me. "Maybe I don't have to use the cards. There's times when I know things without help from them. I know one for sure: you shouldn't be here; it bain't be good."

"What are the things you know?"

She shook her head. "It don't do to tell."

"But if they concern me—"

"You should never have come, that's all it's right to tell you. You should never have listened to him."

"You mean . . . Mr. Seal?"

She was silent, watching me with her glimmering eyes.

"He loved my mother," I said, for the first time using the words without actual hesitation. "I wanted to meet him."

Her hands, with their dirty fingernails, traced vague circles on the top of the pack of cards, as if she were preoccupied. She was muttering to herself, and although I had begun to learn, listening to the broad Dorset burr, to translate the language into my city English, I couldn't understand what she was saying.

Suddenly she lifted her head. "What do you want to know, missy?"

"Livanova . . . my mother. How did she die?"

She seemed to reject my question. "It were all in the papers. She fell."

"But why, when she had such perfect balance? Was she alone when it happened? Or was there someone with her? Could there have been a quarrel?"

"I weren't there when she died."

Watching her strong, dark face, I was quite certain that whatever she knew by her own brand of magic, or more reasonably by whispered fact, she would tell me only what she chose for me to know.

I gave up and changed the subject. "For three days I have been sent a single chrysanthemum with my name on a tab. Why?"

Mrs. Manfred or Bridget had obviously told her about the flowers, for she showed no surprise. "There be things happening here, missy, that be strange, even to me."

"What sort of things?"

"Voices," she said with awe. "Last night there were voices that don't come from mortals. Ever since you came—though it bain't be your fault—there be no peace here at Pilgrim Abbas."

"What have I done?"

She shook her head. "I've tried, missy. I've tried to find that

132

out, but it don't come to me. I hear them voices and they tell me things I don't understand . . . not yet. But I will. I will. My granny heard voices, she that told that Prince Albert would die of the typhoid."

I drew her firmly away from reminiscences. "What voices do you hear, Mrs. Hobbin? A man's . . . a woman's?"

"Both." She looked at me, her expression awed at the proof of her increased powers.

"What do they say?"

"Oh, it be a bit jumbled and they be sometimes whispering and I can't hear, and sometimes shoutin' and I can't hear them rightly then, either."

"But you must hear some of the words."

"Aye, some." She gave me a sideways look. "But I don't tell nothing yet."

"You think they have some message through you . . . to me? Is that it?"

She nodded. "Maybe. But I can't tell until I know what. I might be telling all wrong." She drew a deep breath, leaned forward and touched my forehead. "So broad and beautiful. But I told you, missy, you have the mark there. It don't bode good. Go away. Go back. Follow the west wind."

I looked from her to the door as if expecting to see the west wind's face there. "What do you mean by that?"

"*You* think hard, missy. All I says to you means the same thing. You think." There was a finality in her tone.

I made one more effort. "I looked in a book Mr. Seal has, a book on magic. And it said that the flower spell was for revenge."

"I tell you nothing, *nothing*."

"But you have an idea who—"

"*No,*" she interrupted me violently. "I tell you *no*. But I hear voices . . . them voices." She shook herself out of what was obviously half fear, half excitement at her new-found gift. "Take no notice of the flower nor any other spell. I can't tell you no more."

"Just follow the west wind, you said—and I still don't know what you mean."

She had finished with me; I knew I could learn nothing more. I opened my purse, but she reached across the table and tried to close it. "I don't take money from you, missy. Not from you."

"Then please, for Robin and Lucy. Buy them something."

I put some money on the table and escaped before she could give it back to me.

After the stuffiness of the tiny cottage the air outside was sweet and the fern fronds were golden in the midday light.

"Follow the west wind," Hobbin had said. I looked up through the trees at the angle of the sun. The wind that blew west from the Atlantic would cross Dorset, cross Wiltshire and the Home Counties, going eastward . . . to London. She was right. She had said "Go back." And she had said "Follow the west wind." Two sentences that held the same meaning. Get away from Jessamy; let the west wind blow you toward home, toward safety. But there was no proof that I would be safe even in London. Either I, or Stephanie.

Fabian was still in the practice room when I reached the house. As I passed the doorway I saw him standing at the reading table, a mound of torn-up paper at his feet.

He must have heard me, for he called out, and as I went into the room he asked me where I had been.

"In the forest. And I saw the deer again. They're so alert and nervous."

"Of course they are. Men have hunted the red deer there for a thousand years. The foresters still periodically keep their numbers down, so they have never lost their wariness of humans." He reached over on the table and picked up a small black-leather box.

"I've found something that you'll recognize." He snapped open the lid; there on a bed of white velvet lay a tiny, exquisite model of a yacht in painted enamel and gold. An emerald and a ruby were its port and starboard lights.

"This will take you back some years."

It could well be a trap that I didn't dare fall into, and so it had to be a moment for honesty. "I don't remember."

"Oh, come. It was made by La Vallaine, the Parisian jeweler." He waited.

"It's . . . very beautiful," I said to cover the pause.

"And you still don't remember?"

"No."

He took the model from its velvet bed and held it in the palm of his hand. "Perhaps when something has happened to arouse a deep and distressing emotion, there comes a kind of panacea of forgetfulness. All right, we'll say you have a blank spot in your mind. La Vallaine owned the yacht, *Purple Emperor,* and your mother sometimes went on cruises with him. They always sailed to the lonely places: Sardinia, Corsica or the eastern shores of Turkey. Livanova was gloriously contradictory, enjoying the unspoiled islands while living on La Vallaine's yacht in luxury, with her marble bath and her fine crimson bed. She loved wildness because it touched a streak in her; but she never traveled rough. *Now* do you remember how the little model came into your life?"

"No, not even now."

"Your nurse once took you down to Villefranche," he said with the touch of impatience I always noted in him when he had to explain something, "to see your mother leave on one of her cruises on the yacht. You tried to run after her and fell and hit your head and had a concussion."

"Perhaps that's why I . . . don't want to remember."

"Perhaps. You were only five at the time. She never again let you come to see her off when she went away. In fact, you never lived with Livanova again, did you? She sent you to your grandmother, because she decided that country air would be good for you."

Silence implied the lie. I was silent.

"Take it." He thrust the small, lovely toy into my hands. "It's yours by right. In fact, you'd better look through the things here and tell me what you want. I've written to the solicitor that I understand only the house is mine."

I felt cold inside, as if I had drunk too much iced water. "And you've heard from him?" (Had he said, "Miss Clair is in hospital, Mr. Seal, didn't you know?")

But Fabian answered lightly, "Oh, he's away on some court case for a week. I had a letter from his chief clerk. But I suppose you saw the solicitor at the inquest."

I let a small silence pass between us and hoped that Fabian would take it as assent. Then I said, "I have to contact Mr. Crewe as soon as I get back to London."

Fabian nodded and I breathed freely again. But I faced a serious problem. If I were not out of Jessamy within the week, a letter would probably arrive from the solicitor and reference would be made to the fact that Stephanie was in the hospital. I shuddered to think what the result of that would be. It was therefore desperately necessary for me to find out quickly the real reason why Fabian had invited Stephanie to Jessamy.

I said, "We haven't really discussed things, have we, Fabian?"

"What things?"

"Why, something you wrote that was important."

"I've already told you. I wanted to meet you and talk." His eyes, shining and narrowed, met mine.

I don't believe you, Fabian Seal . . . I don't believe you.

"Now," he said and tapped the small leather box I still held, "go and put that away upstairs and we'll walk along the beach to the village for a drink."

"I saw Hobbin just now."

"And did she offer to tell your fortune?"

"In a way, yes."

"Cards or candles or numbers? I believe she is even prepared to give love potions, only the young of this village are too wise to take them. But she never gives up hope. She is always wandering round the grounds here looking for wild angelica and alder and yew. What did she tell you?"

"To follow the west wind."

"What did she mean by that?"

"She told me to work it out for myself."

"Oh, so now she's becoming obscure. And have you? Worked it out, I mean?"

"Yes."

He watched me. "Well, and what *did* she mean?"

"I think it was a way of saying go back to London."

He seemed to accept the explanation. "Sometimes she has patches of poetry. She once said to Livanova, 'I would draw a circle round you, madame, to make you safe forever.' I don't believe she realized how colorful her words were."

"Or how my mother was one day to need that circle. Only it wasn't there, was it? And she wasn't safe."

Fabian picked up the sketch on the lectern and tore it in two. "Go and put that gee-gaw away and I'll meet you in the hall."

I wondered how much of the long-ago incident Stephanie would remember when I gave the jeweled boat to her.

XV

THE TIDE WAS OUT when we walked together on the wet, firm edge of the beach on our way to the village and Black Agnes. I relived the far-off childhood pleasure of stepping from rock to rock, dodging the tiny pools the sea had left and avoiding slithering on the wet boulders. The smell of seaweed was heady; the tips of the waves curled like ostrich feathers. The sun broke through clouds and shone on a small motorboat. In its wake was a glitter of light, as if the fragments of a comet had been caught and sea-bound.

In spite of his lameness Fabian was more sure-footed than I, and I envied the easy precision of every movement and childishly willed him to slip.

He didn't. It was I who stumbled more than once, scaring the tiny crabs and the pink sea urchins sheltering in the pools.

"You should have learned ballet," he said at my third uneasy leap from one low rock to the next.

"I'd never make a dancer."

"Oh, I'm sure of that. You lack the ability to bear pain."

"Is this another case of taking my mother's opinion of me, or are you forming your own?"

"Both. And they don't fit. I wonder why?"

My heart gave sharp, nervous thrusts. We were facing one another and the sun was in Fabian's eyes. I noticed that he didn't blink, but then, pure clear light could not dazzle a man used to the high places in unpolluted air.

"She never told me that you have a very attractive nose and beautiful hair," he said.

"She probably told you that I liked compliments," I parried, offering lightness for lightness.

"No, but all women do." He reached out and drew a light finger across my hairline.

A flame suddenly ran through me. My fear of him and my fear for my own safety were swept away by a wave that was like a fever of the spirit. Afraid that my expression—my eyes, my whole attitude—might betray me, I bent down quickly and stuck my fingers in a rock pool. The cold water was a balm.

I felt that I knew in that moment why this man had been Tatiana Livanova's lover. He possessed a great sensual attraction. It seemed to come as lightning does, blazing through a storm. In good men, this could be rather like the gift for healing. I had no idea how to describe it in Fabian Seal.

I walked on, scuffing up the hard sand with the toe of my sandal and feeling it seep uncomfortably cold and damp through to my feet. I kicked at a rock and half of it gave way and toppled into a shallow pool.

Fabian was a few paces ahead of me. He turned. "You know," he said, waiting for me to catch up with him, "you walk like a little girl engaged in sulks. Are you sulking? And if so, why? Didn't you like the generalization about all women enjoying compliments? Do you want to be exceptional?"

"That would be very childish, and I'm adult."

"Oh, they sulk too."

"If I look like that, I'm sorry, but it's not the way I feel. I'm enjoying walking by the sea."

He was needling me again. It was as if he wanted to see me in my worst light, like a scientist studying things under adverse conditions. I was resentful of my mother, I was too idle to keep jobs, and now I lacked the capacity to bear pain. He was repeat-

ing a ready-made assessment of the character of Stephanie Clair—
and in that, he was not far wrong. He was merely attaching it
to the wrong person.

"You'll get chilled feet if you keep kicking up that wet sand."

"I like the feel of it. It's astringent, like winter."

We met no one on our beach walk. We could have been the
first or the last people on earth; neither man nor animal nor ship
came into sight, until after another ten minutes Fabian said, "Here
we are," and pointed inland.

The stone cottages of Pilgrim Abbas were visible on the other
side of a wide spread of low salt-burned bushes bent eastward by
the prevailing winds. The square tower of the Saxon church rose
into the gathering oyster-colored clouds.

I stopped as we left the beach for the rough track inland, took
off my sandals and brushed the sand clinging to my damp feet.
Then we made our way up the small main street of cottages of
golden stone and gardens filled with September flowers.

"Black Agnes is sixteenth-century," Fabian said, "and beautiful,
if you like low beams that crack your skull every time you forget
to duck and where you need lights in the corners of the room even
if the sun is dazzling outside. I have no taste for old-world discomfort, genuine or not. But come and see for yourself. At least, Black
Agnes *is* genuine. We'll go in the back way and then you can see
the garden and the lake."

The plot of land outside the inn was bright with creamy Ophelia
roses and green with willows trailing tendrils across the smooth
surface of the lake. A great bird hovered hungrily over the water.

"A heron," Fabian said. "Did you know that it's the bird of
chivalry?"

I watched three swans gliding away from us, dipping orange bills
into the water. "You are full of knowledge," I said, laughing.

"Irrelevant bits and pieces." He turned toward the inn.

There were small tables scattered over a lawn and a few people
sat at them. "I think we'll go inside. It's not particularly warm,
and anyway, you won't be able to see the locals out here. Only
strangers come and watch the swans. The villagers have seen them
all too often and tend to congregate in the fustiest place they can
find, where there's tobacco smoke and the clink of glasses and
scarcely any elbow room."

The locals had already gathered and Fabian was being greeted
on all sides with that mixture of curiosity and caution which villagers show to strangers who come for brief stays.

There was the sound of music from a room beyond the bar, and as we sat down on a dark-red velvet banquette, I said, "Someone's playing Chopin."

"On a not very good piano."

"But playing well."

Fabian laughed. "Why sound so surprised? Do you imagine that cities have the monopoly on talent? Yes"—he was listening—"someone is playing quite well."

The landlord, with a face like a red apple and sparse ginger hair, took our order of sherry for me and a dry martini for Fabian. "I didn't know anyone in your family played," he said as the man started back to the bar.

"They don't."

"Then who?"

The landlord's small bright eyes shot a nervous look at the door. "Oh, just . . . just a guest, Mr. Seal."

"Dominick Hunt?" Fabian asked pleasantly.

"Er, yes."

"Ah . . ." It was a long-drawn sound, as if something long suspected had at last been proved.

For a moment or two the music mingled with the din of voices around us. Then there was a crash, as if the pianist had brought both hands hard and flat down on the keys. Then silence.

I looked at Fabian. He was sitting back in his chair as unconcerned as if his thoughts were a long way away. The drinks came and he lifted his glass to me. "To your future." His eyes met mine with irony.

The door at the far end opened and Dominick came out. He walked toward the bar, paused and glanced about him and saw us. Immediately an expression of utter surprise and affront crossed his face.

Fabian was watching him, and said to me, "I seldom come here. My taste for conviviality doesn't usually stretch to bars, so we surprise Dominick." He beckoned him and raised his voice. "Come and join us."

For a moment I thought Dominick was going to refuse. But he came to our table and sat down, crossing his long legs and frowning at the room.

"The piano isn't as finely tuned as the one at Jessamy, is it?" Fabian asked conversationally.

"No."

"And yet you were practicing on it." The scorn and pity for

an ancient and nondescript bar piano were only too evident in Fabian's voice.

Dominick's eyes flashed. "I couldn't very well work at Jessamy, could I? You were in the practice room."

"I don't need the piano; you know that. Why didn't you say something? It can be moved into another room. Heaven knows there are enough of them in the house."

Dominick looked over his shoulder as if searching for the quickest way to escape. "It won't help now. Nothing will; nothing can. The spark has gone."

"Dear, sweet heaven," Fabian exploded softly. He looked as if he were about to say something even more violent, then with a visible effort, controlled himself.

"Perhaps," Dominick said, ignoring Fabian's outburst, "perhaps I never really had the spark that lifts the musician or the artist out of the ordinary."

"There is a saying"—Fabian tapped the table with an impatient forefinger—"I have no idea who said it or where it was said. But it goes: 'Hope till hope creates, from its own wreck, the thing it contemplates.' "

Dominick appeared to think it over, his eyes resting steadily on Fabian's face. "You've got it wrong, you know. You've always had it wrong about me. You think I'm full of self-pity, but I'm not. I have a desire to succeed and I believe I will." He jerked his head toward the room behind the bar. "It's that piano that depresses me."

"Then use the Bechstein at Jessamy."

"I need to work in peace."

"And there's no peace there?"

"Livanova's dead," Dominick said and left that as his answer.

Fabian allowed a brief silence, and then asked what Dominick would drink.

"Nothing, thanks. I'll walk back to the house. I've some letters to write." He gave me a puzzled look as he rose to go. It was as if he were asking himself how I could sit so seemingly contented by Fabian's side, and I felt as if I had been guilty and needed to be reproached.

A tall, military-looking man stopped at our table and greeted Fabian. I heard his name only vaguely, and as he began talking to Fabian about his recent return from Chile, I glanced out the window.

Dominick passed by. I leaned forward and watched him cross

the road and disappear down the avenue of elms that linked the village with the twisting lanes.

It was odd that I, who spent most of my day among men, worked with them, accepted them and seldom found my pulse quickening at the sight of one, should be so affected by the two men at Jessamy Court—the one whom I distrusted; the other for whom I felt a vague compassion. But not pity. I couldn't pity someone who had such masculine beauty, because on a superficial level, life would be good to him. Yet beneath it, I knew that Dominick was unhappy and uncertain of himself, and from that sprang my compassion, which I knew was a dangerous emotion. I was one of those people who could be trapped by it.

But aware of it, I still wanted to help Dominick. I also wanted to escape from Jessamy Court. I had no idea how to go about the first, nor why I should find the second difficult. I was free to leave.

". . . nice meeting you, Miss Clair."

The voice brought me back with a jerk to the small, low-ceilinged room with the rows of bright bottles and the polished horse brasses hanging on the wall. The military man was about to leave.

Fabian said, watching him join two people at another table, "He has climbed in the Andes, and he's now a farmer in Charminster."

I saw a man pass the window leading a great shire horse, its white mane blowing gently in the wind that had sprung up.

"Has Dominick any family?"

"Dominick?" Fabian asked in surprise, as if for the moment he had quite forgotten who he was. "Oh yes. A sister somewhere in Hampshire and a mother living with a brother in New Zealand."

"I think he must have been unhappy when he was very young."

"Why in the world should you think that?"

"He never laughs."

"Has there yet been anything sufficiently amusing to laugh at?"

"There's usually the odd thing in a conversation. I mean—"

"Yes," he said steadily, "I'd like you to tell me what you mean."

"You've known him longer than I have, is he always so grave?"

"I haven't thought about it. Now try that sherry and stop wondering why Dominick doesn't leap about like a faun in some theatrical woodland."

Fabian was perfectly well aware of my meaning but he had no

intention of being drawn into a discussion about Dominick Hunt.

The sherry was good: light and dry. I tried to relax and enjoy it, telling myself that in a day or two at the most I would be back in London. And I would take with me to the hospital, and the doctor there, the little I had found out.

I would say, "Fabian Seal, who was Livanova's lover for some years, has inherited her country house." I would say, "Livanova was the cause of the accident which meant that Fabian Seal has never climbed again." I might even add, "Someone down there has a kind of vendetta against her—or it could be against Stephanie, or it could have been against me."

The doctor would infiltrate those pieces of information into Stephanie's blank mind and perhaps stir up a reaction that could become the starting point for her recovery.

Fabian reached for my glass. I put my hand over it. "No more, thank you."

"Oh, yes you will," he said lightly.

I felt a sudden, unreasonable anger. "If I say I don't want another drink, Fabian, then I don't. Thank you. But I'm not stopping you from having a second."

"No," he said and stood up and looked down at me. "You aren't, my dear. But I'd like to know just how mellow you could get, and in that state, what you would do and say. It would be interesting. On second thought, I doubt if it would be very good for your liver to get mellow on sherry. We'll try with something different later, shall we?"

I had been forewarned, and anyway, I had no intention of being lured later into more drinks at Jessamy that might mellow me, even if Fabian meant what he said.

"I have to go to Lorne Abbey sometime," he said conversationally, returning with his glass to our table. "Have you ever seen it?"

"No. It's not as famous as Glastonbury."

"It's not so large. But I want to make some sketches there for the second act of the witch ballet. There's a small excavation going on just behind the abbey grounds. They hope to find some medieval tombs—the romantics still harp on the actual existence of King Arthur and his Knights."

"King Arthur was buried at sea," I said, "and three queens came and took his body away."

"My! You do know your mythology." He was mocking me

again. Then he said matter-of-factly, "At best, Arthur was the last emperor of Britain; at worst, just a brave general. But keep your romantic dreams, by all means."

"Thank you, I will."

Again I felt the electrifying sensation of something pulling and tightening between us. A sensation, an undeclared war, a resentment on my part of his curious magnetism.

Fabian looked away first. "Come along, or Mrs. Manfred will be angry at us because the lettuce in the salad is getting limp or the tongue is turning up at the corners. Neither will happen, of course, but she uses such warnings of spoiled food if I'm late."

We walked back along the beach. "Did my mother like the sea?"

"You don't even know that?"

"No, not even that."

"Well, she did. She liked it when it was rough and when the wind blew. Strange for someone living a rather hothouse life. Oh yes, the sea excited her." His voice held a note of nostalgia, which blended in with the hiss of the waves at our feet.

"You loved her very much?" For the first time when speaking to Fabian, I spoke gently, as if I were deeply aware of a mutual loss.

He didn't answer me, but I saw in his eyes the distant memory-look that people had when they were recalling the past. I wondered how much Livanova had taught her young lover about making love and about giving it. It would seem that she was the perfect example of an older woman turning to a younger man, his love the fixative for her beauty, her established fame, her amassed prestige. It was like the scent given to a fully opened rose, the final splendid flowering before the downhill slide.

The tang of seaweed was in the air, and we walked as near as we could get to the lazy midday waves rustling like taffeta at our feet. I dipped my hand into a pool again. A starfish stirred and tiny marine creatures, their bodies translucent, scattered at my giant fingers. I lost my balance and swung wildly left and right. Fabian put out a hand and steadied me. "Why can't you leave that starfish to enjoy its sleep?"

"It was unfair, wasn't it?" I said. "You should have let me tip forward into that pool just to teach me a lesson. It's like the temptation to stroke a sleeping cat. But then, things disturb us too. I don't like thunderstorms waking me in the night."

He ran a strand of my hair through his fingers. "It's the color of heather honey."

Dyed, my dear Fabian . . . Dyed in order to help my act. Do you know that? Or don't you?

He moved toward me, hands on my shoulders, and laid his forehead against my hair. "What do you wash it in? Lily of the valley?"

I couldn't answer him. Again excitement swept over me. All my instincts and my common sense resisted the magic of that close moment. I pulled away from him with the most banal remark I could make. "Don't forget what you told me. Mrs. Manfred will be furious if we're late."

He started to walk on. "You're right, she will. And she's much too valuable to risk losing."

We crossed the beach toward Gideon's Rock. The sparse bushes at the top of the cliff face nodded and plunged in the increasing wind like people gesticulating in a fierce argument. The bushes were gray-green, and I was just about to ask Fabian what they were when I saw that high on the brow of the rock, someone was watching us.

She could only have climbed there from the gentle land side. She stood, her dark hair streaming back in the wind and her blue suit molded to her like a figurehead on old ships. She was too far away for me to see her features but I sensed her absorption in us.

"Who is that girl?"

He looked up. "How should I know?"

I looked along the base of the cliff. "I can't see a car, so she must be from the village."

"Or probably one of the students working on the archeological site at Lorne Abbey. I expect there's a car on the far side of the cliff. Hey, mind that bank. There's a deep drop on the other side and I'd hate to have to carry you unconscious all the way to Jessamy."

We had reached the green wasteland and the girl was lost to our view.

I hadn't noticed the increasingly darkening sky until the rain began to fall. The wind tossed it in capricious spraying gusts, so that one moment I scarcely felt it, and the next, it drenched my face.

"You can run on if you like," Fabian said. "I happen to like rain."

"So do I."

XVI

THE CHRYSANTHEMUM SPELL had faded out, perhaps because I had laughed at it or perhaps because it was clear the message had reached me that through a piece of witchcraft, someone wished me ill.

I had two things to do that morning. One was to telephone the hospital in London. The other was to see Hobbin again.

I left my car at the edge of the forest and walked to the cottage. The great acres of trees were brushed over with translucent light, and the faint wind that stirred the tops of the beeches could not penetrate the quiet path where I walked.

This time no one stood outside the cottage as if expecting me. I paused and called Hobbin's name and thought I saw a shadow move inside.

I stepped over the threshold and looked in. The shadow was

the odd flicker of firelight playing across the empty room. There was a door on the far side which probably led to a bedroom. I called again.

The smell of the stuffy little room was overlaid with the tangy, aromatic scent of burning wood and the only sound was the occasional hiss of flame from the logs. I felt that the fire had been lit for some time and was burning out.

On the small round table pushed against the wall was a very rough picture of a girl with fair hair. It was so badly painted that it was like no one in particular. But the hair fell, as Stephanie's did—as mine did from the moment I decided to impersonate her —smoothly from a side parting.

Lying on the ugly red cloth immediately below the picture was a playing card. The five of spades was set on a piece of dirty white paper on which were drawn twelve circles. I stood, fascinated, counting them.

It could have nothing to do with Stephanie or with me. The world was full of fair-haired girls, and most certainly the artist was incapable of even a remote likeness. The girl could be anyone, the spell cast around her by the card and the circles as likely to be good as evil.

All the same, I fled the cottage, retracing my steps to the car, suddenly unnerved by the loneliness of the forest. I kept repeating a reassurance that this was the late twentieth century and the age of science. I even sang to myself as I drove past the place where the bog lay beyond the hawthorn hedge. But when a squirrel ran across my path, the wheel jerked under my hands; and when I laughed at my own jumpiness, the sound wasn't quite true. For the first time in my life I could understand that people could be brainwashed into believing the unbelievable. I had no intention of that happening to me.

But myself as Rachel Fleming and my life in London was more than a world away.

I drove into Dulverley and called the hospital from one of the telephone booths at the post office. The same sister-in-charge answered me. Stephanie had recovered consciousness two evenings ago and against all advice and persuasion, had discharged herself. The doctor had tried to reason with her, arguing that she was in too weak and agitated a state to be on her own.

But Stephanie had signed herself out and there was nothing anyone could do to stop her. She had protested that she remembered nothing of what had caused her collapse, but the doctor was not entirely convinced. She had been, however, reasonably in control of herself and had said she was going home.

I thanked the sister and immediately put a call through to Stephanie's Chelsea apartment. There was no reply. Finally I put through a desperate call to the only friend of hers whom I felt she might contact, a considerably older woman called Louise Alderney.

"Yes," she told me. "Stephanie called me on the telephone and told me she was going away for a while. She said a strange thing: 'I don't suppose anyone will try and find me. I hope they don't.' I asked her what she meant, but she just said that she wanted to hide away for a week or two, and she refused to explain. I'm sorry, Rachel, I can't tell you anything else."

I thanked her and went out and sat in my car, aware of both the panic and the urgency of the unexpected situation.

Stephanie had recovered. Very likely she had looked for Fabian's letter, and of course, had not found it. I doubted if she had mentioned its loss to the nurse; she would have known that had they found it, it would have been among the possessions returned to her. It was far more likely that hearing I had fetched her things, she guessed that I had seen the letter and put it somewhere. Perhaps, after searching her desk and not finding it there, she had telephoned me. But there would have been no answer, because for the time being I was without my daily help; and if she had called my office, no one there would have known where I was.

Stephanie had told Louise that she wanted to hide away for a while. That didn't sound as if she were coming to Jessamy, because once there, all the villagers would know of a stranger among them. The alternative could be that she had spoken the truth to Louise and that she was hiding from Fabian Seal. Although she no longer had his letter, which was still in my purse, she must have remembered its contents and been afraid of a confrontation. Why that was so, I had yet to find out.

I started the car and drove back to Pilgrim Abbas, and all the way I tried to think where Stephanie could have gone.

When I reached the village general store, I went in and bought some bars of chocolate. It would be useful to have them in my purse in case I came upon the children and could perhaps offer a bribe for some information. Those sly, strange children of the forest were the eyes and ears of Pilgrim Abbas.

The bright-cheeked woman who owned the tiny store asked, "Be that your car outside, Miss Clair?"

"Yes."

"But it be white."

"That's right."

"Now bain't that odd? When you came through here yesterday, I saw you right up the road get out of a black car, and it weren't Mr. Seal's. You stopped and talked to Don Radipole, our baker."

"I don't even know him. I came to the village yesterday with Mr. Seal—we walked over—and had a drink and walked back along the beach. We didn't use a car."

"Don Radipole described you, fair and thin like you are. He said you asked him the way to Dulverley."

"But I didn't."

"That's funny. Then I wonder who it was?"

"I wonder," I said. "Did she say she would be staying in Dulverley?"

"I gather from what Don tell me, yes, she be." Her bright eyes in her pink face looked at me with interest. Anything new, anyone strange was absorbing in this little lonely, lovely village.

So there was a girl like me around.

"I suppose there are plenty of hotels in Dulverley where she might stay?"

"Oh no. There be just three. The inn near the Minster and two just along the main street. You know"—she looked me over and I sensed her slow mind working—"you know, I begin to think that lady we saw were dark and it were that she wore one of them scarfs over her head—pale yellow it were. That's why I must have thought she were fair. But she were slim, like you."

I said, "I saw a dark girl yesterday on Gideon's Rock."

"Did you now? Well, maybe she be the one."

"Yes, maybe."

It took me another five minutes to get free of her and her laden questions about myself, about the great Livanova and my wonderful life in London. At least, by telling her a wealth of fabrications I did her no harm.

It would take me another seven minutes to get back to Dulverley, and I had plenty of time before lunch.

The hotels were easy to find. The girl was not staying at the inn near the Minster, but someone young and dark, who drove a black car, had arrived two nights earlier at the White Hart and had booked a room for an unspecified time. The proprietor refused to tell me her name. If I would care to write a message for her, he would see that she received it. I thanked him and said it was possible I would call again in the hope that I would find her in.

If the girl who had booked in at the White Hart was the one who had watched Fabian and me from the rock, I wanted to know who she was.

People were notoriously inaccurate when they gave descriptions of others—the police knew that. The fair girl had turned into a dark one in the space of a few moments. Equally, the dark one could have been fair, and not the girl on the cliff top at all. A fair girl with a yellow head scarf. In fact, it could have been Stephanie.

Yet I doubted if she had come to Dorset. If she had, her objective would have been Jessamy Court. There would be no way in which she could know yet that I was impersonating her and nothing to stop her coming straight to the house. Besides, she didn't possess a car, nor did she drive.

The way back to Pilgrim Abbas lay past the Heath. I stopped once and listened and heard the purling cry of the curlew, and the wind in the purple moor grass. I had restarted the car and was driving on when I saw Fabian's Bentley parked ahead of me.

The door on the driver's side was wide open and Fabian was bundling a small protesting boy through it. I saw waving arms and legs and a mane of untidy black hair before the boy disappeared into the car. Fabian himself could have been a mirage, for one moment he was there and then, as if with a single movement, he was behind the wheel and driving like the wind down the road.

It was typical of the dreamy village that no one was around to witness that swift, violent scene; it was also fortunate for Hobbin's grandson that I was there.

I didn't stop to think about it. I trod on the accelerator and shot forward, and saw the Bentley swing right and take an unfamiliar road that led away from the Heath and from Jessamy.

My small car sang, loving speed, but it was facing a difficult battle, which I had no intention of giving up. I had good eyesight and I guessed that in that part of Dorset there were few branch lanes where I might lose Fabian. I just had to keep straight on between the undisturbed hedgerows that opened out occasionally to grazing fields and the scattered huddle of thatched cottages with their flowered gardens.

I had no idea where we would end up. All I knew was that a small, frightened boy sat by Fabian's side, and that had I stopped to explain the situation to someone in Pilgrim Abbas, we would probably be too late to give chase. Besides, with Fabian's prestige, I doubted if anyone would believe my story that he had rough-handled a little boy. And even if he had, they would probably decide that Robin deserved it, and since he was the grandson of a witch, the less they interfered, the better.

After several minutes of driving, the car began to protest at being thrashed to its limit. It rounded the often dangerous bends in the lanes with a protesting scream of tires. I assumed that Fabian was too busy keeping Robin quiet to look in his rear mirror and recognize me. I was becoming almost afraid to blink in case in that flash of a moment I lost them down an unexpected side turning.

Once I passed a farm and an old man paused and watched us with amazement as we streaked by. This bird-haunted corner of Dorset was obviously not used to the noise of car engines, and I doubted if one an hour passed that way.

I kept telling myself to stop my frantic anxiety over Robin. He was a strange, sly little boy whom I had met only twice and hadn't much liked, anyway. But he *was* a little boy and vulnerable and capable of being afraid.

I had no idea what would happen when the Bentley eventually stopped and I caught up with them, if I ever did, for the distance between us was widening. I didn't dare take my eyes off the road to enjoy the view through the great oaks of the lovely valley and the blue hills beyond. My thoughts, as I drove, were between anger at Fabian's handling of a child and another, more personal anger at my susceptibility to the almost hypnotic attraction he had for me. I had been in love with men and I knew the emotion too well to believe that I felt that way about Fabian Seal. Whatever it was that drew me to him, it had none of the tenderness I connected with love. I could hate Fabian Seal so easily, and I felt that before I left Jessamy Court that was exactly what I was going to do.

For the few moments that my thoughts had taken over, I had unconsciously relaxed my speed. When I pulled myself together I was at forked lanes and the car was out of sight.

The signpost at the corner was very white, very clear and quite unhelpful. I had no idea whether the Bentley was making for

Maiden Newton or Bridport. Had there been snow on the ground, I could have seen the tire marks, but all I could do was take one lane and hope for luck. I chose the Bridport road, accepting the fact that the sane thing to have done would have been to admit defeat, turn the car around and return to Jessamy. Anyone else would have seized the opportunity of Fabian's absence from Jessamy to pack and escape back to London. But I was held by a hope that by staying I might learn more, and also by Fabian himself, as if he were partly in control of my will. On the face of it, there seemed nothing to link a little boy's enforced journey in a car with Stephanie's unconscious obsession with Jessamy Court. But instinct ruled me rather than cold calculation, and instinct sent me careening in a direction which would very probably prove to be the wrong way.

And then I saw the car. It had slowed down at the point where the road met a wider one. As it did so, the door on the passenger side opened and Robin leaped out. He seemed to somersault twice before he landed and lay quite still in a grassy ditch, his arms over his face.

The Bentley slid forward again, and in a lull in the oncoming traffic on the main road, it swung right and disappeared. I pulled into the side of the lane and stopped and got out.

Robin stirred as I reached him, and seeing me, began to cry noisily.

"Are you hurt?"

He shook his head. His knees were muddied, for there was a thin trickle of dark water in the ditch and his face was streaked with the pale-green marks of wet grass.

"Let's get into the car," I said, "and I'll wipe you down and you can tell me all about it."

I heaved him up and he scuffed by my side. I sat him in the passenger seat with a handful of tissues and told him to wipe his eyes, blow his nose and then tell me where Fabian had been taking him.

The mopping-up process needed some urging from me and I wiped his knees clean to make certain that there were no cuts. The sides of the ditch had been softened by thick grass and it was as if he had fallen on a wet cushion.

"Now," I said when he was fairly clean again, "why were you in Mr. Seal's car?"

He shook his head.

"Oh, come. I saw him force you to go with him. He must have given you a reason."

"I don't know." His eyes began to stream again. "We be scared of him, Lucy and me."

"Why?"

"He be bad."

"In what way?"

"He do witch things, them that my granny wouldn't do."

"But, Robin, that's quite wrong. Mr. Seal is working on a ballet with a witch story in it. You know that, don't you? And you know what a ballet is."

"Course I do. It's them people that dance. *She* danced."

Livanova, of course. I said, "Mr. Seal isn't a magician; he can't make magic."

He gave me a sideways look, and I noticed again how curiously angled his eyes were, like the drawings of Pan in mythology books.

"Robin, will you please tell me where Mr. Seal was taking you?"

He repeated, "I don't know."

"Well then, we'll have to use some other way of finding out. Perhaps Lucy . . ."

"You don't ask Lucy nothing," he flared up. "She knows what I know, but she won't tell, neither."

I restarted the engine, put the car in gear and drove forward toward the main road. I managed to turn and go back down the lane.

"We're going home," I said, "and you'd better direct me, because I'm sure you know these lanes quite well."

"Lucy and me don't walk in lanes, we walk in the forest."

"Ah well, let's just see how often we get lost, and while we're wasting time finding the right roads, you can think again about telling me why you were in Mr. Seal's car. I'll find out, you know."

He was crouched away from me, staring ahead of him, his mouth a long tight line, his whole manner taut and sulky and on guard. I wondered whether I, also, scared him because I was staying at Jessamy Court.

We took only one wrong turning, and all the time his frozen silence and his eyes periodically turning to watch me were unnerving. As we came to the village I decided that perhaps he could be won around to talking to me by the simple process of bribery. The two chocolate bars I had bought earlier might not be sufficient, so I stopped again at the store and bought him the largest package of candy I could find.

While I was paying the shopkeeper with a handful of loose change, I saw his glance wander to a mechanical tiger with bright orange stripes and red eyes. The shopkeeper wound it up and it clattered across the counter, stalking some hidden prey. I said I would take it, then gave it to Robin, who accepted it without thanks and clasped it to him. As I got out my wallet again to pay, he began to slink away.

"Oh no, you don't!" I managed to drop the right amount of money onto the counter, murmured a vague "Good morning" and marched Robin back to the car.

All the way to Hobbin's cottage he ate coffee fudge without stopping, but I was brought no deeper into his confidence. He didn't know where Mr. Seal had been driving him; "I don't know nothing." He popped another huge chunk of candy into his mouth, and I hoped he wasn't going to be sick.

Between munches he repeated that he knew nothing, but I was certain that he knew perfectly well and he wasn't telling because he was afraid of Fabian. I was afraid of him, too, so how much more terrifying must that powerful personality seem to a child?

We plunged into the long green archway of trees.

"I must tell your grandmother what happened."

He sprang forward in his seat. "No. Please, no. Don't 'ee tell her." He clutched my arm.

I shook him off. "If you do that, you'll have us both in the ditch. Why don't you want her to know?"

"She'd be angry . . . me goin' off like that."

"You couldn't help yourself. I saw what happened, and I'll tell her that you were forced into Mr. Seal's car."

"She wouldn't understand. She and him . . ."

"She and him what?"

"Nothing," he said. "I don't know nothing."

And so, with the car full of the atmosphere of lies and evasions and the chewing of candy, we arrived at the path that led to Hobbin's cottage two hundred yards into the forest.

I stopped and opened the door and let the clean salt air seep in. Ellen's Heath lay to our right and a sea mist, luminous as spun silk, hung over the violet patches of heather. Fern fronds stood up like stiffened lace. The hills were shadowy in the distance and the peace was unbroken even by a bird's song. Yet, breath-takingly beautiful though it was, I had a terrible awareness that beneath the surface lay that which Shakespeare had called "evils imminent."

I pulled the car onto the grass; Hobbin's cottage could be seen through the distant trees, gray stone against the green.

"Out you get," I said to Robin, "and go home. Here, take your tiger."

"You won't tell Granny?"

"No."

"Oh, miss"—the dirty little hand grabbed my arm—"you be so kind. You be really kind."

"I hope so."

I was watching for signs of Hobbin, who must, in that deep silence, have heard us approach. But no one came to the open door. I realized that I had never seen it closed.

Robin fumbled with the door handle, so I reached across and opened it for him. "You managed to open Mr. Seal's," I said.

"Oh, I were sitting forward while he were driving and I were feeling all the time. So it were easy when we came to that corner. I were waiting for that."

"Clever boy," I said dryly.

"I be clever, much cleverer than Lucy. Folks round here say she be a bit daft, but she don't be. She knows things, like I do."

"What things?"

He jumped out of the car, grinning at me.

"Oh well, if you want to be mysterious, have fun," I said. "But you had better find Lucy and stay together."

"We was, but she ran off when she see Mr. Seal."

I nearly said, "Wise girl!" but stopped in time.

"Miss . . ."

"Yes?"

"We got something, Lucy and me. We got something but we don't know how to use it." He leaned against the car door, no longer afraid, watching me with bright hope. "You could show us."

"How do you know that?"

"Well, you be grown up."

"So is your grandmother. Why haven't you asked her?"

"Oh no, we daresn't . . . daren't . . . do that."

School, I thought, was teaching him to check his Dorset dialect. But that was no business of mine. I had other things to consider.

"Why can't you tell your grandmother? If what you've got is really yours . . ."

"O' course, miss. O' course."

"What is it?"

He glanced quickly over his shoulder. "Granny ain't in. It be her day to go to the village."

"All day?"

"Well, most. She cleans for them that lives at the Mill House."

I wondered whether an acute shortage of labor had forced them to employ a witch for a cleaning woman.

"So—would you come, miss?"

"Where?"

"In there." He nodded toward the cottage.

I had no wish to see again the table with the red cloth and the painted girl and the five of spades lying within the twelve circles. But it was possible that Robin knew that the girl in the picture was someone from the village and could reassure me. If he didn't, and I still feared it could be a dreadful portrait of me, then he might be able to tell me that the five of spades had no malevolent meaning and the circles were benign.

"All right." I got out of the car. "Let's go."

But when we reached the cottage, he passed the front door and went around the side, stopping by a tall tangle of laurel bushes and fern and ivy. It was a place straight out of a gardener's nightmare, dark and smelling of damp earth and rotting leaves.

Robin paused and looked back at me. "I show you."

He laid the painted tiger and the remainder of the bag of candy on the ground, and then dropped to his knees, parted the knotted jungle of green and began to wriggle through. As I watched him, the tangle through which he went made me think of the plants that formed the wild barrier to the palace of the Sleeping Beauty, a small, threatening screen of dark, dank green. It was a perfect camouflage for a secret place and entirely in character with the strange little boy who was fighting his way through.

The rustling went on for some time, and then I heard the sound of metal scraping and a soft creaking from somewhere behind the screen of laurel and ivy. All I could see of Robin were his heels as he struggled forward on his stomach, giving little grunts as children and old people do when their energies are being used to extreme.

The heels disappeared. "Miss. Come."

I tried to part the bush but could find no place.

From somewhere behind it Robin must have been watching me, for he called, "You can't get in that way, miss. You've got to crawl like I did."

I looked down in vague horror at the parasitic ivy clinging to the wall and the decaying mass of greenery through which I was supposed to follow Robin. "Oh no, I'm not going through that."

"It be the only way, miss. You'll be all right. Me and Lucy do it all the time. We got to keep all that stuff over our door so it be secret."

"Well, I can't crawl on all fours through that, so if you have something you want to show me, bring it out here."

"Please, miss. *Please* . . ."

Swift pictures of ancient graveyards, of horrifying medieval catacombs, of mystic horrors flew into my mind and flew straight out again. If children were familiar with whatever lay beyond the laurel bush and the wet rotting leaves, it couldn't be very terrible. I dropped down, lay flat and wriggled through the undergrowth. Laurels slapped my face; my fingers dipped into the wet earth; tendrils of ivy clung to my hair.

"Don't make a noise, miss," said Robin from somewhere in the green gloom in front of me.

But I was twice his size and twice his weight and the miniature jungle resisted every move I made. I kept closing my eyes against the onslaught of the slapping leaves. Then, when I felt that the only way for me to go was backward and into the clear daylight again, my hand made one more move forward and touched flesh.

"That's *me*," Robin hissed.

I looked down and saw that my fingers were gripped around his ankle. Behind him was a small open doorway.

He turned as I tried to scramble to my feet. "You can't get in that way. You be too big. You got to kneel."

It was the first time in my life anyone had called me big. I dropped to my knees on the sodden earth and followed Robin, edging my way through the thick door that hung on two broken hinges.

The air was damp and sour. I gave a swift thought, as I went through on my knees like someone doing a penance, that a sharp nudge might break the hinges and send the door crashing onto me. I was quite certain that the solid piece of oak could break my bones.

The moment I was through the door, I stood up.

I was in a room with a small high window, so dirty that it was opaque and made even darker by the heavy green bushes outside. Only the barest light drifted in, but on the stone floor I saw some unlit candles set in broken saucers.

"She bain't here," Robin said in a small forlorn voice.

"Who?"

"Lucy."

So whether she was what the village people called "daft," or whether she was what I called "fey," Robin was incomplete without her.

The little stone room held only a shabby folding chair someone had probably thrown on the rubbish heap, a three-legged stool and a packing case that served as a table. On that table was something quite out of character with the tiny, primitive place. It was an old tape recorder with exposed reels and it was set in the place of honor in the center of the packing case.

"Is this your room?"

He nodded. "It be Lucy's and mine. Granny don't know about it, or she may have done once, but she's forgot. She be old, you see, though she be a witch. She hasn't never been here. She be too big, anyway."

He was right. Her large, strong shoulders would stick in that tiny doorway.

"I made that." He pointed to the packing case. I saw that one side was roughly nailed and I realized that the children must have brought it in in pieces and assembled it once they were inside.

"And your grandmother didn't hear you hammering and ask you what you were doing?"

"No. We does things like that when she be out working."

I looked about me. "But there must be some other way in and out of this room."

He shook his head. "Granny'ud find it if there was."

The cottage was very old. Perhaps there had once been a door into the main room, but it had been blocked up and no one living knew about it. I said, to draw Robin out, "And your Granny's magic doesn't tell her you've got this secret room?"

He grinned at me. "Her magic don't touch us. We be family. She don't know yet if me and Lucy be witches too, and we'd scare her. It'ud be fun to scare Granny."

I couldn't imagine Hobbin being afraid of anyone, and asked him, pointing to the recorder, "Where did you get that?"

"It be ours." He was immediately on the defensive. "We didn't steal it. We don't steal nothing, Lucy and me. But—" His eyes softened. A lock of black hair hung over one temple and I could see the beginnings of adult charm creeping over the child image. "Please, miss, you tell me how to use that thing."

"Surely the man in the shop where you bought it showed you?"

"Yes. But Lucy and me have forgot. Please . . ."

When he reached eighteen or nineteen, his strange, secretive eyes and the smile that curved his long mouth would be devastating to some impressionable girls. They even got me succumbing to the extent of going over to the packing case and pressing the buttons of the old tape recorder. I had never had one or worked one, and I pushed the keys as if I were playing a piano. Nothing happened, until I saw that one of them was jammed. A tiny piece of what looked like a matchstick was embedded in the socket.

"Have you got a knife?"

"No."

"Then something long and thin," I said.

He produced a hammer.

"Long and thin," I said. "A pin?"

He felt in the pocket of his shorts and produced some coins, tangled string and a large safety pin, which he handed to me.

I dug around the little key, not quite knowing whether the tape recorder would work even if I released the sliver of wood. At the moment when I almost gave up, the splinter shot out.

"Now let's see," I said. "I'm not certain that I'll be able to help with this."

The wheels whirred and the tape that was on one of the spools revolved. I was about to tell Robin to speak into it, when a high-pitched woman's voice burst out: ". . . and you tell me to leave it all to you. But I can't. I can't. It's gone too far. Jessamy . . ."

So old a tape recorder would not reproduce voices in perfect pitch. Yet one word of that sobbing protest gave me a clue. No one I had met in Dorset accentuated the name Jessamy like the voice on the tape, softening the "J" as Livanova with her French accent might have done . . . *As Stephanie had done when she had murmured the name in the quiet hospital room.*

I swung around to the boy. "Who was speaking?"

My tone scared him and he cringed from me.

"I'm not going to hurt you." I spoke more gently. "But you *must* tell me who was speaking to you."

He fought free of my hand, which was gripping his shoulder, and his little clawing fingers tried to tear at the tape. "I don't know . . . I didn't . . . We didn't . . ."

"Didn't what?"

He gave me a sideways look. "We never heard nothing. We couldn't turn it right, me and Lucy. I told 'ee . . . you . . ." Correcting his dialect seemed to be automatic, for he remembered it even though he was so frightened. I believed him, for he wouldn't have brought me to his secret place had he not badly needed help with the recorder.

The words I had heard must have followed some heated conversation I knew I had to hear. Certainly the tape ran on without any sound but its own faint hum. And then it stopped revolving.

"You must have turned the tape on without knowing that you did."

"We didn't, miss, we really didn't. Don, in the village, gave us a lift in his van from the town after we bought it, and we got it straight here."

"But you must have used it before the knob jammed, or there would be nothing on the tape. Unless—" Another thought occurred to me. "Who did you buy it from?"

"A shop, miss. It was going cheap. It be old stuff."

"Did the man say it was secondhand? I mean," I explained as he stared at me, "had someone else owned it and sold it to the man in the shop to sell again?"

"I don't know, miss."

"But you told me the man showed you how to use it."

"He did. But when that tape went round, there weren't nothing on it. He said, 'There, now. All you have to do is to press this button. And when you want to stop the tape, press this one. You see?' Lucy and me thought we did, but we didn't."

After they had brought it home they must have accidentally turned it on, sometime before the match had become jammed in it. They could have sat with it outside in the forest, but have grown bored and left it with the swift impulsive movements children had, before they knew that the spool was whirring, and so they hadn't heard the woman's voice and didn't realize that they had made the recorder work. Only two people, surely, pronounced Jessamy in that French way; only two people, and it could be either of them speaking—a dead woman or a living daughter.

"Hey—" I flung myself at Robin, who had managed to tear the tapes off the machine, dragging and pulling at them. I heard the whirring of the spools stop and I wondered if he had broken the machine, which I suspected had been patched up for a second-hand sale. "Give them to me."

"No . . ."

"Robin, please. If you let me have them, I'll show you how to start the machine going and how to stop it and remove the tape properly." I didn't care that I had never used one in my life. Somehow or other I would manage, because I had to know what was on the rest of the tape.

But I reckoned without the eel-like movements of the small, thin body. My tenacious hands slithered from him as if he had been greased all over, and he was lying flat and wriggling through the low door before I could get a strong enough hold on his ankles to pull him back. Twice he kicked out at me, and each time the back of my hand was jerked upward and hit against the iron bolts of the door, so that sharp arrows of pain forced me to let go of him.

I flung myself down and crawled through the door, clawing at the laurel, pushing myself along by its short, strong branches. But by the time I had fought through the ferns and the tangle of ivy, Robin was out of sight.

I stood looking about me. Then I called. My voice ricocheted hollowly from tree to tree. The wind in the grass made sounds like brush strokes on a drum. For all I knew, Robin could have clambered into one of the great beeches and was watching me through the branches.

He was obviously determined to keep his tapes, though I had no idea whether it was because he was afraid that if I took them, the recorder would be useless, or whether it was that in spite of his protests, he knew what else was on the used tape and was frightened. All I was certain of was that no amount of calling on my part would bring him to me.

XVII

THE HIGH, NEARLY HYSTERICAL female voice was the only sound I seemed to hear, echoing in my mind. I went back to the cottage and looked through the open door. The room was empty and I doubted if Robin would be hiding behind the far door, which must lead to a bedroom.

I drove the car a short way along the lane and stopped in the heavy shade of some trees. Then I waited and watched. The forest itself was the children's sanctuary, as natural to them as to the deer and the squirrels and the rabbits that lived there.

I knew that the only way I would find Robin would be if Lucy appeared. I felt that he would come out of hiding for her, but the stillness and the emptiness of the forest remained, and I gave up.

Near me a bird I could not identify burst into song. It was like laughter, and as I listened I began to wonder if nerves and imagination had me in a coiled grip, so that I could be losing my sense of reality. The tone on the tape had been untrue, unidentifiable except for that single pronunciation. I needed advice, but I could ask no one to help me get that tape and listen to it with me, because it could be Stephanie speaking, and I was she.

I could see in the driving mirror that someone was coming up the lane, and turning around, I recognized the long, striding figure of Hobbin. On an impulse, without knowing how much or how little I intended to say to her, I got out of the car and waited for her to reach me.

"How be you, missy?"

"I'm fine. I've just seen Robin."

She pursed her lips, looking away into the dense green of the forest. "He be told to get eggs from the village and keep the fire burning—the cottage be damp. And if I don't find them things done when I get home, I'll tan the hide off him."

I doubted if she would find the eggs delivered or the fire still alight. And I doubted, also, if she would ever be able to beat that small, thin eel of a child.

I said, "Is there someone in the village about my age? Fair, like me?"

"Aye, but not so pretty. She be Chrissie Long, working down at the Mill House. Why do 'ee ask?"

I ignored the question. "Does she come to you for . . . for advice?"

"No."

"Then perhaps someone from Dulverley?"

"Oh, I don't know folks at Dulverley." She edged away from me.

"But someone who was a stranger could have been sent to you; someone, perhaps, who had a friend in the village who told her how clever you were at advising people about their lives?"

My flattery did me no good. Her eyes moved from her dark, steady contemplation of the trees and rested on me. "I don't ever talk about them as comes to see me. It be secret between them and me."

"I'm sure, and I wouldn't want to pry. But I thought perhaps someone I might know had come to stay down here and needed help."

It was a weak explanation and it was obvious that she didn't believe me. She fingered the huge shapeless bag she was carrying and didn't take her eyes from my face. "Stop asking questions, Miss Clair. It don't do no good here for you to ask questions."

"I'm sorry, but . . ."

She was out of hearing, walking quickly toward her cottage. It was the same as at our last meeting: nothing revealed, but a warning given. And that meant she knew something that could be dangerous for me. Whether she knew it as a fact, or through reading cards or casting spells, didn't matter. I was determined to make one more effort to find out what it was. I ran across the knobbly ground, with its short, spiky grass, to the cottage.

"Mrs. Hobbin . . ."

She had her back to me and was poking the nearly dead fire. The red cloth was still over the table but the picture of the girl, the card and the circles were all gone.

"Mrs. Hobbin, please, if you can help me . . ."

She turned, poker in hand. She looked taller than ever. "I can't help you."

"Why, when you help so many people?"

"Not *you*." She set the poker down and reached to a shelf, picked up a pack of cards and flung them across the table. "The cards won't speak for you."

"I don't want spells. I want the truth."

"My cards speak the truth."

"Then what does the five of spades mean?"

She gave a long hissing breath. "Why be you asking that? Don't dabble in things you don't understand. Don't try to read the cards."

"Just that one, Mrs. Hobbin."

"It be that book Mr. Seal has—that's it, ain't it? You start reading books on witchcraft and you think you know. I tell you it takes far more than words to be a witch. It be a power inside you, something you can't learn from books. And it don't be evil either, least not always."

"If I had studied the book on witchcraft that Mr. Seal has, I would know what the five of spades means. But I am asking *you*."

With superb and blazing authority she said, "What I do here for them as comes for help is not for anyone else to know."

"The five of spades, Mrs. Hobbin . . ."

"It be someone's fate card. It means, Miss Clair, a wild destiny." She took a step toward me, not quite menacingly yet not particularly friendly. "The five of spades . . . 'tis the Five of Swords. Go home. You bain't be doing any good here. I tell you again, the mark be on your brow." She looked over my shoulder.

I, too, turned. Someone stood behind me.

"Come in. Come in," she said to the middle-aged woman standing hesitantly in the doorway.

I had failed and I was dismissed. I went back to my car with one disturbing thought uppermost. Whether Hobbin had magical powers, whether there were such things—and I was prepared to believe better brains than mine who acknowledged the existence of the enchanter--the fact remained that Hobbin knew I was in danger. And was trying to warn me. Yet the more I thought about it, the less I believed it was concerned with her simple spells and charms. She lived close to Jessamy Court, and ever since infancy she must have known a great deal about the people in it, not only from the villagers who worked there but also from her own sharp observation. I had no idea whether or not she liked me, but it seemed that each time she spoke to me, there had been a queer, paradoxically harsh compassion on her strong face. *Follow the west wind, Miss Clair.*

Looking back over our brief, tense confrontation, I realized that expressions of fear had kept crossing her face, but I would not have thought that Hobbin knew fear. Then I remembered how, the last time we had met, she had spoken of the voices she had heard—the extension of her powers, which obviously both excited and awed her. Voices: a man's and a woman's.

I drove back to Jessamy through the fine, soft mist from the sea. It had come in on the tide and would drift away as gently as it arrived. I slowed down as I came to the straight lane that led to the house. I stopped the car and looked out at Gideon's Rock and thought of the girl with the blown dark hair who had watched Fabian and me.

There seemed to be a battle between the light mist and the imperceptible breeze, for everything I looked at appeared to sway slightly. It was as if some metamorphosis were taking place, like a dream scene in a film when a shot of the picture, quivering and out of focus, was distorted.

I was in that moment aware of the change around me and in myself. Every day it was becoming easier to be Stephanie. The thought frightened me, not only because I dreaded a lost identity but also because I should be facing the fact that I had failed to discover more than a few superficial facts concerning Stephanie and her link with Jessamy Court. Since the house, as such, had never been of much interest to her, I was certain that there were deeper things involved in her breakdown, and it was becoming obvious that I possessed neither the subtlety nor the courage to find out what they were.

I was still afraid of asking the wrong question, or making an unheeded statement that would give me away. *And yet, with that fear always with me, I didn't leave Jessamy.*

I was immobile, with a queer, helpless acceptance of the fact that by remaining, I might be denounced by Stephanie herself at any moment.

And yet I stayed . . .

The strange sensation was growing on me that Fabian was not a man I had met for the first time only five days earlier, but someone I had known before.

To me, Rachel Fleming, he was just a name and a stranger. But Stephanie could have known him, without ever having told me. And in the curious semi-transference of myself into Livanova's daughter, it was possible I could sense this.

A herring gull, its great wingspan stretched, plunged through the sky, diving into the water for the hermit crabs that lay in the rock pools. The swift, faultless action gave me a sense of the power of even a bird to be utterly itself. It was my lesson, and I needed one. I had to hold on to being myself, too.

I looked down at my hands, broad and slightly tanned, at the antique silver ring I wore. They were *my* hands, *my* ring . . . Reassured by the sight of them, I restarted the car and drove through the gates.

The door of the practice room was open and the lights were on, each reflected in the great mirrors and making the lovely lily ceiling glow. The Tibetan bell stood on the trestle table among the litter of sketches.

Fabian was standing by the reading desk, turning the pages of the book of witchcraft, his back to me.

"In some ways I'm a traditionalist," he said, "but I dislike the classic tutus. They would be impossible, anyway, in this ballet with its mirror images. The costumes, like the dancers, must be completely fluid. Don't you agree?"

It was unnerving to realize that without turning to see who was standing there, he had known that it was I who watched him. But if it had been Mrs. Manfred, she would probably have said, "Excuse me, sir, but . . ." and then asked her question. And Fenney, the gardener, would have done the same. I doubted if Dominick ever came near the practice room when Fabian was there. So that meant the footsteps stopping at the door were obviously mine.

"I saw you, Fabian."

"I'm glad I'm not invisible."

"I mean I saw you earlier this morning, in your car."

He placed a slip of paper in a page as a bookmark. "Did you?" He was disinterested.

"Robin was with you."

"Oh yes?"

"You pushed him into your car and drove off. I followed you because I saw the way you rough-handled him and—"

"And what?"

"I was worried. You were very harsh with him. And I saw him fall."

He looked at me for the first time. "My dear Stephanie, I assure you murder wasn't in my heart. Had it been, I'd have chosen a far more subtle way than making off with him in broad daylight in a car everyone knows is mine."

"All the same, you could have killed him."

"Oh yes, you're right, I could." His mouth was smiling but his eyes were cold and hard. "We all have our faults, and one of mine is that when I'm angry, I can be quite lethal."

"You almost were. When Robin fell from your car, you didn't even stop to see if he was injured."

"He wasn't."

"How do you know?"

"Because I saw you go to him and I saw him get up. He hadn't even sprained an ankle. Tell me, do you like this particular blue?" he pointed to a streak of it at the side of a sketch lying on the table.

"Yes. But about Robin—"

"Blue, according to witchcraft, is a protection against evil. Light a blue candle for safety, Stephanie."

I walked away from the table without answering.

"You didn't tail me very well, did you?" he said. "You need some lessons in strategy."

"If I hadn't been there, would you have gone to help him?"

He laid the sketch down very carefully. "Are you cross-examining me? Because if you wish to, I must warn you, I shall consult my solicitor. That's the normal procedure." He was still laughing at me.

I demanded with cold, mounting anger, "You don't mind if I ask you why you bundled Robin into your car as you did?"

"I don't mind in the least, but I haven't the slightest intention of answering you."

I was using the wrong tactics. I said more softly, "I'm sorry if I sound interfering, but he *was* very frightened."

"He had no need to be. He has at least nine lives. Besides, he has probably tried his grandmother's broomstick and fallen off before he got used to swinging over rooftops, so he has learned how to fall softly."

"Can't you be serious?"

"Perhaps I am."

"Oh no . . ."

He had turned his back on me. Suddenly his arm shot out and made a violent half-circle across the trestle table. The Tibetan bell spun through the air and crashed to the floor. It made its own lovely, vibrant protest.

"Damn everything . . . damn all things . . ."

"You damn the world because a little boy has made you angry?"

He picked up the bell and stroked it with strong square fingers. "You can put your own interpretation on what you saw. But you've never been exactly right about things, have you? You always jumped to wild conclusions, didn't you, Stephanie? Livanova's bitter daughter!" The words came from him with an almost sinister quiet.

I walked past him to one of the mirror walls. "Does it show on my face? The bitterness, I mean."

"Not yet. But it will."

"Oh no . . ." My wild protest was out before I could check myself, but it was felt too much: it came with pain, the kind that Stephanie would feel. My nails dug into the palms of my hands as I fought to lose identification with Livanova's daughter and find myself.

"What's the matter, Stephanie?"

(That's what's the matter. *Stephanie* . . .)

"Nothing," I said aloud, "except that I don't like being called bitter."

"I've never believed that as much of our character as people make out is inherited. It's a good excuse for virtues and vices. But some things are. Your father was a bitter man. He expected perfection from Livanova and couldn't take less. And when your turn came, you couldn't take less than perfection from her, either. You never once gave her the benefit of the doubt, did you? You wasted so much of your time being sorry for yourself for having a mother who had a life of her own. Why the hell didn't you go out and make a useful existence for yourself?"

My suspicion that Fabian knew I was not Stephanie did a half-turn. He spoke with such intensity that it was difficult to believe he was just cleverly playing my game for his own reasons. I was certain of nothing except anger at his attack.

"Did you ask me down here just to plan this attack on me?" My eyes and my voice blazed. "If so, it would have been better if you had put it all in a letter. Then you'd have been spared the irritation of having to look at me."

His movement toward me was so swift that as he seized my shoulders, I gasped. If my eyes and voice had blazed at him, his held a terrible, quiet fury. "Dear God, you little fool. I loved your mother. *I loved her.* Don't you realize what you might have been to me? My stepdaughter."

He flung me from him and I staggered against the table, my arm catching the edges of some sketches and scattering them on the floor. I bent to pick them up.

"Leave them . . . I said *leave them.*"

"If you spoke to my mother like that, I don't wonder she left you. You don't own the whole world; you don't own anyone or anything except . . ."

"Except what?"

"A talent, and your possessions, which now include this house."

I stood rooted to the floor, willing my expression and my shaking limbs not to betray me. He must not see that he had this powerful emotional effect on me. With what small strength I had left I turned and marched away from him, the hammering of my heels pretending a strength of purpose I didn't possess.

"Stephanie."

It isn't my name. Just for once refuse to acknowledge it. Walk out of the room and don't look back.

But at any moment something might be said or done that would make clear to me—and then to the hospital in London—the shock-link between Jessamy Court and Stephanie. Because of that, pride had to exit as gracefully as possible. I turned at the door as Fabian called me again.

"What did Robin tell you?"

"What are you afraid he told me?"

"I'm afraid of nothing. But I'm interested."

I leaned against the doorpost and folded my arms. "He wouldn't talk because he was frightened, but he took me to look at one of those old-fashioned tape recorders he had. He didn't know how to work it."

"Oh? And did *you*?"

"I found out by accident."

"So Robin was happy?"

"There was a tape already on one of the spools. Someone was speaking."

Fabian made neither sound nor movement and yet I sensed a tightening of the atmosphere, a sharp rise in tension.

"Did you recognize the voice?"

"No."

"Children's chat."

"No."

He said, "I suppose it's sheer curiosity that makes me ask what the voice was saying."

Oh no, my dear Fabian, it isn't . . .

"A woman was speaking," I told him, "but I didn't understand what she said." And that, I thought, was true in a way, because I had no idea of the reason for the hysterical outburst.

Fabian appeared to accept my explanation. He picked up the sketches I had knocked to the floor and said, "Children have expensive tastes these days."

"Yes, but I wonder how Robin got hold of the money. Even an old tape recorder costs something, and Hobbin must be very poor."

"He's the grandson of a witch." Fabian snapped his fingers. "Magic could be the answer."

"Did you give him the tape recorder?"

He raised his eyebrows. "Now, why would I do a thing like that?"

"Because if you had once had one, you would probably throw it out and use a cassette."

"That's right. I often play back conversations I've had with Hannaford or Gilderoy. It's not only helpful for reference, it's also amusing to listen to our temperamental arguments. Do you think me temperamental, Stephanie?"

About as temperamental as a subtle, stalking tiger. "Oh no. For an artist, you've very level-headed."

"As a man who climbed mountains, I had to be."

He was changing the direction of the conversation again, countering question for question, telling me nothing. He was too devious for me.

Mrs. Manfred was waiting for me in the hall; something silver gleamed in her hand.

"Is this yours, Miss Clair?"

I had no need to handle it to know. It was the small silver compact Jock Graham had given me the previous Christmas. "Where did you find it?"

"Hobbin brought it. She said you dropped it in her cottage."

"But I didn't—" I began, and then a sharp stab of alarm silenced me. I reached out for it, and as I did so, Mrs. Manfred turned it over in her hand. On the other side were my initials in tiny green stones: *R.F.*

"Thank you," I said. "I'd have hated to lose that. It . . . it was given to me . . ." I left the rest of the sentence in the air, hoping that she would think it was a secondhand gift.

"Excuse me, Miss Clair, but I must make out my weekly grocery order." Always correct, always just sufficiently deferential without in the least being subservient, Mrs. Manfred walked silently away from me toward the green-baize door that led to the kitchen quarters.

I went into the empty drawing room. If I had even half believed in magic, I would have been convinced at that moment, for I knew perfectly well I hadn't dropped the compact out of my purse when I was in Hobbin's cottage. It was silver and fairly heavy and I would have heard it fall.

I wandered around the room and stood looking into Livanova's cabinet of fans. I had taken my powder compact out of my purse the previous day to check the clasp, which was not closing properly. I remembered leaving it on the highboy in the bedroom, that I had forgotten to put it back in my purse.

And someone had seen it there. Mrs. Manfred, for one. There could be others, too, for while I was out, anyone could have entered my room. Someone searching the room out of curiosity or because of something said or done which was suspicious. The search could have been for a letter that was not addressed to Stephanie, or a diary with another name in it. Or even something in a handwriting that did not match that on the letter from Stephanie, which Fabian, or someone else who suspected me, could have seen at some time in Livanova's possession.

I had been so careful about those things, but I had given no thought to the initials on my powder compact. Instead of leaving it where it was, whoever had found it had taken it and dropped it outside Hobbin's cottage. I could make two guesses as to why that was done. Either it was to prove to me that someone knew I was not Stephanie and was giving me proof, or it was dropped there as a message to Hobbin, although I could think of no reason why it was intended that Hobbin, and not someone living in the house, should find my compact.

It was useless to stand there conjecturing. I rushed out of the room and up the stairs to fetch my coat, and then, not caring whether I was seen, made my way to Hobbin's cottage.

From the smell that hit me as I stood knocking at her open door, she was cooking some kind of stew with onions. She looked up, saying nothing, a huge wooden ladle in her hands.

"I believe you found my powder compact," I said, "but I don't think I dropped it here."

She nodded. "Oh, but you did, it were on the floor."

"Are you sure you didn't find it somewhere else?"

She put the ladle into a bowl of water, swished it around and wiped her hands on a cloth. "I've been in this room ever since you left, and if I say a thing, it be true. You understand? I tell no lies."

"Someone came to see you as I left. How did you know the compact was mine and not hers?"

"Because I saw it while she were here. It were just outside the door and it weren't hers."

"The initials on the compact are R.F. Why did you think it was mine?"

"You and her be the only ones who come here just now."

"Someone else did," I said, "whether you saw them or not. And whoever it was, brought the compact with them and planted it here for you to find."

"Then it be yours?"

"Yes," I said as airily as I could. "It's mine. Take no notice of the initials, Mrs. Hobbin."

172

"No, missy, I don't."

It could mean nothing, or it could mean a very dangerous situation for me. I did the only possible thing. I ignored the danger and brazened it out. "Well, at any rate, I'm glad to have it back. Thank you for bringing it round."

It seemed that the cottage in the forest was not nearly as isolated as it appeared to be, for I saw her eyes go past me to the door. I turned.

Fabian said, "Why, Stephanie, have you come to hear from Hobbin whether you're going to marry your dark lover?"

"I've come to thank Mrs. Hobbin for finding something I seem to have nearly lost. My powder compact."

"Really." His face was shadowed by the dark little room. "Let me warn you never to drop anything you value in the forest, because like the desert, it's doubtful you'll find it again."

"I still can't think how I dropped this one." I took it out of my purse and held it for him to see, the initialed side hidden in my palm.

He picked it up and then laid it back again in my hand without turning it over. It could have been deliberate, as if he knew what was inscribed on the other side and, in his own devious way, was letting me know.

"It's all right, Mrs. Hobbin, I haven't really come to see you," he said. "I happened to be passing and saw Miss Clair. I was badly wanting to find her, because she said she would like to come with me to Lorne Abbey this afternoon."

"But I didn't. I—"

"Come along. There's lunch to be got through. I've ordered it early, since it's a fair way by car and I want to get there while there's still enough light to sketch."

I knew that his fingers on my arm would tighten as soon as I tried to get free of him, and I knew, too, that nothing could be gained by remaining any longer at the cottage.

We were well out of Hobbin's hearing when I said indignantly, "You didn't ask me to go to Lorne Abbey with you this particular afternoon."

"Didn't I? Well, I fully intended to." He let go of my arm. "Anyway, it's a lovely day, so we'll go."

XVIII

SITTING IN FABIAN'S BENTLEY was the nearest thing I would ever get to car luxury. But it failed to make me feel secure. I said, as I settled in the passenger seat, "Robin was the last person to sit here, wasn't he? And he was very frightened."

"But you're not."

"No. Why should I be?"

"That's a question for you to answer, my dear," he said and started the engine.

It took us nearly three quarters of an hour of smooth, swift driving to reach Lorne Abbey.

The few tourists were already leaving and the bookstall at the walled entrance, which sold various histories of Lorne, was closed. Not that Fabian needed a guidebook; he was interested in the atmosphere, not the past. And anyway, he knew a great deal about the abbey, which he told me as we wandered among the stone ruins of the great church that had been in its full glory in the twelfth century. The only part that was in any way recognizable was the fine arched Lady chapel and the large porch outside that had once been the main door, which, Fabian told me, was called the Galilee and was used in ancient days as a stage for festivals. The late-afternoon sun had turned the age-darkened stone to pale rose. I could understand why visitors flocked to the magnificent, legend-haunted Glastonbury that was not so very far away and did not come to Lorne. The ruins were less magnificent, less vast, because Lorne had suffered far more from fire and battle than had Glastonbury.

Fabian paused, in his explanations, seeming to forget me, and looked about him, frowning into the low red sun. "I want an unfolding panorama. Distance beyond distance, ancient stones and flaming sky reflected in mirrors into a kind of dream of infinity." Then, as if remembering me, he pointed to a few ancient graves deep in the beautifully kept lawns out of which the ruins rose.

"They say that Sir Lancelot, King Arthur's knight, is buried here. I doubt if many believe it. But since Glastonbury insists on the graves of Arthur and Guinevere, Lorne must have its romantic knight, too." Then, as we reached the far end of the ruins, he said, "And this is just a brief glimpse of the outer wall—nothing, as you can see, but a few low piles of stone." He turned his back on me. "Over there you'll find the archeological site. Go and have a look. I'm told they have unearthed three ages: the late Bronze, the Dark Ages when the Vikings came and the age of the building of great abbeys."

He had a drawing pad in his hand and he dug in his pocket for one of the thick crayon pencils he used. The swift slashing lines were already covering the top page of the pad before I had left him.

The site of the "dig" was just beyond the abbey. Fences and ropes formed a barricade around a comparatively small area. There was a hut at one end of the trenches, but the door was closed and there was no light. The archeologists and the students must have left earlier. Inside the little hut would probably be the finds of the day—pottery and tools and perhaps the jewels of women who had lived there more than a thousand years ago. I remembered reading about Troy, for so long supposedly a legend and in the end proven to be a fact. Perhaps the Knights of the Round Table were more real than was supposed; perhaps there was a Holy Grail to be sought and a sword that only one man could handle.

Earth cleared from the deep ditches revealed rough stonework and there were niches which might have held urns and cooking pots, now almost certainly carefully itemized and stored.

I stood on the bank of a deep trench and looked along it. On a small rise at the far end stood a pillar of mottled stone, and as I neared it I saw jagged sides, as if pieces had been broken off. It was fairly obvious that what I was looking at was an ancient cross, although whether Saxon or Celtic, I had no idea. It was tilted slightly forward, and with the flat landscape behind it, stood stark against the reddening sky.

"There's a carving on that." Fabian's voice came unexpectedly from behind me.

"You walk like a cat."

"I'm sorry, but grass isn't exactly a sounding board. That cross is rather interesting. The inscription on it is in Latin. Is your Latin any good?"

"I've almost forgotten the little I knew, but it's a challenge, isn't it?" I looked back at him, laughing.

"Of course it is. Go down and see if you can decipher what's written there. I tried the other day, and I can't."

"The guard rope is all around it to keep inquisitive people off the site."

"I know. But I have permission to wander here as I like. The leader of the excavation, Tom Bradford, is a lecturer at the University of Dorset and a friend of mine. He knows that no rope will keep me away from something that interests me, so he has ceded what you might call 'game, set and match' to me, which means that I can go wherever I like. I've reassured him that I won't make off with Celtic jewelry or an incense cup. Come on," he urged me. "Don't look as though I'm asking you to jump off a mountain."

People had fears of heights, fears of darkness, fears of being in lonely places. I disliked jumping. Once, when I had gone to Switzerland with my family, we had walked down a mountain path and had had to jump a small mountain stream. Everyone else leaped clear; I landed slap in the middle of the stream and my face was slightly slashed by the small sharp rocks.

I looked down at the deep trench, which my imagination turned from its few yards into half a mile, and said, "I always have to steel myself for a jump. I'll probably count twelve first, so you'll have to be patient." I began slowly, "One . . . two . . ."

"Come away from there. Hey, you over there, get back . . ."

The voice checked my counting, and startled, I lost my balance and reeled sideways, slipping on loose earth.

A man was running toward us, still shouting, "Get the hell out of there. Do you hear? *Get . . . out.*"

My feet slithered on the dry soft earth. There was a crash, and as I lost my balance on the sliding soil and fell against the side of the trench, there was a tremendous thud that shook the earth around us. I lay quite still, looking over my shoulder. The stone cross had crashed and lay at the bottom of the trench, half hidden in the great mass of earth it had disturbed in its fall.

The man had raced around the end of the trenches. "Good God, Mr. Seal!" He was gray-haired, overweight and panting from his run. "What in heaven's name made you go through the ropes?"

"The simple answer is that I always have." Fabian was hauling me out of the loosened earth at the side of the trench, which fell away each time I fought for a foothold. I kept staggering and slithering, and Fabian breathed at me, "Dig your heels in, damn it. *Heels . . .*"

"Give me your other hand." The man who had shouted to me reached out and held me with a grip like a vise. Together they got me to the top of the trench and I felt rather like a sack of vegetables being hauled into a truck. That was the funny side. But behind the hysterical desire to giggle, lay shock.

The stranger was saying, "The few who are allowed on the site to watch the excavation were warned this morning not to come near the top of this first trench. Surely they called you about it?"

"No," Fabian said succinctly.

"We had thought the trench was safe, but then last night the earth began to slip away. We boarded up most of it along this part of the trench and reckoned we could do the rest in the morning. We were certain that the cross would be perfectly safe for another day or two, provided the earth around it wasn't disturbed."

"A delusion, obviously," Fabian said, "since Stephanie was only standing at the top of the trench."

"That's just it. The earth at the top end of this trench is loosened. We reckon that at some time or other in the past, great floods must have moved the soil and undermined the foundations of the stone. Then the soil settled again, and when we first excavated here we saw no sign of erosion. I'm sorry . . . you aren't hurt, are you?"

"No, but only thanks to my own dislike of jumping even a few yards," I said and looked at Fabian. "If I had jumped when you told me to, I'd probably be dead by now."

Although the low sun cast a rich glow over everything, I had a feeling that beneath the softening effect of the light, the lines of his face were taut with the shadow of anger.

"Why the hell don't they put up signs, warning people?"

"Because, my dear Fabian, sightseers usually respect rope barriers."

"You damned well know they don't. Particularly visiting students. Of all the bloody incompetence . . ." He pulled himself together with an effort. "By the way, Stephanie, this is James Tallent, curator of the Sedge-Barrow Museum. James, this is Miss Clair, Livanova's daughter."

I had been leaning against a tree, my hands cupped around my face as if trying to hold in the terrible accusation that could have burst out: *You knew of the danger here,* didn't you, Fabian? You *were* warned. What did you want? A broken leg? A broken neck?

I said shakenly to James Tallent, "Thank you for being around."

"Oh, I was stamping the ground in that group of trees over there. I think they've grown over another ancient burial place."

I shuddered at the gruesome thought, then I said, "Neither of us saw you, did we, Fabian?"

"No."

Suspicions and counter-suspicions tore through me as I rested for support against the old tree.

That was a chance taken on the spur of the moment, wasn't it, Fabian? Then, common sense mocked my silent accusation. He could have had no sinister intentions when we set out for Lorne, nor when he had come so quietly behind me. How could he have, in such a place where anyone might have seen us? But I had been wandering for some minutes by myself and had seen no one. The place had seemed completely isolated; Fabian had joined me, and with one movement of his arm, could have killed me. But, argued my common sense, he couldn't have been certain where I would have landed when I jumped or exactly the spot in which the stone would have fallen. But I was wrong there, too. For Fabian had climbed mountains, he was experienced. The tilt of the ancient

Celtic cross pointed to the angle of its fall just as I, turning toward it to jump, must have leaped right in its path. Fabian knew . . .

And afterward? At the inquest it would have been said that a young woman filled with foolish curiosity, defying her host's warning not to go near the top of the trench where the cross stood, jumped down to see if she could read the words carved on it. And no one would ever believe that Fabian, a one-time mountaineer, respected and admired, had not warned me.

I'm safe this time . . . But, dear God, I've got to get away. Stephanie might need help, but I was no heroine and I loved my life.

My thoughts swung wildly, like a pendulum, and I realized suddenly that James Tallent had stopped his conversation with Fabian and was speaking to me.

"I really am sorry, Miss Clair. I can't think how they missed warning Fabian. I suppose it's because, although he's a friend of Professor Bradford, who is heading the excavation, he's not an archeologist. The university and the schools had been warned. But of course, by tomorrow the place would have been made safe. It takes time to do that and it's too tricky for our staff to work in darkness. They are archeological students but they aren't yet qualified to dig trenches without someone watching and directing them."

I was staring down at the thick stone pillar torn from the loose earth by my stumbling at the top of the trench. Safe for a thousand years, and then you, Rachel Fleming, go and dislodge it without even touching it.

Fabian was saying, "When I went to dinner with Tom Bradford the other night, he told me that they had even found pieces of matting, over a thousand years old, and graves, some Romano-British and some pagan. Bodies had been buried with a coin still in their mouths—to pay their entrance fee to eternity, I suppose."

The keeper was not to be diverted. He shot me a careful look. "I think, Fabian, that Miss Clair is still a bit shocked. Why don't you come along to my place and have a brandy."

"No," I protested, "thank you, I'm quite all right." I managed a smile.

Fabian put an arm around me and I trembled and drew away, leaning against the tree with the rough bark.

The sky was deepening and streaks of orange and flame fanned out behind the dark ruins of Lorne Abbey, so that the whole scene before us was like something out of *The Twilight of the Gods* with Valhalla in flames. I could almost believe that I would hear Wagner's music thundering across the quiet and ancient land.

Fabian said, "Come along, we'd better go. We've done enough damage here."

"Well, thank God you weren't injured, Miss Clair. That's all that matters."

The three of us walked back together to Fabian's car. There Tallent stood, giving us a brief salute as the Bentley moved away.

This time, Fabian, there were no children around to blame.

We talked in occasional desultory sentences on the way back to Jessamy. I sat with my head averted, watching the tiny villages and the green valleys flash by. But all the time, above the purr of the car, I seemed to hear the tremendous thud of the Celtic cross as it hit the spot where I might have landed.

After the flaming sunset across Lorne, the twilight came gently and darkness was complete by the time we turned in at Jessamy's gates.

There was a light in the drawing room and one of the French doors was open. I thought, as I went toward the terrace steps, how beautiful were the small, slender stone columns that supported the covered terrace and, startled, heard my own voice. I had had no plan to speak. The words came as involuntarily as a cry of fear or of pain.

"Did you really not know the warning about the Celtic cross? *Did* you, Fabian?"

He was a long time answering me. He stood in the shadows and I felt that he was thinking hard. Then he asked softly, "And did *you* think I wanted to see just how big a thud the cross would make if it fell—like a child knocking down a pile of bricks?"

He would always floor me, using the question-for-question tactic. I turned away from him, but he stopped me with both hands on my shoulders. He turned me around roughly and kissed me. I fought him with my fists, but I couldn't match his strength.

Afterward I remembered Mrs. Manfred's face at an upstairs window; I saw the light streaming out from the drawing room; I smelled the soft salt air. Fear and excitement raged inside me as I struggled to get free.

But it was Fabian who thrust me away. "First Livanova and now her daughter . . . Oh no! I leave that sort of entanglement to the romantics."

He strode away from me, and I called after him, not caring who heard, "You talk of an entanglement, but it isn't. It's a solo. Just you, Fabian. An entanglement takes two. Tomorrow, when I leave here, I shall cease to remember you."

He swung around. "There's not a cat in hell's chance of that."

"Do you imagine you have the power to control my thoughts? If so, you may as well know that you are quite wrong."

"We have a permanent link," he said. "Your mother."

It was a confrontation, and I believed that at last I understood the reason he had asked me to Jessamy. He had a score to settle with Livanova for what she had done to him. But the score did not end with her death. It was too terrible for that. *I shall never climb again* . . . So, like a sequel, Stephanie had to suffer too. To be watched and frightened and mocked with kisses. Or it could be that I was being paid out for not being Stephanie.

I walked away from him, up the steps and onto the terrace. I hesitated instead of escaping to my room, and part of the reason was that my shaking legs wouldn't carry me that far.

I had my back to the house, looking out over the invisible Heath. He walked so lightly that when I felt his hands draw me back against him, it seemed that he must have used a kind of magic to get from the lawn to the terrace.

"Please let me go."

He laughed as I dug my elbows into him. "You forget, I've climbed mountains. I'm hard and tough. Your elbows are like thistledown." He took one hand from my arm and ran his fingers through my hair. Then, as I jerked my head away, he let me go. I crossed the drawing room and entered the hall; from the place above the mantel, Tatiana Livanova looked down at me. Her eyes seemed alive and too knowing, always reminding me: "You aren't my weak and wailing daughter, Rachel Fleming."

I fled from those extraordinary painted eyes.

Dominick was playing on the white piano in the practice room. I went up the stairs, and the music, which I did not know, followed me, crashing and splintering the quiet of the house.

My bathroom had pale-green walls and soft mauve fittings and I lay in the water that I had extravagantly scented as if I lay in a pool in an orchid garden. But the bath was not fulfilling its function of relaxing me. I heaved myself out as tense as when I had climbed in.

A tall mirror gave back my reflection, gleaming wet and pale-skinned, hair clinging to my neck. The huge towel hung around me, trailing on the floor like a mermaid's tail. And all the time I bathed and dressed I struggled not to think of Fabian; not to try to unravel the reason for his mockery of me; not to let it matter that contact with him was like a flame inside me. "It's too stupid; like being an adolescent again . . ." I hummed to stop myself from thinking, and then became silent, irritated with myself because I could never sing in tune.

When I was dressed and ready to go downstairs, I opened my door, and Jupiter, proprietarial and as smoothly golden as bronze, entered my room. I stroked him, but he rejected me with a soft yowl and bounded out again.

To my left was a passage leading to the rest of the bedrooms, and as I followed Jupiter, I heard voices coming from a room with an open door.

"She were asking for Mr. Seal."

"But who *was* she?"

"That I don't know. She never gave her name. But she knew him all right, so he must know her."

"And he were out all afternoon?"

"Yes. I'd made scones for tea, but he said, all of a sudden, that he were going out and that he were going to find Miss Clair and take her along."

"And what did he say when you told him she had called?"

"He said that if it was urgent, she would call again."

"Did you tell him how she were crying?"

"No. Why *should* I worry him?"

"I know what you mean. Oh, he being in the theater world and all they pretty girls running after him. Madame used to laugh about it, don't you remember?"

"And now the poor lady only just dead, and they come running."

"Hush . . ."

I had moved and a floorboard creaked. The conversation closed and Mrs. Manfred appeared, and without turning her head to look along the passage, went down the stairs.

I stood very still, waiting for her to reach the kitchen. Bridget was in one of the rooms to my left. I glanced at my watch. Fabian never liked eating before eight o'clock and there was still a quarter of an hour to go.

I leaned against the doorpost and examined my nails. Fabian

had decided very suddenly to spend the afternoon away from Jessamy, and a girl had called. Someone Mrs. Manfred didn't know, so it could not have been anyone from the village. But possibly the girl who had watched us from Gideon's Rock.

Bridget, sandy-haired and charmingly freckled, came toward me. "You been to Lorne Abbey, Miss Clair."

"Yes."

"My son be workin' there. He cuts the lawns."

"They were beautiful," I said.

She looked pleased. "Oh, he be a good lad, my son Charlie."

I stood aside for her to go into my room. As I went down the stairs I heard raised voices from behind the closed drawing-room doors, and although I couldn't hear what they were saying, I realized that Fabian and Dominick were having a row.

Not all the lights were turned on in the hall and it looked dark and peaceful. I paused momentarily on the stairs, uncertain whether to walk in on the two men or remain in the hall until they had fought it out.

While I still hesitated, I saw something move slightly. Mrs. Manfred was near the drawing-room door, pressed so flat against the paneling that she looked like a not very alluring figure painted on it.

She glanced up and saw me, and went swiftly, without a word, toward the kitchen. I thought, in that flash when our eyes met, I saw alarm on her face. But it could have been just the heavy shadows of the half-lit hall.

I walked as noisily as I could down the remaining stairs and across the hall. The angry voices ceased as my footsteps rang out, and when I opened the double doors the two men were standing with drinks in their hands as if they were old friends meeting on a warm September evening. The soft lights fell on Fabian's smooth dark hair and on the crisp quills of Dominick's corn-gold head.

"Ah, Stephanie." Fabian smiled at me and waved me to a chair.

Dominick was twirling his glass around and around, letting the light fall on the pale-green liquid of his favorite gin-and-lime. He was no actor, and when I looked more closely at him I saw the aftermath of anger on his face, shadowing it with a tension around the mouth and coldness in his eyes.

"A dry martini?"

"Please," I answered Fabian and sat down.

"Did you look out of your bedroom window? It was a lovely

night when we were on the terrace, wasn't it? Now the moon is even brighter. That's one topic the poets can no longer be romantic about—always provided that you consider modern poets romantic."

His self-possession was faultless, his cool reminder of our terrace wrangle outrageous. I took the small crystal glass from him and despised myself for warming to the smile he gave me.

> Where the apple reddens, never pry,
> Lest we lose our Edens, Eve and I.

The words were irrelevant, for my Eden was not here with Fabian. Yet while I drank my martini, the devil drove me into the dark dream of a tempting yet frightening impossibility.

The room was very quiet, and looking around, I saw that Fabian had left us.

Dominick got up and went to the French doors and flung them open. "Sometimes I can't breathe here. Do you mind?" He looked over his shoulder at me.

I felt the cool wind on my face. "I like it," I said and joined him. "After London, the air here is so clean and fresh."

"The air is one thing; the atmosphere generated by personality is quite another." He seemed to regret his quick retort and touched my hair. "It's wet at the ends," he said.

"I slid too far down in the bath. That's the trouble when small women lie in big baths." My voice was light, but I was remembering Fabian's fingers through my hair.

"Strange you're so fair," Dominick said, "when Livanova was so dark."

"My father was fair." My father . . . *But, Rachel, your father has dark-red hair like autumn beech leaves and he won't be pleased if he has to bail you out of prison for impersonation.*

"You have something of Livanova about you, though," Dominick was saying, "and something that, after the picture she painted of you, is very surprising."

"Is it?"

"Her spirit. It was wonderful, so proud and imperial."

"There's nothing imperial about me," I said.

"Oh, but there is. I think it's the way you walk and the poise of your head."

"Walking tall." I laughed. "It's a trick to fool people into thinking I've more inches than I have."

"And then . . ."

Fabian entered, cutting through whatever other pleasant compliment Dominick might have been handing me.

Tomorrow I would leave for London. I walked through the open door onto the terrace and watched black spears of tree branches being teased by the wind. I had never before lived in such grand surroundings, but my days at Jessamy had given me no love for the place. In spite of that, somewhere deep inside me was a curious feeling that once gone, I would look back on these days as a nostalgic memory, a sense of some marvelous possibility lost in a welter of fear and suspicion, a might-have-been destroyed by the need for masquerade.

Fabian's voice came from inside the room. ". . . damn fool, going to practice on that tin piano at the inn when you have the Bechstein here. I've told you . . ."

"You've told me and I've given you my answer," I heard Dominick say. "And I intend to continue with the tin piano, as you call it."

When I reentered the room, Dominick was not there, and he only reappeared when Mrs. Manfred rang the Tibetan bell for dinner.

She stood at the serving table, and as I passed, she raised her eyes and smiled at me. Listening at the door was probably a pastime of hers, working as she did in an isolated community where gossip was the bread and breath of life. I would have to guard myself against seeing suspicious actions where there were none. When she set before me the little dish of pink shrimps curled up in an avocado, I glanced up at her and wondered what her feelings were about the two men who lived at Jessamy.

After dinner Fabian left us to visit an old man who had been a choreographer at the time of Diaghilev and Nijinsky and now lived in seclusion in a cottage on the road to Broadmayne.

It crossed my mind that for a host, Fabian took supremely little trouble with his guest. It was likely that he thought Dominick, being nearer my age, would supply the entertainment for me, but it was far more likely that everything was planned to undermine my enjoyment. I was never to be quite certain what he would be doing or where he would be. It could even be that I was to be left alone in the house just to see what I would do, what rooms I would enter, what I would try to discover. And while I did so, thinking myself alone, someone perhaps was watching me.

XIX

DOMINICK AND I had coffee together, and on an impulse I asked him to play for me.

He said almost violently, "I'm sorry, but I can't. Not tonight. I want to get out of here. I want to walk. Come with me."

"Yes."

He left me to fetch his favorite turtleneck sweater, and as I waited, the quiet of the house beat around me and I felt a rising panic. It was as if the walls and furniture had eyes and were watching me, as if someone had appointed inanimate things to be my guards. I was poised for escape and yet I could not leave.

There was no sound of Dominick. I walked restlessly from room to room, and nowhere was there either sound or movement. I went through the swinging door into the kitchen, looking for

Mrs. Manfred. The room was as empty and as still as the others. It was large and the walls were pale yellow. The enamel pots and pans were neatly stacked on shelves; the working surfaces of the two tables were clear of everything except a bottle and yesterday's newspaper. The bottle was labeled *Blackthorn Cider* in large painstaking letters. So while we had our apéritifs in the drawing room, Mrs. Manfred had her little nip as she finished cooking.

I looked through the newspaper; the outside world on which it reported was utterly remote from my existence at Jessamy.

"Are you ready?"

I shot around. Dominick was at the kitchen door. "Oh, you startled me."

"I'm sorry, but I wondered where you had got to."

"I never seem to see the newspapers," I said lightly. "I just wondered if there was one around."

"Fabian gets three a day. He likes to read all the theater and art reviews. Today's are probably somewhere in his room. Why not ask him?"

"Oh no, I was just killing time waiting for you. It's not important. In a way it's rather pleasant not being harrowed by news," I said, knowing perfectly well that I would rather sit comfortably and read of other people's experiences than suffer the emotional strain of my own.

When Dominick asked me which way I would like to go, I chose the forest, wanting its stillness rather than the fret of the sea. We zigzagged between the trees, walking carefully because the chunky boles of the beeches were hazards for our feet. The moon scarcely penetrated the interlacing branches and we walked like shadows, not speaking and with an almost self-conscious distance between us, as if we were being careful to respect each other's living space.

In some strange way the sense of timelessness which I felt in the forest brought a new awareness of the man who walked with me. It was as if we were drawn together by escaping from the house where clocks beat away the moments of our lives. I had been aware of Dominick's aloneness ever since I came to Jessamy, but in the forest it took on a new dimension. He was no longer just a young man with magnificent looks and a fair talent. He was someone suddenly tossed out into a world that was heavily competitive; he had lost his job and also the roof over his head.

Two men had suddenly come into my life and both of them had aroused my emotions—one filled me with excitement; the other, with compassion. But I had nothing to fear, since in the morning I would be gone. I could have sung aloud with relief, and yet beneath it was an ache for something so nearly touched, so nearly experienced. Because I could not bear to analyze that deeper, more despairing emotion, I was grateful that Dominick broke the silence.

"You haven't said whether you received any more single chrysanthemums."

"No, just three—and then whoever sent them must have got tired of it. After all, if you're trying to impress someone or frighten her, and it has no effect, there isn't much use in continuing."

"Thank heaven for that."

I stepped cautiously over the tree roots and thought back over the days at Jessamy. The sending of the flowers had ceased, but immediately after had come the incident at the bog. The elementary witchcraft act had developed into the more sinister thing it had predicted. The game had ceased; the serious part had begun.

I felt Dominick touch my hand lightly. "I wish you could have come down here when your mother was alive. It's a tragedy that you and she seemed to have lost one another somehow on the way of your growing up. And now, as for me, now . . ."

"Now what?"

"It's all too late. Then I had great hopes for my own career. I no longer know where I'm going or what's in store for me. It's strange that when Fabian arrived, the lives of all of us changed."

"But his coming here wasn't what changed things for you. Livanova . . . my mother didn't die here, she died in London."

He moved a little away from me and his voice was strained, as if he hated what he was saying. "If they had really come together again after that long separation, Livanova would have stayed. She wasn't dancing that night."

"You think she gave him permission to work here because she wanted everything to be right again between them, but when they met at Jessamy, they quarreled again?"

"I don't know."

"But you were here. You must have seen, have heard."

"I left them alone. They spent most of the time in Livanova's sitting room upstairs, anyway."

"She must have told you how long she intended to stay."

"Oh, she never explained. She came and went like a bird, swift and light and graceful."

"I wonder whether the police are fairly certain they know what happened that night, but just can't prove anything?"

He hesitated before answering me, and I felt him turn my way as if trying to see my face. Then he said, "They are very thorough."

We had come to a slightly thinned-out part of the forest and I could barely make out the dim shape of a fallen tree in the silver light.

"Let's sit here," I said. "This new ballet, *The Witch and the Maiden*—did my mother talk to you about it?"

"Scarcely at all. She wrote that Fabian was to work on the costumes and sets for it, and that he was coming to Jessamy to get away from London and the endless meetings because he liked to work on the initial stages on his own."

"She didn't say 'We're friends again,' or anything like that to you?"

"Why should she? I was just her accompanist here."

"Perhaps"—I stared into the forest stillness—"she expected to be given the leading role."

He didn't answer me.

"She would be too old for it, though, wouldn't she?" I was being deliberately persistent.

"Oh, Livanova would never be too old for even the youngest parts. She could create youth where others who were young just looked it and that was all. Fabian Seal wouldn't dare refuse her if she had wanted the part of the Maiden."

I was unable to visualize Fabian capitulating to anyone, even to a great ballerina he had loved.

"She could have wanted the part badly. Fabian told me that everything about the ballet is going to be on the old grand classic scale—great music, great dancers, a glittering Covent Garden scene. So Mother probably asked Fabian here hoping she could persuade him to insist to the Company that she dance the leading role."

Dominick said unhappily, "It could be. But we'll never know now."

"There are so many cases that happened years ago where the police files have not been closed and never will be." I hugged my arms across my chest and looked up into the moon-blanched leaves of the beech trees. "Dominick, listen . . . just listen. It sounds awful, but I've got to talk to someone. You understand?"

"Of course."

I was grateful that he made no attempt to touch me, to lay a hand over mine, to make this a personal, emotional thing.

"Suppose Livanova— Oh, let me call her that, everyone does. Suppose she issued an ultimatum to Fabian sometime in London: 'If you will persuade the committee to let me dance the role of the Maiden, I will give you Jessamy Court.'"

"That's impossible. She would never—"

"Just for the moment imagine that it *is* possible. Suppose she actually did that, and then came down here and found that Miranda McCall was going to dance the leading role?"

"She wouldn't, she couldn't, sign away the house she adored."

"She adored her own immortality, her public image far more."

We sat in a rather terrible silence. The cold seemed to drift in from the sea and curl around the great trees, curl around me.

"Then suppose she had told Fabian she'd left the house to him in her will. Then discovered that the role of the Maiden was not for her and went back to London furiously angry, hurt . . ."

"But *not* suicidal," Dominick said fiercely. "She would never want to end her life."

I hadn't suggested that, either, but I stayed silent.

It was curious and dreadful sitting in that silvered clearing and seeing Fabian everywhere. I felt as if I were the devil's advocate, arguing his destruction.

This was what I had come to Jessamy for, but every word I uttered and every supposition I made was a betrayal of my own essence where Fabian, the man, the mountaineer and the artist, had taken root.

"There *was* one thing," Dominick said. "That afternoon the drawing-room door was open, and as I came across the hall I heard Miranda McCall's name."

"Livanova talking?"

"No, Fabian. I heard him say something that ran like this: 'She's like Taglioni, whom neither you nor I are old enough to have seen. But McCall can do what she did, and what Nijinsky did. She has the power of appearing to hover at the top of a leap.' Livanova said, 'That's just a trick,' and Fabian answered her, 'I know. It has to do with breath control. But the public love it. And a bewitched girl needs that trick.' That's all, because then they saw me. But it didn't sound as if they were quarreling."

Because Livanova had already seen Dominick and had too much pride to parade her anger and humiliation in front of him.

McCall can float, and you can't, Tatiana Livanova . . .

"If only I could get away," Dominick cried. "I'm living at the moment on Fabian's charity."

"You're so wrong. This is still my mother's house. It takes a long time to probate a will."

"That's only the legal side. Fabian knows—everyone knows—that the house is his."

I frowned into the night and heard myself ask a question I hadn't even been aware I was formulating. "What is it that hangs over Jessamy?"

Dominick made no attempt to pretend he didn't understand. "Fear," he said without hesitation.

"That sounds very melodramatic."

"Oh, I don't mean someone's walking around with a dagger in their hands or that there's a ghost in the attic. It's a kind of climate, an aura, if you like."

"What kind of fear?"

"I don't know. But sometimes thoughts can create an ambience for good or evil."

"Or we could both be letting the 'bell, book and candle' of Fabian's work influence us. That, and the fact that a supposed witch lives almost on the doorstep."

"If it were just that, one could laugh at it."

"Can't you?"

"Can *you?*"

"No," I said, "but then, all old houses must have strong atmospheres. So much has happened in them: life and death and all the things in between."

"There was atmosphere when Livanova lived here, but it was so different. Then it was a kind of scent of greatness. Now—Oh, don't let's talk about it. I wonder"—he looked at me steadily—"if you regret coming?"

"You mean . . . ?" I broke off, waiting, letting Dominick explain.

"Coming to the house that should have been yours?"

We had started to walk again, and I said lightly, "Oh, I don't want Jessamy." I sounded completely uninvolved, momentarily throwing of my identification with Stephanie. I was myself, Rachel Fleming, walking between the dark beech trees with a man I liked and flattered that he liked me. I even gave a casual thought to the fact that Stephanie would have said the same thing. But I

191

realized I was wrong in thinking that. Of course she would want the house, for the estate would bring a great deal of money on the market.

In the meantime I had no idea where Stephanie was. The fact that I had not yet been denounced seemed to indicate that as she had told Louise, she was actually in hiding. If that were so, I was temporarily safe from recognition, but I remained in danger from whatever it was that threatened Stephanie.

The old cliché about the tangled web of deceit certainly applied to me, and the enclosing darkness made it very tempting, as it had done once before, to tell Dominick the truth. It would be a tremendous relief to be Rachel Fleming to him. But before I could find the courage, he said, "Would you like to go to Dorchester tomorrow? I'm afraid you'd have to use your car, but I could show you round. It's very historic."

"I'd have liked that, but I shan't be here; I'm leaving in the morning. I thought I'd make an early start before the traffic gets too heavy."

"Have you told Fabian?"

"Not yet." *Not until the very last moment, when there will be no time to stop me.*

"I think he expected a longer stay."

"I know he did."

Dominick swung around on me. "Stephanie, don't." He seized my wrists. "Don't leave me."

"But I must go sometime."

"Stay a little while longer. I had a letter this morning from my London agent about the ensemble. They haven't replaced their pianist yet, and if I'm lucky, I'll be wanted almost at once. If you could wait, we could go to London together." His eyes caught a glint of the capricious moonlight. They were pleading with me.

Somewhere near us leaves rustled. I looked up and could feel no wind. It could, of course, be some small wild thing creeping through the night in search of food.

"Will you wait?"

I should have been able to say, "I'll give you my address, my telephone number. We'll meet." But I couldn't.

He misunderstood my silence. "You think that all I feel is just that you are a link with Livanova. That's it, isn't it? But it's not so. There's a kind of alchemy that draws two people together. You and I . . ."

I am Rachel Fleming.

But I couldn't say it.

The forest night glimmered and the rustling began again. I looked up, but the branches on the trees didn't move. There was no wind, and a rabbit or a hare would be too wild and shy to stay around where we walked. Someone was near us in the blackness, their feet brushing the undergrowth.

The children, perhaps. Robin and Lucy, inquisitive as monkeys, or Hobbin looking for hemlock or belladonna for a spell no one wanted. Or Mrs. Manfred taking the air for half an hour. Or Fabian . . .

"Listen," Dominick said and laid a hand on my arm.

We stood as still as the dark columns of the trees around us, and I could hear my heart thudding as if I had been running hard.

Dominick said, "I've a feeling that we haven't been alone. If we want to talk, we'll be safer in the house. At least we'd know if anyone was around. Let's go back."

I turned obediently, stumbled against the bole of a great tree and was flung at Dominick. He steadied me, pulled me close and said, "Don't go back to London, please . . . at least, not yet."

"I must." *Because, my dear Dominick, I like my life too much to lose it by bravado.*

He put a hand across my shoulders, but I pulled away from him and walked on.

"If you go in that direction," he said, "you'll get hopelessly lost. There are miles of forest that stretch from here to Avon Hill. Only the deer would find you."

"How do you know the way back to Jessamy?"

He jerked his head upward. "By the direction of the moon. Hobbin taught me that when I first came here. I went for a walk one night and lost my way and ended up hours later near her cottage. She taught me the lore of navigating my feet by the moon's direction in its various quarters."

"Then which way do we go?"

"Turn left," he said and propelled me through a forest clearing and into the denseness of the trees again.

"Do you know Hobbin well?"

"No," he said and took my hand lightly, as if we were children. "And I don't particularly want to. I saw the effect she had on Livanova."

"My *mother?*"

"Oh, she was very superstitious, though she never went in for things like spells. But she always consulted Hobbin before a new season started here or in Paris, or wherever she was to dance."

"But Hobbin didn't tell her that she would die alone in her London apartment."

"Who knows what she said to her? But if she did, I'm sure that was one thing your mother would never have believed. The public had willed her to be immortal and she thought she was. I'm sure that the cards or numbers or whatever Hobbin uses can't tell anyone what's going to happen to them."

Star-crossed Hobbin had said to me and touched my forehead. And, dear God, star-crossed was what I seemed to be.

"Fabian believes in certain magic," I said.

"Magic . . . sorcery . . . all that sort of thing?" he said. "Oh no, that isn't what Fabian believes in. His brand of magic is . . ." He stopped and was silent for too long.

"Is what?" I urged.

"Correctly channeled energy, that's how he put it to me once. A subconscious force made conscious and used in whatever way is wanted. I've heard that it can be deadly."

"You're being very extravagant with words. *Deadly?*"

"It can manipulate. You can't understand, can you? I can't, either. But I believe it works. One evening when Livanova was in a depressed mood, she said to me, 'Fabian is my dark fate. He doesn't have to speak. He can make me do exactly as he wants.' She was such a powerful person, but I remember, also, how she said only once had a man ever dominated her, and somehow I knew she was speaking of Fabian. We used to have long talks, too, about magic. She believed in it."

"But you don't," I said. "Dominick, you couldn't. Not in these realistic days."

He said, "I never did until I came here to Jessamy. But it's not something you can convince others about, and you're a skeptic, aren't you?"

"I have yet to be convinced," I said and didn't add that I was very afraid that I might be.

He stopped again and turned to me. "Shall I really tell you why I want you to stay down here until I can come back with you?"

"I thought it might be because you liked my company."

The lightness of my words didn't touch him. "It's that, of course. But because of that, I'm anxious for you. I want you to be where I can keep an eye on you. It has to be here for the moment, because for a year and a half Jessamy has been my home and I've accumulated quite a lot of stuff. I can't just walk out with one suitcase; I must clear everything I possess. When I actually leave, a friend in Dorchester has promised to store my things until I can have them in London. It's not much, really, just some pieces of Victoriana I rather like, and some books. Stay with me until I've made those arrangements—I hope it'll only be a few days—and then we'll go back together to London."

Whatever the odds against being safe in a huge, indifferent city, London was my home and familiarity bred a sense of security. I turned my face away from the intense pleading I knew must be in Dominick's eyes. The trees were thick where we now walked and we were heavily shadowed.

"Let's not talk any more now," I said and kept stumbling in the thick darkness over the great tree roots. Each time Dominick steadied me I felt his hands tremble. I understood how he must feel—anxious and alone and suddenly without security.

His need for attachment reached out to me. The emotion someone had called "a profound and dangerous pity" was growing stronger, but the fact remained that I could not be of any use to him, for in my state of masquerade, I was in my way as helpless as he was in his.

As if by silent agreement, we changed the conversation. We spoke impersonally, wondering how old the trees were and what birds slept with folded feathers above us and whether predatory owls were watching us.

As we came out of the forest I said, "Perhaps it was Hobbin we heard back there in the woods."

"Perhaps," he said, sounding unconvinced.

That night as I lay in bed I heard Fabian come up the stairs, listened to his quick, uneven footsteps, then the closing of a door, audible only because the world around the house was so still.

I had no idea of time. But like the mysterious, unknown moment when sleep comes, so I had no idea when the truth hit me that I was in love with Fabian Seal. For a while I accepted it and felt that because I was leaving Jessamy and would never see him again, the scar was neither deep nor permanent. I had been in love before; I would love again. All emotion needed to be fed and this was one I intended to starve. As I swung in the twilight world between waking and sleeping, I repeated to myself all the shades of meaning that people called love: affection, devotion, passion, infatuation. None of them fitted what I felt for Fabian.

Restless, I heaved myself up in bed. I hadn't closed the curtains properly and the nearly full moon shone on me. I saw my reflection in the dressing-table mirror. My skin was turned to silver in the moonlight and my hair looked as pale as pearls. The moon had transformed me into something far more ethereal, far more enchanting than I, Rachel Fleming, had ever been or would ever again be. And half stupefied by sleep, I wished that Fabian would walk in and see me, unreal and alluring by a trick of the moon.

I turned and hid my face in the pillow. It was human to wish some man to see you at your best but that reflection of myself in the mirror was no more real than a mirage.

I leaned up and thumped the pillow. So far as Fabian was concerned, the essential moment would never come. To feel this kind of emotion for someone who was not trusted was like mixing a love potion for Beelzebub. I said to myself, "It's all this damned hocus-pocus magic," and went to sleep on the thought.

XX

I WAS BREAKFASTING in my room the following morning when I heard the Bentley start up and purr down the drive. I rushed to the window and watched it disappear around a curve in the avenue of limes. I finished breakfast quickly, dressed and then went in search of Mrs. Manfred.

She was coming out of Livanova's suite.

"Good morning. That was Mr. Seal's car I saw drive away."

She nodded. "That's right. He said I were to tell you that he'd be out for some time—maybe all morning and part of the afternoon, since when there are meetings to do with county affairs, he lunches at Lys Manor."

The sense of hours of relief from the strain of the last few days decided me against rushing away. I would go in search of the children. Somewhere there was a tape with voices on it. But there would be no time to make a long search. In order to be absolutely safe from the risk of Fabian's returning too soon, I would give myself only an hour. Then, whether I found the children or not, I would leave. It was a coward's way, but it was also my only escape from a predicament that was now out of hand.

One thing troubled me. I would have liked to have explained to Dominick. After our walk together the previous night, I knew that he believed I would remain at Jessamy until he was ready to leave. I hadn't actually promised that, but I had left a kind of assenting silence on the air after he had suggested it. He would be disappointed and perhaps a little hurt, but the truth would affect him even more deeply.

So far the gods—whoever the gods were—had watched over me. But I couldn't reasonably expect their constant surveillance; I had to make efforts to safeguard myself.

The fact that Fabian had not knocked on my door and called to me before he left was a small point. It was characteristic of him that he should come and go as he chose, his own master, his own motivater.

I packed quickly, moving as quietly as I could, waiting for Dominick to leave for the village and the piano at Black Agnes. With Fabian away, it was just possible that he would practice that morning at Jessamy, in which case I would have to make certain that the music was being played fortissimo when I crept out of the house.

I was folding a dress when Dominick knocked on my door and called, "I thought I'd just tell you, I'm going to the village. But I won't be long."

I opened the door a few inches, holding it so that he wouldn't see my open suitcase on the carved chest near the window.

"We'll meet later," he said, and I bade him goodbye with a tinge of regret that I would never see him again.

I went to the window and watched him take the short cut across Ellen's Heath. He had a firm walk, and as his figure diminished into the distance, he seemed as lonely as the landscape. I opened the window and leaned out, shivering a little. The scene had the unreal beauty of an English September morning. My immediate world of lawns and trees and the glimpse of the sea was like a reflection seen in a misted mirror—ivory and gold. It had probably been raining in the night or else the dew was heavy, for there were bright splinters of water on the leaves of the nearest trees and minute pools lay like disks of silver on the path below my window. It was all so still: mist-wreathed and haunted.

I heard Mrs. Manfred's footsteps outside the door and turned quickly away from the window to stop her coming into the room for my breakfast tray. My toe caught the corner of the white goatskin rug and I fell with a thud and slithered across the parquet floor.

"Miss Clair . . ."

"I'm all right."

But my words were muffled by the sound of the door opening. I had picked myself up as Mrs. Manfred dashed in, and was standing quite steadily on my two feet. Her eyes wandered to the open suitcase.

"I caught my toe in the rug," I said.

She ignored my explanation. "You are packing?"

"Yes, I have to leave for London this morning."

"Does Mr. Seal know?"

"No."

"But you can't go like that. I mean—"

"I know what you mean, Mrs. Manfred, and I'm sorry, but since Mr. Seal isn't around, I can't tell him, can I?"

"You could get him at Lys Manor."

"No . . . oh no."

"He'll be very angry. He knows that I could find Lord Homer's telephone number."

I said quickly, "He'll only be angry with me for what he will see as my lack of courtesy. He couldn't possibly be angry with you, so don't worry. I'll explain in my note to him."

She said coldly, "Surely you could wait until he comes back?"

"I don't know how long he'll be gone."

"Some hours," she said.

"Then I can't wait. It's a long drive to London. As I've said, I'll leave a letter for him."

"It's not the same."

It wasn't, but I didn't need her to tell me. Nor did I relish the way she looked around the room as if I had corrupted it. She had always been polite to me, always considerate, but I had never believed that she liked me, and I knew why.

"I'm disappointing you, aren't I, Mrs. Manfred? I'm sorry I'm not more like . . . Livanova. That's what you hoped, isn't it? Because you were so fond of her."

"She was wonderful." She crossed the room and picked up the breakfast tray. Then she set it down again and looked at me across the huge bed. "You call her Livanova?"

"Yes, but then, everyone did."

"*He* didn't."

"Who?"

"Mr. Seal. He called her by her Christian name because he loved her. I called my mother Mum because I loved her. You call yours . . ."

"Mrs. Manfred," I said firmly, "I'm sorry if the word—or rather, the name I use—offends you, but I can't argue about it."

It was as if now that she knew I was leaving and she would never see me again, she felt she no longer needed to hide her feelings. Her eyes tried to outstare me and then looked away. "What am I to tell him?" she demanded.

"I'll explain it all and you don't have to worry. I shall point out that I have to go back to my own life, and anyway, I know he didn't expect me to stay for long." Suddenly, on an impulse, I asked, "Why did he invite me here, Mrs. Manfred?"

The immobility of her expression had vanished. She looked angry and distressed. "Because"—she swallowed twice—"because he wanted to meet you . . . naturally."

I would have liked to point out that there was nothing natural about Fabian Seal, that he was as devious as a labyrinth. Instead, I gave up the argument. She had no intention of discussing Fabian with me.

"If you should want any help, Miss Clair."

"Thank you, no."

The door closed behind her.

When I had finished my packing, I went to the little carved mahogany desk and wrote a letter to Fabian.

> Please forgive me for leaving this way, but I am anxious to get back to London and you drove off before I came downstairs and could explain. This is a very beautiful part of Dorset and I am so very glad to have seen it.
>
> Thank you for your hospitality,
>
> Yours,
>
> Stephanie

I put a postscript:

> I am sure *The Witch and the Maiden* will be very successful. I shall try to go and see it.

As soon as I had sealed the letter and written his name on the envelope, I had second thoughts. I ripped it open, unfolded the sheet of notepaper and stared at the handwriting. Mine, not Stephanie's.

I went downstairs, found the small back room where I had seen the typewriter, and pulled off the cover of the machine. Notepaper was in a top drawer, and the address in dark red on gray paper took me back to the afternoon when, standing by Stephanie's bed, I had read Fabian Seal's invitation.

I typed out what I had already written by hand, my ear trained toward the door in case Mrs. Manfred or Bridget should pass by and see me, although the sight of my using a typewriter in full view of anyone who might pass had such an innocence about it that I was quite certain no one would think it odd.

I signed the letter with a scrawl of a signature, as like Stephanie's as I could manage, and sealed the envelope. The discarded letter I tore up and put in my purse. Then I put the sealed envelope on the side table between the two terrace windows in the drawing room and secured it with a silver paper knife. I had slipped some money in another envelope and left it in my bedroom, with a message to Mrs. Manfred to buy herself something she really wanted and thanking her for all she had done for me. A personal leave-taking was beyond me and I was equally certain that she had no desire to take my hand and wish me well. To her, I was Livanova's bitter daughter.

If I could have stood outside myself and watched as I crept down to the hall with my suitcase bumping against each stair, I would have seen it as something out of an old-style comedy. But I was in no mood to be amused.

I put my suitcase in the trunk of the car, and since the morning was fairly warm, flung my coat across the passenger seat. I was ready to slip behind the wheel and drive off as soon as I wished.

But first I would try and find the children. I crossed the corner of the Heath and entered the forest, making for Hobbin's cottage. No sounds came through the open door. Robin and Lucy's playground was not there, where a witch's eye could watch them.

I kept calling them, but the only answer I received was from a solitary bird high in the trees. I even went around the side to the tangle of laurels that led to their secret room, calling them softly, luring them with the promise of the chocolate still in my purse. "I have something I want to give you." But they were either not there, or not to be drawn.

I turned away, and walking under the archways of the trees, I remembered what Fabian had said about not losing anything in the forest because I would never find it again. Searching for the children proved his point. For in all my walks there, I had never found a path and the massive blue-gray trunks that were made almost luminous in the filtering half-light had no distinguishing features. Once again I saw in the distance the red deer, and once again they caught the scent of man before I could get close to them. They faded swiftly into the background like shadows on a golden screen, and I was alone again.

I kept looking at my wristwatch, knowing that I needed to be well away from Jessamy by the time Fabian returned. Then, just when I had decided to give up the search for the children and go home, I saw them.

I stepped behind a tree and watched. Lucy's hair fell over her left shoulder, hiding all except the angular profile. She was kneeling on a bank, her shoes kicked off, her bare feet tucked into the long grass. Robin's skinny little body was curled up beside her. He had made himself into a ball like a hedgehog and his chin was on his hands, his face rapt.

They were both quiet and very absorbed, and watching them, I realized that I had never heard them shout or even laugh aloud. It was not the quiet of perfect behavior but of secrecy, of existing in a world separated from that around them.

I moved out of hiding, and as I drew nearer I saw that they were crouched over some plaything that lay on the bank between them. Then, with their strong animal sensitivity, they became aware of me before they could possibly have heard my footsteps. Their heads shot up simultaneously and they listened, as the red deer had listened, alert and very still. Robin looked over his shoulder and saw me.

His reaction was complete indifference. He turned back to whatever was absorbing them, and as I approached and stood over them I saw that they had a pack of playing cards so dirty that the designs were scarcely recognizable, the hearts and diamonds almost as black as the spades and the clubs.

On a large sheet of crumpled brown paper the children had drawn circles, and in the center, much as the five of spades had lain in the twelve circles in Hobbin's cottage, was a torn and badly stained seven of diamonds.

"Are you telling each other's fortunes?"

"No, we be learning."

"Learning?"

The boy traced one of the circles with a forefinger. "It be our Great-Granny's own spell, but she was awful old and she died and we be trying to remember how she said it goes."

"And you know?"

He looked at his sister. "What I forgot she remembers, but she don't remember all."

"You think that between you, you've got it right?"

He nodded.

"What is the spell?"

He sat back on the bank and looked at me, his eyes taking on the reflection of the russet leaves above his head. "If we tell what we be doing, it don't be a spell."

"Oh, I see. But you could just tell me one thing, whether it's good or evil."

"That be just it. Great-Granny knew how to turn a bad spell into good."

"Just with cards."

He produced a sprig of a tired and drooping plant from his pocket. "It be thyme. We have to do things with this too. But we can't with you watching us."

"I'm sorry. But do tell me, is this spell to be put on someone you know?"

"Yes."

I wanted to ask "Who?" but I knew perfectly well they wouldn't tell me. Someone hated at their school perhaps, or a disliked relative. It was useless to conjecture. I said, "I was wondering what had happened to that reel you had on your tape recorder."

His eyes swiveled to avoid mine. Lucy shook back her hair and swung around on her thin little bottom so that her back was to me.

"The tape," I insisted. "What happened to it?"

"I dunno."

"Oh, I think you do. You can't have lost it, since it was so important to you that you ran off with it before I could play it over again."

"It be mine . . . ours," he amended, glancing at Lucy.

"I know, and I don't want to take it from you. I would just like to hear it again, that's all. You see, I think I know whose voice you had picked up on it—probably by accident." It was a half-truth, after all.

"It be no good now."

"What do you mean no good?"

"Fenney says it be all wiped out, the things on it, I mean."

"Fenney?"

Robin twisted himself around so that he sat cross-legged on the bank, his long mouth curved into a secret smile. There was a kind of innocent superiority about him. His none too clean brown shirt and shorts blended so completely with the background that if he had a flute in his hands and cloven hoofs, he could have modeled for Pan.

The silence curled about us without even a bird's song to break it. Lucy had found an insect and was teasing it with a blade of grass; Robin looked up into the branches of the beech above them, watching something I couldn't see.

"Fenney?" I asked again. "How does he know anything about the tape recorder?"

"Oh, we didn't know how to use it nor how to put the round things back."

"The reels," I offered.

He ignored me. "So we asked Fenney. He knows everything about everything."

"So Fenney has your tape recorder."

Robin nodded. "He be mending it for us."

"It wasn't broken."

"He said it were. And then he be going to show us how to use it."

"Why did you run away when I wanted to hear the first part of that tape?"

"It be ours, not yours."

"I know, but I only wanted to listen. And you did ask me into your special room to help, didn't you?"

"Lucy said I shouldn't have. Secrets should be secrets, and you bain't of us."

"Able to do magic, you mean?"

"Fenney don't know nothing that way, either, but he be clever putting things together and making things grow. He talks to the flowers."

204

"Does he? And where does he live?"

He pointed diagonally. "Down there by the water."

By the stream that fed the River Brit.

"I think I'll walk over and see him," I said.

Neither of the children showed any interest.

"Is it far?"

"Dunno," Robin said unhelpfully, and then said something that was like a foreign language to me.

"What was that?"

His long mouth grinned. "I be talking real Dorset then. They don't like it at school."

"Will you translate it for me?"

He said, "No. 'Tis a secret when I talk that way."

He had defeated me, he and his indifferent, suntanned sister. I said goodbye and went off in the directon of Fenney's cottage. I was quite certain that like his grandmother, Robin imparted knowledge in an obtruse way. Hobbin had been poetic. "Follow the west wind" she had advised and I had interpreted it correctly. But Robin had intended his strong dialect to be unintelligible to me, and he had succeeded. He had spoken either in a mood of mischievousness or showing-off. I tried to make sense of it as I walked off in the direction of Fenney's cottage. It had sounded like "not as far as the crows can fly."

I found Fenney's cottage more by luck than by Robin's casual pointing hand. A patch of crimson and yellow drew me, and nearing it, I saw behind the dahlias and sunflowers a cottage even smaller than Mrs. Hobbin's. It stood by the stream, and the tiny garden path led to the lane down which anyone from Jessamy had to go to reach the village. I wondered how far the cottage was from the bog.

Fenney was doing something to his bicycle, which was propped up against the gray stone wall of the house.

I called "Good morning" and he looked up, jerking his bushy eyebrows; he seemed formidable until I looked at his eyes and saw that they were kind.

"Do 'ee come with a message from the master?"

The master. Fabian . . .

"No. Robin told me you were mending a tape recorder he had."

"That be right. It be a good little thing once it works."

"What's wrong with it?"

"Those two," he said. "They played around with it and broke it. But 'tis easily mended when I got time."

"There was a used tape already on it."

He shook his head. "There weren't nothing on that tape, and it be so messed around, missy, all twisted, that I couldn't do nothing with it. I be going into Dulverley and I be getting them another. They give me the money. Don't knows where they gets it from, and being them, they don't tell."

"Services rendered to someone," I murmured.

He didn't quite catch what I said and cupped a hand to his ear.

"I just thought they might have earned the money running messages for someone."

He made a sound rather like the hoot of an owl, and his weather-beaten face creased into a mass of little grinning lines. "They run messages? Why, they be as proud as the deer in the forest, they two."

I looked around. "Your flowers are lovely. It's a pity they don't have any at Jessamy Court."

"Oh, Madame Livanova never wanted flowers. She liked green, green all round. She even said she'd have the maple cut down, but I said, 'You does that, my lady, and much as I would kneel at your feet, I wouldn't cut another blade of grass for 'ee.' And so, she never cut it down."

"Your chrysanthemums are fine."

"Aye, and someone else had the same idea, missy. They picked some, they did. Don't know who, but I stopped that. I wrote big letters on some cardboard and stuck it on a pole in the middle of the chrysanth bed. It said: *I'm watching you. So don't pick my flowers.* It stopped 'em, missy. It did an' all."

And that could have been the reason why I received no more. That, or the other reason I had already decided on, that someone knew I had got the message and so had moved on to the more dangerous game.

His shrewd, narrow eyes watched me. He had bicycle clips in his hand. "I be just going to Jessamy," he said.

"That's all right, I won't keep you. But tell me one thing. When the children brought the tape recorder to you, did you play the used tape at all?"

He shook his head. "I tried, but it weren't no use. It were torn off the reel."

"You didn't hear any words?"

"No."

"Thank you," I said and left him.

The way back was easy. All I had to do was follow the tawny line of ferns that ran alongside the bushes that bordered the lane. It had taken me half an hour to find the children and Fenney's cottage, and I had achieved nothing.

I had a very fair sense of direction, and soon I came to a deep curve in the hedge that seemed similar to the one where the light in the lane had waved me to a stop and I had found the bog.

It was daylight and I felt no fear, only a curiosity to see what the place looked like. It was safe to walk where the trees grew. But when I came to the end of their line, I stepped cautiously toward the lane that was hidden on the far side of the hedge. The bog was somewhere between myself and the hedge, and I was certain of the place when I came to where the curled brown fern fronds drooped limply and the ground squelched a little beneath my feet. The bushes in front of me must have only the thinnest foothold and the bog would be on the other side. I parted the bushes carefully and looked through.

It lay quiet enough and the daylight found no reflection in the patches of blackish water. The tiny hillocks, the children's Little Purple Men, were gray-green and I supposed that only some unknown summer flower gave them their name. The bog was small and made a ragged circle, the edges merging with the bushes. It was a dark place, sinister to me because I knew what had so nearly happened there. It had a strange smell, not, as I would have expected, of rotting vegetation but faintly apple-scented.

I moved away from it, and keeping near the invisible line of the lane behind the hedge, found my way back to Jessamy.

Mrs. Manfred came riding a bicycle down the lime avenue, and I realized that until then I had given no thought as to how she went to and from the village. I drew back into a thicket of rhododendrons as she approached; there was nothing more we had to say to each other.

I left the curved gravel drive and took the short cut across the lawn to the garage. The house stood in the morning light, the sun on its old golden stone, its gables like the three points of a crown against the hyacinth sky. The leaves of the creeper that twined around the slender pillars supporting the terrace roof had not yet turned their autumn red.

Tatiana Livanova was right. There was nothing quite so beautiful or so restful as a green garden. The fact that there was no silence that morning did not detract from the serenity, because the sounds were high and far away, made by the herring gulls and the rooks in the tall trees.

I would never see Fabian Seal again. The thought should have made me glad; I should have been able to sing with relief that whatever lay behind the things that had happened to me—and heaven knew whether they were curious accidents or whether someone had made deliberate attempts on my life—I was safe. And strong, and young and happy.

Happy. The word seemed to catch in my throat as though I had tried to speak it aloud. I knew perfectly well that when I returned to London, I would have to make an effort at something that had previously been effortless. I was going to have to work at happiness, and to live as if Fabian Seal had existed in some troubled and nostalgic dream. The only way to peace of mind, until time itself quieted the memory, was to forget him. Heaven help me. He was the one unforgettable man . . .

I went past the garage and the silver birches to the strip of wasteland before the gentle landside of Gideon's Rock. Sea-lavender and sea-pink clung to the few stony outcrops. And at the foot of the cliff, walking head down, clutching straggling tendrils of some green plant, was Mrs. Hobbin.

Like the children, she knew I was there before she could possibly have heard me, and turned. I had never before seen her in the clear light, and now, free of the shadows of the great beeches, I felt the tremendous radiation of her vitality. The forest had subdued it, but out here in the open country, it was like part of the bright aura of the day.

"I'm going back to London this morning, Mrs. Hobbin."

She nodded approval. "So you listen to what I tell you. That be good; 'tis wisdom to listen to the warnings of them as knows." She held up the flagging green leaves. "I be gathering wild herbs."

"Mrs. Hobbin, those voices you said you heard—"

She stiffened. "They be no concern of yours, missy."

"I have a feeling that you heard actual voices."

"Of course I did. I told you. It be something special given to all our family and it grows stronger as we gets older. My granny were ninety when she heard voices of some as lived a thousand years ago."

"What I'm trying to say, Mrs. Hobbin, is that actual living people were speaking." I watched an expression of angry pride cross her face. "I'm sure you have wonderful gifts, wonderful knowledge, but when you heard voices in the forest they were on a tape recorder. You know what that is, don't you?"

"Of course I do. There's one at the mill, where I work on days. But them voices were real, I tell you. Voices talking to *me*."

"Of course it's possible. But I'm just suggesting it's more likely you could have heard a tape being played."

She gave me a dark, scornful look. "As if I'd have one of them. It'ud be like me having a piano." She shook her head slowly and her rich black hair slipped from its coil. "I *know* voices tell me things. It's just that I don't yet understand what they say. It takes a long time to learn the way 'they' talk to you."

" 'They,' " I said, "could be voices distorted on a bad tape recording."

I saw the way her eyes darted among the grasses and the nettles, more intent on searching for herbs than trying to prove her witch's power to a skeptic like me. But the slightest hint, the most unconsidered remark that could give me a clue to the voice on the tape, was important. I would never tell of the children's secret room, but it was more than likely that sooner or later Hobbin would find out about the tape recorder, and by telling her, I was merely precipitating what was inevitable.

"The children . . ."

Suspicion burned in her eyes. "What about them?"

"They have a tape recorder."

"That they haven't. Where'ud they get the money for one? I'd like to know that, missy."

"They could earn it by running errands."

"Them?" Her raucous laughter rang out, mingling with the fretted cries of the gulls.

"I have a feeling that the children could have left the tape somewhere near your cottage," I persisted, "and could have accidentally picked up two people's voices."

"You be quite wrong, missy. It weren't like that at all. The voices were voices *for me, missy. For me* . . ."

"Very well, if you think so." I turned to leave her, and she raised her voice.

"Where did they get that tape thing from?"

"Mrs. Hobbin," I said as clearly and calmly as I could, "it was necessary for me to tell you about the tape recorder. I had to find out whether the voice *I* heard on it was, perhaps, one of the ones you heard. But if the children have something you don't know about, please let them be. I'm quite certain they earned the money honestly. It's a very old machine, and children enjoy their secrets. Please don't ask them about it."

She laughed at me. "And you think they'd say anything if they didn't want to? I tell you, missy, I talk a lot about boxing their ears, but I wouldn't never do it. They have their own ways of paying people back." She paused and looked at me speculatively. "What did you hear the voices saying?"

"Only one voice, Mrs. Hobbin. It was a woman's, and she said, 'It's gone too far. Jessamy . . .' Did you hear that?"

She said cautiously, "They be voices, a man's and a woman's."

"And they said . . . ?"

She looked over my head, her eyes dreamy. "They don't be human, missy. They tell me things and one day I'll understand."

"The voices, Mrs. Hobbin, *the voices.*"

She gave a nod of resignation. "The woman said something like you say."

"And the man's?"

"I don't know—"

"What did he say?"

"It did sound like he said 'Go away, Go away' over and over again. I know it were a message for me to tell someone to go away."

"Who were they, Mrs. Hobbin?"

"They never tell us who they be. You see, missy, folks don't know anything about us. Witches don't *look* into the future; they try to change what's there. Maybe the voices were telling me how to change things for you. Could be because of you that the voices came to me."

Realism was warring with witchcraft. She would never understand, and I gave a tentative thought to the fact that perhaps I wouldn't, either.

One small piece had fitted into the puzzle. The woman on the tape had been talking to a man and the man had told her to go away. I couldn't see how it helped, and I left Hobbin to search for herbs and walked back to the house.

The car stood there, hood pointing outward, and it would be the easiest possible thing to get in and drive away and never even glance back in the rear mirror for a last glimpse of the golden brick house.

But the easiest thing didn't happen, for the car wouldn't start. I coaxed and bullied, began by being patient, because it had been running so well that I was certain there was nothing really wrong. Then I became irritated, and that didn't help, either.

I got out, opened the hood and looked inside. But it was a completely futile act, for I knew almost nothing about the mechanics of an engine.

Fenney was cycling up the drive. I waited until he had parked his bicycle by the wall that enclosed the small kitchen garden, and then I went to him.

"My car won't start and I don't know why. Could you help me, please?"

"There be petrol?"

"Yes, plenty."

"I don't know much about cars, miss. But I'll have a look for you." He came over, ducked his head and peered at the engine, muttering to himself. He said at last, "I think you'd best call the garage and get Bob Hopkins out to have a look."

I ran indoors to the telephone, and Bob Hopkins, who owned the garage, said, "I'll be over and have a look at it straightaway."

"Thank you."

There was the first touch of autumn chill in the air, and I sat on the wooden seat in the shelter of the wall, hugging my coat around me, feeling my whole body taut for sudden flight. And that, above all else, was what I wanted . . . what had to be.

The minutes before Bob Hopkins arrived seemed interminable. My throat felt dry and I longed for coffee, but I wanted to ask no favors in a house from which I was escaping, cowardlike, with a note left on a table and a suitcase smuggled out.

I was alone and outwardly quiet, but despair still weighed against my relief at leaving Jessamy. I closed my eyes and saw Fabian. Now that I was free of him, I could crush suspicion and let my mind circle around the Fabian who excited and amazed me. The many-gifted man with his agile, paradoxical mind, at once clear-cut and devious, both deprecating and mocking toward me; the atmosphere he created when he entered a room, making everyone else seem insignificant when measured against this not very tall and certainly not handsome man. His magnetism was something I did not understand any more than I understood his belief in magic—if, indeed, he did believe in it. As I sat in the cool sunshine, I wondered whether it was a pretense, a ruse, to alarm me. A sophisticated man telling me that he believed magic existed, that there were powers in some people beyond the normal: powers that could be good, powers that could destroy in revenge.

His image hurt too much and I opened my eyes. *His* lawn lay before me, *his* avenue of limes, *his* single blazing maple.

A car was coming down the lane. I sat up, tense and listening, and when it came into sight, I saw with dismay that Bob Hopkins had brought a break-down van. Fenney, too, had heard it and was crossing the lawn.

"Don't know what's wrong," he said to Bob Hopkins. "Don't know much about cars, anyway."

"Well, we'll see, shall we?" Head and arms disappeared under the bonnet. "Well, I'm damned!" He emerged again. "Someone has removed the rotor arm, so of course it won't start."

"But nobody would . . ." I looked from him to Fenney.

"Maybe it be them children."

"They wouldn't know a rotor arm from a cylinder," Bob said. "I'm afraid that's that for today."

"But I *must* get to London."

He shook his head. "We'll have to send to Dorchester for a new part."

"Then is there a car I can rent?" I sounded desperate because I *was* desperate. "I mean, I could leave mine with you and come down and collect it in a few days' time?"

"We're a very small village, we don't have spare cars."

"Then could you take me? Please . . ."

"I couldn't leave the garage that long, and you've missed the connection at Dulverley for today. The only train now for London is one that passes through Dorchester—"

"Then please take me there."

"Dorchester is a very long way, Miss Clair. I'm alone in the garage and I've got a heap of work. The farmer's estate car needs servicing and I've got Dr. Piper's old Ford to patch up again. He won't buy a new one and he has to do his rounds on a bicycle. Those two jobs must be done today."

"Then I'm stuck?"

"I fear so. We might be able to get the new arm down in a couple of days. That's the best I can suggest."

In these times of connecting planes and fast intercity trains, Bob was accentuating the isolation of Pilgrim Abbas. I knew that Black Agnes had no guest rooms, and anyway, I would not be far enough away from Jessamy Court if I went there. I knew, too, that I couldn't carry my suitcase all the way to Dulverley, nor did I see any prospect of hitchhiking, even if I had the courage to do so, on those lonely West Dorset roads.

I gave in because there was no alternative. "So we'll have to tow my car to the garage. Let me take my suitcase out and I'll be ready."

I left Fenney to help Bob fix the towing chain and went into the house by the French window on the terrace. I had no idea where Bridget was, but I dumped my suitcase back in the guest room without anyone's apparently knowing that I had ever taken it out, and went back to the car.

The more I thought about it, the more resentful I felt. Bob could surely have spared the time to drive me as far as Dulverley. But I had to see the whole thing in a different and less personal perspective. I was reckoning without the leisurely pace of everything in this village and also without the fact that, to Bob, I was just a casual visitor, a woman to whom today was just a day and tomorrow would do as well. The doctor and the farmer who relied on him, and on whom he relied, came first. Five days in Pilgrim Abbas had taught me to understand a little of the workings of people outside the fret and rush of the cities.

The solitary, frightening fact was that at some time during last evening or in the night, someone had deliberately immobilized my car. It hadn't been an attempt to cause me to have a bad accident, since the car wouldn't even start, but it made it impossible for me to leave Jessamy that day. And that had been exactly what was intended.

Only Dominick knew I had planned to leave, and I could not believe that he would ever attempt anything drastic in order to keep me at Jessamy. He would hope that whether I left that morning or waited until he was ready to leave, we would most certainly meet in London.

I remembered the sounds we had heard in the forest the night before. Someone had been there in the darkness listening to us, and knew my plans.

Bob and Fenney were standing by the truck and their voices came clearly in the deep silence that had followed the spasmodic fret of rooks and gulls.

". . . did it deliberately. But why?"

"Maybe it *was* the children, not knowing what they were taking, just taking something."

"I don't believe that," Bob said. "And who'd come out here just to steal what he could steal locally? There bain't anyone else living round here."

"Aye. It be strange."

They saw me and broke away. I said, "I heard that. It's strange to me, too."

"You'll report it to the police, won't you, miss?" Fenney said. "If we be getting villains in this village, it be bad for us all. I don't want no one taking my bike. Her wheels be a bit shaky, but I be fond of that old girl, I be."

"I'm sure this is an isolated incident," I said.

"Why be you sure?" The eyes peered at me, bright and clear as a young man's.

"Just a feeling I have, Fenney," I said.

Bob got into the truck and I sat behind the wheel of my car trying to concentrate on the none too easy task of steering a car on tow.

We crawled between the limes, and each leaf blade swung almost imperceptibly in the faint breeze that had sprung up. Below the trees, the spiderwebs hanging from leaf to leaf swung like delicate mobiles.

I could not guess the answer to the question of why I was being prevented from leaving Jessamy Court. A faint suspicion occurred to me that Bob could have been persuaded not to be cooperative and drive me to Dulverley. But I was fairly certain that for one thing, whoever had done this had not needed to resort to asking favors. He knew the village and its business too well, knew even that Bob had two emergency jobs to be done that day. Besides which, one look at that gentle, open face was sufficient to tell me that no one would ever bribe Bob Hopkins.

As I came out of the garage, I saw Mrs. Manfred some distance up the road, standing near the village store talking to two women, one of whom held an ebullient puppy on a chain. I turned and walked the other way, occasionally looking over my shoulder. I didn't want to pass her and perhaps have to explain to strangers why I was in the village. I doubted if they had noticed a car being towed; the garage was at Jessamy's end of the village, well away from where they stood.

At the end of the village street, where it opened out into a beautiful wilderness of purple ling and copper-tinted fern fronds, I looked back again. Mrs. Manfred was riding away and the little brown dog was yelping and dancing on the end of its leash.

I turned and retraced my steps. I wanted to telephone London and find out if anyone knew by now where Stephanie was. But since it was impossible to get into Dulverley without my car, I would have to risk being overheard in the village store. Its two bow windows were full of all and everything, from packages of candies to a few paperback books. The two women and one man customer inside all stopped talking as I entered. I gave them a bright smile and asked if I could use the telephone.

"It be there, miss." The apple-faced woman pointed to the end of the counter.

It certainly was too public. I explained that the calls would be long-distance and that I would find out from the local exchange how much I owed her. She nodded and smiled and returned to her conversation in the soft Dorset burr, with the "s's" like "z's" and the "ee's" for "you."

I telephoned Stephanie's number, reassured that if she were there, she would recognize my voice and there would be no need to give my name. I let the ringing continue for some time, but no one answered. When I called the hospital I was put through immediately to the sister-in-charge. I kept my voice as low as possible as I asked if they had news of Miss Clair. I avoided giving my name by saying, "I came to see her and spoke to Dr. Wilde."

The nurse said, "Yes, of course I remember. But I'm afraid we have no news. Miss Clair is out of our care now."

Of course, by walking out she had taken over responsibility for herself. They were far too busy with their very sick patients to have time to try to keep track of her.

I knew by the whispered spurts of conversation behind me that the ears of those in the shop were tilted toward me, and when I paid for my calls they watched and I knew they were intrigued. I doubted, though, whether they had actually heard what I said, for a farm cart had rumbled down the street at the moment I had asked about Miss Clair. The little gods of luck had most certainly watched over me that time.

XXI

I WALKED DOWN THE STREET. A horse looked over a wooden fence and I stopped and patted him and talked to him, ready to do anything that would keep me away from Jessamy Court.

Beyond the yard where the old horse dreamed was Black Agnes. Although I couldn't hear music being played, I was fairly certain that Dominick was there and that the little parlor was at the back, where the windows, looking out onto the lake and the indifferent swans, would be tightly closed against the cool, crisp morning.

I hesitated, wondering whether to find Dominick and tell him about my car. But again, cowardlike, I put off the moment of telling him that I could not wait until he was ready to leave Jessamy Court.

I crossed the road just beyond Black Agnes and entered the

forest. Just as faces varied, so did trees, but to me every one seemed identical with its neighbor: blue-gray trunk and dark-green leaves, rapier-sharp at the tips. Every bole was black and powerfully humped, every bank was as green as an emerald.

For ten minutes, while my feet rustled last year's leaves, my mind could not free itself from Fabian. Twice in my life a man had asked me to marry him and each time I had refused and said, "When it's real, I'll know." I knew now that my certainty had been blind arrogance; my stay at Jessamy had made me wiser. Love wasn't something that sailed serenely through adversity; it wasn't even a romantic, singing thing.

"For love is heaven, and heaven is love . . ." Oh no, dear Sir Walter Scott, that line may look deliriously beautiful when written down, but it isn't true. Love is illogical; it's a challenge and a battle.

I knew, for my feeling for Fabian was all those things. And taking them one by one, the challenge was unacceptable; the battle was one that I had to win, for my love was also my enemy and he lived in an impenetrable fortress. He was the dark, secret side of the coin which fate, or life, had flung down between us.

No, Fabian Seal, I don't love you. I just feel your incredible magnetism, and away from you, the magnet will have, must have, no power over me.

Head down, watching for forest hazards, I argued with myself, but could not find peace. No herd of deer appeared to take my mind off myself and the birds had either sung themselves into silence in the dawn chorus or were hopping around distant cottages for crumbs.

Then, when I came to the clearing where the forest pool made a circle of thick brown velvet, the silence was broken. I heard the high, unnatural barking of a dog, followed by cat sounds and then of cattle joining the mocking, unmusical chorus. After the cacophony of simulated animal noises came soft giggles.

Robin and Lucy were above me, curled up in the forks made by tree branches.

I called up to them, "Can you make bird sounds too?"

Lucy cupped her hands and hooted in a very fair rendering of an owl.

"Very clever," I said and began to walk on.

"Miss . . ."

"What is it?"

"We be waiting for you."

"How did you know I wasn't at the house?"

They came down from their tree hiding place with a swift grace and stood side by side, looking at me.

"We saw you go off with Bob Hopkins," Robin said, "and we was waiting for you."

"So you've said. But why?"

Lucy put up her hands and undid a scarf that had been knotted around her neck.

"We knows who this belongs to," she said and held it out to me.

It had been twisted so tightly that the pattern was lost, but as it unfolded, the charming silk square became familiar. I took it and looked down at the pattern, deep yellow zigzag lines on a paler yellow ground. There must have been thousands of scarfs with this particular design—including one Stephanie used often to wear over her hair. But Stephanie had once dropped a cigarette on hers and burned a tiny hole. I ran my fingers round the edges and found it.

"Where did you get this?"

"She dropped it."

"Who is 'she'?" There was still a chance it wasn't Stephanie. Coincidences happened in life.

"Don't know who she be," Robin said. "But she be in the forest and she be watching you."

"If it's someone who lives round these parts, you must know her name."

"She don't live round here. But she watches you," they said again with malicious delight.

"You must have some idea who she is."

They remained silent. There was a strange and not altogether unpleasant earthy smell about them, as if they lived in burrows under the trees.

"Why did you tell me about the scarf?"

"We found it; we don't steal things."

"I'm sure you don't. But I'd never have known," I said to Lucy, "that it wasn't yours unless you told me, would I?"

"We don't want nothing they'd say we stole," she said, her eyes flashing.

"Then what do you want me to do?"

"Give it to her."

218

"But I don't know who she is."

"You will, miss. She watches you."

"It doesn't follow at all; she hasn't made herself known to me yet."

"She will," they said again. "We asked the cards. They told us."

I pushed the scarf into Lucy's lean brown hands. "I don't want it. Take it, and if you see her, give it back to her. Did she drop it in the forest?"

"Yes, while she were watching you."

I had thought myself so alone, so wrapped around in the safe enchantment of the ancient trees. So Stephanie watched me. I, priding myself on my masquerade, had blundered along a blind path.

The children were looking at one another, nodding silently at some secret agreement. Then Lucy spoke. "Miss, *you* take it." She pushed the scarf back at me. "And do what we tells you and it'll be all right for you."

"What must I do?" They were only children, but I was suspicious of their narrowed, knowing eyes.

"It's Great-Granny's spell," Robin said, "and it works. We tried it once and he died. He called us awful names because we don't like school and houses and things like that, and we made him die. We can tell you how to do it. You just go to somewhere where she you hate will be walking and you drop something that's hers —like the scarf—and you set fire to it and you say 'Go. Go. Go.' And you find she'll die."

I gave a deliberately visible shudder. "That's quite horrible."

"You do it, miss, before *she* does it to you."

"How do you know she isn't a . . . a friend?"

"She don't look a friend, and we know. We be learning magic."

Robin urged, "Do what we tells you. Burn it down there." He pointed to a huge tree standing where the Heath began. "That's where *she* watches you."

"Does your grandmother know her?"

"No, but Granny were standing at her cottage and we was just behind, near our secret room, trying to work that tape thing. And then it started moving and we heard words. And Granny heard them too. And she put up her hands and shouted—it were funny, the way she shouted, 'They've come. They've come to me, like to my granny.'"

The mimicry of a frightened woman's hands clutched to her head was perfect.

"Who are 'they'?"

"The voices. Great-Granny used to hear them and Granny got all excited. And then the tape thing stopped and we was scared in case Granny would think we was playing tricks. She be awful when she be angry. So we hid and we never told her about the thing we'd bought."

I said to Robin, "You managed to rewind the tape so you were able to use it. Why did you ask me to help?"

"No, we couldn't, we just wound it back to see what'ud happen, and nothing did. Then it got stuck."

"With the piece of matchstick. I see. But I don't understand why you tell me this now."

"Because Granny knows somehow that it weren't the voices she heard but only us with the tape thing."

"Was she angry?"

"A bit. But we told her we knew spells and could do them, and she got quiet and didn't say anything more to us. I guess she thought we'd put a spell on her."

"Miss," Lucy urged. "You do what we tell you; you burn that scarf where *she* walks."

I said, "For one thing, I'm not at all sure 'this' she you talk of is out to harm me. For another, even if she is, to will her to die is horrible."

But someone wished you ill, Rachel, and that's what you were trying to escape from. But 'they' stopped you. "They." "She." No longer quite so anonymous.

I tossed the scarf onto the low branch of a tree. "Either take it, Lucy, or leave it there for it to be found by—well—by someone else."

I walked away from them.

"Miss . . ."

They called after me with an unusual softness for children, but with a curious command. I turned and waited.

"Don't you want to know why we told you these things when we wouldn't tell you before?"

"Why?"

"Because you don't tell us we're mad; you talk to us."

"Mad? You and Robin?" In spite of myself, I burst out laughing. "For heaven's sake, no one would say such a thing."

"They do. They call after us, 'Here come the witch's mad lot.' But we bain't mad. We be wise in ways they don't know of."

I was held for a moment or two, fascinated by the sight of them. For suddenly they were no longer just two rather tatterdemalion children dressed in brown shirts and shorts, watching me in that silence they were so able to keep far longer than most adults. They glowed with an unconscious theatricality, in a shaft of light filtering through the branches, and I saw in them a beauty I had never seen before and would probably never see again. It was as if their own magic practices were working on me, for there was nothing beautiful about their strange tilted eyes, their dark skins, their straight tangled hair and long thin mouths. When the boy grew older, his features would sharpen and he would wear a satyr's face. As for the girl, I couldn't see her as a complete adult. She was Robin's shadow, and as such, I felt that he would never be quite free of her. It would be another case of the power of the weak over the strong.

"Goodbye," I said and left them.

They watched me go, but when I half looked around, they were not there. The scarf hung clear and yellow from the branch of the beech tree.

So Stephanie had come to Pilgrim Abbas, to Fabian. It was more than possible that they shared a secret and shared it in fear. Otherwise, there would be no reason for Stephanie to stay away from the house or for them to hide their knowledge of each other from Dominick and from me.

And those times when Fabian said he was going to see Freyberg or to a local council meeting, he could have been secretly meeting her.

I remembered the dark girl watching us from the top of Gideon's Rock, the dark girl who had been seen talking to the village butcher. A dark girl—or a fair girl wearing a wig? Stephanie. Until I had visited her in the hospital, I hadn't seen her for some time, during which she could have taken a driving test and bought herself a car.

I had come within sight of the house and I stopped and looked across the bright green lawns, and another thought hit me. Fabian had said, "First Livanova and now her daughter." Youth stealing from maturity. It could so easily be that which had broken up the resumption of Livanova's affair with Fabian. Leaning against one of the great trees that stood on the edge of Jessamy's estate,

I faced the fact that a meeting between Stephanie and Fabian and a love affair between them could have been the reason she had stopped coming to see me. After the bitterness she had shown toward him, she would be nervous of telling me of that emotional involvement. And when Fabian had said that to me, it had been with the derisive knowledge that I was not Stephanie. Yet he hadn't exposed me as a cheat.

Whatever his motive, he would act as he chose in his own good time.

The slight west wind rustled the leaves over my head and I looked up as if I expected to find the children watching me from the branches. Remembering them, I realized that this particular old tree could be the one they had pointed out as being the place where "she" had watched me. I looked down at the black boles and the brown earth.

The children had said, "Burn the scarf there, where she has stood, and say 'Go. Go. Go,' and she will die." Their great-grandmother's spell, something made up by her to frighten simple villagers. Nothing more. Yet I shot away from the tree as if the burning had already begun.

No one was around as I reached the terrace and entered the drawing room. The note I had written for Fabian was still secured by the silver knife. I picked up the sheet of paper, slid it into my purse and went to my room.

Mrs. Manfred was dusting the dressing table. She wheeled around as I entered the room and stared at me.

"I'm afraid something has happened to my car. I've just had to have it towed to the garage, so I won't be leaving today."

"That's good," she said. "So I don't have to tell Mr. Seal that you were even thinking of going."

"Oh, I shall tell him. I'll have to. You see, the reason I couldn't get away this morning was because someone had stolen a vital piece of mechanism from my car."

"Stolen?"

"Yes." I outstared her.

"Nobody steals things here, Miss Clair."

"It's said that there's always a first time. And this was it. Do you know anything about cars?"

"No."

"Then it won't mean anything to you if I tell you that the rotor arm was taken. It immobilizes the engine."

I crossed the room to the closet, took out my suitcase and opened it. My nonchalance was pure play-acting. I wasn't merely nervous. Now that I was back in the house, I was acutely frightened again, and there was only one person who might help me. Since Mrs. Manfred had said that Fabian would be lunching at Lys Manor, I would see Dominick first and I would tell him what I had intended to do and what had happened to my car. It was possible that he knew someone living around Pilgrim Abbas who could take me to Dulverley, where I might stay overnight and catch the train to Dorchester and the express to London in the morning. There was still a possibility of escape.

Mrs. Manfred crossed the room and stood for a moment by the open door. "It would be better if you didn't tell Mr. Seal you were planning to leave without a word to him," she said coldly. "Madame would never have done it that way; but then, she would never have left him."

For a moment or two after she closed the door I saw no connection, but gradually I realized how words, tossed at random, became links in the chain. Livanova would never have left Fabian. So when the famous love affair ended, it must have been he who left her. For Miranda McCall . . . For Stephanie . . . When dramas happened in the lives of famous people, the world usually knew about them. But those two had kept their secret well, concealing the tensions and emotions that tore at them—Livanova probably out of the fierce pride that would not accept rejection, and Fabian out of an old loyalty.

I unpacked only as much as was necessary for the day. The room, which I had thought so charming when I first entered it, had become claustrophobic. I glanced at my watch and saw that it was only half past eleven. The glorious morning beckoned, and wrapped in my coat I went down to the terrace, sat in the sun and waited for Dominick. Time crawled, and behind my seeming quiet, I was alert and afraid.

I knew someone was behind me the moment I turned from watching a rabbit sitting on the far edge of the lawn, licking its paws.

"I thought you were going to be away for hours," I said to Fabian.

"Then I hope it's a pleasant surprise that I'm not. What have you been doing with yourself this morning?"

It was probably the sunlight that made his eyes seem over-bright and his face tight, as if he were holding hard to an emotion he had no intention of expressing. Anger, perhaps, or bitterness, or suspicion—I couldn't interpret what it was he hid.

He repeated, "Well, what *have* you been doing?"

Trying to run away from you. I said aloud, "I wanted to use my car this morning. But instead, I had to be towed to the garage; someone has stolen the rotor arm."

"Who the devil would do a thing like that?"

"Perhaps he did." Nerves were making me flippant. "The devil, I mean."

"Suppose we talk sense."

"That's what I'm doing. Sometime last evening, or during the night, someone immobilized my car."

He was standing very still, his eyes steadily on my face. "Where, by the way, were you intending to go?"

"To London," I said.

He showed neither surprise nor acceptance of the fact. Instead, he looked at his watch. "It's only twelve o'clock, but suppose we have a drink and talk this out?"

A drink or a coffee . . . Always some action that would ease a situation. Only, nothing could destroy the suspicion and dull the depths of my curious despair. *I love you, Fabian Seal. And I don't trust you.*

"There's nothing to talk out," I said after too long a silence. "Unless you have any idea who could have done it."

"You said you were going to London."

"Yes."

"Without telling me?"

"I'm sorry if that sounds ill-mannered. It does, of course. But I had left you a note, explaining. I've got it here . . ." I began to open the clasp of my purse.

Fabian stopped me. "I don't want to see it. But why do you think someone wanted to stop you from leaving?"

"I've told you. I don't know."

He said, "I'm afraid even if I offered to drive you to Dorchester, you're hours too late for the train."

"There's one later, though, isn't there? I seem to remember . . ."

"But I can't take you, I have something important to do this afternoon. I'm afraid, my dear, you are stuck—until tomorrow, or whenever your car is ready."

"They're going to call me and let me know."

"In the meantime it's a lovely day, but it's cold. Shall we go indoors?"

"I don't think I want a drink."

"That's all right; neither do I. Apéritifs should never be taken too early in the morning, the palate isn't ready for them." He had perched himself on a corner of the carved desk. "And by the way, I've had an inventory made of the things here that belong to you. It was completed before you arrived, but I only received the copies of it this morning."

"From . . . from the lawyers?" I could barely get the question out.

"No, from a Dulverley typist I sometimes use. Your mother stated in her will that I was to decide what I wished to keep and let you have the rest. Not a very fair thing to do. But I've made a pretty extensive inventory. I presume you'll sell the lot, and you won't starve on the proceeds." He crossed the room with his light, limping step. "The inventory is in my room. I'll get it."

I went to the desk between the windows and waited.

XXII

THE FOOTSTEPS crossing the hall weren't Fabian's.

"Oh," Dominick greeted me. "You should be out enjoying the sunshine."

"I have been. Were you at Black Agnes?"

"Yes, frustrating though it is to play on that piano, I tried. But I had one piece of good news while I was there. I got through to London, and Palmer tells me there's a real chance that I'll be auditioned for the ensemble Christopher Trench is forming. You've heard of him?"

"No, I'm afraid not."

"He's a fine musician and came in second in the International Competition at Munich two years ago. He would be one of the world's leading concert violinists, only he can't memorize big works."

"I'm so glad for you."

"What's this you're glad about?" Fabian asked from the doorway.

Dominick told him as sheets of beautifully typed paper were dropped onto my lap. "Here you are. Read it later." He went toward the terrace window and I looked past him into the distance, seeing the great beech tree under which, the children had said, "she" watched us.

Fabian let out a sharp exclamation. "Damn the man! Doesn't he know he's attacking the main stem?" He shot out of the door toward Fenney, who was happily snipping off some bare wisteria wood.

I collected the sheets of paper in my lap and folded them. "Someone has deliberately damaged my car," I said to Dominick.

He had been crossing to a chair, but as I spoke he swung around in blank amazement. "For God's sake, who? And how?"

I told him what I had told Fabian.

"But why?" He sat down heavily in the chair and asked incredulously, "Who in the world would come out to a place as isolated as Jessamy for that?"

"Obviously not someone who wanted a rotor arm. I think it was done to stop me from going to London."

"But you aren't leaving yet?"

"I'd planned to go this morning. I'm sorry. I was being a coward and slipping off without telling anyone, but I felt I had to get away—and what has happened proves how right I was."

"Even so, who knew?" He shook his head in sheer disbelief, and then jerked himself out of the chair. "Of course. Last night in the forest we thought we heard someone. Do you remember?"

"Only too well."

"We guessed it might be Mrs. Manfred or Hobbin or the children, but they surely wouldn't know the mechanics of a car."

He ran his hands through his thick hair, shining in the sunlight shafting across the room. "You've told Fabian, of course."

"Yes."

"Did he offer any explanation?"

"No."

"Or suggest that it must be reported to the police?"

"Not that, either."

"Call the police now."

"I know—without knowing *how* I know—that it won't do any good."

We both looked toward the open terrace doors. Fenney was loping across the lawn and Fabian was standing in the sun looking toward Gideon's Rock.

"But I told you, didn't I, that I'd also planned to leave here as soon as I could?" Dominick's voice came to me with reproach.

"I can't wait indefinitely. I have to get back to London; my home is there and . . . and my job waiting for me. It wouldn't have made any difference to us if I'd left this morning," I added as I felt his disappointment in me. "We could have met . . ." (*And that is a lie, Rachel Fleming.*)

Dominick said suddenly, "I've got an idea. Hobbin is always wandering in the forest. She could have been out last night and seen someone, and that someone could have been whoever watched and listened to us."

"Oh, please leave it. My car is out of action and there's nothing to be done." I was too late with my protest. Dominick was across the room, going by way of the front door, avoiding Fabian and obviously not wanting to explain his sudden exit.

"Stephanie." Fabian called me from the terrace, and when I joined him he was still looking out at Gideon's Rock. "Do you know what those birds are?"

A flock was wheeling, heavy-winged, across the shoreline. "They could be eagles, only there aren't that many in England, are there? Or storks . . . I don't know."

"Wild geese," Fabian said. "They're rare around here. And I expect the wildlife sanctuary at Abbotsbury has already seen and recorded them."

Fabian followed their flight across the sun. He was totally at ease, but by his side, I felt so awkward and restless that I had to make conversation, spinning out the time until Dominick returned.

"You're lucky. You must have seen so many wonderful sights. Animals . . . birds . . ."

Fabian perched on the stone balustrade, leaning against one of the slender columns, his face half turned away from me, so that it was hard against the sunlight. "I have seen gazelle in Iran leaping across the plains so swiftly that they were like birds flying. I have seen kingfishers like blue streaks of light. When I traveled, when I climbed, I saw wonderful things." He seemed to have gone, in his mind, away from Dorset into the enchanted places.

"And when the ballet is finished, will you go away again?"

"I don't know. How can I tell what my life will be in six months from now? Do *you* know what will be happening to you, say, next March?"

"No, I don't. Have you decided whether you'll keep Jessamy?" It wasn't an idle question to mark time. I wanted to know. Anything, the least remark, could become a link in the chain between a girl and the house behind me.

"Perhaps I will, perhaps not." He answered coolly; there was no sentiment about Fabian Seal. He sat still and calm and seemingly prepared to wait where he was, enjoying the midday sun, until Mrs. Manfred summoned us to lunch.

I was so near him that I needed to make only the smallest movement to touch his hand resting on one of the little rope-patterned pillars. I kept my eyes fixed on the distance beyond the lawns where the heather grew thickly, yet I knew that more than anything else, I wanted physical contact with him. An emotion that had both longing and anger in it, an elemental urge that wanted, above all, for Fabian to take me into the forest or into his bed and make love to me. But it would have been important to my pride for me to have been the one to have driven away out of his life, for *me* to have left *him*. It would have seemed, both at the time and in retrospect, a fine personal triumph.

Not that it was going to happen, for Fabian had no desire for me.

I saw something move at the edge of the forest. A stag ventured onto the heath, lifting its head and sniffing the air.

Fabian saw it too. "The herd's ancestors lived here when Shakespeare was a boy," he said. "It's a marvelous thought, isn't it, the idea of continuation?"

He wasn't watching me, so I had no idea whether he saw me nod my head, but he asked, "Do you want to carry on your line, Stephanie, with children who resemble you, or perhaps Livanova? Sometimes characteristics miss generations."

I said half angrily, back with Stephanie's bitterness, "If I had children who were like their maternal grandmother, then they would never want children of their own, so the line wouldn't be carried on, anyway. They would be like her; they would want only their own immortality."

"They could do worse than that. The world can stand a little less of the commonplace. It's the difficult people who stimulate us and take us out of our complacent half-sleep; it's the difficult people who shake us out of our preconceived ideas of ourselves."

His face was still turned from me, and I felt that he was telling his thoughts aloud and my presence was just incidental.

"Are you still in love with her?"

He slid down from the balustrade and walked away from me. "Even her daughter has no right to ask me that."

"I'm sorry."

"No, I don't think you are." He reached out and snapped off a dried-up leaf of creeper and crumpled it in his fingers.

I had pierced his armor, but I couldn't recognize what showed through, because everything that was said and done had to be judged from the theory that he knew I was not Livanova's daughter. And so I watched and listened through a mist of uncertainty, particularly because, on his own admission to me, he had woven a circle around himself to guard his freedom.

The Tibetan bell rang from somewhere in the house, the sweet light tone hung on the air, and turning as I heard it, I saw Dominick crossing the drawing room.

He gave me an imperceptible shake of his head, which meant that either he had been unable to find Hobbin or that she had seen or heard no one pass her door the night before.

Fabian saw him, too. "I didn't know you were a sprinter," he said pleasantly as Dominick joined us, breathing heavily as if he had run a race that was too hard for him. "You should do some climbing."

"No, thanks."

"You don't know its exhilaration until you try. It keeps you fit. Or rather, you have to be fit to attempt it. Have you ever climbed?"

"I've tried a few easy ones in Wales and in the Lake District."

"Would you like to try that?" He nodded toward Gideon's Rock.

"No. I'm an amateur."

"And I'm lame, so that would make us even, wouldn't it?"

Dominick looked at him. "You can't mean you'd take that on. You'd be mad."

"I'd be prepared to try if you would." Fabian laughed. "With your physique and my experience, I guess we'd make the top."

"Have you ever climbed it?"

"Before my accident it would have been too tame; since that time I've tried to forget the urge always to get to the top of something by the most difficult route. But it's a beautiful day for a try."

"It's just a steep hill from the land side, but it's pretty devilish from the shore."

"Not entirely. The body of the rock is difficult, but you'd find the two wings fairly easy," Fabian said.

"After the Andes, I can't see Gideon's Rock satisfying you."

"It won't. Small climbs are no panacea for a mountain-hungry man, but it could take the edge off the longing."

"It's years since I climbed even Welsh cliffs."

"Then maybe I'll be whetting your appetite again and giving you a hobby that will last all your life."

I sensed the pull of Fabian's stronger will. "You challenge me and I accept," Dominick said.

"The bell has rung for lunch," I said.

"Oh, that's all right," Fabian said easily. "It's cold food today —salmon, I believe. It will keep. Besides, I want my lunchtime martini before we eat. Let's go in."

I walked away from them. "I don't want a drink, thank you."

"Where are you going?"

"Just walking," I called back.

I crossed the garden and went through the copse of silver birches. Standing on the stretch of wasteland, I looked up at the gentle green slope of Gideon's Rock.

If one had enough breath, one could run up it from the land side. I went around the base and walked over the fine sand to the sea's edge. From there the body of the rock rose sheer, broken only by clefts and protrusions made by the Atlantic weather battering it for thousands of years. The two wings did not reach quite the same height and were less vertical, with ledges and indentations that offered easier footholds—easier, I decided as I went back to the house, for a mountain goat. But I shuddered for Dominick.

Fabian said as I entered the drawing room, "Ah, Stephanie. Will you change your mind and have a drink?"

I thanked him, shook my head and turned to Dominick. "Have you really climbed?"

"Oh yes, on school holidays. Thousands do it."

"I've just been to have a look at Gideon's Rock."

"It's no worse in places than some I scrambled up when I belonged to our college climbing club," he said lightly.

"But that was years ago—"

He gave me his slow, gentle smile. "I'm not that old."

"You know I didn't mean that," I said, angry and frightened. "But people need to train."

"To climb a rock?" Fabian inquired.

I turned to him. "Yes, to climb a rock. I've read reports of climbers falling because of dizziness and vertigo."

"Oh, I'll be there. If he falls, I'll haul him up," Fabian said, making it sound as if I were fussing over something that was scarcely more dangerous than walking over Ellen's Heath.

"It isn't a joke for either of you," I said angrily. "Fabian, how *could* you think of climbing?"

His eyes were narrowed in the way I had grown to recognize as cold and glittering dislike of interference. "You don't imagine I'm going to hurtle to my death from some simple rockhold, do you?"

"You could," I said. "It's different now from when you used to climb."

"Because I'm lame? That accident didn't atrophy my brain as well, my dear. So shall we not discuss it?"

He defeated me every time. I turned away and heard the lunch bell ring again.

Fabian finished his drink and set down his glass, and his tone was light again. "Let's go, or the salmon will return to its river."

I made a pretense of eating, but I was too anxious to be aware of the taste of the food. Superimposed on everything I looked at, I could see the stark gray face of the cliff. The conversation was sporadic. I felt that neither of the men wanted to talk about the thing uppermost in their minds, but that the scaling of the rock was of greater importance than appeared in the casual challenge.

Behind Fabian's suggestion and Dominick's acceptance was a purpose that I, as an outsider, could only sense. They were out to prove something—or achieve something—and this climb that seemed a sunny afternoon's adventure had undertones that were intensely important to them. I tried once again over lunch to dissuade them, but Fabian merely reacted as if I were rather a bore and Dominick quietly changed the subject.

The men ate lightly and we lingered over coffee. It was nearly three o'clock when Fabian said he was going to find windbreakers for both of them. "If the wind gets up when we're halfway to the top, the cold could affect your grip."

Dominick and I were in the hall. The flowers in the blue bowl had been removed and a cushion of Ophelia roses set in their place. The two chrysanthemums I had put there had been thrown out with the Michaelmas daisies, and as I thought of them, they were like part of some odd, disturbing dream.

Dominick sat on the window seat with his fingers splayed out, so that the sun shone through the leaded panes onto them.

"My hands," he said. "That's the only thing that worries me. I've got that audition in London next week. I can't risk injuring them."

"Then tell Fabian you've changed your mind about climbing. It's crazy and you know it. Why did you agree to go with him?"

He said quietly, "His will is stronger than mine."

"Oh, for heaven's sake, surely you can say no. And it isn't too late now."

He shook his head. "You don't understand. Livanova didn't either, and in a way, neither do I. But if Fabian decides on something that involves you, you can't refuse. It's as if— Oh, never mind."

I did mind. "It's as if what?"

"I don't quite know how to explain it, but Fabian has powers we don't understand."

"All he's got is a strong will, and it's up to you to challenge it."

"You dismiss it as easily as if you had snapped your fingers. But you've felt his power over people. I know because I've watched you."

I didn't want to discuss my own weakness about Fabian. "If you don't want to climb that damned rock," I said, "then say so. I fail to see any magic about a man's determination to get his own way."

"Do you?" His voice took on a burning intensity. "Do you think that anything that has happened while you have been here has been by accident? Do you think that there's nothing in the world but the things you see, the thoughts you hear spoken, the wishes people tell you about? Oh God, Stephanie . . ."

"What are you trying to say?" It was obvious, but I asked because I had to hear it from him.

He was looking out the window, flexing his fingers as if preparing them for the gripping of the hard cold ledges of Gideon. "There are powers most people don't know about. Don't you realize that even science has begun to think again about everything being explainable by its own technical terms? Don't you know that logic can be smashed by things you and I can't begin to understand?"

"So we're back to magic." My mockery was purely superficial and beneath it was a sense of suffocation. It was as if the unexplained things of the world were drawing nearer, accentuating mysteries that were frightening—and daring me to disbelieve.

"People far wiser than we are believed in magic. Shakespeare did; George Bernard Shaw did."

It was as if Fabian had forced his own deep theories on him, for Dominick's whole manner was that of a man facing something he dreaded and yet was powerless to avoid.

"You've never talked this way before about 'powers.' It's like some sort of intellectual virus you've caught from Fabian. I just don't understand."

"Perhaps I don't, either," he said like a man in a trap.

On an impulse, I went to him and caught his arm. "Don't make this climb. Tell Fabian you have to be careful of your hands because of the audition. It's true, anyway. *Tell him.*"

Instead of his usual passivity, Dominick shook me off. "I can't. I have to prove something to myself—and perhaps to Fabian too. I'm sorry; it must seem to you that I'm talking in riddles."

I walked to the great double doors and opened them, standing in the cool air and letting the sunlight pour on me. I neither moved nor spoke until I heard Fabian return, and as he joined Dominick, I swung around and faced them both. "Why don't you two men behave like adults and stop making a game out of something dangerous for both of you?"

"Dangerous. Climbing a rock?"

I tried to outstare Fabian. "People have been killed doing less."

"Oh, people have been killed falling down a flight of steps." Fabian leaned against the refectory table and smiled at me. "The rock is child's play to me, and if Dominick does what he's told, he'll be perfectly safe. And I'm quite sure he won't be foolish."

The words, for all their assurance, had a sinister ring. People didn't do foolish things deliberately; impulse or emotion drove them. Behind Fabian, I saw the little crowned head of Tatiana Livanova and her painted eyes met my living ones. I had an odd, irrelevant thought. I wondered if the painting was among the items in the inventory Fabian had handed me and which I had not yet read.

"We'll probably start our climb in about half an hour." Fabian tossed two windbreakers on the refectory table and the pale-rose

234

petals quivered in the disturbed air. "Are you coming to watch us, Stephanie?"

"No."

"Livanova would have," Fabian said. "She would probably have cheered us on. She might even have sat on a boulder combing her long hair like a mermaid, and she would have loved every moment of it. She had no fear for others or for herself."

"Perhaps, if she had, she might not have died," I said and walked out of the hall and up the stairs to my room.

XXIII

I LAY ON THE BED taut and uneasy, listening to the men talking below and aware that although the conversation sounded as if it flowed with harmony, it was only distance that gave that impression. Talk was never easy between them, the one because he didn't trust Fabian, the other because he seemed to take a perverse delight in this mistrust.

I heard them cross the hall, their footsteps dying away along the passage that led to the kitchen quarters. Fabian had said that there was climbing gear somewhere in the vaults. I closed my eyes and pictured the scene. Dominick would be trying on various climbing boots for a pair that would fit him, and I prayed that he wouldn't find any. I saw in my mind's eye, the coils of rope, the various paraphernalia they might take with them, although Fabian had laughed over lunch at Dominick's mention of what he called "hardware." He had said, "It's a cliff, not Everest."

An hour passed during which I felt that I was chained to the bed by a fear so illogical, and yet so real, that I didn't dare stir from the room that had become my sanctuary.

As silence fell on the house, I guessed they had left for their climb, and for all I knew, it could be quickly over. My common sense told me that nothing terrible was going to happen. In spite of his lameness, rock-climbing was easy for a mountaineer of Fabian's caliber. Yet the fear persisted, perhaps the more keen because I knew that Dominick was there against his will. This was not so much a feat of achievement as a triumph of will.

I hated the clock in the hall below that kept chiming the quarters, the halves and then the hour. I had no idea whether Mrs. Manfred had left for her usual afternoon visit to relatives in the village, but I had a feeling that I was entirely alone at Jessamy.

At last I could bear the isolation no longer. I got up and ran out of the room and down the stairs. The sun had moved sufficiently across the sky for the great hall to be in shadow. Jupiter lay in the terrace doorway, supine and relaxed, his throat vibrating as if he were purring in his sleep.

I crossed to the Heath, wanting to put distance between myself and the men on the rock. My feet made whispering sounds on the stiff purple clumps of heather and the dried fern fronds, and nothing broke the golden peace of my external world. But I walked with a knowledge that tore at me with its tensions. All that had happened, and might be about to happen, had been planned. My car had been tampered with so that I could not escape involvement with whatever was to be the outcome of this afternoon.

Ellen's Heath seemed endless, stretching away between low hills like a hyacinth carpet under the soft polished light. Time dragged, and I tried to imagine how far the two men had got on Gideon's inflexible face. I had seen boys climbing minor cliffs, clinging and shouting to one another, but I had never seen grown men on a real climb.

I came at last to the place where the forest cut like an arrow into the Heath, and unable to bear my own company any longer, I returned to the beeches. The wind that had begun as a soft sea breeze when Fabian and Dominick had set out had become stronger, and the branches of the trees swung above me in a green, drunken dance.

She was standing right in my path, dressed in a woollen suit the color of apricots. I remembered going with her to buy it. Her wig was long and dark brown, but as I watched, she reached up, whipped it off and threw it on a bank of last year's beech leaves, where it lay like a furry animal, asleep. Her hair was a halo of pale gold.

I said her name on a breath: "Stephanie."

The way she leaned against the tree had led me to expect vituperation and reproach, or at least complete command of a situation where I was so blatantly at fault. Instead, she held out her hands, and I realized that she was shaking violently and that the tree was her support.

"I've got to find Dominick . . . Help me, Rachel."

"You know him?"

"Don't ask questions now, just tell me where he is."

"Probably halfway up a huge cliff called Gideon's Rock. But you know it, don't you, Stephanie? You watched Fabian and me from there a few days ago."

"I've *said* don't waste time on questions."

"Oh, we've got loads of time. I doubt if Fabian and Dominick will finish their climb for some while yet. So suppose you tell me first why you came here without calling at Jessamy and making yourself known?"

"Not now. Not now . . ."

She tried to pull away from me, but I held tightly onto her arm. "We'll go to the house," I said, "and you can start from the beginning and tell me."

"*No.*"

"Look"—I was trying hard to be patient—"we both have some explaining to do, but I feel mine can wait longer than yours."

She was very pale and her eyes were wild and restless, darting at me and away, her body resisting me and yet unable to fight my determination to keep her with me.

"Were you really unconscious when I came to see you in hospital?"

"There were a few moments when I was aware of what was going on. But before I could say one word or even make a sign with my hand, I went blank again."

"And as soon as you came out of shock, you left the hospital."

"It was horrible—something seemed to click inside me like a gate opening and I began to remember things. I knew then that

I couldn't stay. I didn't want any treatment. I just had to get out of that place."

"Why?"

"To find Dominick."

I was walking her quickly toward the house, but she drew back when we reached the lawns and leaned against me, shuddering.

"Tell me, do you drive a car?" I asked.

"Yes. I bought one some time ago. I'd passed my test . . ."

"You kept very quiet about it." I remembered how everyone had had to listen repeatedly to the triumphant fact that I had passed my own test the first time.

"And you've been staying near here."

"Oh no, not too near, not in the village. That would have been dangerous—villagers watch and talk."

They did.

I gave her a slight push to make her stand on her own two feet and began to walk toward the house. Even when we reached the drawing room I didn't relax my guard over her. I stood between Stephanie and the open terrace window. I knew her too well to risk her trying to escape if I asked a question she didn't want to answer.

"Now, suppose we both do some explaining."

A flash of spirit burst through her and she said defiantly, "I think I have the right to ask the first questions, don't you? For instance, why are you here calling yourself by my name?"

"You've been talking to the villagers."

She leaned, slim and tense, against the wall. *"Why?"* she whispered.

"Because the doctor at the hospital couldn't get through to you and we were both certain there was a link between the shock that made you collapse and Jessamy Court. The name of the house was the only word you uttered and I could think of no other way of helping you. The doctor said that the longer you remained like that, the more difficult your chances of recovery. The solicitor was away for a week and I couldn't wait for him to return—he couldn't do anything for you, anyway. So I rang his office and told them where you were and then I came down here. I had the seven days during which the solicitor was away in which to try to help you."

She closed her eyes. "This . . . damned . . . house . . ."

"But it wasn't the house which made you ill."

"I don't remember what happened after the street went round

and round and I heard hammering in my head. After that, everything was a blank."

"But you recovered, and just walked out of hospital."

"It was like waking from a nightmare. Only . . ."

"Only what?"

"The nightmare went on." Easy tears sprang to her eyes. "Rachel, I'm so afraid."

"Of what?"

"Of the whole terrible business. Dominick was right. I know he was. He told me to stay away."

"Dominick and you?"

"Yes. We . . . we knew one another."

For a moment I was speechless, hearing the echo of Dominick Hunt's voice calling me Stephanie, taking my arm gently as we walked in the dark forest, being kind . . .

"You'd better start from the beginning."

She took a deep breath. "It all happened months ago. I asked Mother to let me come down to Jessamy Court, but she never would. So one day I came without telling her. She was away, dancing in Paris. I called at the house, and the only person here was Dominick. He was kind. Mrs. Manfred was out and Fabian wasn't around because he and Mother hadn't made up their quarrel—if they ever did. Dominick took me all over the house. He said, 'It will be yours one day, so you may as well see it. It's lovely.' And then we went and sat in the forest and talked a lot."

"And you met after that?"

"Yes."

"Down here?"

"No. In London. We didn't dare be seen together in the village. People talk."

"Are you telling me that you contacted him after you left the hospital?"

She was leaning against a heavy chair, looking frail and thin and helpless. "Yes, I telephoned him as soon as I got back home. And then I came down here to see him. He was angry about that. He said it was dangerous for me. He told me to go away and wait."

"For what?"

"Until he had found out everything he had to." She leaned her head back against the ruby-velvet curtain and closed her eyes. The tears squeezed out slowly under her golden lashes.

I heard my own harsh question. *"What was it Dominick had to find out?"*

She opened her eyes slowly and her voice was a whisper. "Why . . . why . . . my mother was killed."

My heart stopped beating for a flash of time and then began to thud. "Why do you use the word killed as if what happened was deliberate?" I heard myself asking the question, and dreaded the answer. But I had to know. "Stephanie, *why?*"

She ran her fingers through her hair with a jerky, frantic movement. "Dominick believes that . . . that Fabian . . . killed my mother."

"No. Oh *no!*" I heard my own violent protest "I won't believe it."

"It's awful for us, too." She turned her face away.

"Give me one good reason for what you have just said," I shouted at her.

"I can't. That's the frightening thing. I . . . we . . . can't."

"Of course you can. *Why,* Stephanie? Look at me. *Look at me.* Why?"

She said weakly, "We were going to meet at Mother's apartment that night."

"Livanova invited the two of you?" I asked incredulously.

"No."

"Go on, then. What do you mean?"

"Oh . . . on the day she died, Mother sent for Dominick. She wanted him in London to hear the orchestration for one of her newly choreographed dances. Dominick knew that Mother would be going out later and he planned to say he wanted to stay behind at her apartment at Briand House and try over the new music on the Bechstein she keeps in her London practice room. And then, when Mother had left that evening, I was going to meet him there."

"In your mother's home?"

"We were in love, and we could so seldom be together." She looked at me, pleading for understanding.

I stood quite still by the open terrace doors, feeling numb inside at what she was so artlessly telling me. Fabian could have been the last person to see Livanova alive. And Dominick had known from that first late afternoon that I was not Stephanie Clair.

"I waited a little way away from Briand House," she was saying, "until I saw Mother's car come out of the drive. I watched the chauffeur turn the corner and then I went up to her apartment. I didn't know she had changed her mind about going out and had sent the car away. Dominick opened the door to me and I flung my arms round him. I said something, oh, I don't know what—

something about being with him, loving him. And Mother came out of the drawing room—" Stephanie stopped and her fingers plucked at the silk cord of a cushion. "It . . . it was awful."

"Why?"

She raised her head and her face seemed suddenly to lose its clear contours, so that her beauty dissolved. "Mother laughed. Rachel . . . she stood there laughing at me. She said, 'You little fool. Dominick is *my* lover.' "

First the mother; then the daughter.

"There was an awful scene. Mother dragged me into the drawing room and said in that hard, mocking voice of hers, 'You think you have my lover? What more do you imagine you have of mine? Jessamy? Well, dear, you are in for a very great disappointment. Nothing of mine will be yours except the allowance I give you. Nothing, my little thieving daughter.' It was horrible. I ran out of the room and heard Dominick say something to her and then call to me. He caught me up in the courtyard and we sat on the rim of the fountain there and he was sweet to me, but I couldn't stop crying. He told me that he had never said he loved my mother. I knew he was speaking the truth and that she had made it all up because she couldn't bear that anyone could care for me rather than her."

"What has all this to do with Fabian?"

"We were sitting there together when we saw him go into the apartment block. We sat under the trees by the fountain for some time. And we saw Fabian come out and walk away very quickly. He kept looking around him as if he were trying to get away without being seen. And then Dominick and I left. If ever Mother sent for him to come to London, she put him up at a hotel, but we couldn't be seen there together. Nor could we go to my place that night because I had a girl staying with me for two nights. So we just went for coffee and then we walked and talked about it, and Dominick said that whatever happened, he loved me. The doctor gave the time my mother had died as around eight o'clock. That was just about when we saw Fabian leave Briand House."

"You're forgetting Miss Westerman, your mother's housekeeper in London," I said.

"It was her evening off."

So they had been alone in the apartment, Livanova and Fabian. Inside me a wild voice protested. *It mustn't be Fabian . . . it can't be Fabian . . .*

"Why didn't you say all this at the inquest?"

"How *could* we? Fabian arrived at Briand House almost at the moment when we left. We could easily have been suspected, and Fabian swore on oath that he had not seen Mother since she left Jessamy that morning. And he's so well known and admired; he would always be believed. If we had said we had seen him going into the block, we would have been questioned as to why *we* were there. Fabian would win. He would always win."

Outside the clouds were gathering, blown by the wind, and the swallows began their agitated low wheeling from the bushes to the eaves of the house.

Stephanie put her hands to her face and spoke in quick, muffled words. "When the solicitor talked to me after the inquest, he looked at me as if he suspected me of knowing something I hadn't told. And if anybody actually suspected us, we couldn't prove our innocence."

"That's ridiculous. The police have ways—"

"You don't understand. Rachel, we *did* quarrel with Mother. We *were* there. And our fingerprints would have been—oh, on things we had touched."

"So would Fabian's and Miss Westerman's."

"But *mine* were there too. Oh, Rachel, I was so alone and so frightened even before that awful thing happened. It had to be so secret because Dominick said it would be dangerous to tell anyone, even my best friend—you—about our being in love. He said that Mother would be angry and he might lose his job. He never dreamed that when she *did* know about it, she would laugh at us. I was terrified. I thought: If anyone finds out, they'll think that we'd had some terrible quarrel and . . . and we attacked her. After all, Dominick and I *were* angry that night."

"Just angry. Nothing more than that?"

"Rachel, how can you ask?"

"All right. So after her death you felt everything was building up into something so big you couldn't face it."

"That's right. That's exactly right. I couldn't bear to stay alone in my apartment. I ran out into the street and then everything began to swim round me, and I kept thinking: Who am I? Where am I? I no longer knew. It was days later when I came to in the hospital."

"When you left there, what did you do?"

"Everything crowded back and I got a taxi home and called

243

Dominick. Someone who said she was a housekeeper answered. I pretended I was speaking from his agent's office in London, and when he came to the telephone, he told me that someone was at the house pretending to be me. He said he didn't believe you were anyone sent by the police because you didn't seem the type, but he couldn't be sure. He thought you were just an inquisitive friend, and when he described you I knew who you were."

"You told Dominick I was Rachel Fleming. And then . . . ?"

"He was angry and as scared, in a way, as I was. He said you had to be watched as well as Fabian and that I must stay away and leave everything to him."

And so he played a charming companion to my masquerade. Had he not been so seemingly open and friendly with me, I would not have minded so much. Then, trying to be fair, I saw that he could be just as bitter at my deception.

"Mother could never bear that any man near her could love someone else. Perhaps that was Fabian's trouble, too. That he wanted another woman, someone younger, and that's why they quarreled and he killed her . . . oh, accidentally."

"Don't dare say that again. Do you hear?"

"But, Rachel, it's the truth, only we can't prove it." She stared at me, and I knew she was puzzled by my violence.

I didn't care. The challenge of Gideon's Rock had suddenly become terrifying. Livanova was dead, but hatred and revenge could stretch beyond death.

I leaped over to the chair where Stephanie crouched. "Come on." My voice was rough. "We're going to find them. Oh, for God's sake, you've been asking me to take you to Dominick. Don't hang back now." I dragged at her arm.

Stephanie gasped little phrases as we ran. "The solicitor . . . saw me . . . after the inquest. He . . . said in a horrible hard voice, 'We'll have to have a talk, Miss Clair.' He said it as if . . . he suspected me of . . . not telling the truth . . ."

"Save your breath for running," I called from a few steps ahead of her.

"And there was . . . Fabian's letter . . . I've lost it . . . But I was afraid . . . of him . . . I *am* afraid . . . of him."

And with all that fear piling up inside her she had escaped into her limbo world.

We raced together across the lawn and through the silver-birch copse. Suddenly she stopped and her voice came in little whispered gusts. "Let me go on alone. Don't come with me."

"It's out of your hands. I'm involved too."

I dragged her on, and she gave wails of protest, fighting my grip on her wrist. "Let me go. I won't run away. I can't. But you're too fast for me. I . . ." She tripped over a clump of dock leaves and cried out, although she couldn't have been hurt. "Don't go so fast, Rachel . . ."

I had given no thought to the fact that she had so recently been in hospital, and for all her desperation, had not my stamina.

"Take some deep breaths," I said, "and try to keep calm. It won't do any good if . . ."

"*You* tell *me* to keep calm?" she gasped up at me. "You're in far more of a hurry even than I. Why? What are you afraid of?"

"We haven't time to stay and talk."

"Oh, please stop, Rachel." She was running without lifting her feet sufficiently, so that she kept stumbling like a sprinter in the last stages of exhaustion.

"Stay there," I called back, running ahead of her.

We had reached the strip of wasteland, and Stephanie sank into the long grass, panting and sobbing. But as I began climbing the slope of the rock, she was screaming out to me to wait for her.

"Rachel . . . Rachel . . ."

I ignored her. I had no clear thought in my mind as to why I had to be there when the men completed their climb. It came from an urgency that was intuitive.

The tall coarse grass whipped my legs, the seemingly gentle slope took on a terrifying gradient as I tried to run up it. I went as far as I could to the nearest wing of rock where there were wind-torn bushes to cling to. Then I dropped on my stomach and crawled to the jagged, needle-sharp crowns of rock. Beyond them were a few feet of grassy cliff before the final drop. Herring gulls rode the waves and circled the cliffs, resting like pieces of swansdown blown by the wind on the gray ledges.

I had expected to see the men roped together, but they were climbing separately although fairly close. Dominick was nearest me on the low eastern wing and had almost reached the top. Fabian was on the harsh center face, hands clinging to clefts, feet on edges of rock that seemed, from my angle of observation, too sheer for balance.

Although I couldn't take my eyes off them, I tried to keep out of sight, sheltering in the shadow of a salt-burned bush. Dominick was moving carefully, searching for his own holds, but either he —or Fabian for him—had chosen a route which I could see from where I lay was extremely easy, with ledges and clefts like a step-ladder, so that unless he looked down and became dizzy, his way was safe to the top. I knew very little about the sport, if this was indeed a sport and not a kind of lunacy of reckless men. The way Dominick balanced himself before changing his weight, the way he kept his eyes on his next move instead of looking up at his final goal, seemed to me to be the acts of someone who had learned at least the rudiments of climbing and remembered them.

I was careful not to let either man see me, in case I broke their concentration. I felt a little like a tortoise, my own head shooting out of my bush shelter to watch, then darting back as their heads went up for their next hold.

Stephanie hadn't joined me, and I had no idea whether she was still at the foot of the rock or if she had gone around to watch from the beach. In that moment I didn't care.

Tension held me in a vise of fear. The bright morning was hidden under a gray billowing pall of racing clouds. The wind had grown fiercer and crashed against the rock in great gusts, tearing around the crevices in long-drawn wolf howls, drowning even the screaming of the gulls. In between the bursts of wind there was such quiet that I could hear the scraping of Dominick's climbing boots.

He had heaved himself closer up the rock face and I could hear his grunts and gasps as he forced his body into the next position. In another three or four moves he would reach me. I shifted my position, wriggling to the right, nearer the great cleft which cut into the limestone, partially separating the wing from the main body.

Fabian was three quarters of the way up, and even to me, knowing virtually nothing about climbing, the longer I watched, the better I could see the difference between them. For Fabian was moving with an easy rhythm, his face tight not with anxiety but with concentration, his arms and legs stretched effortlessly. Even there, on Gideon's ruthless face, the lame man had an almost catlike grace. Dominick, on his easier climb, looked more strained.

Each move they made held intense absorption, but every time I turned to watch Dominick, my eyes were drawn back to Fabian. So, watching him, I missed the reason for the scream.

246

It came in the lull between two gusts of wind from somewhere far below us, a high woman's scream that disturbed the gulls and sent them swooping with the heavy alarmed beat of their white wings.

"Dominick . . . don't . . ." Those were the words that followed the scream.

I levered myself up from my crouched position and looked over the cliff face; my heart, my nerve ends, my whole body atrophied in a lightning grip of fear.

As another gust of wind parted the scraggy branches, I saw that a piece of limestone rock, which he must have been clutching, had partially broken away in Dominick's hands. I saw him lean for support against the rock face and I knew I dare not cry out or I would startle him and he could hurtle to his death.

Only Fabian could help, or since Dominick was so near the top, I might be able to if I edged nearer the cliff point. Even so, Dominick was a big man and I couldn't possibly drag his weight up to safety unless he could help himself, and he was gripping the rock as if his fingers were bound to it.

I crawled a few inches closer, looking toward Fabian. He was making no attempt to go to Dominick's aid. Instead, he was spread-eagled and totally still on his own precarious footholds.

I looked back at Dominick. His right hand was clawing at the rock and was so close to me that I could have touched the white knuckles. Then, simultaneously with a sudden movement of his arm, the scream from the beach came again.

Dominick was breathing heavily and little hissing sounds came with his efforts. I inched my way forward and saw with horror that he wasn't trying to find a handhold for the final hoist to the top, but was tearing at the piece of loosened rock. I saw it come away, bits of earth and thin blades of grass clinging to it.

Dominick's right hand had a firm grip on the topmost ledge; the one holding the rock moved, swinging outward, but sufficiently slowly for his balance not to be upset. Then I saw the arm start to make an arc through the air.

I acted in a flash, without conscious decision. Dominick's arm was at the top of its swing and closest to me as my hand shot out and crashed against his. Alarm and sheer amazement weakened his grip and the great stone fell. Because he hadn't seen me crouched just above him, I had caught him off his guard.

The rock dropped, bouncing against the limestone wing, the sound lost in the gusty howls of the wind.

In horror and fascination, I watched Dominick regain the balance he had so nearly lost as I hit his arm. He shouted something, but the wind took his words away. He stumbled on the next two footholds, each time clinging to the rock face. Then, recovering both his nerve and his balance, he heaved himself to the top and lay sprawling near me.

I moved, and he turned his head and saw me. His face was so contorted that no beauty remained.

"Damn you, Rachel, damn you for interfering."

He staggered to his feet and began to run. I lay paralyzed. The complete reversal of all the opinions I had formed about his character, the dreadful suspicions that had torn into my opposing emotions, stunned me. For that moment I was beyond making sense of the brief, horrifying incident. Then another thought shook me into action. Fabian was still on the cliff face. It was possible that he had seen Dominick's arm lifted for the throw, and turning on the rock face to avoid the aim, had lost his footing.

I looked over the edge and was sickened. I could not see Fabian. An outthrust of the wing could be hiding him from me, or he could have fallen.

I scrambled to my feet and climbed on shaking legs to the place beyond the buttress where Gideon's Rock was highest and the cliff itself steepest.

The wind tore sideways at me as I reached the topmost spot. I dropped to my knees and crawled again as near the edge as I could go. In those terrifying moments it flashed through my mind how perfect was the self-control needed in dangerous situations. For Fabian was climbing again, his movements smooth and unhurried.

I looked for Stephanie on the beach, but couldn't see her. It was possible that she was somewhere far below, watching. But more likely she had come running to the land side of the rock, had seen Dominick and had gone to him.

"I must find Dominick . . ." Her cry to me was in the wind as it fought to tear my hair from my head. My thick sweater felt no more protection than a piece of gauze. I had to wait for Fabian, and while waiting, I faced the shocking truth that Dominick had tried to kill him. It would have been such an easy way, there on the cliff face with no witnesses. A rock thrown and missing, and then another try, and if that failed, another. For there was no way that a man, even an experienced climber, could escape an attack on a place like Gideon. But two people had been watching them.

I had sensed from the very first the tension between them. It must have grown and burned inside Dominick, this hatred for Fabian because of a desperate certainty that he was in some way responsible for the death of the woman who gave him his livelihood. All I could feel was a thankfulness that by my frantic act I had stopped the final effort of revenge.

I looked over the high ridge and was certain that Fabian hadn't seen me. To me, as he leaned out slightly from the wall of rock, looking for the next handhold, he seemed frighteningly alone. Behind him were the gray clouds. And the sea reflected their color, only the tips of the waves softening the effect, lacy as waxen honeycombs, stretching far out to where two ships passed on the horizon.

Looking back from where I lay, I could see only the tops of the silver birches and the crowning points of the three gables of Jessamy Court. The grass under me was damp with sea mist and windblown spray; my hair streamed back and my ears felt frozen. But I could not leave until Fabian reached the top of Gideon's Rock. It was as if I had come to Dorset and found a great door closed upon an ugly secret. Every day fingers had pushed the door a little wider, so that I was able to see more clearly the emotions and the hatreds that had not ended with Tatiana Livanova's death.

I put my head down on the grass, almost welcoming the spiky discomfort as a physical pain to stop a deeper emotional one.

"What in God's name is going on?"

My head shot up and I saw Fabian. My limbs were so stiff that I got up awkwardly, the wind trying to push me down again.

"Why did you scream like a banshee?" His casual, almost flippant question was a curious anticlimax. Either Fabian hadn't seen Dominick's attempt on his life, or he was purposely playing it down.

Before I could speak, he asked, "And where the hell is Dominick?"

"I don't know. When he reached the top he just ran."

"Why are you here?" He waited. "Well, why?"

"I had to wait to see . . . if you were all right."

"What did you think was going to happen to me on *that*? That rock is almost a boy's third lesson in rock climbing. So, my dear Stephanie . . . ?"

"I am not Stephanie."

"I don't care what name you choose to be known by, and it's not important."

"Fabian, please listen."

"No, *you* listen. I'll come to you later. In the meantime, I know perfectly well that Dominick tried to unbalance me on the rock. But his aim was bad and he missed. We'll start the explanations from there. When he aimed again, someone knocked the piece of rock, or whatever it was he had, out of his hand. I couldn't see who it was. Was it you?"

"Yes. But, Fabian, I'm *not* Stephanie Clair."

"Then who are you?"

"Rachel Fleming."

"And who the devil is she?"

"Stephanie's friend."

"Don't tell me I've been entertaining a stranger as Livanova's neglected daughter? Oh, I don't believe it. And the ruse doesn't work, anyway, my dear. It's not a very intelligent way of wriggling out of an involvement."

"I don't know what *you're* talking about, but I'm talking about *me,* and I'm telling you the truth."

"We'll get through the stories later, Stephanie-Rachel." He pushed me forward. "Now get going. Go on. Down there, back to Jessamy."

"Fabian, I've got to talk *now.*"

"Damn it, can't you get your priorities right? Do what I tell you. Go the way Dominick went. You must know where that is, since it's been your meeting place."

"How do you know that Dominick and Stephanie met?"

"Oh, I like fitting pieces of a pattern together, and quite suddenly I learned a lot of things. But we're wasting time. Help me find Dominick."

"I haven't any idea . . ." The wind snatched at my words as Fabian passed me.

We were moving very fast down the slope. Once or twice I stumbled, but Fabian was too far ahead to notice. By the time I reached the stretch of wasteland Fabian was through the copse of silver birches, and when I arrived at the house, he was nowhere in sight.

XXIV

I WENT ONTO THE TERRACE and into the drawing room, listening for three people. The wind fretted at the windows as I crossed the silent hall and went down the passage to the kitchen. It was very tidy and glowing with cleanliness. There was a melon in a white dish and a magazine on the rocking chair in the corner. Mrs. Manfred had probably gone to the village. Jupiter lay asleep on the window sill. I wanted to pick him up and hold him close to me, as something warm and stable and uninvolved. But I left him and went back into the hall, paused at the bottom of the stairs and listened.

There was no sound from overhead. All I heard was the loud ticking of the grandfather clock. I opened the door of the practice room, and in the only light which came in from the hall, I saw my reflection in the three great mirrors as dim as if I were a ghost walking in the windowless room.

There was a movement. Someone came from behind the door, closed it and stood against it.

"Thank God you've come," said Dominick. "I thought I'd have to go out and look for you."

"You tried to kill Fabian when you were on the rock."

"It was the maddest impulse of my life. He was there, without any means of escape, and it seemed a way out for your safety. Does what I did sound so terrible?"

"Yes—terrible. It's not for you to take the law of life and death into your own hands."

"For God's sake, Rachel, face facts. *Your* life was in danger from him. Doesn't that change your judgment of me?"

"Yes, but not to the point of accepting an attempt to . . . to murder." I leaned against the great wall of glass near Fabian's worktable. The room closed round me, and I, who had never fainted in my life, felt faint. "Let's get out of here. I don't care what's outside, but I can't stay in this room."

Dominick flicked the switch by the door. The chandelier sprang into dozens of glittering facets which turned his hair to a blaze of corn-gold and flung the molded flowers on the lily ceiling into rich relief.

"Is that better?"

I ignored the question.

"Why did you pretend to believe I was Stephanie?"

He drew in a slow breath, as if he had been running hard and was trying to steady his racing heart. "I have to justify that point, don't I? I'm sorry. I knew you weren't Stephanie. You see, we had met."

"Yes, she told me."

"What else did she tell you?"

I ignored the question, and insisted, "Even if you didn't want to say anything in front of Fabian, why didn't you tell me when we went for a walk on that first night that you knew I wasn't Stephanie?"

"I thought you were here as some inquisitive so-called friend who had discovered that Stephanie was frightened out of her wits and had read the letter Fabian wrote to her and decided to interfere. I don't like inquisitive people. But I had no idea who you really were until Stephanie called me when she left hospital."

"You knew she had had a kind of blackout?"

"No. But when I couldn't contact her, I guessed she had gone into hiding. She scares easily, and it would have been typical of her, when I warned her that for the time being it would be unwise for us to meet, to rush into hiding."

"Fabian didn't know," I said. "Or did he?"

"I'm quite certain he thought you were Stephanie, so I waited to see what he would do. You took a terrible risk, you know."

"From Fabian." I leaned for support against the table. The two words I spoke mingled with the noise of the trestles giving way under my weight. The light wooden frame collapsed and drawing papers, pens, crayons scattered over the floor. I left them there and backed against the wall.

"From Fabian," I said again.

"Of course. That's why when Stephanie came down here and we met in the forest, I told her to keep away and that while Fabian believed that you were Stephanie, she was in no danger."

"What danger? Fabian had the house. What more did he want?"

"Payment," Dominick said, "for what Livanova did."

"Leaving him . . ."

He shook his head. "Retribution. The accident that lamed him: that's the reason Fabian never forgave her and in the end killed her."

"How can you possibly know that?"

". . . and then, because that was not revenge enough, he wanted to destroy her daughter. You—as Stephanie."

I was like a piece of frozen rock against the mirror wall. I closed my eyes and then, because all I could see was Fabian's face, I opened them again and looked with relief on Dominick's brightness.

"Do you know what Livanova did?" he asked.

"I don't want to hear any more." I turned my head away from his cold blue eyes.

"What's the matter with you? If he has caught hold of your emotions and your imagination, then the sooner you get over it, the better. Listen . . . *listen,* Rachel. Fabian told Livanova he was going to climb again in Peru, and there was a row. She knew that he would probably never come back to her. It was his way of breaking off an affair that ate into his freedom. And she couldn't bear it to be the end. He was on the point of leaving Jessamy and his car was outside. While he went to get his bags, she got into his car, and when he reached the drive, she ran him down—here, at Jessamy. She said, 'Now you'll never be able to leave me.' It was hushed up, and that seemed to be one thing in Fabian's favor. But he had his own plan of revenge. There is no forgiveness, you see, in a man like Fabian."

"Why didn't you tell the police all this?" I asked.

"We suspected, but we had no proof. That's why I remained down here to watch Fabian, to wait until he made a mistake. And then . . ."

"Then?"

"You came walking into his trap for Stephanie. He wanted her down here." He lifted his shoulders as if releasing some tension. "But now you're safe and it's Stephanie who could be in danger if she makes herself known to Fabian. That's why I've got to find her." He put his hands on my shoulders. "I'm going to leave you here while I look for her. And I'm going to lock the door so that you'll be safe."

"Don't do that. Dominick, *don't* . . . Whatever might happen to me, leave the door unlocked. Please."

His hands were gentle on my arms. "It's only for a little while. Then, when I find Stephanie, I'll bring her here and cope with Fabian. I'll have to get help from Dulverley."

"The . . . police?"

"Of course. But trust me. You're safe here."

The door closed and I heard the scrape of metal, as if the key hadn't been turned for many years.

I leaped across the short space and twisted and pulled at the door handle, but it didn't give. Dominick could not know my hatred of locked places.

Three times I hammered on the door and called, but the huge panel of mahogany would neither yield to my pressure nor would anyone hear me unless they were very close.

The great room seemed to grow smaller and press in on me as the minutes went by; my own mirrored images came closer, so that I had a terrifying sensation that when those three reflections met in me, I would die. It was a fear as absurd as a superstition, but in the silence and my aloneness within that locked room, the slow panic rose so that my heart thudded and every breath was painful.

When I first heard a sound at the door I thought it was in my imagination. But when I looked, I saw the ornate brass handle move, at first slowly, then impatiently.

I crouched down and peered through the keyhole. I could see nothing. Someone had come looking for one of us, and finding the door locked, had gone away.

I was wrong. Sounds came again from outside. Someone was fitting a key in the lock. I sprang away, stumbled against the collapsed trestle table, pressing myself against the mirror wall, hands either side of me, stiff and straight, as if I were made of wax.

My heart was no longer thumping like a drum. It had become quiet, as if it had passed the edge of fear and was accepting an inevitability that was also atrophying my brain. Beyond terror was limbo. In the great practice room, under the lily ceiling, I felt like a prisoner, past hope of reprieve, waiting for my inquisitor and perhaps my destroyer.

"What in the name of goodness made you lock yourself in?" Fabian asked.

I couldn't take my eyes from his face. Every muscle appeared tight and his eyes were brilliant. "How did you get the key?"

"Oh, every key fits every lock in this house. Come on." He reached for me, and I avoided him. He thrust a hand toward me, and I backed away. "For God's sake, don't stand there. Get out, girl. Quick."

Of course, he had to escape before Dominick found him. And it was possible that I was to be the hostage.

A bleak flutter of optimism broke through me. I must escape from Fabian and I could, because desperation would make me run faster. I took great leaping steps to the door, but as I reached it, it closed; the lock clicked. Once again the key turned, this time imprisoning us together.

I could think of only one person who might hate me for what I had done. Stephanie couldn't yet fully understand the reason for my impersonation. I called her name, but as I shouted at the thick door, my voice sounded like the bleep of a fledgling and my hammering had a muffled cotton-wool sound.

I cried out as Fabian came behind me and pushed me away. "It's as solid as Gideon's Rock. Don't waste your strength."

"Who . . . who is on the other side?"

"I'm the biggest bloodiest fool! God in heaven," he exploded, "how could I fall for that?"

"For what?"

"Walking into a trap, of course."

"I don't understand."

I doubted if he even heard me. He was looking around the room, swinging on his heels from left to right and back again. "Short of dynamiting that door—and I'm quite certain there is no explosive among the props here—we'll have to find another way of escape." He walked over to the mirrors and frowned at them. "The windows. I remember seeing them before the mirrors were put in. But which walls, damn it to hell, which walls?"

I watched him slide back the glass doors, step through and test the walls. Afterward I was to try to think what it was which linked that moment with the one where I stood poised for a jump on the excavation site near Lorne Abbey.

Fabian was dragging out props, tapping the walls behind them. Little tubs of artificial trees, a gilt chair, a tiny table that only dwarfs could sit at, cushions, a silver wand—all the discarded props of old classical ballets were flung out, and went skidding across the floor. He came out, stepped over the pile of things that had once seemed magic on a stage but now looked, as they lay discarded, merely dusty and, somehow, sad. Then he pulled back the second glass panel, dragging aside Livanova's costumes. They fluttered and fanned out as he pushed through them, and watching the disturbance of that world of myth and faery which Tatiana Livanova had ruled for so long, I heard myself ask, in a clear, carrying voice, a question I hadn't even thought was in my mind, "Did you really forget the warning about the dangerous trench at Lorne Abbey, where the Celtic cross was?"

He stepped back into the room; his eyes, catching the light from the chandelier, were yellow-green fire.

"Surely you must know?"

"Know what?"

"That I was out when the call came and the message was given to someone else to give to me—and wasn't."

"Mrs. Manfred?"

"No."

"But why would anyone, deliberately, not give it to you?"

"Your grammar is appalling," he said, walking toward the wall on our left and sliding the glass back.

"I wish you'd explain. How . . . ?"

"Stop asking questions and let me think. The important thing is to get out of here." He glanced at me over his shoulder. "And don't keep looking at the door. I've told you, that's no escape route."

"There's no answer, then, to my question?"

"The question . . ." he began and then didn't finish his sentence. "I've got it! There's a window here, just where this mirror joins the wall. I remember now." He strode across the room, glanced down at the collapsed trestle table and the scattered drawings, and said, "That was careless of someone." Then he picked up the chair.

"What are you going to do?"

"Smash the glass wall, of course."

"You can't. If that crashes, it will kill you."

"My dear Rachel—that's your name, isn't it?—I'm not going to be ass enough to let it collapse on me. Nor do I intend to be incarcerated in this Alice-in-Wonderland room forever. Now, get out of the way. Not there—I shall try to smash it so that it falls that way. Get right back, as far as you can."

He swung the chair and as it crashed into the mirror he leaped away. The glass splintered, and I turned my back, covering my face. When I looked again, there was a gaping hole; beneath it, glass lay like a cascade of glittering ice.

"I was right," he exclaimed in grim triumph, "and I even remembered how high the window was from the floor. Look, you can just see where it's been boarded up. One more go at it and we'll be able to get to the window and prise those boards away—they're only strips of plywood." He flung the chair at the mirror again and more glass splintered. "I think that's enough," he said and slid the chair across the room. Then he seized a small stick and chipped away the jagged pieces caught in the window frame.

"Someone's outside," I cried. "Listen."

We stood looking at one another in silence, ears strained.

The sound came from beyond the boarded-up window: "Rachel. Rachel. Fabian . . ."

"It's Stephanie," I said.

She must have heard the crashing of glass and raced around the corner of the house to the place from which the sound had come. I ran across the room, but pulled up short as my feet crunched on the edge of the pile of broken glass.

Fabian thrust me roughly away. "Don't be a little fool. Wait. Some of those jagged pieces will cut through your shoes. Stay back and stop rushing at things. I'll clear a way and . . ."

257

The voice outside broke through again. "Rachel, get out quickly. You must. Dominick . . ." The name ended in a small scream.

Fabian found a long-handled broom that had probably been used in the Cinderella ballet. Splinters of glass clung to the bristles and shone in the light; the glass made a soft hissing sound as Fabian piled it to one side.

"I can't clear it completely because it clings to this damned broom," he said. "You'll have to walk carefully." He stepped through the hole he had made in the glass wall and struggled with the latch that had become jammed in the warped window frame.

Cries and shouts came to us from beyond the window. I heard a high, hysterical voice that I could only just recognize as Stephanie's, but the sound became fainter, and finally there was silence outside.

The ancient, obstinate frame gave way at last, and as Fabian flung the window open, I took a great gulp of air.

Fabian climbed through first and glanced about him. Then he reached toward me. "Give me your hand, and be careful how you step over those splinters of glass. When you're outside, throw off your shoes or you'll cut yourself and everything else you walk on. Now come on."

Fabian helped me onto the sill. I had to push through branches of a lilac that, allowed to spread too near the wall, was thrusting through the window.

The quiet beat about us, heavy with menace. We were in an untended part of the grounds at the western side of the house, where the berserk lilac bush and rhododendrons and prickly holly made a jungle of green. As I fought through it all to reach the tamed garden beyond, there was an acrid, smoky scent in the air, as if somewhere near us Fenney had started his autumn bonfires.

Free of the bushes, I stepped over furze and bracken. The fire scent became stronger.

Fabian had paused, lifting his head. Then he gave a loud and violent curse, "Hell and damnation!" and tore past me, flinging aside everything that blocked his way. With one great burst of speed I tried to catch up with him, and immediately fell full tilt into a rotten tree stump. Fabian was already way ahead of me. I picked myself up, flung off my shoes and left them as Fabian had instructed me, in the bracken. Then, ignoring the sharp stones and wet slippery leaves of the undergrowth, I raced on.

If Livanova had wanted a wild garden beyond the neat lawns

and the yew hedges, she certainly had it on this far side. Evergreens, thick tendrils of ivy and laurel hindered my speed, and by the time I reached the front of the house I knew that the smoke was not from a bonfire. It drifted past the front doors like small twists of black veiling. I raced up the steps.

Stephanie was inside, crouched by the open double doors. Fabian had found a fire extinguisher and was squirting chemical at a blazing armchair that had been pulled into the center of the hall. The yellow brocade was burned away, revealing the blackened stuffing of cushion feathers and frame.

He saw me and said, "Get that girl out of the way. She has twice almost had herself sprayed with chemical."

"Then stop trying to put it out." Stephanie leaped up, screaming at him, "Let it burn. Let it all burn . . ." She turned on me as I tried to hold her back, sobbing and struggling. Her loveliness was spoiled by the frenzy in her face and her hair was as wild as a mad woman's. But she knew what she wanted. She was desperate to destroy Tatiana Livanova's house.

"Wasn't I clever?" She was gloating without joy. "I found the straw in the garage."

In spite of her frenzy, I was stronger than she, and gradually I subdued her sufficiently so that she collapsed helplessly into wild weeping and protesting.

"I didn't mean to let Jessamy burn with you and Fabian inside. That's why when I heard a noise, I came to find out if you were there, but I couldn't open the door. And there was no key."

The floor was icy cold to my feet, but I held onto Stephanie.

Fabian was saying, "I left the key in the door."

"But *he* came and found it there and took it. He wanted you both— Oh, never mind. Don't ask me . . . don't ask me anything. You're safe. You can get away. But let Jessamy burn."

"Jessamy," with a soft "J," as Livanova spoke it; as the voice on the tape had spoken it. "Let *J*essamy burn . . ."

"Stephanie, listen to me." I tightened my hold on her. *"Be quiet and listen.* The house isn't yours to destroy even if you wanted it. And it certainly wouldn't burn down with *that* effort."

I glanced involuntarily at Livanova's portrait. The dark eyes in the strong face looked down at her sad and lovely daughter: "Stephanie always was a fool." For a moment I thought that by some necromancy, it had been Livanova who had spoken.

Suddenly Stephanie stiffened in my arms and cried out Dominick's name. He stood behind us on the steps of the house.

"You should have let her jump into the fire and then we'd all be relieved of that hunk of trouble. Here, let me deal with her."

He reached out and grasped Stephanie's shoulder. She moaned with pain, "Leave me alone."

He swung her roughly around and bent her arm backward. She screamed and tried to tear herself away from him. Fabian started to move toward them but I was nearest. I didn't stop to think. I saw Dominick pull tighter on Stephanie's arm.

For the second time, I hit him. It wasn't a very hard blow, but because I was small and he was tall, and because his attention had been on Fabian, it caught him off balance in the solar plexus. He reeled back, looking at me, a curious smile on his face, his eyes a little out of focus, almost as though he was drunk.

For the next few seconds, or minutes—time lost its meaning—everything was confusion and noise, screaming and sobbing, shouting and coughing in the last smoke from the unimpressive little fire.

The first clear words I heard after my ungentle punch was Dominick saying to Fabian, "And now I've come for what is really mine."

"Which is . . . ?"

"The letter. You have it. I want it."

"Where do you think I keep it?" Fabian had turned off the extinguisher and set it down in a corner of the hall.

"Go and get it—now. And I mean now. I'll come with you."

"You'll have a damned long way to go." Fabian was very calm. Stephanie stirred in my arms. "Fabian, give it to him. Please."

"You've done enough damage. Now shut up." Dominick's gentle, almost tentative voice was gone. I remembered an old Spanish proverb that spoke of the two faces of man: the bright, open side and the dark, secret side. That was what Dominick was showing us, coldly, quietly blazing. "That letter."

"Oh, you can have it, but you'll have to be patient."

"I'm not. I want it now. Where is it?"

"With the police. And they're on their way here."

As if Fabian had timed his words perfectly, I heard a car in the distance. Dominick heard it too. He swung around, took a flying leap and began to run toward the forest. Then he veered off to the left and raced across the lawn, past the blazing maple, and disappeared around the far wing of the house.

In that split second of changing his direction, he must have realized that the forest was the obvious place where they would look for him.

Fabian was standing near me, very straight and still, making no effort to go after Dominick. And as we stood there in moments of seeming suspended time, I heard another car start up.

I swung around. "Fabian, the garage . . . your car . . ."

"Probably," he said with disinterest. "But as he doesn't really drive, he'll probably crash it. Let's thank God it's the Bentley and not our necks."

"But we could stop him by cutting across the gardens and into the drive."

"If you want to get run down, fair enough. But I don't. And there is only one way here where wheels can go, and that's down the lane. They can't miss him there."

"They." The police.

Stephanie was lying full length on the top step, like a child in a tantrum, weeping, not in temper but with the hopelessness of despair.

I looked down at her and felt no pity. "The tale you told me back there in the forest was all lies, wasn't it?"

"I had to tell you something—anything—to keep you from knowing the truth. Rachel, understand—" She broke off, coughing. "Please try to understand."

The smoke and stench of chemical still hung around us, making speech difficult. "Get up." I heaved at her ungently.

"Leave me alone."

Fabian went past us. "For God's sake, get that girl and yourself out into the air." He ran down the steps to meet the police car coming up the drive.

"Don't let them take me away." She gave little choking wails. "Rachel, don't . . . He'll get me, somehow, because I've ruined everything for him. But I can't live with it, not now."

"You accused Fabian of murder. And for that I don't care at the moment whether you choke yourself silly. But I don't want to, so get up and come into the fresh air."

"I can't move. *That* isn't a lie, Rachel, I can't. My legs have just given way."

"Well then, you can tell me the truth through coughs." I very nearly hated her. The compassion I had for so many years felt for her was only a faint stirring. If it had vanished altogether, I believe in that moment I would have wanted to drag her out to find Dominick and leave her to his fury. As it was, I said again, "The truth, this time."

"I thought it need never be known. But out there on the cliff, I saw . . . I saw that it wasn't over. Fabian must have suspected something and that's why Dominick realized that he couldn't wait any longer for . . . for the plan to work. So he had tried to kill Fabian."

"What truth are you talking about?" I was gripping her so tightly that I must have been hurting her. "Stephanie, *tell me*."

"When Mother laughed at me and said that awful thing, 'Dominick is my lover,' I put out my hands and pushed her hard. I wanted to hurt her, Rachel, *I wanted to hurt my mother*. But she only staggered back. I knew she must be shaken by knowing about us, but she acted—oh, she acted marvelously. She stood against the mantel, still laughing and saying, 'You stupid child, as if you could hurt me.' Then she said again that Dominick was her lover. He kept shouting at her that it was a lie. But she gave one of those sweeps of her hand I knew so well—it meant that you were less than the dust to her. She said to Dominick, 'Don't forget, you are my paid employee as well as my lover. I brought you out of the cold, my darling . . .' And then Dominick hit her. She looked suddenly frightened and ran out on the balcony. That's when he hit her a second time, and she fell. And she didn't move again. We never meant . . . we didn't mean to hurt her. We . . ." She stopped speaking and her head rolled to one side. I willed her not to faint, not to lose consciousness, not to escape from me.

"Why did you come down here?"

"Because I had to see Dominick. To know what he was going to do. He kept talking on the telephone of a plan, but he wouldn't tell me what it was, and I was frightened." She paused, and then added in a curious slurred voice, as if she were talking in her sleep, "I knew that Mother had willed the house to Fabian, because she told us when she laughed at us—that night. But she said that if he died, the house would be mine."

"Yours and Dominick's," I said.

She nodded. "But after the inquest everything went wrong. I had a dreadful fear that there were people who knew, or guessed, the truth. I was terrified. In the end I was even frightened of Dominick."

"As you were innocent, you could have told the truth to someone you could trust."

"Who?" Her voice was plaintive and protesting. "I was there when Mother died, but what proof did I have that Dominick killed her and that I was just a witness? Besides, it wasn't deliberate. He didn't mean to do that awful thing. He just lost his temper because Mother laughed at us. On the rock with Fabian it was different. You *must* see . . ."

"Oh yes, I see. He intended to kill Fabian. It would have been a climbing accident. A lame man. A distraught friend giving evidence after a fatal fall. Hints about Livanova and Fabian. Then admitting that not all had been told at the inquest on your mother's death because you were afraid you would not be believed. And don't look like that, as though I shock you. It's true, isn't it? Oh, heavens, two innocents—you and Dominick—revealing all about a man conveniently dead." My voice came, torn and harsh at the very thought of what might have happened had I not been on Gideon's Rock.

Stephanie was pulling agitatedly at my sleeve. "Understand, Rachel. Please understand. Mother's death wasn't *planned*. It *was* an accident, and after it happened everything became too much for us. How do you know how you'd react if you were scared?"

"I'm scared now," I said, "for you and for Dominick."

She buried her face in my shoulder, moaning.

"You came once to the house, didn't you? You asked for Fabian."

"I suddenly felt that if I didn't tell someone the whole truth, I'd go mad. Mother had said that Fabian was strong. I thought: I've got to take a chance that he will understand and forgive— and keep our secret. But when the housekeeper opened the door I came to my senses. I knew no one would understand, so I turned and ran. Rachel, I love Dominick so much."

"But does *he* love *you?*"

"Of course."

"Well, you should know, I suppose. But you always did choose the wrong people for friends and lovers, didn't you? And if you two had married, how do you think you could have afforded to live at Jessamy?"

"Oh, we wouldn't. There was the letter."

"What letter?"

"The one that was sent to Dominick—or should have been. Fabian has it. It will make everything all right for us. You see . . ." Her voice faded to silence.

263

"Stephanie." I gave her face a few light slaps.

"Dominick wants the house," she said with an obvious effort, and then her eyes glazed and closed. She fell heavily against me and her face had taken on the same frightening indifference I had seen at the hospital. It was washed free of all emotion, all expression.

I bent down and asked, slowly and clearly, "Why did Dominick want the house?"

I waited for her answer. In the distance I could hear the wail of an ambulance. Here, where we crouched, the scent of burning had been dissipated by the wind.

"Stephanie."

But I saw that there was no way in which I could arouse her. The fates had given Stephanie one glorious blessing. When life became too difficult, she could escape into unconsciousness. It was no act.

The ambulance stopped and Fabian came up the steps. He took a long look at her. "At least they won't have to take her struggling," he said.

"Why did you send for the ambulance?"

"Because one of us would need it," he said shortly. "Violence was in the air."

It was all so neat and quiet and tragic. The men laid Stephanie on the stretcher, tucked a blanket around her and carried her down the steps. Her hair fell about her, and I knew, as I laid my hand against her face, that she had no idea what was happening to her.

Fabian said, "Get away from this filthy smell."

"I shouldn't leave her . . ."

"Do you think she knows whether you're with her or not? And if *you* don't mind the sight of that hideous object that was once a chair, I do. Go along. I'll be with you as soon as the police have done with me."

I went to my room and found some shoes. My feet felt ice-cold and sore. I cleaned my face, and as I put on fresh make-up, I remembered that my powder compact had been taken from my room. Without doubt, Dominick had watched me go out and then had gone to my room. He might have thought that I had made some incriminating notes about him, and seeing my compact with the initials on it, had decided to give me a small fright. Nothing dropped on Hobbin's bare doorstep would remain unseen for long.

The smell of smoke and chemical was also trapped in the drawing room and I crossed to the terrace doors and opened them and stepped outside.

I could hear the men's voices in the drive, the slam of a car door and then the ambulance's siren. I went quickly down the steps and around the side of the house.

Fenney was weaving his usual crooked way up the drive and only the persistence of the ambulance siren urged him to the side of the road to let it pass.

I avoided Fabian and the policemen talking at the front steps and walked toward the forest. I wondered how far Dominick would get in Fabian's powerful Bentley. He must have waited, hidden in the laurel bushes, until the police car had pulled up at the front steps and then raced into the garage. Although he had told me he didn't drive, he must have known enough to start an engine and steer and thus make his escape—or crash.

The great branches closed over my head as if guarding me from the outside world. The forest was what I most needed. I had to recharge my exhausted energy and control my wild and bewildered emotions.

It was Dominick who was most clearly in my mind. His immediate acceptance of me as Stephanie had been a magnificent piece of acting. I recalled how he had entered the room on that first evening when Fabian had introduced us. Dominick had commented that I held out my hand as Livanova had done. How well his light laughter had covered up the shock at being faced with an impostor.

Looking back over my days at Jessamy, I was amazed at the risks I had taken. But the one who had been the best actor was Dominick Hunt: Dominick, the grave, the cunning, the gentle and the mad. For who, if he were sane, would kill for a house isolated in the lovely wilds of Dorset?

I felt no sense of alarm as I walked in the forest. I was certain that the police had seen which way Dominick had gone and had followed him. The only sounds I heard were the bird's songs and all I could see were vistas of great beech trunks and a heavy canopy of golden leaves. I must have walked almost in a circle, for I found myself near Hobbin's cottage, and as I passed the open door, I saw Fabian and the children inside.

Robin's slanting eyes caught sight of me first, and then Fabian turned and beckoned.

On the table in the center of the room was the tape recorder. Hobbin stared at it, fascinated, and then turned to me.

"You was right, missy. You was right. I didn't hear voices like my granny. *That's* what it was." She jabbed a thick finger at the little silent machine. "Him that was as bright as Lucifer, he had the devil's sweetness on his lips, but I knew he were bad. I told that to Madame once, but she laughed at me. She said, 'Perhaps I like them bad, Hobbin. And he's young and beautiful.' If she'd only listened, she'd have been alive today."

"I liked him, too," I said. "*I* thought him a good and charming man."

"But Madame were wise, she knew he were bad. You are so young, missy. You did not see the blackness behind the gold." She raised her eyes to the smoke-stained ceiling. "I saw how you and he walked and talked together, and I warned you."

"Yes, you did."

"No one listens to witches," she broke in half angrily. "People say they bain't be trusted. But when 'they' warn us, it be our duty to tell who's in danger. We name no names, leastways, only to them as is like Madame was. I knew she wouldn't go round tellin' what I said and makin' mischief. With you, missy, I didn't rightly know. You be a stranger. But now it's over and you be safe and he be goin' behind bars."

In the brief ensuing silence the children looked at one another.

"And now," Fabian said to them, "you can tell Miss Fleming what you know. Robin, come on. You're the eldest. You begin."

But even Fabian could not make the children feel guilty. "We was playing a game, Mr. Dominick and us—we always call him that." Robin turned brightly to me. "That night you came down here, miss, he said you'd come to stay and he wanted you to believe in magic and we was to help."

"It were a fun game," Lucy said. "That were all. And secret. We wasn't to tell Granny nor no one."

"Start with bog," Fabian said.

"Oh, we was just to throw the light on there to make you think the place were witched . . ."

"*Be*witched," said Fabian.

". . . and tell you we heard someone around. We didn't really, only Mr. Dominick said you was from the big city and people like you always thought you was clever and we was simple idiots. He said, 'Let's show her that there's things in the country she can't know about, magic things.' We was just to scare you a bit."

"It wasn't as simple as that," I said. "Whatever way Dominick explained it to them, he really intended me to go after the light. When I told him about it on the drive back to Jessamy, he said that I could have been dragged under in that horrible place. And it would have been a long time before they came and rescued me."

Fabian said, "How shocked he must have been, then, to have seen you waiting for him at the station when he arrived like an innocent from London."

I said to Lucy, "Did you pick Fenney's chrysanthemums?"

She giggled and glanced at her brother.

"All right. You did," I said. "And was it you or Robin who drew a picture of me and set it up here for me to find?"

"We did that," said Lucy, nodding. "He wanted you to think there were witches doing things to you. We watched and saw you see it, and then we took it away. You were frightened." She turned her face to me. "You were, weren't you?"

"Not much," I said.

"It were a spell of Great-Granny's to make someone think they was haunted."

"It were nothing of the kind," Hobbin shouted at them. "Your great-granny never did haunting things. That don't be the witch's way."

Lucy said, "All right. Then it be *our* way, because Mr. Dominick were kind to us and gave us money for that." She jerked her little pointed chin at the tape recorder.

"Which I saw Robin playing with in the hedge by the lane," Fabian said. "When he saw me he hid it and ran off. He runs like a cheetah, that grandson of yours," he added to Mrs. Hobbin. "I caught him up in the village—empty-handed."

"You thought I'd stole it," Robin said indignantly. "And you was going to take me for a drive and make me tell you where I got it. I weren't going to, though." His eyes flashed defiance.

"I'm sorry, but I did think something like that," Fabian said. "And I apologize. I'll make it up to you somehow. But you should have let me see it and not hidden it before you ran off. If I'd had a look at it and had seen that it was a very old type of tape recorder, I mightn't have been so suspicious."

"Me and Lucy couldn't tell anyone about our game with Mr. Dominick and . . . her . . ." He gave me a sideways glance. "It were our secret. I told you."

"And now let me tell *you* something," Fabian said pleasantly. "Never run away if you're innocent. Only the guilty try to escape."

"That thing be ours, Lucy's and mine."

"Of course it is. Keep it. Keep it." Fabian turned to Hobbin and then to me. "Well, now you know. This is where it all began, here with Dominick meeting the children in the forest and drawing them into some secret game. Then, Rachel, making his final plan for you and me." He looked through the door to the dark canopy of the beeches. "This, too, is where it must all end. Mrs. Hobbin"—he glanced at her—"please, no tempers lost or boxing of ears after we've gone. Do you understand?"

"But they've been and done mischief, Mr. Seal." She gave the children a scowling look, and they looked brightly back at her.

"What was done by an adult in evil was aided in innocence by these two. All children are, on occasion, little monsters, but they grow out of it."

"As you say, Mr. Seal," she answered with exasperated resignation.

"Good." Fabian took my hand and we stood for a moment outside the cottage. Then he called over his shoulder, "I doubt if Dominick Hunt is anywhere near the forest, but until I send you word that they've found him, don't let the children go out. Do you hear?"

She nodded, and I heard the cottage door close as we walked away.

"How did you guess the children were involved?"

"There was no one else," he said. "Or if there was, I decided to eliminate them first."

"I tried to talk to them about the voice on the tape and they wouldn't tell me anything. They weren't secretive when you came along."

"No, they weren't."

"Then how did you get the truth out of them?"

"Magic," he said.

I stepped over the boles of an ancient beech tree. In spite of all that had happened, the violence and the hatred that had stormed through the afternoon, I was too aware of Fabian's nearness. I loved it and dreaded it and wondered if Livanova had ever felt as I did. But whatever the prima ballerina and the "three-gifted man" had been to one another was their shared and secret knowledge, and I would never know.

"Magic," I said thoughtfully, "but you weren't so clever about Gideon's Rock. You nearly lost your life there."

"When you climb mountains you take risks. I'm a gambler, and it worked. It was the best place to confront Dominick with the facts. You can't turn and run from a rock face. I didn't reckon, though, that he would try to stone me off."

"You wrote to Stephanie that you and she had something important to discuss. You've never told me what it was."

"It was precisely nothing," he said. "Just a ruse to get her here because I knew, as I'm certain the police knew, that she wasn't telling the whole truth at the inquest. I worded the letter in a way that I felt sure would bring her down to Jessamy. And it did—or at least, it brought someone." He glanced sideways at me.

"Stephanie was lying in hospital completely helpless, not knowing what was going on around her. She was quite genuinely in some kind of shocked state, and the doctor needed help to get through to her. I'm sorry, Fabian. I cheated, didn't I?"

He said, laughing, "Don't think my pride is hurt that I was fooled. It's rather a case of gambler meets gambler, isn't it?"

"What happened at Lorne Abbey really was an accident, wasn't it?"

He shook his head.

I protested, "But Dominick couldn't know we'd go there that day and that I'd be tempted to jump down to look at the Celtic cross."

"I mentioned that I was taking you that afternoon and he suggested I show you the cross. He said it had wording on it and was interesting." Fabian gave me a faint smile. "At the moment when you hesitated to jump, the gods must have been on your side. But it was just one of the opportunities Dominick seized on to endanger your life. I think, my dear Rachel—I like that name—that he played every trick, as an idea came to him, in a sort of hit-and-miss effort. You probably avoided a few more attempts on your life through sheer luck and his random plans. I suppose we'll never know what they were."

"When he was supposed to be practicing on the piano at Black Agnes, he could have been watching me."

"Sometimes, yes."

I stared ahead into the green gloom of the trees. "I wonder what will happen to Robin and Lucy."

"Nothing much. There's no bad in them. But if you play games with children and promise them little luxuries as payment, then they'll keep your secrets and use a bit of their own vivid imaginations just to color the adventure."

"Dominick immobilized my car."

"I did that."

I stopped still and stared at him. "Why?"

"To keep you here, of course."

I felt suddenly unsteady as I waited for him to speak. And when he remained silent a wild hope caught me by the throat: perhaps he didn't find it easy to explain why he wanted me to stay.

"Why?" I asked again.

"I knew the truth by then. The solicitors wrote to me this morning enclosing two letters that had been sent to them by a European Alliance Company that wants Jessamy as a Congress Headquarters. Dominick had replied to their original letter, saying that Livanova was willing to sell provided the price was right and that, as she was leaving almost immediately for a European tour, she was placing the matter in his hands to deal with. A note of authorization signed by Livanova was enclosed with Dominick's letter to the European Alliance Company. The company received this correspondence the day *after* she died and it was sent on to the solicitors. They, in turn, sent it to me, since Jessamy would become my property. It arrived this morning in its original envelope with Vincent Crewe's covering letter. And that was the master key that opened the way to the truth of what had happened on the night Livanova had died."

I stared at him, uncomprehending, but he was too absorbed in the puzzle to interrupt his narrative.

"I knew perfectly well that she would never have considered selling Jessamy. She loved it too much and she had no need of the money. So I began to wonder why that letter was written and whether it was actually her signature. From that, I tried to think how selling the house would benefit Dominick, since with Livanova living there, he had a very comfortable roof over his head which he would lose if the house was sold."

"From the way he talked of Jessamy, I think he loved it."

"Or its value on the market," Fabian said. "Let's take it from there. The terms of the will were clear. I inherited the house, but if anything happened to me, it would become Stephanie's. That thought brought me to a suspicion that you—as Livanova's daughter, my little blond cheat—might all the time have known Dominick and shared some plan with him."

The dry leaves of the beeches rustled under our feet like forest whispers as a background to the terrible truth.

Fabian continued, "Tell me, do you look closely at a postmark on an envelope?"

"No. I doubt if many people do."

"Exactly. They slit the flap, take the letter out and throw the envelope away. But in this case the two secretaries, the company's and the solicitor's, were well trained. Dominick's letter agreeing to the sale came through both those offices, and then to me, in its original envelope."

Again Fabian paused. I felt that he was guarding himself and that behind the steady voice was an emotion for the dead ballerina he had trained himself never to show to anyone. When he spoke his voice was calm and without any hint of personal feeling. "I looked at the letter again," he said, "the one agreeing to a negotiation. It was dated the day of Livanova's death, but it couldn't have been sent that night, otherwise it would have caught the first collection the following morning, which is at nine o'clock. Instead, the envelope was postmarked 'One P.M.' So Dominick might have posted it after her death. That wasn't certain, but I *was* certain that she would never have signed that note of authority for him to negotiate the selling of Jessamy. She had once said to me, 'Whatever I lose, there are two things I shall always keep. My dancing and my house.' Besides, she would have consulted her lawyers had she, on some wild impulse, decided to sell."

The pause was a long one. I was vividly aware of the man by my side. The fire of his affair with Tatiana Livanova could have been extinguished long ago, but something remained to be haunted and outraged by her death.

I stepped around a great fallen tree branch and gave an irrelevant thought to the fact that Robin and Lucy could have broken it climbing there. The thought passed and I was back with the realization of how small and seemingly insignificant were the things that could damn and denounce. The unknown typist in Vincent Crewe's office had, by enclosing the envelope with the letter which was supposedly sent by Livanova, confirmed suspicion of Dominick Hunt. It could never now be known whether an answer had been dictated, giving a clear "No" to the offer to buy Jessamy Court, or whether Livanova had even seen the letter.

It no longer mattered. The vital point was that Dominick had known she was dead when he posted the letter agreeing to the negotiations for selling the house.

"When you went out early this morning," I said to Fabian, "did you go to the police?"

"Yes. In Dulverley. And while they were getting handwriting experts to examine Livanova's supposed signature on the note of authorization, I took Dominick to Gideon's Rock. You know the rest."

"Will you sell Jessamy?"

He didn't answer me. After all, I was an outsider and it wasn't my affair. We walked in another long silence. Between the trees in the distance I could just see the russet lines of the house with the three gables standing up against the wind-torn sky.

Everything around me seemed suddenly somber, sharing my sense of loss. But I couldn't lose what I had never had. I knew now that Fabian's interest in me was because he had believed me to be Livanova's daughter and a probable suspect for involvement in her death. I would now leave Jessamy Court, and if ever I came into his mind, it would be only as a link between the dead ballerina and her daughter.

Somewhere on the main road came the sound of a car's siren, thin and screaming, breaking the heavy peace.

"They've found Dominick?"

"Perhaps," he said.

We fell silent again as we crossed the dividing line of coarse grass and honeysuckle bushes and neared the smooth green lawn of Jessamy.

Mrs. Manfred was on the terrace and a man was standing by her side.

"Now will come the police questions and the army of the law for the trial."

"Of Dominick. But not of Stephanie?"

"Of both of them."

"She'll never be in any state to be cross-questioned. She'll escape them each time they try. It's strange, but her strength lies in her weakness."

Before Fabian could comment, Mrs. Manfred had come running across the lawn to us, her skirt billowing out, her usually neat hair in flying wisps.

"Oh, Mr. Seal, I've just got back. I don't understand. They do

272

say down in the village that there be things happening here. Fenney says something awful be going on."

"I'll tell you later," Fabian said. "Is that Inspector Craig on the terrace?"

"Yes, he be waiting to see you."

Fabian walked quickly away from us, calling back, "Mrs. Manfred, would you get some ice, please? We'll need a drink."

As she scuttled away toward the side of the house and the kitchen, I went slowly up the terrace steps into the drawing room. In spite of the out-flung French windows, the smell from the fire still hung on the air like demon's scent.

I looked at my watch. It was seven o'clock and I wanted to go to the hospital in Dulverley, to be with Stephanie. I felt that someone should be responsible for her. I would have to ask Fabian to take me later.

That would be my final duty. And when that was over, it would be like a page turned on a brief and tragic emotional episode in my life.

I would be back in London in twenty-four hours. A week later Jock Graham would be asking me how I enjoyed my holiday, and the rest of the staff would be demanding why I had been too mean to send them postcards of wherever I had been. They would know soon enough why, for I was quite certain that I would be involved in the inquiries, unless Fabian and his lawyers were very clever and kept me out of a limelight I didn't want.

I was tired, physically and emotionally. I could hear voices from the dining room on the far side of the hall, but I had no idea when they ceased or when the inspector left, for I was immersed in an intense and poignant sadness. Not that, for all its beauty, I loved Jessamy, but that I knew it was the end, almost before the beginning, of something that could have been so important to me.

To want something and to work ceaselessly for it can have its reward. But to need another human being is different—and nothing can be achieved unless the need between two people is mutual. It hurt; it hurt so much that I didn't hear anyone enter the room. When a hand touched my shoulder I started.

Fabian was behind me. "I'm afraid it's going to be rough for a while."

"They've found Dominick?"

"Yes."

"What will happen to him?"

"A trial." Fabian sounded tired. "But don't let's dwell on it. I've had enough for one day without delving into detailed explanations." He spoke briskly, and I felt that for Fabian, I was already part of an experience that was over.

He was called to Dulverley police station later that evening. Dominick had not been able to control the powerful Bentley. He had smashed it at the fork of the two lanes and had been taken, uninjured, into custody. A police car was coming for Fabian.

"I should go with you," I protested as he waited for it to arrive.

"I think your part in all this is over," he said. "I may be back late, but if you're hungry, start dinner."

I didn't. I waited for him. But all through the meal and afterward, as we sat together and talked, I felt that he was only waiting politely for the evening to be over.

"I must leave early tomorrow," I said. "It's a long drive."

He did not ask me to stay, and exactly fourteen hours later Fabian said goodbye to me on the steps of Jessamy Court.

His last words, called through the open window of my car were, "You should take up acting. If you ever do, I promise to go to the first night of whatever play you're in. Goodbye."

I saw Fabian again at Dominick Hunt's trial. He had been convicted for the manslaughter of Tatiana Livanova. Stephanie had rallied sufficiently to appear in the witness box, but she had collapsed again while being cross-questioned and was removed to a clinic for psychiatric treatment.

During the trial Fabian and I had greeted each other, exchanged about half a dozen words, and then gone our separate ways. Jessamy Court, Gideon's Rock and the golden beech forest might have been features of a dream.

The first night of the new ballet *The Witch and the Maiden* occurred three months later. I longed to see it, but I knew that I was not prepared to be harrowed by the disturbing memories it would resurrect. But I couldn't resist reading an interview by a Sunday newspaper reporter with Miranda McCall, who had had rave notices in all the reviews and had taken the ballet world by storm.

"It's all due to Fabian Seal," Miranda had said. "He'll be very angry with me for telling you this, but I want people to know. You see, I'd been at ballet school for some years, and then my parents died in a car accident. The school was expensive and there was no longer any money for me to continue. Fabian found me one night outside Covent Garden crying my eyes out because I had just seen the new production of *The Sleeping Beauty*. He took me to his house, sat me down, made coffee for me and listened to my story. I *had* to be a ballerina, I told him, even if I starved for it. He merely said briskly that a starving ballet dancer would fall flat on her face at the first effort of a pirouette. Then he took me home, and I was sorry he had been kind because it made me more unhappy than ever. But not long after that, he came to the school and watched us at ballet class. After that, I was sent for by the Ashenden Ballet Company and I became a pupil there. Mr. Seal did that for me. He also arranged for me to stay with someone he knew—and I hope Mrs. Carlson, who looked after me, will read this and realize how grateful I am to her as well as to Mr. Seal. I've been looked after so wonderfully for the past six years—with no strings attached anywhere and no publicity for Mr. Seal. He quietly paid my bills because he believed in me. I hope in dancing the Maiden in this ballet I've given him the kind of thanks that will please him. He'll probably be furious with me for making this public, but I don't care."

Jock Graham had once used the word "devious" to describe Fabian. He was wrong. What Fabian needed was that nothing—and nobody—bind him. He had to have complete freedom to do as he wished without interference or comment.

Miranda McCall's face looked out of the photograph accompanying the interview—a dark little face with slanting deer's eyes and a pointed chin; young and radiant. She and her words brought Fabian too near to me, and I took the newspaper to the kitchen and put it with a pile I was throwing away.

Six months later he telephoned me.

"Come down to Jessamy this weekend. If you don't, you'll never see it again."

His voice on the telephone, void of any kindly preamble, hurt and annoyed me even more than his news shocked me.

My answer was terse. "If you're thinking of pulling that beautiful house down, then I hope the authorities step in and stop you."

"Nobody is pulling anything down. I'm handing it over as a center for handicapped people. And before you comment on my generous gesture, let me be quite frank and tell you that I find I can't live here myself and I don't need the money it would bring on the market. The choice of the particular charity is purely because of Livanova's physical perfection."

"Why ask me down?"

"Are you coming?"

I was, and I said so.

There should have been a kind of glorious chorale bursting inside me on my journey to Pilgrim Abbas. Instead, I knew that I would have been wise to have refused to go. Six months had not been long enough to weaken Fabian's power over my emotions. Driving over the high ridge of Salisbury Plain, I knew that it was going to hurt far more to see him than to have kept away. I was a fool and I knew it, but not once did I think of turning back.

The cherry blossoms were in full bloom, the white stitchwort starred the lanes and the grass was bright green after the April rains.

The gray stone griffins still looked sightlessly over my head as I drove through the tall gates. Between the trees in the distance I saw the three crowns of Jessamy's turrets.

Fabian was standing at the double doors. He came down the steps to greet me. "Are you tired?"

"Not in the least."

"Good." He took my suitcase from me and led me into the house.

The drawing room was exactly as I had seen it before. Livanova's showcase of jeweled and painted fans stood just out of the direct sunlight; the fragile copy of the ancient Oriflamme banner hung from the far wall and the French doors were open to the terrace. Outside, in the hall, the grandfather clock struck the half hour after six.

I gravitated to the same chair to which I'd always gone when I entered that room. For a while we talked, avoiding all mention of Livanova and the tragedy of death and greed and fear. The house had not lost the aura that two strong personalities had spread there, and the same questions that I could not ask before milled around in my mind behind our casual conversation. I would never know how deeply Tatiana Livanova had been loved by Fabian. He had to be accepted on his terms and there was no key which would open the secret places of his mind.

He crossed the room and handed me a dry martini. "You see, I haven't forgotten." Then, instead of letting me take it, he put

276

it down on the small table by my side, drew me to my feet. "I thought I was free, but I'm not. In these past seven months you have upset my thoughts, crept into my working life, disrupted my leisure. Looking at you now, I'm quite certain that none of that is any surprise to you."

I walked away from him. It was useless to dissemble. He knew perfectly well that eyes didn't lie and the April light had shone straight into mine.

"Will you marry me?"

I fought the impulse to rush to him as if I were afraid he might change his mind. Instead, I stood where I was, half turned away from him, staring through the open French door toward the forest.

"Since you won't come to me," he said, "then I must come to you."

I trembled as he put his hands on my shoulders.

"Well, Stephanie-Rachel?"

"You don't say the right words."

He laughed. "Is that what's making you hold out against me?"

"Yes."

"For God's sake, what more can you want from a man who has fought a six-month battle against you and has admitted defeat?"

There would be many battles of will between us in the years to come, but I had won this time and I intended to savor my victory to the full. I felt as light as the white, flimsy clouds that drifted above Jessamy. I turned to him and laughed. "Very well, my love, I'll marry you. But I don't know that I will ever forgive you for wasting six months . . ."

"There's a time for talking, Stephanie-Rachel," he said, "and this isn't it."

And after that he said all the things I had longed for him to say.

ABOUT THE AUTHOR

ANNE MAYBURY is the author of *The Midnight Dancers, Walk in the Paradise Garden, Ride a White Dolphin, The Terracotta Palace, The Minerva Stone, The Moonlit Door* and *I Am Gabriella*. She lives in London, overlooking the towers of Westminster Abbey, St. Paul's and the Houses of Parliament. An indefatigable traveler, she knows best the English countryside, including the wild Dorset, about which this book is written.